FALLING IN LOVE WITH ABE

He surprised her by driving to Canajoharie Falls, where they enjoyed a picnic and hiked the trails. They had a lovely day together. Before they needed to get back for the afternoon milking, they took a short walk to admire the falls.

"Anna Mary." Abe turned and gazed at her with admiration. "You look so beautiful standing there with the spray behind you."

At the desire in his eyes, Anna Mary's pulse matched the rapidly pounding water. She'd always compared her beauty to that of other girls and found herself lacking. But Abe saw both her inner and outer beauty, and had eyes only for her . . .

BOOKS BY RACHEL J. GOOD

HIS UNEXPECTED AMISH TWINS

HIS PRETEND AMISH BRIDE

HIS ACCIDENTAL AMISH FAMILY

AN UNEXPECTED AMISH PROPOSAL

AN UNEXPECTED AMISH COURTSHIP

AN UNEXPECTED AMISH CHRISTMAS

AN AMISH MARRIAGE OF CONVENIENCE

HER PRETEND AMISH BOYFRIEND

DATING AN AMISH FLIRT

MISSING HER AMISH BOYFRIEND

Published by Kensington Publishing Corp.

MISSING HER AMISH BOYFRIEND

RACHEL J. GOOD

ZEBRA BOOKS
Kensington Publishing Corp.
www.kensingtonbooks.com

ZEBRA BOOKS are published by

Kensington Publishing Corp.
900 Third Avenue
New York, NY 10022

All Kensington titles, imprints, and distributed lines are available at special quantity discounts for bulk purchases for sales promotion, premiums, fund-raising, and educational or institutional use.

Special book excerpts or customized printings can also be created to fit specific needs. For details, write or phone the office of the Kensington Sales Manager: Kensington Publishing Corp., 900 Third Avenue, New York, NY 10022. Attn. Sales Department. Phone: 1-800-221-2647.

Zebra and the Z logo Reg. U.S. Pat. & TM Off.

First Printing: September 2024
ISBN-13: 978-1-4201-5648-5
ISBN-13: 978-1-4201-5649-2 (eBook)

10 9 8 7 6 5 4 3 2 1

Printed in the United States of America

CHAPTER 1

A leafy canopy overhead shielded Anna Mary Zook from the hot afternoon sunshine as she stumbled deeper into the woods. The sturdy trunks of majestic oaks offered strength, a strength she desperately needed and wished she could draw on right now.

Why, God, why?

The bracing aroma of the pines scattered among the broad-leafed trees normally soothed her frazzled nerves and calmed her spirit, but today it did little to quell the storm raging within.

Nothing like finding your boyfriend concealed behind a tree with the biggest flirt in the *g'may*. Humiliation washed over Anna Mary.

Over the past six months they'd been courting, she'd confided in him, told him many of her secrets, her heartaches, and her dreams—things she'd told no one, not even her best friend, Caroline. She'd shared some of her pain with him, and she'd leaned on him as she dealt with her mother's depression, her family money worries, and the heavy responsibility of caring for four younger sisters without a *daed*. Caroline knew some of Anna Mary's stresses over her homelife, but other than what she'd told her best friend and her boyfriend, Anna Mary bore all these burdens alone.

And now he'd betrayed her.

The last time they'd been at a Sunday singing, that flirt Rachel had been surrounded by a bevy of boys. Anna Mary had commented on it, and her boyfriend—at least she'd thought he was her boyfriend—had assured her he'd never be interested in Rachel. Less than a week later, he and Rachel were hidden in the woods, exchanging enamored smiles.

Then, instead of apologizing, he'd stalked off, accusing her of not trusting him. That had wounded her more than his flirting. He'd two-timed her, but somehow, he'd put her in the wrong. And instead of supporting and comforting her, he'd been more concerned with his own hurt feelings. Or had it been guilt?

Anna Mary tripped over a tree root and tumbled to the ground. She pulled herself to a sitting position, her back against the rough bark of an oak, and gave in to the tears.

Lord, please help me deal with this betrayal, with Mamm's depression, with caring for my little sisters, and with all the work still left to do when I get home. You promised not to give us more than we can bear, but I'm at my breaking point.

After crying a little longer, Anna Mary stood up and brushed off her dress. She'd promised to ride home with her supposed boyfriend, but maybe she'd ask Caroline to take her instead. Unless he was waiting to apologize. Even if he did, Anna Mary wasn't sure she could trust him.

She'd always sensed an underlying connection between him and Rachel, an unspoken bond, even though the two of them avoided looking at each other. That reluctance to look at Rachel hinted at a deeper connection, something hidden and meaningful. Anna Mary had never asked about his past. Maybe before her family moved here five years ago, something had happened between him and Rachel.

He couldn't have dated Rachel, because, back then, none of them had been baptized yet. Still, maybe he'd had a crush on her and she'd broken his heart, the way she did with so many of the *buwe* at church. Worse yet, maybe he harbored deep feelings for Rachel and would never get over her.

Anna Mary glanced around. She'd been walking for a while but hadn't reached the volleyball field. Was she even walking in the right direction?

She sent up another prayer. *Lord, please show me the right path. In the woods and in life.*

Abe King chided his cousin Tim. "You shouldn't have been so mean to that girl Caroline from the other team."

A sullen look on his face, Tim growled, "I already said I forgave her. Now will you let it drop?"

"You should have apologized to her too."

"Me apologize to Caroline? After all she's done to me? You've got to be kidding."

Abe prayed for patience. "What exactly has she done to you? Besides winning the volleyball games?"

"And gloating about it," Tim groused. "Next time, she won't be bragging about winning the game."

Gritting his teeth, Abe tried to talk some sense into his cousin. Tim, with his petty feuds and hair-trigger temper, always tried to pay people back for what he saw as insults.

Although Abe agreed Caroline showed off whenever she made winning shots, she'd fallen in a mud puddle trying to save her team's final point. And she'd set it up for a teammate. Tim had been laughing so hard at her predicament, he'd muffed the return. Abe had tried to save it, but the ball had grazed the top of the net and dropped on their side.

Tim walked toward the parking lot, kicking pebbles and grumbling. "Instead of Caroline, why don't we talk about you losing that final point?"

As usual, Tim blamed everyone but himself. Abe didn't want to argue, so he didn't point out that Tim could have spiked the ball if he hadn't been mocking Caroline. "*Jah*, sorry about that."

"You should be. We could have beaten them. And we will next time. Sooner or later, I'm going to beat that girl."

Abe had his doubts. Tim was a skillful player, but Caroline had a natural ability Tim lacked. Abe kept those thoughts to himself. "You know, if you dropped your rivalry with Caroline, you might play better."

Tim stopped walking and snarled, "Are you saying I played poorly?"

"*Neh*, I didn't say that at all. You're the best player on the team. But sometimes your temper gets in the way of your better judgment."

"At least I don't hit weak shots into the net."

"True." Abe didn't want this to escalate into a full-blown argument. "I'm sure you'll be glad when I head back to New York."

They'd reached the parking lot, and Tim scuffed the toe of his sneaker in the gravel. "Naw, I'm not. I'll miss you."

Tim's honesty surprised Abe. Usually, his cousin bluffed and pretended not to care about anything.

Warmth filled Abe. "That's nice to know."

Tim went on as if he hadn't heard. "You're the only one who listens to me. I don't really have any friends."

"But your teammates follow you around."

"Mostly just to see what I'll do. They like that I'm not afraid to do things they're too scared to try."

Abe's heart went out to his cousin. "Maybe you could find other ways to lead."

Tim stomped toward the buggy. "You sound like Onkel Myron. I don't need people telling me what to do."

Abe sighed. The moment of closeness had vanished. He should have kept his mouth shut. He gave advice when he should keep it to himself. Tim liked to spout off, and all he wanted right now was a listening ear.

A rustling in the trees to his left startled Abe. From all the twigs snapping underfoot, it sounded like a lumbering bear. He froze. Snuffling? Bears snuffled, didn't they? Did the Pennsylvania woods have bears?

Loud voices penetrated the woodsy silence, broken only by birds tweeting and small animals scampering in the bushes. Someone was arguing.

"*Danke*, Lord," Anna Mary whispered.

Sniffling, she headed toward the noise. It seemed to be fading. She had to find her way out. She crashed through the undergrowth and emerged near the parking lot.

Grateful to be out of the trees, she'd forgive anyone and everything. Including Josh. Was that him waiting there for her?

Anna Mary charged in that direction, but it wasn't Josh. That tall boy from the other team stared at her wide-eyed. Tim's cousin Abe.

He laughed. "Am I ever glad to see you! I thought a bear was about to attack."

Her face reddened. Had she thrashed around like a

bear? She couldn't look him in the eye. "Sorry. I got lost in the woods and raced toward the sound of voices."

"I'm glad you found us. We're the last buggy in the parking lot. I'd hate to think of you spending the night alone in the woods."

"The last buggy? Everyone's gone?"

Abe nodded. "*Jah*, only Tim and I are still here."

Panic filled Anna Mary. Where was Josh? Caroline? Were they both so upset they'd left without her? How would she get home? She could walk the eight miles, but she needed to start supper, and she shouldn't leave Mamm alone any longer.

"Are you all right?" Abe studied her with concern.

"I—I, um . . ." How could she answer that? Her eyes stung, and she blinked to prevent tears from falling.

"Were you planning to walk home?" he asked gently. "Or did you miss your ride?"

Josh was supposed to drive her home, but . . . "I think he left without me."

"Oh, you're dating that good volleyball player. Josh?"

"I was. I'm not so sure if I am anymore," Anna Mary blurted out. "W-we had an argument."

"Sorry." Abe's sympathetic look stirred feelings she'd tamped down.

"It's not your fault," she mumbled. "I got upset." Now that she was over her scare of being stuck in the woods, Josh's smile at Rachel seemed a small and petty thing to fight over.

"So he left without you?" Abe sounded indignant.

"I guess so." It didn't seem like Josh to be so unkind, but he had stalked off when she'd said she couldn't trust him. She shouldn't have said that. She'd blurted it out in anger.

"Come on." Abe beckoned to her. "I'm sure my cousin will drive you home."

"Your cousin?" Anna Mary's stomach curdled. *Ride with Tim?* She'd rather walk the eight miles.

"He's not a bad guy once you get to know him."

Anna Mary hesitated. A guy who mocked her best friend every chance he got? One who made vicious shots on purpose?

"It's all right. Besides, we can't leave you here. How far away do you live?"

"Eight miles."

"You're coming with us. I'll make sure Tim drives carefully and minds his manners." Abe's lips curved into a rueful expression. "At least I'll try."

Anna Mary laughed. "I don't think Tim likes taking advice."

"You're right. But he wouldn't leave anyone stranded."

"I hope not." Although Tim was the last person she wanted to ride with, she needed to get home as soon as possible. And for some reason, this Abe intrigued her. She'd like to get to know him better.

They walked in companionable silence to the buggy.

Tim's eyes bugged out. "You poached someone else's girlfriend? Does she know you're heading back to New York soon?"

"Relax. She missed her ride, and I told her my cousin's a gentleman who'd be happy to take her home."

Fleeting expressions crossed Tim's face—annoyance, uncertainty, pride, then resignation.

Anna Mary almost fled, but Abe's presence steadied her.

"*Jah*, come on. We don't have anything better to do."

To Anna Mary's surprise, Tim didn't poke fun at her for getting left behind by her boyfriend. In fact, once they pulled out of the parking lot, he participated in the *getting-to-know-you* conversation Abe began.

She found out about Abe's family in New York State, and she told him a little about her family, leaving out Mamm's troubles.

"Is it hard for your *mamm* being widowed twice? My *daed*'s struggled with loneliness since Mamm died two years ago."

Something about the understanding in Abe's eyes as he turned his head to look at her gave Anna Mary the courage to be honest. "Ever since my stepfather died, some days she's so depressed she can't get out of bed."

"That's too bad. It must be hard on you. I guess you have to take care of everyone."

"*Jah.*" The empathy in his eyes almost made her cry.

Tim cleared his throat. "At least both of you have a parent."

That brought Anna Mary up short. Should she ask what he meant? Did he want to talk about it? "I'm sorry, Tim."

His brittleness returned. "I'm not. Sometimes you're better off without them. And who wants siblings?" Despite his bravado, his voice shook a little, and Anna Mary detected a deep loneliness underneath.

Abe changed the subject. "Do you enjoy other sports besides volleyball?"

Anna Mary admired his tact and his consideration for his cousin's feelings. "Well, I'm not very good at volleyball. Not like Tim and you."

Tim's self-satisfied smile returned. Although his attitude grated on Anna Mary, she was glad to see the droopy lines around his mouth disappear, and his eyes no longer held the faraway sadness. She shifted on the back seat so she had a better view of Abe.

"I'm a little better with baseball."

Abe turned to smile at her. "I prefer baseball too. I wish I could stay longer so we could set up a game."

Disappointment snaked through Anna Mary, surprising her. She'd only just met Abe, but she didn't want him to go. Her conscience jagged her. *You shouldn't be feeling this way about another man. You already have a boyfriend.*

But did she?

"What about Caroline?" Tim broke into her thoughts. "She have a boyfriend? What about that guy that came to watch the game?"

Anna Mary shrugged. As far as she knew, Caroline had never gone on a date with anyone, but Anna Mary worried about Tim being interested in her best friend. Better not to give him any encouragement. He bugged Caroline with his taunts and bragging.

"We beat her in the second game today," he boasted. "And next time, we'll win all three."

"She's a good player," Abe admitted. "And so's your, um, boyfriend."

Anna Mary winced. Josh might be her ex-boyfriend after today. She shook her head. *Neh*, Josh would do the right thing. He'd apologize and ask for forgiveness. And she'd do the same. They'd make things right.

"Does Caroline live near you?" Tim asked.

She hesitated. Why did Tim want to know? Did he plan to play a prank on her? He'd been furious she'd beaten him at volleyball. "Um, she doesn't live too far away."

"Not going to tell me where?" Tim shot her an annoyed look.

Anna Mary wished he'd keep his eyes on the road. He was already driving faster than she liked.

Abe laughed. "Anna Mary might wonder what you plan to do to her friend."

"Someone needs to take her down a peg or two," Tim snapped. "She thinks she's such a great volleyball player."

"Well, she is," Abe said mildly.

"But she doesn't have to brag about it all the time. She's insufferable."

"She's really very sweet and caring." Anna Mary wouldn't let him criticize her best friend. Caroline might be mouthy at times, but she'd do anything for people.

"Wish she'd show that side to me," Tim grumbled.

"She might if you were kinder to her," Abe pointed out.

Tim lapsed into sullen silence.

They had several more miles to get to her house, and Anna Mary didn't want to sit in uncomfortable silence, so she addressed a question to Abe. "What do you think of Lancaster?"

"I like it. I come here whenever I can." Abe tilted his head toward Tim and tried to send a message to Anna Mary with his eyes. "I need to check up on my cousin from time to time."

"*Neh*, you don't," Tim growled. "You just want to get out of all your work at home."

Anna Mary wasn't sure she'd interpreted Abe's meaning correctly, but it seemed he was concerned about Tim. Did it have anything to do with Tim not having parents? She didn't want to ask after seeing how upset Tim had gotten about that subject earlier.

"What do you do, Abe?" From what she'd seen of Abe, Anna Mary didn't believe Tim's dig about Abe avoiding work.

Tim harrumphed. He liked to be the center of attention. Had she hurt his feelings by talking to Abe? She'd have to include him in the conversation more, even though she only wanted to find out about Abe.

"We have a dairy farm, so it's hard on Daed when I come to Lancaster for visits."

"Abe's lucky." Envy laced Tim's words. "He's the youngest, so he'll run the family business someday."

"You know you can always come to New York and join me. I'm happy to share the business."

What a generous offer! The more Anna Mary got to know Abe, the more he impressed her.

"Easy to say when you know I'll never leave Lancaster."

She wondered why. Tim didn't have family here or seem happy in Lancaster. And she could tell Abe meant what he said.

"Where do you work, Tim?" Anna Mary hoped it might distract him.

"I'm stuck inside a prison. All blank walls and no windows. Doing stupid, repetitive work every day."

"He works at a factory that manufactures farm machinery," Abe explained. "He alternates between the different shifts, including the night shift sometimes."

"I see." Maybe losing sleep at night caused Tim's grumpiness. Anna Mary felt sorry for him. No parents, an unpleasant job, a challenging work schedule, and losing volleyball games. Maybe she could convince Caroline to be kinder to him.

The buggy approached Rachel's house. Anna Mary intended to glance away, but a familiar head of brown hair caught her eye. She sucked in a breath. Her stomach clenched. *NEH!*

CHAPTER 2

There on Rachel's front porch, Josh sat laughing and talking with Rachel. They both glanced at the buggy, but Josh didn't even bother to wave. He must be too caught up in their conversation.

Abe's head whipped around. "What's wrong?"

Tim had noticed and slowed the horse. "Well, lookie there. Seems like your boyfriend is having fun with another woman. Don't blame him. She's real pretty, ain't she? I wouldn't mind—"

"Tim!" Abe's short, shocked exclamation cut off whatever else his cousin had planned to say.

Anna Mary snapped her head forward so she didn't have to watch Josh enjoying that flirt's company. Anna Mary's eyes stung, and she pinched her lips tight. It was bad enough Josh had humiliated her like this, but having Tim see it and spread the news . . .

Even more embarrassing, Abe had just seen her rejected by her boyfriend. What must he think?

"*Ach*, Anna Mary, I'm so sorry." Abe's soothing voice sounded as if he really cared.

As much as she appreciated his kindness, being jilted stung. And Rachel?

"She's such a flirt," Anna Mary muttered.

"Wish she'd flirt with me." Tim sighed dreamily.

Abe poked his cousin. "Would you stop? This is hard enough for Anna Mary, and you're only making it worse."

Anna Mary loved how Abe stood up for her. Maybe if Josh was moving on, she should too. But even as she thought it, her heart ached. Josh had told her he'd never be interested in Rachel. He'd lied.

"Oh," Anna Mary exclaimed, "that's the turnoff to my house." They'd almost driven past it. She should have been paying attention.

Tim jerked on the reins, and they came to an abrupt stop. Anna Mary pitched forward. Abe threw out a protective hand, and she banged into his strong, tanned forearm.

"Did I hurt you?" he asked when the buggy stopped shuddering.

"I'm all right." But she wasn't. She hadn't hit too hard, but she rubbed the place that had made contact. If she hadn't been thrown backward so quickly, she might have let her face rest against—

Anna Mary Zook, what are you thinking? You have no business letting your mind go in that direction. Besides, you have a boyfriend.

But did she? Even if she didn't, she shouldn't be longing to touch a man she'd just met. Or any man, for that matter. Even if he was tall and handsome and very, very nice.

She dropped her fingers to her lap, but she couldn't

slow the rapid pattering of her pulse. She'd been angry at seeing Josh with that flirt, but what was she doing?

Shame heated her cheeks. She had no right to condemn Josh if she did the same thing.

To prevent another accidental bump, Anna Mary kept a close eye out the window so she could direct Tim before they reached the turns. "My house is the light gray one after this cornfield." She pointed to the right.

When they pulled into her driveway, she couldn't wait to hop out and run inside. To get away from her embarrassment and her roiling feelings. Abe slid the door open and got out so he could pull the seat forward.

He gave her a gentle smile. "Will you be all right?"

She gulped and nodded. His flushed cheeks and the slight sheen on his face revealed he was still overheated from the game. She should be hospitable.

"It's hot out here. Would you both like to come in for some lemonade and cool down a little before you start back?"

Sure, Anna Mary. You just feel sorry for them.

"That sounds nice," Abe said.

Tim ducked his head so he could stare out the passenger door. "You got any sisters?"

"Four of them."

"What are we waiting for?" Tim hopped out and tied the horse to a post. "Where are your sisters?" he asked eagerly as they headed for the door.

As the other two trailed Tim across the overgrown lawn, Abe leaned closer and whispered, "Your sisters are younger than you, aren't they?"

Anna Mary nodded. "Sarah, the closest in age to me, is twelve. The other three are five, three, and two."

"Tim's going to be disappointed."

"I know." Anna Mary couldn't keep the note of satisfaction from her voice. "Sorry. I shouldn't have said it that way."

"It's all right. Tim's my cousin, and I love him. But I can see he annoys people. He's had a rough life, and he's always trying for the attention he never got."

Tim bounced impatiently on the front porch. "What's taking you two so long? I want to meet your sisters." Then his eyes narrowed. "*Ach*, Abe, you trying to move in on a girl whose boyfriend dumped her?"

Abe winced, and so did Anna Mary, inwardly. She'd forgotten about Josh until Tim brought it up. Now it hit her full force. She sucked in a breath. *Josh and Rachel.* He'd looked happier than she'd ever seen him.

"I'm sorry, Anna Mary." Abe's soft, understanding voice seemed to come from a distance.

She struggled to pull herself back from the shame of being cheated on and the fears of life without Josh. Until now, she hadn't realized how much she'd depended on him for emotional support. Caroline helped as much as she could, but she was a talker, rather than a listener. And Anna Mary often needed a listening ear.

Abe must have sensed her worries. "Will you be all right?"

"I-I'm not sure," she admitted honestly. "It's not easy handling everything on my own."

His expression softened. "I wish I could be here for you."

Anna Mary almost blurted out, *I wish you could too,* but she caught herself in time.

Suppose Josh regretted what he'd done and came to apologize. She'd have to forgive him. Better for her not to give in to the feelings Abe stirred in her. Maybe she was only drawn to Abe because he offered sympathy and understanding. Or because she was so hurt by Josh's betrayal.

But Josh wasn't here now, and Abe was. And he'd said something kind and caring. She needed to respond. Ducking her head so he couldn't see how his words affected her, Anna Mary choked out a *danke*.

Tim hopped from one foot to the other. "Are you two going to stand there the rest of the day staring into each other's eyes? It's not like you're going to be around here long, Abe. Flirting with her is a waste of time."

Heat flashed into Abe's face. Did Anna Mary think he'd been flirting? He'd only intended to be kind. She seemed so troubled, and he wanted to lift some of the burdens weighing her down.

"I didn't— I wasn't—" Abe stuttered out.

"I know," Anna Mary said softly. "I try to ignore most of what Tim says."

Relief washed over Abe. "A wise idea."

He didn't want Anna Mary to think he'd try to take advantage of her situation. She'd looked so devastated to see her boyfriend enjoying someone else's company, anyone would have wanted to comfort her.

But if he were honest with himself, he had to admit he'd been drawn to her before he knew about her boyfriend. That attraction had only increased the more time he spent around her. And learning about all she had to cope with had brought a strong desire to care for her.

"I wish I could do something to help you," he blurted out before thinking.

She stared up at him with such appreciation, his heart almost stopped beating.

He reminded himself he'd be headed back to New York soon. Even if she wasn't courting someone, he'd have no chance. He lived too far away, the dairy business required long hours, and he couldn't visit very often. Anna Mary needed someone who'd support her day in and day out, someone who could be here in person.

Tim yelled from the porch again. They had to get over there before he broadcast more embarrassing comments to the neighborhood.

"We'd better not get him too upset." With his eyes, Abe begged Anna Mary to hurry.

She must have gotten his message, because she rushed toward the house. "Tim," she scolded in a sweet voice, "my *mamm* might be sleeping."

Anna Mary's gentle voice tugged at Abe, but it made no impact on his cousin.

"At this time in the afternoon?" Tim sounded incredulous.

Abe elbowed Tim. "Anna Mary told us her *mamm* isn't doing well. Have a little respect."

"Respect?" Tim's voice grew shrill. "Nobody respects me. You made me stand here waiting while you tried to steal someone else's girlfriend." He sneered. "Not that her boyfriend's very faithful, but still—"

Tim yelped when Abe's elbow jabbed him in the ribs again. "What was that for?"

"For being rude."

Anna Mary's clipped response caught Abe by surprise, and he laughed. She had some vinegar in all her sugary sweetness. He liked that.

"Me, rude?" Tim puffed up. "I think it's rude to make

guests wait while you dilly-dally with another man who's not your boyfriend."

Anna Mary's cheeks pinkened to a lovely shade of rose. She lowered her head. "You're right. I'm sorry. Will you forgive me?"

Abe was torn. As much as he appreciated this gentle side of her, he didn't like the way his cousin was treating her. He frowned at Tim, but his cousin appeared stunned by the apology.

"The correct answer is '*Jah,* I forgive you,'" Abe prompted.

Tim parroted the words.

"And," Abe suggested, "you could also ask for her for-giveness."

"For what?" Tim's sullen expression showed he wasn't about to admit to any faults.

With a sigh, Abe bit back his criticism. No need to provoke his cousin into a temper. Tim would take it out on Anna Mary, and Abe wanted to protect her.

The front door eased open, and a frightened girl peered out. She looked about twelve. "Mamm's asleep."

"I'm sorry." Abe wished he'd silenced Tim earlier. "We didn't mean to disturb her."

Tim's lips twisted. "Of course you didn't. You'd never disturb anyone."

The bitterness in his tone told Abe the ride home would be miserable. As much as he'd like to spend more time with Anna Mary, it might be best to get Tim away from here before he took his annoyance out on her family.

Abe cleared his throat. "If your *mamm*'s not feeling well, maybe we should go."

The disappointment in Anna Mary's eyes cut straight

to his heart. He hadn't meant to hurt her. Perhaps she didn't get a chance to have much company. He should have thought about that.

"We could have lemonade on the porch. If we keep our voices down, we won't disturb Mamm." Anna Mary stared up at him pleadingly.

He hesitated. "If you're sure."

"I can bring some lemonade out to you." The girl in the doorway smiled at Abe and gave her older sister a loving glance. "Anna Mary's always so busy, she doesn't have much time for company, except for Josh."

She clapped a hand over her mouth. "I didn't mean . . ."

"It's all right, Sarah." Anna Mary's eyes reflected the same love as her sister's. "If you could bring us some lemonade, that would be great." She waved to some rockers at the other end of the porch. "And I'll be in to fix supper soon."

Tim followed Abe and Anna Mary across the porch and sank into a rocker with a pout. "I thought I'd get to meet your sisters. Why are you hiding them away?"

"Don't worry." Anna Mary's eyes danced. "I'll have Sarah bring everyone out to meet you."

"Not your *mamm* too, I hope," he growled.

Abe caught Anna Mary's sense of fun and smiled back at her. When she beamed at him, his insides somersaulted. *Uh-oh*—he'd better get himself under control. No point in falling for a girl who lived hundreds of miles away. One who might make up with her boyfriend. But somehow, Abe's heart didn't heed the warnings his mind kept sending.

Sarah returned with a pitcher of lemonade, three glasses, and a platter of cookies. She pushed against the door to open it, and Abe jumped up to help her.

"Here, let me take that." He reached for the heavy pitcher, and with his other hand, he held the door.

Tim shook his head. "She's much too young for you, Abe."

Abe shot him a frown. "What? You only help people if they give you something in return?"

But Sarah did give Abe something in return. A grateful smile and a shy *danke*.

She looked so much like her sister. She, too, would be a beauty someday. And both sisters had the same sweet, caring dispositions. The two of them had a lot to bear, but it didn't show in their calm demeanors.

Tim pinned Anna Mary with a sharp look. "What about—"

"Oh, right," she said. "Sarah, Tim would like to meet the rest of the girls."

Leaning back in his chair with the three cookies he'd grabbed, Tim grinned. "I sure would."

"I'll be right back." Sarah set the cups on the table and headed inside.

A short while later, she returned, ushering two small blondes in front of her. In her arms, she held a toddler with a thumb thrust in her mouth. The small girl rested her head on Sarah's shoulder and eyed everyone sleepily.

"Hannah just woke up from her nap," Sarah said apologetically.

Tim choked on his cookie. Abe pounded him on the back.

"Those—those are your sisters?" Tim looked dumbfounded.

"*Jah.*" Anna Mary's sly smile made Abe chuckle.

"They're so cute," Abe said.

Tim rolled his eyes. "Maybe if you like—"

Abe halted him with a sharp look. He didn't know what Tim planned to say, but he had no doubt it would be insulting. These adorable little girls didn't deserve his cruelty.

"Cookies," one said.

"These are for our guests," Anna Mary explained, and all three little ones stared at them longingly.

It flashed through Abe's mind that they might not have money for treats. He regretted taking two cookies. He'd already eaten more than half of his first one, but he held out the other and glanced to Anna Mary for approval. "I could share this one with them."

The gratitude in her eyes confirmed what he'd feared. They had no more cookies. Only then did he realize Anna Mary had taken no cookies for herself, but Tim's plate still held two. Abe doubted his cousin would give up both of them, but maybe he'd be willing to part with half.

Abe broke his cookie in two and handed the pieces to two of the girls. Then he turned to Tim. "Maybe you could break one of yours in half to share with the other two sisters."

Tim growled and began to protest, but stopped under Abe's stern glare. Reluctantly, he snapped a cookie into two pieces and handed them to Sarah and the toddler.

Sarah flashed him a delighted smile. "It's all right. You don't have to give me your cookie."

To Abe's surprise, Tim growled, "Take it."

Although his manner wasn't gracious, it took a lot for Tim to make that sacrifice. Abe knew Tim had often gone hungry when he was younger, so he guarded his food like a hawk.

"*Danke.*" Sarah took the half he held out. She closed her eyes as she ate, as if enjoying every bite.

Tim watched her, and his face softened a little.

Leave it to a sweet little girl to get to his cousin's heart. Perhaps there was hope for Tim after all.

CHAPTER 3

Anna Mary couldn't believe the change her sister made in Tim's attitude. "Sarah, why don't you sit with us for a little while?"

"But what about supper?"

"It's all right," Anna Mary assured her. "We can have soup and salad. I washed some lettuce and vegetables before I left for the market this morning." She waved her sister to the empty chair beside Tim.

Sarah sank into it with Hannah in her arms. Tim held out a hand to prevent the toddler from falling. Sarah's grateful expression and soft *danke* melted his usual sullen expression into a semblance of a smile.

Abe leaned close to Anna Mary and whispered, "Tim and his sister were separated when she was young. She'd be about your sister's age now. He's never stopped searching for her."

Poor Tim. Anna Mary's heart went out to him. "What happened?"

"It's a long story. I'll tell you sometime."

Anna Mary's heart jumped at the thought that Abe planned to spend more time with her. Then she chided herself for thinking about someone other than Josh. She excused her reaction by telling herself Abe was only a friend and he'd be gone soon. But her conscience bothered her.

Abe's voice dropped even lower. "Tim's had a hard life."

"I'm sorry to hear that." She couldn't even imagine being separated from her sisters.

Tim's sharp voice sliced into their conversation. "What are you two talking about? Did I hear my name?"

"You certainly did." Abe grinned at him. "Should we talk louder?" When Tim frowned, Abe turned to Anna Mary, "I couldn't believe Tim's spike in the second game. He won the game for us. And that sideways roll. Wow!"

Tim stared at them suspiciously, but Sarah lifted awestruck eyes to his face.

"You must be a very good player," she said softly.

To Anna Mary's surprise, Tim blushed.

"I guess," he said carelessly, waving off the compliment.

Abe lowered his voice. "Sorry, Anna Mary. I didn't mean to remind you of your loss." He stood and announced, "We should go and let you get your supper ready."

"Nice meeting you," Tim said to Sarah. He even smiled slightly at her and the younger girls.

Sarah beamed and stared after him, dazed. "I hope you come to visit again."

"We will," he promised.

We? Anna Mary's spirits soared as high as her sister's.

Abe stared out the window at Anna Mary as Tim turned the buggy into the street. She stayed on the porch, waving until they disappeared from sight.

"Stop mooning over that girl." Tim's voice cracked through Abe's hazy daydreams. "She already has a boyfriend."

But what if her boyfriend fell for that girl he was talking to on the porch? Then Anna Mary would be free to date. Except Abe wouldn't be around. He'd be leaving soon.

"Want to stop for something to eat?" Tim asked.

"*Neh*, we should go home and fix something for your *onkel*." Abe had noticed that preparing meals regularly made their *onkel* less *grexy*.

Neither Tim nor his *onkel* had picked up many cooking skills over the years, so they relied on casseroles donated by neighbors or on fast food. After his *mamm* had passed, Abe had taught himself to cook some of Daed's favorite dishes. Their *onkel* Myron seemed to like them too. Maybe they reminded him of childhood and that softened some of his crusty bachelor ways.

Tim huffed about Abe's suggestion, but he headed home. "As long as you're the one doing the cooking," he grumped.

"I plan to. I don't feel like having hard-boiled eggs and cold cereal," Abe teased, then wished he hadn't when Tim's face hardened.

Tim and his *onkel* often had that or sandwiches for all three meals some days. They heated canned soups or spaghetti rings when they were ambitious.

"I could teach you how to make a few casseroles," Abe offered.

"What fun!" The sarcastic edge to Tim's voice made it clear he had no interest in learning. "Besides, why should I learn to cook? It's not like my *onkel*'s ever done anything for me."

Abe ground his teeth together. "He puts a roof over your head."

"And takes most of the money I make to do it."

"It's only fair that you pay something when you have a job."

Tim jerked on the reins to stop the horse at a stop sign and glared at Abe. "He takes so much I can't save enough to move out on my own."

Not wanting to argue, Abe tamped down his irritation. "Why don't you talk to him about it?"

"Like he'd agree to me moving out. He wants to keep me under his thumb."

I can understand why. Tim would bristle if Abe said that aloud, but his cousin had been a handful when their *onkel* adopted him at age seven. In the ten years since then, Myron had kept a tight rein on Tim. Still, that hadn't stopped Tim from getting into trouble. Even now, Tim hung around some of the worst-behaved *youngie* in the *g'may*, and he tried to show off for them, which led him to do foolish and dangerous things.

Usually, when Tim started getting out of control, Myron invited Abe to visit. Abe couldn't always come because scheduling skilled workers to take over his chores at the dairy farm proved difficult. Abe's older brothers pitched in when they could, but they had families and businesses of their own. Whenever Myron contacted them, though, Abe's *daed* insisted they should help. Myron was Daed's younger brother, so Daed wanted to assist however he could.

Tim's face set in grim lines. "I have to work the midnight-to-eight shift on Saturday night. Myron's going to have a fit."

Abe sighed. Myron had always been strict about following the *Ordnung*. No working on Sunday allowed.

With dairy farms, cows still had to be milked, so Abe had learned to be flexible. But he didn't do any work other than what was strictly necessary.

Tim had no choice on his hours. The factory rotated workers and set their schedules. Myron scolded Tim for working on Sunday and for missing church if Tim slept in after being up all night.

Abe bit back a sigh. He didn't look forward to playing peacemaker tonight to avoid fireworks between Tim and Myron. He liked mediating people's disagreements as long as they acted civil when they discussed their problems, but Tim and Myron—

Abe cut off his criticism. He shouldn't be thinking negative thoughts about others. He had plenty of his own faults. God would want him to concentrate on his own failings rather than his cousin's or his *onkel*'s.

Maybe the first fault Abe should deal with was his attraction to someone else's girlfriend. Still, he worried about Anna Mary and wanted to help her and her sisters.

Tim turned into the driveway and groaned. Myron stood by the barn, arms crossed, waiting for them.

"*Ach!* I forgot I promised to bring the buggy back right after the game ended. Now I'm in for it."

As soon as Tim pulled the horse to a stop, Abe jumped out.

"Myron, I'm so sorry. A girl got stranded at the volleyball field, and I forced Tim to take her home. It's my fault we're late."

"So . . . Tim's courting some girl?"

"*Neh, neh.* We didn't know her. She lives near the Green Valley Farmer's Market."

"You went all the way out there? Now the horse is probably too tired to take me to my meeting. And I'm late. I won't have time to stop for something to eat."

"I'm sorry. I didn't know."

Myron's mouth pinched into a tight line. "But Tim did."

Tim took his time tying the reins to the hitching post near the front walkway. Knowing Tim, he'd say something to inflame Myron's temper. Abe needed to defuse things.

"I bought some ham and cheese when we stopped at the Green Valley Farmer's Market earlier this week. Let me make you a sandwich to take."

"I don't have time," Myron grumbled.

"It'll only take a minute," Abe said, then hurried to intercept Tim. "Hey, Tim, I could use some help making sandwiches."

A relieved look crossed Tim's face. Instead of heading down the driveway, Tim veered up the front walkway and rushed inside.

"You're a miracle worker," Tim said when Abe reached the kitchen.

"We'll see." Abe plunked jars of mustard and mayo on the counter. "You get out the bread and spread those on two sandwiches. I'll take care of the ham and cheese."

In short order, Abe grabbed the two sandwiches and a bag of chips. He jogged outside and handed them to Myron, who was struggling to unknot the reins.

"How does he get them so tangled?" Myron groused.

"Here." Abe handed Myron the food. "Why don't you eat those while I get this undone?"

Myron bit into the sandwich. "Um, that's good," he said around a mouthful of bread.

Some of Myron's grumpiness might be traced to his poor eating habits. If he had regular meals, it might soothe his temper. It would help Tim too.

Poor Tim had grown up with irregular meals, and when Myron got too engrossed in a woodworking project, he forgot to eat altogether, leaving Tim to fend for himself. A bachelor used to keeping his own hours, Myron often didn't remember to keep an eye on Tim or set regular hours for meals and bedtime. Tim suffered from neglect and carelessness, even though Myron didn't intend to be cruel. He was just too absorbed in his work and his own sorrows, and he hadn't known how to raise a young boy.

Abe's parents had often begged Tim to come and stay with them, but Tim refused. He wanted to stay in the Lancaster area in case his sister ever returned.

As he headed back to the house, Abe prayed that Tim and Myron could work out their differences and that his cousin would settle down and join the church—another sore spot between Tim and Myron.

Tim surprised Abe by setting out two sandwiches for each of them. He even put out pickles, red beet eggs, and chips.

"Wow." Abe grinned. "A whole feast. Want me to heat up some soup?"

"Sounds good." Tim settled onto a kitchen chair.

While he stirred the soup, Abe wondered aloud, "Do you think Anna Mary and her sisters have enough to eat?"

"Why wouldn't they?" Tim stuffed his mouth with a huge bite of sandwich.

"I thought we might have eaten the last of their cookies. And I wondered if they had enough food for supper because—" Abe didn't know how to put his concerns in words. It was more a vague sense he had.

"Because why?"

"Well, with their *mamm* not always getting out of bed . . ." Abe shrugged. "Just kind of a feeling I had."

"Anna Mary's working. I'm sure she can handle it. Besides, if they don't, the church will help."

"The church didn't always help you."

Whenever Abe had come to visit Tim when they were younger, Mamm had packed cartons full of homemade soup, applesauce, pickled eggs, and home-canned chicken and fruits and vegetables, along with jars of peanut butter, boxes of cereal, and assorted snack foods.

Tim waved his sandwich in the air. "That's only because the church didn't know. Myron had plenty of money for food. He just didn't always remember to buy groceries."

"What if the church doesn't know about Anna Mary's family? I'd hate to think of Sarah or the other little girls going hungry." *Or Anna Mary.*

At the mention of Sarah's name, Tim chewed thoughtfully. "You really think they might not have enough food?"

"I don't know, but I'd like to find out. I don't think Anna Mary would admit it, but Sarah might. What days is the market open?"

"Tuesday, Thursday, Friday, and Saturday. Why?"

"Since you're on the night shift now, why don't we stop over on a day Anna Mary's at work? I bet you can convince Sarah to tell you the truth."

Tim's chest puffed up a little. "She did seem to take to me, didn't she?" Then his face fell, and his eyes took on a faraway look.

Abe ached for his cousin. Tim must be thinking about his sister, wondering where she was and if she was all right.

"I guess we could do that," Tim said finally. "I don't want to think about those girls going hungry."

Tim often came across as self-centered and uncaring, but he did have a good heart—if people knew how to tap into it. It seemed Sarah had done that.

Although Abe wished he could spend more time with

Anna Mary, it would be better not to. She'd soon mend the rift with her boyfriend, and Abe would head back to New York. But he wanted to do what he could to help her and her family before he went home.

After Abe left, Anna Mary's spirits plummeted. She chided herself. She had no business thinking about Abe, not when she was supposed to be courting Josh. *If* they were still dating. The image of him on Rachel's porch started an ache deep inside.

I can never compete with Rachel's beauty or her appeal to men.

Not long ago, Josh had assured Anna Mary he'd never be interested in Rachel. How had things changed so quickly? All it had taken was the soft touch of Rachel's hand on his arm for him to follow her home and—

Anna Mary shoved the memory from her mind. She couldn't think about it. Josh deserved a chance to explain, but her heart sank. What if his only explanation was that he'd fallen for Rachel and wanted to break up?

Sarah touched Anna Mary's arm. "Are you all right?"

"I'll be fine." Her words came out more sharply than she intended. "Sorry, Sarah, I didn't mean to snap at you. I'm just . . ." She fumbled for an explanation. Her heart—and pride—ached too much to talk about Josh. "I'm just tired." That was certainly true.

"Me too." Sarah's shoulders slumped. "Mamm stayed in bed all day. She's not doing well. I should have gotten more of the chores done, but Beth accidentally over-turned the mop bucket. While I cleaned that up, Emmie tried swinging from the clothesline. She broke it and hurt herself, and she and all the clothes and diapers landed in a mud puddle, so . . ."

"Oh, Sarah." Anna Mary wrapped an arm around her sister's shoulders. "I'm so sorry. I never should have gone to the volleyball game."

"*Jah*, you should. You don't get to have much fun."

Although her sister was right, Anna Mary shouldn't be enjoying herself while Sarah did all the work. And right now, Sarah needed Anna Mary even more than usual because Mamm always struggled with depression this time of year. Around the anniversaries of Daed's passing and her stepfather's death, along with Mamm's two wedding dates, their mother spent weeks barely able to get out of bed. Those four times a year, the girls were left with the extra responsibilities of caring for her, cajoling her to eat, to dress, and to leave her bedroom—attempts that were rarely successful.

Now that Anna Mary had started working at the market, all the work fell on Sarah. Anna Mary really needed to be here to pitch in, but her market job would put food on the table and help pay bills. She did as much as she could at home when she wasn't working, yet it never seemed to be enough.

Thank goodness this weekend was an off-Sunday. They wouldn't have to drag Mamm out of bed and get her dressed or struggle to get the little ones into church clothes. Even though they couldn't do chores on Sunday, Anna Mary took over all the childcare duties, giving Sarah time to relax.

Josh usually visited on off-Sundays, but Anna Mary wasn't sure whether or not to expect him. What if he spent the day at Rachel's?

By the time Sunday rolled around, that worry had become a full-blown fear. As the hours ticked by, Anna Mary tortured herself with pictures of Josh enjoying Sunday dinner at Rachel's, strolling with her in the woods behind her house, laughing and talking with her on the front porch again . . .

Anna Mary had plunged so deeply into gloom she almost missed Sarah's soft call.

"Josh is here." Sarah led him into the kitchen, where Anna Mary was washing the last of the dinner dishes.

"It's so nice out today, you should sit out on the porch," Sarah suggested.

Her sister's words jagged Anna Mary's conscience. She didn't want to be reminded of Josh sitting on Rachel's porch or of Abe's visit yesterday and how she'd been drawn to him. Even worse, they'd finished most of the lemonade and all the cookies Anna Mary had baked for Josh earlier in the week. She'd have no more flour to make more until she got paid next Saturday.

She shuffled her feet, embarrassed she had nothing to serve Josh because she'd given his cookies to Abe and Tim. Shame filled her at the feelings that welled up inside whenever she remembered Abe's kindness, his smile, his understanding.

She should confess all this to Josh, but a sudden spurt of anger stopped her. What about him? How dare he come over here acting like nothing had happened after flirting with Rachel yesterday, sitting outside with her, laughing and talking?

Why was she worried about a brief conversation with Abe after Josh had stranded her at the volleyball field? After he'd humiliated her by sneaking into the woods with Rachel? After he'd spent the rest of the afternoon with Rachel? And for all Anna Mary knew, with the way he and Rachel had been enjoying each other's company, Josh could have stayed there all evening.

Her temper boiled up and over. Instead of coming clean about her own wrongdoings, she went on the attack.

Accusations flowed from her mouth before she could stop them.

"Why didn't you come over here last night?" He usually helped a bit with Saturday chores.

Josh shifted uncomfortably. The guilt on his face convinced Anna Mary he was hiding something. And she was pretty sure his secret was his interest in Rachel. That hurt so much, she kept up her attack.

"So, what were you doing at Rachel's?"

Instead of looking into Anna Mary's eyes, Josh stared at the worn linoleum. "I had to go there. Mamm offered to look after Rachel's *mamm* so Rachel could go to volleyball."

Before she could stop herself, Anna Mary's voice rose in a shriek. "You were at Rachel's *before* and *after* volleyball?"

"I only dropped Mamm off before the game."

"And you didn't see Rachel at all?"

"Not really. I carried Mamm's tote bag into the kitchen. I might have exchanged a few words about the game with Rachel. Nothing important." He took a deep breath. "You don't have anything to worry about. Mamm was right there."

"Your *mamm* wasn't with you two after the game, was she?" Bitterness laced Anna Mary's tone.

When Josh hung his head, it pierced Anna Mary's heart. He must have something to feel guilty about.

"Mamm wanted to spend more time with Rachel's *mamm*, so she suggested Rachel and I have lemonade while we waited. Rachel seemed reluctant, but she did it."

"Reluctant? Really?" Each word came out choppy and furious. "Then why were the two of you smiling and laughing and—"

"I don't know what Tim told you, but . . ."

That sent her over the edge. "Tim? Why would I need him to tell me?"

Josh didn't answer. Instead, his brow furrowed.

Anna Mary couldn't believe it. "You watched the buggy go by and didn't even recognize me? I thought you didn't wave because you were so caught up with Rachel."

"You were in Tim's buggy? It's not easy to see into the back seat. I saw your color hair but—" He stumbled to a stop. "I didn't think you'd be riding in Tim's buggy, so . . ."

So, he'd ignored her? Anna Mary couldn't believe it. Josh had been so caught up with Rachel, he hadn't recognized his own girlfriend?

He shifted from foot to foot. "If I'd known it was you, I'd—"

Anna Mary cut in. "You'd what? You'd have flirted with Rachel inside the house instead of on the porch?"

"We weren't flirting."

But his face flamed red, revealing his lie.

"Really?" At her icy tone, he ducked his head and made some flimsy excuse about a childhood memory.

That sliced through her, reminding her she'd lived in Honey Brook when he was growing up here. She'd never been a part of the youth group's closeness. The rest of them had so many shared experiences that didn't include her. If it hadn't been for Caroline reaching out, Anna Mary might never have made friends. Being Josh's girlfriend had secured her a stronger bond with the buddy bunch. Now that bond had frayed. Did he even want to date her anymore? Or would he rather be with Rachel?

Anna Mary was so busy wrestling with that possibility, she barely heard Josh's question. Had he asked about why she rode with Tim? Like he didn't know.

"You drove off and left me at the field. Everyone but Abe and Tim had driven off, and they went out of their way to make sure I got home."

"What? You were still at the field? I looked all over for you. I thought you were still angry with me so you'd gone home with Caroline."

"I told you I'd go home with you. I wouldn't have left without saying anything. No matter how upset I was."

"I know you wouldn't. I'm sorry. For everything. Will you forgive me?"

Anna Mary turned her back. She couldn't face him after his apology. Her own guilt weighed her down. Most of her anger at Josh had been directed mainly at herself. She'd done things that made her ashamed, and she'd assumed the worst about Josh. All her regret collided with the stress of taking care of Mamm and her sisters, the worries over having enough food for their next meal, the nervousness about the new job at the market . . .

She swiped at the tears trickling down her cheek. *Stop feeling sorry for yourself. Plenty of people are much worse off. Like Tim, who has no parents or siblings.*

"Maybe you need some time?" Josh asked gently.

"*Jah*," she choked out.

She needed time. Time to get over her jealousy. Time to sort out her feelings for Josh. And for Abe.

"I'll go now. Maybe we can talk again later in the week."

Anna Mary's throat had swollen shut, blocking off an answer.

After waiting a few moments and getting no response, he headed for the door. When it closed behind him, regret pooled in her stomach, soon to be replaced by relief.

She struggled to understand her tangled emotions,

but all she could do was sink down on the couch and let the tears fall. Anna Mary had no answers to the many questions niggling at her brain. The biggest ones concerned her future. Was she shedding tears over losing Josh? For not having a chance to get to know Abe? Or for a home situation that might never allow her to marry?

CHAPTER 4

Tim spent the rest of the weekend grumbling about Caroline's boyfriend.

"You jealous?" Abe finally asked.

"'Course not." Tim acted indignant.

Yet, before Tim turned away, Abe caught a glimmer of disappointment on his cousin's face. Had Tim fallen for Caroline?

"You know, if you treated her nicely, she might go out with you. You two have a lot in common."

Tim whirled around. "We do? Like what?"

Abe regretted his comment. He couldn't exactly say, *You both want to be number one. You both like to show off. And you both brag every time you score points*. He fumbled for a response. "Um, you both like volleyball. You're both great players. And you both like to win."

"Yeah, I guess." Tim looked glum. "I'm much better than Caroline, though, right?"

No way could Abe lie, but he also couldn't hurt his cousin's feelings. "I hope you beat her next time."

"Oh, I will. I have no doubt about that." Tim sneered at Abe. "If you don't muff the final point again."

"I'll try not to."

"See that you don't." Tim started out of the room. "That guy Caroline's dating from the market . . . I wonder where he lives."

Abe hoped Tim didn't plan to do something to sabotage Caroline's relationship. Yet, ever since Abe had seen the guy, something about him had been niggling at the back of his mind. Suddenly, it clicked into place.

"I know who he is," Abe blurted out. "He's from Fort Plain."

"What? The guy who came to the field? You know him? What's his name?"

"I don't remember his name, but I recall seeing his face in the newspapers."

"Your bishop lets you take pictures?"

"*Neh.* It was his mug shot."

"He's a criminal?"

If only Abe had kept his mouth shut. He'd been so startled about figuring it out, he hadn't thought what Tim might do with the information.

"Come on, Abe. Don't clam up on me now. What'd the guy do?"

That part Abe remembered clearly. An accident that killed an old man. The news had been plastered over all the papers for months before the trial. Abe hadn't followed it closely, but he remembered the driver had been jailed.

Tim was shaking Abe's arm. "What happened? Tell me."

Against his better judgment, Abe answered, "A hit-and-run."

"He ran someone over with his buggy?"

Abe shook his head. "*Neh*, he was driving a truck without a license."

A long, low whistle came from Tim's lips. "So, he killed someone?"

"*Jah*, an old man."

"We have to let Caroline know. She shouldn't be dating a killer."

His heart heavy, Abe agreed. He didn't want to be the one to tell her, but she should be aware of the man's past.

"Caroline will never believe me without proof," Tim said ruefully. "Was it in the paper?"

Abe nodded. "Our local paper had stories about the crash and the trial." He hadn't paid attention after the first article caught his eye.

"Let's go to the library tomorrow. Maybe we can find it online."

Reluctantly, Abe followed Tim into the library the next morning, and the reference librarian helped them find the archived article on the computer.

Tim nodded in satisfaction. "That's him. He looks older and tougher now, but prison'll do that to you."

Abe shot him a look. "You sound like you know what it's like. You been hanging around with criminals?"

To his surprise, Tim flushed. "None of your business."

"Tim." Abe's warning was low and fierce. "Don't get into trouble."

"I won't," Tim blustered, but he didn't sound convincing.

"You'll never have a chance with Caroline or any decent Amish girl if you head down that road."

"Who says I'm even interested in Amish girls?"

Abe dragged in a sharp breath. "You're not planning to turn *Englisch*, are you?"

Tim only shrugged.

If Daed or Myron had any idea Tim was considering leaving the Amish, they'd keep a closer eye on him. Abe had to let Daed know. Daed could decide what to tell Myron. Abe didn't want Myron to go into a panic and come down even harder on Tim. That would only make his cousin more likely to rebel.

Unlike Abe, Tim hadn't been baptized yet, so he wouldn't be shunned, but it would break Daed's heart. He'd tried to be a long-distance parent to Tim and to support Myron with raising the young boy. And Abe couldn't bear to think how Myron would react.

Tim interrupted Abe's thoughts. "Maybe I could find my sister if I were *Englisch*."

"What makes you think she's *Englisch*?"

"I don't know. None of it makes sense."

"That's for sure. But you can still search for her even if you join the church."

With a loud huff, Tim crossed his arms. "You promised not to pressure me."

"I'm not. I'm just pointing out that wouldn't make a difference."

At Tim's scowl, Abe dropped the subject and left it with the Lord.

Please, God, keep Tim from doing anything foolish or turning his back on the faith.

As soon as Abe prayed, an idea popped into his head. Tim had seemed his best self around Anna Mary's younger sister, Sarah. Maybe if they spent time with her, it might keep Tim in line. At least, it was worth a try.

Abe tried to ignore the way his own heart skipped a beat at the possibility of seeing more of Anna Mary.

* * *

On Monday, Anna Mary woke early and weeded some of the garden before breakfast. She and Sarah started on the laundry, which was doubly difficult because, with a broken clothesline, they had to find ways to hang the clothes in the basement until Anna Mary had the time and money to replace it.

Meanwhile, Emmie caused her usual mischief. That kept Anna Mary from completing all the jobs she'd planned to get done. She stayed up until almost midnight mending Hannah's two threadbare dresses. They'd been handed down through all four older girls, and now they were so worn they tore easily.

After rising before dawn on Tuesday to do more weeding, Anna Mary dragged into work at eight, overwhelmed and exhausted.

"What's wrong?" Caroline's sharp question pierced Anna Mary's misery.

She shouldn't carry her edginess into work, but try as she might, Anna Mary couldn't manage to paste a smile on her face. Instead of being honest about her roiling feelings, she snapped at Caroline about abandoning her at the volleyball field, even though Anna Mary knew full well Caroline had expected Josh to take his girlfriend—that is, if Anna Mary still was his girlfriend—home.

"What?" Caroline took a step back. "I thought you were riding with Josh."

"You thought wrong." Anna Mary regretted the bitter edge to her words.

Caroline didn't take offense. Instead, a concerned frown pulled her brows together, and she responded gently, "What happened?"

Her friend's kindness sliced through Anna Mary. She hung her head and avoided Caroline's eyes. After picking up a stack of trays, Anna Mary set a napkin and plastic silverware packet on each one, trying to get her emotions under control. It didn't help much, and she choked out, "I suppose some of it was my fault for getting jealous. Josh stormed off. I'm sure he thought you were still around and would take me home."

"I'm so sorry." Caroline reached out and hugged Anna Mary. "I never would have left if I'd known."

"I know you wouldn't. I don't blame you."

Feeling guilty after criticizing her friend for something that wasn't her fault, Anna Mary backed away from Caroline's embrace. She swallowed the lump in her throat. "We'd better get to work. It's almost time for the market to open."

Caroline studied her. "I'll shred cabbage while I listen."

Anna Mary's lips twisted a little. When did Caroline ever listen? Her friend must have picked up on her skeptical expression.

"I promise to stay quiet." Caroline placed her hand on her heart, obviously forgetting she had a knife in her hand.

When Anna Mary sucked in a sharp breath, Caroline lowered the sharp blade to the cutting board.

An unusual silence grew between them as Anna Mary filled tray after tray without speaking. Surprisingly, Caroline stayed quiet and waited.

Finally, Anna Mary confessed, "Josh accused me of not trusting him. I should have told him I did, but I pointed out he and Rachel had hidden in the trees."

"*Ach!*" Caroline clapped a hand over her mouth, but then she shot Anna Mary an encouraging glance to get her to continue.

"Things got worse from there." Anna Mary nibbled at

her lip for a moment before bringing herself to admit the rest. "I—I saw him with Rachel before the singing at Yoder's a few weeks ago. I never said anything, but Rachel had her hand on Josh's arm and—"

"Rachel does that with a lot of people. It's just her way."

"You don't understand. Maybe if you had a serious boyfriend, you'd know how I feel."

At Caroline's quick intake of breath and hurt expression, Anna Mary regretted snapping back. She'd hit Caroline in a sore spot. Anna Mary's own pain was no excuse for being cruel.

Dropping the tray she held, Anna Mary rushed over and hugged Caroline. "I'm so sorry."

Caroline stood stiff, her back rigid.

"Please will you forgive me? I didn't mean to hurt you."

After a few seconds, Caroline thawed and returned the hug. "I'm sorry you think Rachel has come between you and Josh, but you have nothing to worry about."

"Maybe I do. Rachel's so pretty and lively. I'm dull and plain."

"That's not true. Besides, if Josh preferred Rachel, he'd be taking her home after the singings instead of you."

"I guess." Anna Mary tried not to think about the joy on Josh's face as he laughed with Rachel. "Maybe he will now that we've fought."

"I doubt it."

But Anna Mary wasn't so sure. Caroline hadn't seen Josh and Rachel on the porch together. Anna Mary had never seen him so relaxed and . . . and . . . glowing. That was the only word that came to mind. *Glowing.* Anna Mary's mind shied away from even better descriptions. *Enamored. In love.*

* * *

Tim shook Abe awake at six-thirty on Tuesday morning. "Let's get ready. We need to go to the market. I want to get there when it opens."

"Shouldn't you go to bed? You worked third shift, didn't you?" Abe was still groggy, but he was sure Tim normally would still be asleep.

Even so, Abe should have been awake long ago. At home, he got up at four to milk the cows. He shouldn't get into the habit of oversleeping.

"*Jah*," Tim said, "but I want to get to Hartzler's Chicken Barbecue stand before the market opens, and we need to muck out the barn before we go."

Abe's eyes flew open. Anna Mary worked at that stand. As much as he wanted to see her, going to the stand where she and Caroline worked would be a terrible idea. "You can't give Caroline that news while she's at work."

Tim stuck out his chin belligerently. "Why not?"

"It's not fair to upset her during the workday."

"How else am I going to let her know? Anna Mary wouldn't tell us where she lives." Tim poked Abe in the ribs. "If you don't get up, I'll go without you."

No way would Abe let Tim taunt Caroline in the market. He needed to be there to keep the two of them from fighting. Abe hopped out of bed.

Tim's laugh followed Abe as he hurried to wash and dress. "Figures you wouldn't want to miss seeing Caroline's friend."

That isn't the only reason I'm going, Abe insisted to himself. But he couldn't deny it was the main one.

They arrived at the market soon after it opened, and Abe trailed Tim to the Hartzlers' stand. Anna Mary's brows rose in surprise as they approached, and at the welcoming message in her soft brown eyes, his pulse sped up. He paid no attention to Tim's banter—or more likely bickering—with Caroline until Tim called her closer.

"I have something important to tell you," Tim insisted.

Caroline tossed her head. "I'm not interested. I don't want to hear gossip."

"I don't think you want me to blast this so everybody hears."

Reluctantly, Abe pulled his gaze from Anna Mary's and whispered to Tim, "This isn't a good time." He angled his chin toward the customers lined up at the counter.

The man behind the counter evidently agreed. "Excuse me. We have people to wait on."

Anna Mary's cheeks pinkened, making her look even prettier, and she mumbled, "Sorry."

Abe's face probably matched hers. The man must be her boss, and they'd interfered with her job. Abe stepped aside to let the people behind him reach the counter. But his cousin continued blocking their access.

Tim blurted out, "I came to tell Caroline her boyfriend just got out of jail."

"Boyfriend?" The man stared at Caroline with a stunned expression.

Anna Mary turned to Caroline with a shocked face. "Jail?"

Clutching a container of salad, Caroline charged over to the counter and glared at Tim. "Stop spreading lies! You have no proof." She slammed the metal bin into the refrigerated case with such a loud clang that Tim jumped.

That little scare served his cousin right. Abe couldn't believe Tim had started this in a busy market while Caroline was working.

Tim smirked. "I do have proof. Well, at least my cousin Abe does." Tim jabbed Abe with his elbow. "Tell her, Abe."

The distress on Anna Mary's face made Abe feel sick. He shuffled his feet. "Not now, Tim."

But his cousin ignored him. With a smarmy grin, Tim confronted Caroline. "Abe's from New York State, and he recognized your boyfriend from when he was in the Fort Plain newspapers a few years back."

Caroline pinched her lips together and stayed silent.

"I can tell from your face you didn't know," Tim gloated.

Abe had to stop this train wreck of a situation. "Tim, not now. Not here." Abe sent an apologetic glance to Anna Mary. He hoped she'd realize he had nothing to do with this.

Well, that wasn't entirely true. He'd brought up the accident and the prison sentence, even if he hadn't remembered Noah Riehl's name until they'd found the old newspaper article.

"Tim." Abe clamped a hand on his cousin's elbow and steered him away, but Tim couldn't resist shooting one final triumphant smile at Caroline.

Ignoring Abe's plea, Tim broadcast in a loud voice, "Caroline needs to know her boyfriend killed a man."

Chattering customers fell silent as Tim's announcement rang out, and Anna Mary sucked in a shocked breath.

"You take that back." Her face red, Caroline appeared on the verge of tears. "That's not true."

Tim only shot her a self-satisfied smile and strode toward the exit.

As he and Abe disappeared through the door, Caroline muttered, "He made that up to upset me."

"Caroline," Anna Mary whispered, her tone desperate, "I don't think Abe would lie."

Caroline waved a hand, dismissing Anna Mary's comment. "You couldn't know that from one ride home with him."

Anna Mary had to be honest. "It wasn't only a ride home."

"What?" Caroline skidded to a stop.

Anna Mary gulped at her friend's incredulous expression. She hadn't planned on telling anyone about what had happened after the volleyball game, but she needed to defend Abe. She didn't know why that was so important to her. Perhaps because he'd been so kind, so honorable. She didn't like him being associated with Tim's underhandedness when she could see Abe had been uncomfortable with his cousin's actions.

"Tim and Abe drove me home from the volleyball field after Josh left me. I invited them in for lemonade."

Caroline stared at Anna Mary.

Anna Mary shrugged, trying to make it sound like no big deal. "They were hot and sweaty after the game, and they'd gone far out of their way to drop me off."

"You asked Tim into your house after the way he treated me?"

"He's all right once you get to know him. And Abe . . ." A smile curved Anna Mary's lips as she remembered their time together. "I've never met anyone so nice."

"Even Josh?" Caroline sounded shocked.

Anna Mary stared at the floor, afraid her friend's probing gaze might expose the truth. "I was upset with him that day."

"I see."

From her tone, Caroline saw a lot more than Anna Mary intended her to see.

Caroline's brother Gideon cleared his throat. "Do you two plan to wait on anyone today?" The stiffness of his shoulders and the tightness of his jaw revealed he was swallowing back a lecture because they had customers. He didn't glare at Anna Mary the same way he did at Caroline, but knowing Gideon was unhappy increased Anna Mary's guilt. She rushed to dip out salads. She couldn't afford to lose this job.

CHAPTER 5

On Thursday morning, Abe and Tim headed for Anna Mary's house. Part of Abe's plan to keep Tim out of trouble was to get him engaged in helping this family. Abe prayed encouraging his cousin to see Sarah as a substitute younger sister might bring out his brotherly feelings and reveal his caring side.

Tim was still pouting. He'd gone to the library yesterday and asked the librarian to print out the article about Caroline's boyfriend. He'd been determined to wave it in her face this morning, but Abe insisted they head over here first.

Tim stalked up to the front porch. "This better not take long."

"Relax. You said the market's open from eight to eight today." If Abe's strategy worked, though, maybe Tim would forget all about his plan for revenge.

Sarah opened the door, and her eyes widened. "Anna Mary's at work."

Feeling a little awkward, Abe smiled. "*Jah*, we know. Could we come in?"

Her eyebrows drew together in puzzlement. "Sure."

She opened the door and motioned them inside. "Mamm's still in bed," she whispered.

"I'm sorry." Abe's heart went out to her mother. His *daed* had gone through a rough time when the date of Mamm's death arrived last year. Daed never stayed in bed, but he'd grown silent and morose.

Sarah closed the door and turned to face them. "I wish I could bake cookies for you, but Anna Mary won't get more flour until after she gets paid this week."

Tim's lips set in a grim line. So he'd gotten the same message as Abe. These girls had little money. Did they have enough food?

Abe shuffled, unsure how to bring up that subject. "We stopped by to see if there are jobs we can do to help Anna Mary."

Tim's frown showed he wasn't happy with that, but Abe wanted to do what he could to help.

"I don't know." Sarah appeared hesitant.

"Your sister works hard, and I feel the Lord is leading me to do something to—"

Sarah's face brightened. "You might be the answer to my prayers. Emmie broke the clothesline a few days ago, and I can't figure out how to fix it."

"I'm sure we can help with that." Abe grinned, ignoring Tim's grimace. "Lead the way."

Sarah took them to the backyard, where Abe examined the post. The wood had rotted through, making it impossible to rehang the rope. "It split here." Abe pointed out the damage. "Maybe it should be replaced."

"*Ach!* We can't af—" Sarah clapped a hand over her mouth. Despite the worried look in her eyes, she brightened. "If you can just prop it up for now, God will provide."

A wail sounded from the house.

"That's Hannah. I have to get her before she wakes Mamm." Sarah dashed toward the back door.

Abe turned to Tim. "Can you get new metal posts and a plastic-coated clothesline at the hardware store? Along with enough cement to fill the holes?" Abe pulled out his wallet and handed Tim more than enough money to cover the cost. He held out some extra. "Maybe you could get a few things for their pantry and refrigerator."

"Me? What about you? No fair making me do all the work."

"I'll dig new holes for the posts. And if I finish before you get back, I'll weed that section of the garden." One third of the plot had been cleared of weeds. Abe figured that's where Anna Mary would start after work. "Unless you'd rather do it?" He reached for the money.

Wrinkling his nose, Tim snatched the money away. "Never mind."

By the time Tim returned, Abe had the holes ready and had started on the bean patch. As soon as they cemented the poles into place, Tim strung the clothesline, while Abe returned to weeding. In a few more weeks, Anna Mary would have a bountiful harvest that would last throughout the summer and into the fall with plenty of vegetables to can.

"Come help me finish the garden," Abe called after Tim finished.

"That's girls' work."

"Well, I didn't have any sisters, so my brothers and I had to do it."

"I didn't have a sister either," Tim said sullenly.

Abe regretted bringing that up. He should have kept his mouth shut.

"Didn't you have to weed Myron's garden?"

"*Jah*, as punishment." Tim growled under his breath. "Why'd you have to bring that up?"

"Come on. We can do a few of Anna Mary's chores." Sensing that wouldn't soften Tim's reluctance, Abe added, "It'll help Sarah. She has a lot to handle while Anna Mary's at the market."

Tim made a face but joined Abe in the garden. As they weeded, Tim grumbled. "It's too hot to be doing this, and I have to go into work tonight."

"What else would you do with your time?"

"None of your business."

Abe smiled to himself. Actually, this gardening might keep Tim from getting into more trouble today than just annoying Caroline.

Two hours later, Sarah popped out to check on them, and she blinked at the posts. Then she bit her lip. "I hope Anna Mary won't be upset," she mumbled. "I—I didn't mean for you to replace the posts."

"Don't worry about the cost. It's a gift." Abe hadn't meant to make her worry.

"A gift? But—" She looked dazed. "*Danke*. Would you like some lunch?"

"We brought some from home. There's enough for everyone, so I hope you'll share it with us."

Abe ignored Sarah's faint protest and headed for the buggy. While she went to change Hannah, he carried a large cooler into the house, while Tim hefted an enormous cardboard box filled with fruits, vegetables, and canned goods. The little girls stared agog as they peeked inside.

As Abe unloaded milk, meats, and cheeses, he encouraged Beth and Emmie to race to put everything away before Sarah returned with Hannah. They giggled at the game. By the time Sarah entered the kitchen, the refrig-

erator and cabinets had been filled, and her sisters had set
out plates for the thick sandwiches, red beet eggs, and
chips Abe had prepared for everyone.

Watching the little faces lit up with delight at the food
he'd laid out, Abe's chest twinged. They eyed it all hun-
grily but bowed their heads for prayer. Even Tim looked
a little touched to see how they tore into their meals. And
he didn't protest when Abe suggested helping the girls
with all their indoor chores. Abe only wished he could
see Anna Mary's face when she returned home to completed chores and food in the kitchen.

Fridays were always so busy at the market, Anna Mary
barely had time to breathe. Customers ordered large take-
out orders for the weekends, and even those who weren't
buying barbecued chicken often bought large containers
of macaroni, potato, or broccoli salad for cookouts. So
when she saw a familiar person heading through the
doors, she groaned.

Caroline followed Anna Mary's gaze and echoed
Anna Mary's moan. But Anna Mary perked up as a tall,
dark-haired man trailed Tim. Her heart hip-hopped when
he beamed in her direction. They were coming this way.

Once they got to the stand, Abe attempted to hold his
cousin back, but Tim squeezed past the other customers
and waved a sheet of paper in front of Caroline. "Here's
something you need to read."

Abe winced and mouthed to Anna Mary, *I'm sorry. I
thought he was going to slip that to her. Not show it to
everyone.*

She smiled to show she understood, while Tim pressed
closer.

Ignoring Caroline's dismissive attitude and hints that

he was blocking customers, he stuck the paper under her nose. "Just read the headline."

The bold words "Drunk Amish Man Kills Senior Citizen" emblazoned across the top dragged Anna Mary's attention away from Abe. She gasped. The article seemed to be about that Noah Riehl Caroline was interested in.

"I already know all about it." Caroline waved a casual hand. "That article got the facts wrong."

Anna Mary barely heard her friend sparring with Tim, declaring Noah was innocent, and claiming she'd already read the article he'd brought. Anna Mary's attention was on Abe. After all he'd done for her and her family yesterday, she wanted to thank him, but he'd never hear her over Tim's tirade. Plus, she needed to wait on customers.

She gave Abe an apologetic smile and hurried to the back with an empty macaroni salad pan to refill. As she pulled out another premade batch from the refrigerator, she couldn't help overhearing Caroline arguing with Tim.

It really bothered Anna Mary that her friend seemed to be making up lies to defend this auctioneer she barely knew. One thing Anna Mary had always admired about Caroline was her complete honesty. *Jah*, she often blurted out things she should keep to herself, but she told the truth, even when it was unpleasant. Everyone knew where they stood with her. Until now.

Did falling for someone make you dishonest? A sharp pang shot through Anna Mary at the memory of Josh with Rachel on her porch last weekend. He'd tried to pass it off as only being friendly. But on Tuesday afternoon, Cathy Zehr, a thirty-something *alt maedel* and the local gossip, had told Anna Mary she'd seen Josh coming from Rachel's house on Monday with a big grin, and earlier that day, Cathy made sure to inform Anna Mary, Josh had helped Rachel deliver quilted pillows to a market stand. Despite being at the market, he hadn't even come by to talk to Anna Mary. Why would he be doing those things unless he was interested in Rachel?

Tears stung her eyes. *If he'd rather be with Rachel—which it definitely seems he would—why doesn't he just tell me?*

Anna Mary winced. She hadn't admitted her attraction to Abe.

Guilt flooded through her. The Scripture was right. She needed to take the beam from her own eye before pointing out the mote in Josh's.

Caroline and Tim had progressed to hurling insults at each other by the time Anna Mary returned. Her eyes blurry with moisture, she rushed to put the heavy metal container in the refrigerated case out front as Caroline threw one last barbed comment at Tim and turned to flounce off. She and Anna Mary collided. Caroline grabbed for the container's edge and righted it before it spilled.

"Good catch," Tim called. "Maybe we should play baseball together sometime."

Caroline ground her teeth together.

Though Anna Mary knew she shouldn't be critical, the question on her mind flew from her lips. She kept her voice low to prevent Tim from overhearing. "Why are you making things up to defend Noah?"

"I'm not. I asked him, and he told me the truth about the accident."

"Really?" Anna Mary couldn't believe it. Why had Caroline kept all this from her? "When did you talk to him?"

"Yesterday."

How had Caroline seen him yesterday with the market

closed? And why hadn't she mentioned anything about it today? Since when did they keep things like this from each other?

Anna Mary's conscience poked at her. *You haven't been telling her your secrets.*

"What are you two girls whispering about?" Tim demanded. "How handsome we are?" He gestured toward himself and Abe.

"You wish." Caroline's cutting remark was edged with ice.

Anna Mary sucked in a breath. "Caroline, how could you?" She didn't want Abe to think she agreed with her friend about him.

Tim didn't act offended, but Abe glanced away. The last thing Anna Mary wanted to do was hurt him after all the kind things he'd done.

Caroline whispered, "Tim has a big head. Somebody needs to put him in his place."

"That's between him and God." Annoyed, Anna Mary shoved the macaroni salad into place and swished around Caroline. Her eyes on Abe, Anna Mary apologized. "I'm sure Caroline didn't mean it. She was just teasing."

Thank heavens, Caroline kept her mouth shut, although she appeared to be fuming.

"Hey, Caroline," Tim called. "You gonna apologize too?" When she ignored him, he shrugged. "Guess I won't invite you to another volleyball match tomorrow, then."

"That's all right. I have more important plans," Caroline said airily.

Tim sneered. "A date with your ex-con boyfriend?"

"*Neh*, a trip to New York. And now if you don't mind, we have customers who'd like to order."

"I do mind, but just to show you how thoughtful I

am—" He stepped aside with a flourish. Then he caught Anna Mary's attention. "The rest of your team want to play?"

Shocked by Caroline's bald-faced lie, Anna Mary couldn't respond at first. Why hadn't Caroline just said she couldn't make it or that she had chores to do? Why tell such a fake story?

Abe shifted, drawing Anna Mary's attention. When he smiled as if hoping she'd agree, she found herself answering, "We'll be there, with or without Caroline." She couldn't believe she'd just said that.

"I hope it's with." Tim shot Caroline a cheeky smile. "I love how she dives into mud puddles." Abe elbowed Tim and frowned, but Tim kept going. "Without her, your team will get creamed."

With a wave, he turned to leave. Abe followed, but gazed at Anna Mary over his shoulder until they exited. Her spirits dipped as the door closed behind him. What was going on with her heart and her emotions?

Anna Mary turned to find Caroline studying her with a thoughtful expression. Embarrassed, Anna Mary jabbed at her friend. "I wish you wouldn't lie like that to Tim."

"I didn't tell any lies today."

"*Ooo*, Caroline. You fibbed about going to New York."

"*Neh*, I didn't. Mrs. Vandenberg is taking me after work tomorrow. We'll be back on Monday. We're going to Fort Plain." Caroline paused to ring up an *Englischer* Gideon had waited on.

Anna Mary wrinkled her brow. "Fort Plain? Abe's from there. You plan to visit the Amish community?"

At Caroline's *jah*, Anna Mary tamped down a flicker of jealousy. Why was her friend going to Abe's community? Not that she'd want to go while Abe was here visiting, but still . . .

The rest of the day, they stayed too busy to talk. As they cleaned up after closing, though, Anna Mary brought it up again. "Why does Mrs. Vandenberg want to see the Amish in Fort Plain, and why is she taking you along? You don't know anyone there, do you?" *Other than Abe, of course. And he's in Lancaster now.*

With a fierce expression, Caroline responded, "She thinks Noah is innocent, and I'm positive he is. We're going to get proof."

Noah? Caroline planned to go all that way to try to prove the auctioneer hadn't killed a man? Anna Mary wasn't sure the trip was a wise idea, even if Mrs. Vandenberg was involved. The elderly woman was known for her matchmaking talent, but surely she didn't plan to encourage a relationship between Caroline and an Amish man with a past like that.

As they worked, Anna Mary tried to steer Caroline's thoughts in a different direction by bringing up Tim's interest in her. He might not be so bad after she got to know him. And it might be fun to double-date.

Anna Mary brought herself up short. What was she thinking? Instead of picturing herself on a date with Josh, she'd seen herself smiling at Abe in the back seat of Tim's buggy.

CHAPTER 6

When Anna Mary arrived home after work on Saturday, she stopped in surprise. Mamm sat on the couch, propped up by pillows. Although her face was wan and her eyes were distant, it was the first time she'd been out of bed in more than a week. Anna Mary rejoiced. This was usually the first step back to participating in family life and transitioning back into her mothering role.

What happened? she mouthed to Sarah. It normally took a few weeks before Mamm reached this point.

Sarah grabbed Anna Mary's elbow and dragged her into the kitchen. "Abe came over this morning after you left for work and talked Mamm into letting me help her get dressed. Then he walked her into the living room. She's been there all day."

"I can't believe it." Anna Mary had sweet-talked, begged, and coaxed Mamm to get out of bed every morning, but she'd never responded. Yet, she'd complied with Abe's suggestion.

Anna Mary smiled. He had a way about him that made people want to cooperate.

"And that's not all." Sarah's face glowed. "He mucked out the barn and played games with Emmie and Beth to keep them occupied so I could do the chores while Hannah napped." Her eyes glittered with unshed tears. "It was the first time since you started at the market that I got all my jobs done."

"I'm sorry, Sarah. I wish I could be here to share the work, but I'm so glad Abe made things easier."

"I'm not blaming you, Anna Mary. I know you have to work. But Emmie usually gets into so much trouble by spilling or upsetting things, I spend most of my time cleaning up her messes."

Anna Mary smiled ruefully. She knew just how much trouble her younger sister caused. God bless Abe. What a wonderful gift he'd been to their family!

With Mamm out of bed, Anna Mary skipped the volleyball game. She regretted not seeing Abe or thanking him, but she needed to spend time with Mamm.

But the rest of the weekend, Anna Mary drifted off into daydreams about Abe. Every time she passed her weed-free garden, her heart filled with gratitude. Every time she opened the cupboards or refrigerator, she thanked God for His and Abe's kindness. And when Mamm allowed Anna Mary to help her dress for church, Anna Mary hummed a hymn from the *Ausbund*.

She wished Abe went to her church so she could see him. Only to thank him, of course. But Sundays also meant going to the singing with Josh.

By the time he arrived in the late afternoon, Anna Mary's topsy-turvy feelings had her so on edge, she hit him with a barrage of questions right after he walked through the door.

"I thought you said you weren't interested in Rachel. Why were you at her house on Monday? And why did you have a big smile on your face?" Anna Mary sounded like a jealous nag, but she couldn't stop her outburst.

"And why did you go to the market with her on Tuesday? Cathy Zehr said you helped her carry in her quilts and pillows."

Josh took a step back. Color flushed his face, and he seemed a little defensive. "On Monday, I went to Rachel's house to repair the barn roof. It had a huge hole that was letting in water."

"And that's why you were smiling afterward?"

Josh hesitated and shifted from one foot to the other. "I'm pretty sure as I headed home, I thought about you. And maybe sugar cookies."

"Sugar cookies?"

He waved that away, but she eyed him carefully and waited, letting him know she expected an answer.

"It's nothing."

From the way he fidgeted, Anna Mary could tell there was more to the story.

Finally, he confessed, "Rachel gave me a bag of cookies to thank me for the repairs. They're my favorites."

Anna Mary couldn't believe it. "You never told me that." Never once had Josh mentioned he liked sugar cookies. She always made drop cookies, like oatmeal or, when she could afford it, chocolate chip. "How did Rachel know that?"

Again, he flapped a casual hand as if it weren't important. "We used to play together when we were nine. That was before you moved here, I guess."

"I see." Anna Mary infused those words with all the fears and suspicions swirling through her. "So, you were smiling about sugar cookies from Rachel?" *Or were you smiling because the cookies came from Rachel?*

Josh adopted a conciliatory tone. "I'm happy for sugar cookies from anyone, especially delicious ones from you."

Oh, really? Anna Mary planted her hands on her hips. "I never made you sugar cookies."

"I, um, only meant I'd be happy to have them if you did." He quickly tacked on, "But all your cookies are delicious. I like every kind."

Anna Mary blinked, trying to assess his truthfulness. She felt like a grouch making such a big deal over a few cookies, but those cookies definitely meant something to Josh. Something more than a sweet snack. And added to that were all the times Josh had been spotted with Rachel. Cathy Zehr had made sure to tell Anna Mary all the details.

A horrible dread in the pit of her stomach made her wonder if there'd also been times he hadn't been seen. He still had more to answer for. A lot more.

The Tuesday trip to the market with Rachel bothered Anna Mary. Josh always started jobs at six in the morning with his *daed*'s construction crew, and his *daed* was strict about not missing work. Josh had hardly ever visited Anna Mary at the market. How had he gotten time off?

She didn't bother asking that. She was more interested in the answer to a different question. "And spending time with Rachel at the market?"

"I ran into Mrs. Vandenberg, and she told me to take those pillows. I couldn't refuse, could I?" Josh flashed her a *what-did-you-expect-me-to-do?* expression.

Everyone obeyed Mrs. Vandenberg. She owned the market, and despite being a frail lady in her nineties, she commanded great respect. Everyone always complied with her requests.

Josh doing what she asked was understandable, but even more fear snaked through Anna Mary. Mrs. Vandenberg had another, more important role at the market. She'd matched dozens of couples. If she threw two people together . . .

Anna Mary couldn't control her alarm. Her voice slid up the register to nearly hysterical. "Mrs. Vandenberg paired you with Rachel?"

"Paired us?" Josh stared at her as if she were *verrückt*. "I only walked a short distance to the craft stand."

"You don't understand. Mrs. Vandenberg is a matchmaker. Caroline told me every couple she's matched has gotten married."

Josh laughed, which only upset Anna Mary more. "Mrs. Vandenberg wouldn't pair up someone who already has a girlfriend. Besides, she'd have do a lot more than that to get me together with Rachel."

Anna Mary frowned. His words should have reassured her, but her panic had grown. Had Mrs. Vandenberg's request been part of a matchmaking plan?

She tried to calm herself and ask logical questions. "Did you come to the market with Rachel? Or did Mrs. Vandenberg ask you to go there to meet her?"

"*Neh* to both."

"Then why were you at the market?" Anna Mary crossed her arms and hoped she didn't sound too petulant. "You didn't stop by and talk to me."

"I came to see you."

He did? She couldn't believe his *daed* had let him. But that wasn't the most pressing question she wanted answered. "Why didn't you come up to the counter?"

"You were busy."

That was no excuse. "We could have talked for a few minutes between customers."

Josh's brows drew together in a frown. "You weren't waiting on customers."

"Huh?"

His eyes filled with hurt. "Looked like you were pretty busy with that guy from volleyball—Abe."

Anna Mary gasped. "Josh, that's not true. And you know it. I didn't even say anything to him." At least she didn't think she did.

"Your eyes and smile seemed to do the talking."

"I can't believe you said that. I was only trying to thank him."

"He obviously appreciated the thanks." The sarcastic bite in Josh's words cut deep.

"*Ooo*, that's mean. You know I'd never—"

Josh held up a hand. "Of course not. And neither would I."

That brought her up short. "I guess not," she mumbled, although she didn't sound very convincing. Perhaps because of her own guilt. And some huge doubts about how Josh really felt about Rachel.

He pointed to the clock on her living room wall. "We'd better get going, or we'll be late for the singing."

Anna Mary didn't want to be responsible for either of them getting reprimanded, so she hurried to help Sarah get everything in order for the evening. Mamm had gone straight to bed after church, but the sisters did the dishes and got the younger girls ready for bed.

Josh helped, the way he usually did. Anna Mary was grateful for his assistance, especially because she hadn't been very nice to him. She wanted to apologize and set things right, but her guilty conscience stood in the way.

They went out to his buggy together, but their unity had been broken. And rather than mending the cracks, they'd only widened them. If she didn't confess to her attraction to Abe and ask for forgiveness . . . if she couldn't get over her jealousy of Rachel . . . and if neither of them could trust the other, how could their relationship work?

Silence reigned in the buggy as they traveled to the singing. After they arrived and played some volleyball, they filed inside. Josh took the last seat left on the *buwe*'s side, far from hers. Although she shouldn't be relieved, she was . . . until she realized who else sat at that end of the table.

Rachel, of course.

Not that Rachel paid much attention to Josh. Most of the time. But a few times, she seemed to be sneaking peeks at him through her lowered eyelashes. A slow burn began in Anna Mary's stomach and seared its way up until she was steaming.

Tonight, she didn't even have Caroline here to distract her. Anna Mary hoped her best friend would get the answers she was seeking in New York. With those newspaper clippings Tim had copied, it seemed more likely Caroline would get her heart broken, if she'd fallen for that Noah. What Anna Mary couldn't figure out was why Mrs. Vandenberg had taken Caroline there. Unless she thought Caroline wouldn't accept the truth without proof.

Lord, please help Caroline not to be too disappointed if things don't turn out the way she hopes.

During the break for refreshments, Anna Mary clenched her teeth as Rachel sat at the table, appearing fragile and beautiful. *Buwe* flocked around her, offering her food, vying for attention. She had so many admirers. Why did she want Josh?

He stood rigid beside Anna Mary, purposely looking everywhere but at Rachel. That only made Anna Mary even more sure something was going on between them. When two people couldn't look in each other's direction, it meant they'd either just broken up or they had something to hide.

Meanwhile, the other girls in the group iced Rachel out. They'd done the same at the church meal that morning. By now, everyone had heard about Rachel and Josh in the woods. Gossip still flowed freely tonight. Cathy Zehr's stories were making the rounds. Other buddy bunch members gave Anna Mary sympathetic glances and shot daggers at Rachel. Maybe that's why Rachel had stayed seated while others milled around getting refreshments. Still, she didn't lack for attention with all the males doting on her.

Anna Mary drew in a relieved breath when they returned to the singing. She kept her attention on the hymns, but the more they sang about faith and truth and God's will, the more ashamed she became. If she hoped to mend the rift with Josh, she had to be honest and let him know someone else had distracted her. Then she'd ask for forgiveness.

On the way home after the singing, she tried to confess several times, but the words stuck in her throat. Finally, she turned to him, determined to do it, but he cleared his throat and spoke first.

"Anna Mary, we didn't get to finish talking before the singing. I'm sorry my actions upset you."

She sniffled. "It wasn't you so much as it was Rachel. She's such a flirt. Did you see how she kept all those boys waiting on her, bringing her food and everything?" As soon as Anna Mary said it, she wished she hadn't. She'd been planning to admit her own faults, not point a finger at someone else's.

Josh asked mildly, "Do you think she really likes all that attention?"

"Of course she does. If she didn't, she'd tell them to go away." But Josh's question made her think. Rachel didn't go out of her way to attract attention. Maybe she couldn't help the way *buwe* clustered around her.

That didn't make Anna Mary feel any better. None of the boys had ever sought her out. Except Josh.

And Abe, a little voice reminded her.

Abe didn't count. He didn't live around here, and he'd soon be gone. If she lost Josh, she might never marry. No husband. No children. No family.

Josh took a deep breath and blurted out, "Speaking of Rachel, I'm scheduled to do repair work on her roof this week. I wanted to let you know so you won't be upset about rumors of me being at her house."

"What?" Anna Mary shifted in her seat to stare at him. She couldn't believe this. Was he deliberately planning ways to see Rachel? "How can you do this to me so soon after all the other things that happened?" Anna Mary cringed. She sounded bossy and jealous.

"It's not like I have a choice."

His family's construction company worked on multiple sites at one time. One or two of his brothers could handle Rachel's roof. "Why don't you ask your *daed* to let you work on a different job?"

Josh stopped the buggy at a stop sign near her house but didn't meet her eyes. "Daed didn't book this job," he mumbled. "I did." At her sharp intake of breath, he hastened to explain. "Not with Rachel. Someone else asked me to do it and is paying for it."

Anna Mary narrowed her eyes. "Just you? Not your family business?"

He focused on turning his horse onto the narrow lane that led to her house before answering, "*Jah*, it'll only be me. It's not a big job. Shouldn't take more than a few days."

"You'll be at Rachel's for several *days*?!" Anna Mary

winced. She hadn't meant her question to come out so sharp and cutting.

"I'll be on Rachel's *roof* for a few days."

His matter-of-fact tone and emphasis on the word *roof* did little to ease her anxiety.

"But you'll still have to see her." And what about during his breaks and mealtimes? Would Rachel flirt with him outside? Ply him with his favorite sugar cookies?

Visions of Josh's relaxed, happy face as he and Rachel sat on her porch spooled before Anna Mary's eyes. Suppose they did that every day?

"I'll knock on her door the first day to get permission to store the shingles in their barn and find out what times will be best so I don't disturb her *mamm*. After that, I'll be coming and going without being around her."

Josh tried to reassure Anna Mary by making the job sound routine, but she couldn't shake the pictures from her mind. She wished she could act more reasonable, but this was Rachel they were talking about. It seemed every *bu* in the *g'may* had a crush on her, even some who had girlfriends.

Trying not to sound as desperate as she felt, Anna Mary asked, "Can't you ask the person who's paying you to get someone else to do the job?"

He shook his head. "If she gets upset with us, Daed might lose a lot of work. She hires us for many different jobs."

Anna Mary frowned. "She?" When he didn't answer, she tilted her head, encouraging him to answer.

"Mrs. Vandenberg," he muttered.

"Mrs. Vandenberg?" The name came out as a screech. "She had you carry Rachel's pillows? And now she wants you to work at her house?" If that wasn't a clear sign the woman had started matchmaking . . .

Josh stared over at her with a puzzled expression. He obviously wasn't reading the signs the same way she was.

Anna Mary had to explain. "What if she's doing this to match you up with Rachel?"

"She'd be making a big mistake. No matter what she does, I could never get together with Rachel."

"Why not?" Anna Mary eyed him with suspicion.

He couldn't meet her eyes. "Something happened between us years ago. Before you moved here."

"You . . . you . . .?" she faltered.

Evidently, Josh read the meaning in her expression. "*Neh.* Absolutely not. Nothing like that."

"Oh." Anna Mary relaxed a little. "She flirted with you like she does with all the boys, and then she turned you down?"

He shook his head. "I never joined that group of admirers."

"What happened, then?"

"It's a long story, and I need to get home. Daed wants to start extra early tomorrow because we lost roofing time when it rained Friday and Saturday. We got interior work done on the Myers's house, but . . ."

As he turned into her driveway, she pleaded, "Just tell me a short version of the story."

"It occurred so long ago. Better just to forget it."

"But I can't forget it if I don't know what it is."

His laugh sounded forced. "That's true." He waved a hand to quell her protests. "It doesn't matter to *us.*"

She studied him with worried eyes. "You won't go in her house?"

"I don't need to go inside for anything."

"You'd better not." Anna Mary hated how demanding she sounded. Here she was giving him an ultimatum when she should be giving herself one. She hopped out of the buggy and hurried toward her house, her thoughts churning.

Were her fears about Josh leaving her for Rachel more about her own unfaithfulness than about his?

CHAPTER 7

Shortly before the market closed at four on Tuesday, Mrs. Vandenberg stopped at the stand and beckoned to Anna Mary. Gideon nodded, giving her permission to step away from waiting on customers to meet with the elderly woman.

Mrs. Vandenberg rooted through her large purse and pulled out an envelope. "I wonder if you could do me a favor, dear."

"I'd be happy to." Did this have something to do with matchmaking? Visions of Abe danced in her head before she brought them under control. Why had he come to mind? She and Josh were dating. At least she hoped they were. Maybe Mrs. Vandenberg would help them get their relationship back on track.

"You live near Rachel Glick, don't you?" Balancing on her cane with one hand, Mrs. Vandenberg clutched an envelope with Rachel's name on it in slight shaky, but perfect, penmanship.

"*Jah*." Images of Josh and Rachel laughing together on Rachel's porch flitted through Anna Mary's mind. She struggled to hide her jealousy.

"Could you deliver this to Rachel on your way home?"

Anna Mary's stomach twisted. She couldn't say *neh* to this sweet old lady who owned the market, but Rachel? What excuse could Anna Mary give? She'd rather face a poisonous snake or . . .

Mrs. Vandenberg's sharp eyes raked over Anna Mary's face. "Sometimes we need to face up to our fears."

Startled, Anna Mary took a step back. Had this *Englischer* read her thoughts?

"It's important for Rachel to get this message before suppertime."

With trembling fingers, Anna Mary took the letter Mrs. Vandenberg extended.

The elderly *Englischer* patted Anna Mary on the shoulder. "You're braver than you know."

Anna Mary wasn't so sure about that. Even thinking about approaching Rachel turned her legs to mush. How could she face the person who'd flirted with her boyfriend, who'd made him happier than she'd ever seen him?

As she hobbled off, Mrs. Vandenberg called over her shoulder, "We humans make plans and think we know best, but trust your future to God. He's able to do much more than we can ask or think."

Puzzling over that, Anna Mary headed back to take customers' orders. Hadn't she already done that? Perhaps the *Englischer* meant the meeting with Rachel.

Her face curious, Caroline scurried over. "What did she give you?"

Wordlessly, Anna Mary held out the envelope.

Caroline sucked in a breath. "Do you think she's *fer-hoodled*? Maybe she got you mixed up with Rachel. After all, she is in her nineties."

"*Neh*, she asked me to deliver it." *And no way would anyone confuse me with Rachel.* Rachel was everything

Anna Mary was not—a slim, petite, gorgeous strawberry blonde. Anna Mary, with her dark hair and eyes, had a sturdy farm-girl build.

"But why?" Caroline demanded. "That doesn't make sense." She made a moue of disappointment. "I was hoping it would be something about you and Josh."

I was too—or maybe Abe and me? That was impossible. He couldn't move to Lancaster, and Mamm would never travel to New York State. Mamm had cousins who'd settled somewhere around that area, but she absolutely refused to leave town to visit them.

With a sigh, Anna Mary tucked the letter into the pocket of her spring jacket. Usually, the last hour of the day inched along, but today it flew by. She dragged her feet with the cleaning, but even that moved swiftly.

"Look at all the chicken we have left." Gideon frowned. "I usually plan better than this."

"Anna Mary can take it home," Caroline suggested. "Your sisters like barbecued chicken, don't they?"

"*Jah*, they love it. But I couldn't take all five of those chickens."

"We're not open tomorrow. And our family is tired of chicken." Gideon packaged it up along with a huge foil package of fries.

Torn between shame and gratitude, Anna Mary took the large shopping bag he'd packed. She hoped Gideon hadn't made this mistake on purpose to feed her family.

Even though she should hurry home with the meal, Anna Mary dawdled over cleaning the refrigerated cases because she dreaded stopping at Rachel's. When she could delay no longer, Anna Mary forced her feet to the employee exit as if she were heading to a disciplinary meeting with the bishop. Not that she'd ever had one, but this must be what it felt like.

As she waited in rush hour traffic at a stoplight, a still, small voice spoke to her heart, nudging her to ask Rachel for forgiveness. Anna Mary had often gossiped about and criticized Rachel. Mrs. Vandenberg's message about courage played through Anna Mary's mind. Perhaps this was what the wise old lady meant.

After pulling into Rachel's driveway, Anna Mary tied her horse to the hitching post and walked toward the porch. The same porch Josh had been sitting on with Rachel.

Resentment rose inside Anna Mary, blocking off her good intentions. And when Rachel opened the door, looking somewhat disheveled, but still so beautiful, the words of apology died on Anna Mary's lips. Her throat tight, she could only hold out the envelope.

Behind Rachel, a man's voice called out, "Did you want me to put the casserole in the oven?"

A very familiar man's voice.

"Was—was that Josh?" Anna Mary asked.

Rachel appeared to be fumbling for words.

Josh, holding a little boy, stepped out of the kitchen. "Rachel, I put the casserole in. Hope that was—" He stopped short. "A-Anna Mary? What are you doing here?"

"I should be asking you that, don't you think?" She thrust the envelope in Rachel's direction without meeting either of their gazes. "Mrs. Vandenberg asked me to drop this off. I thought it was an odd request, but now I know why."

Guilt chased across Rachel's face, and she clutched the letter so hard it crumpled.

Anna Mary's eyes stung. She couldn't believe it. Josh had said he wouldn't go inside, hadn't he? He'd broken his promise.

"Anna Mary." Josh's words came out like a plea.

Was he going to try to justify this?

But she couldn't face him. Not now. Not like this. Not with Rachel watching. As he neared the doorway, Anna Mary whirled and fled.

"Wait," Josh called after her. "I can explain."

Her voice thick with tears, Anna Mary replied, "You have no excuse." She yanked her horse's reins from around the post and jumped into her buggy. Then she turned her horse around and galloped off.

Although he worried about overstaying his welcome, Abe prolonged his visit at Anna Mary's house until almost suppertime. He lingered over a few repairs Sarah or her *mamm* wanted done, but Anna Mary still hadn't come home. He'd expected her long before this.

Not that he had to leave. Nobody was waiting back at the house. Tim had moved to a different shift, so he didn't need to be picked up until later this evening. And a widow from church had invited Myron for dinner, so Abe had planned his day to have as much time with Anna Mary as possible, because he'd head back to New York soon. He'd been hoping to get invited for supper, so he'd brought extra groceries, just in case.

While he waited, Abe chatted with Anna Mary's *mamm*, Esther, and played a simple board game with five-year-old Emmie and three-year-old Beth. As the game grew lively, Abe had to focus more on the board. Esther's head drooped against a throw pillow.

"Would you like me to help you back to the bedroom?" he offered.

She sighed and closed her eyes. "I'll try to stay awake until Anna Mary comes home."

To keep her alert, Abe restarted their conversation. "You mentioned relatives in Stone Arabia? That's not too far from where I live."

A faint smile curved Esther's lips, and her eyes fluttered open. "*Jah*, my cousin Delores. We were best friends growing up." She exhaled a long, sad breath. "She moved to New York after she married. I really miss her."

Hope bubbled inside Abe. "Do you ever visit her?" Maybe it would be another opportunity to see Anna Mary.

"*Neh*, I haven't seen her in almost twenty years. We write letters, of course, but it's not the same."

"It's beautiful country up there. Maybe you should go to see her. I'd be happy to show you around." *And to spend more time with your daughter.*

"I couldn't do that. It's much too far. The trip would be exhausting." Just thinking about it seemed to drain her. Once again, she sank back against the cushions, and her eyes drifted shut.

Abe tried not to let his disappointment show. All the excitement flowing through him over the idea of Anna Mary's family coming to New York leaked out.

Outside, a buggy clattered up the driveway at a reckless speed. If Abe didn't have Tim's buggy, he'd suspect his cousin. He jumped to his feet. There must be an emergency.

"I'll go out and see what's wrong," he announced and rushed to the back door.

Sarah, who was changing Hannah in a bedroom, called out a *danke*. "I'll be right out."

Abe skidded to a halt at the sight of the heaving, sweat-slicked horse. When he spied Anna Mary's stricken face, he dashed toward her. "Are you all right?" He longed to open his arms and draw her to him. Instead, he grasped his suspenders to prevent his hands from moving.

"Josh," she croaked.

"He's hurt?" Even if the man was his rival, Abe would race to help him.

Anna Mary shook her head. Then, as if each word being pulled out of her caused agony, she explained, "He . . . he's at Rachel's . . . house. Inside. Holding a little boy. I don't even know whose boy it is." She rubbed her eyes and hung her head.

Abe's hands clenched into fists. How dare Josh hurt Anna Mary this way? "*Ach*, Anna Mary, that must have been awful."

"It was. I—I don't know if I can ever trust him again. He promised he wouldn't go inside her house."

"Then he shouldn't have. When you make a vow, you need to keep it."

She nodded and turned damp eyes to Abe, and again, he fought the urge to fold her in his arms. He reached for the buggy shafts.

"Let me help you unhitch the buggy and rub down the horse while you tell me about it."

Anna Mary's face burned with shame. "I shouldn't have driven the horse like that." *Jah*, she'd been upset, but she had no right to mistreat Brownie.

She ran an apologetic hand down her horse's neck. "I'm so sorry, Brownie." She'd never done that before. "I won't ever do that again, I promise."

Abe finished unhooking the buggy and dragged it into the barn while Anna Mary ran the chicken and fries into the house and then led Brownie to a sunny spot by the barn. By the time he joined her, she'd rinsed off the horse and regained some of her composure. Although how did you recover from your boyfriend's betrayal?

Following her lead, he picked up a sweat scraper and started on the other side of the horse. "Want to talk about it?"

Not really. She didn't want to admit how painful it had been to see her boyfriend with another woman.

"Up to you. I'm happy to listen if it'll help."

Maybe talking about it would put it in perspective. From the first time she'd met him, Abe had been kind and caring. He didn't seem critical or judgmental.

So Anna Mary spilled her heartbreak. And her fears. Every time she hesitated, Abe sent her an encouraging glance over the horse's back, and she continued.

The rhythmic stroking motions soothed Anna Mary as well as the horse. Or was it Abe's acceptance? Perhaps both. Being able to tell someone the truth about the situation made a huge difference. She appreciated his willingness to listen.

"*Danke*, Abe. I feel much better. You're a good listener."

"I'm glad it helped."

"It did."

Without being asked, Abe helped her feed the horses once she led Brownie into his stall. Then he turned to her.

"I'm so sorry your boyfriend hurt you, Anna Mary. You didn't deserve that."

But maybe she did. Maybe . . .

"Hey, don't blame yourself."

Had Abe read her mind? "But I told him I didn't trust him." Anna Mary couldn't meet his eyes.

"Even if he was innocent, he should have realized how his actions looked to others—and especially to you."

"And I lost my temper today. I should have given him time to explain." But she'd been so hurt and humiliated.

"You can ask for forgiveness. And it's always good to hear the other person's side of the story, but—" Abe broke off and stared at the ground.

"But what?"

"It's not my place to say this, but if he's not treating you right, you deserve better. You're too nice and sweet to stay with someone who isn't faithful and kind." Abe's face turned fiery red.

At his gentle tone and caring words, Anna Mary blinked furiously to hold back her tears, but one trickled down.

He gazed at her with such sympathy, she wished . . .

She stopped her fantasies. She and Abe couldn't possibly be a couple. Even if he fell for her, she could never leave Mamm. Plus, she'd made a commitment to Josh. The two of them would have to break up before she'd be free to get involved in another relationship.

Spending time with Abe, who always gave people the benefit of the doubt, made Anna Mary aware that she'd automatically assumed the worst about Josh. He'd tried to explain, but she hadn't listened. She'd taken off in anger.

Seeing him with Rachel, looking like the two of them were husband and wife with children, cooking a meal together . . .

Anna Mary's eyes burned with unshed tears. They looked so good together. And the little boy had been clinging to Josh as if he knew him well and trusted him. That couldn't possibly be the first time they'd been together, could it?

"Supper," Sarah called. "The chicken and fries are hot, and I made a salad."

"We have cookies too," Anna Mary said to Abe, "thanks to you. I hope you'll stay for dinner."

"I shouldn't."

"By the way, where's Tim?" She couldn't believe she'd talked this whole time without once wondering about his cousin's absence.

"He's at work. I need to pick him up later."

"Then you can stay? Or do you need to make a meal for your *onkel*?"

"*Neh*, he's gone out."

"Then please stay." Perhaps she was playing with fire, doing the same thing she'd accused Josh of doing, but she held her breath until Abe accepted her invitation.

CHAPTER 8

A mass of feelings churned Abe's insides. Although more than anything he wanted to accompany Anna Mary inside, to sit at the table with her family, to spend more time with her . . . he'd make a mistake if he agreed to eat with her.

She and her boyfriend might make up. Perhaps Josh had an innocent explanation for being in another girl's house like that. For Anna Mary's sake, Abe hoped so.

His blood boiled, though, when he thought about Anna Mary being mistreated. He didn't want to encourage her to go back to someone who hurt her the way this boyfriend had. If Josh didn't truly love Anna Mary with all his heart, Abe hoped her boyfriend would break things off.

Sure, and that's the only reason you want them to break up, his conscience chided.

Abe wished he could be here for Anna Mary if her relationship ended. But he'd be leaving soon.

When she turned to him with a pleading expression, as if she relied on him to be her lifeline, all his defenses broke down. She needed support and comfort right now, and at the moment, he could give them to her. He headed into the house beside her.

Anna Mary glanced up at him with such a trusting, grateful expression, his breath caught. And she walked so close, each swish of her dress sent a whiff of laundry soap wafting from the fabric. He swallowed hard. Her soft hand swung only inches from his. He longed to reach out and take it in his.

Please, Lord, help me keep my longings under control.

Still, his mind played through images of Anna Mary as his wife—the two of them walking hand in hand to their home. A home with several children. Sitting at the table with her by his side. Praying together. The two of them tucking the children into bed at night.

As he pulled open the screen door to let her into the kitchen before him, he remained immersed in his fantasy. Sarah's cheery greeting broke the spell Abe had woven. For a moment, he remained suspended between future dreams and present reality.

His *mamm* had often warned him about daydreaming. She'd worried he spent too much time on what he hoped for rather than what was happening around him. He was in danger of doing that now, and he didn't want to miss one minute of being in Anna Mary's company.

"Abe?" Sarah stared at him, perplexed.

"*Jah?*"

She must have asked him something and been waiting for a response. With difficulty, he dragged himself back to the warmth of the kitchen. To Anna Mary bustling around, setting things on the table with Hannah clinging to her skirt. Nearby, Emmie carried two bottles of salad dressing to the table. Beth handed silverware to Anna Mary.

He laughed nervously. "Sorry. I got lost in thought."

Sarah's sweet smile lifted her lips. "I do that too sometimes. I asked if you were staying for dinner." She glanced at Anna Mary, who'd added an extra plate and glass to the place settings. "I guess the answer is *jah*."

Abe's heart swelled within him as he focused on Anna Mary's competent hands, flashing in and out.

"I'm glad you're staying," Sarah said shyly as she carried a platter of cut-up chicken parts to the table.

"So am I," he replied. A joyful song swelled in his chest, longing to break free at the happiness filling him. "Should I get your *mamm*?"

Anna Mary's head snapped up, and she gaped at him. "Mamm?"

Sarah beamed. "Abe encouraged Mamm to get up this morning, and she's been enjoying his company all day."

"And I've been enjoying hers."

"Mamm's been up and talking to you all day?" Anna Mary stared at him, dumbfounded.

"*Jah*, she has." Sarah set the platter on the table. "She's really taken to Abe. They talked all about Aenti Delores and our other New York relatives."

The admiration shining in Anna Mary's eyes made Abe concerned she viewed him as a hero. "I didn't do anything."

"You did too." Sarah turned to her sister. "He has a way of making her feel comfortable and relaxed."

"I know what you mean," Anna Mary murmured as she poured water into the glasses.

If Abe stayed here any longer, he'd end up as what his *daed* warned against—bigheaded. Too full of *hochmut* to fit through the door. He had to get out of here.

"I'll go get Esther, shall I?" He hurried through the doorway and into the living room, hoping Esther hadn't sunk back into her depression after they'd left her alone.

Her eyes shut, she lay slumped against the couch cushions. He hated to wake her, but it would be good for her to eat something—she looked so frail—and to be with her family.

He bent over and touched her shoulder. "Esther?"

Groggily, she lifted her eyelids and stared at him uncertainly.

"I'm Abe. Anna Mary's friend. We talked about Stone Arabia and Delores earlier."

A little light flickered in her eyes. "Delores? Is she here?"

Abe hoped he hadn't confused her. "*Neh*, she's not. You told me about her."

"I did?" Esther's hand fluttered to her forehead.

"It's all right," Abe assured her. "I've come to take you to the kitchen for supper."

"I'm not hungry," she murmured.

"You need to eat something. Anna Mary brought delicious barbecued chicken home from work." He sniffed the air appreciatively. "Can you smell it?"

"I guess." Her eyes drifted shut.

"Here. Let me help you."

He took her arm gently to assist her from the couch. After she rose, she leaned heavily against him for support.

A lump rose in Abe's throat. How this made him miss his own *mamm*.

Esther tipped her head to study his face. "Where's Josh?"

"I don't know." *And neither does Anna Mary.*

That realization sent rage spiraling through Abe. Was Josh still at Rachel's house? Abe knew one thing for certain. If he were Anna Mary's boyfriend and had been caught at some other girl's house like that—not that he'd ever put himself in such a compromising position— he'd have raced over here to ask forgiveness. And give an explanation, if there was one. Instead, Josh had never shown up. Poor Anna Mary.

Abe tamped down his irritation. *I have no right to judge. Suppose Josh had rushed after Anna Mary and been in an accident? Or what if he'd gotten an emergency call? And how can I criticize him when I'm here having dinner with his girlfriend?*

When Abe and Esther entered the kitchen, Anna Mary's face lit up at the sight of her mother, bringing joy to his heart. He was glad he could do something to make Anna Mary happy.

He helped Esther into her chair and took the seat Sarah indicated, thrilled to be part of this family. It had been lonely at home with only him and Daed at mealtimes now that Mamm was gone and his brothers had all married. Often, they just grabbed reheated leftovers after work.

Abe enjoyed the liveliness as Anna Mary's two younger sisters scrambled into their places, chattering away. And little Hannah, excitedly banging her spoon, made him smile. Only when his brothers and their children visited did Abe's house ring with laughter and teasing. Tonight was a special treat.

They bowed their heads for the silent prayer, and once Abe lifted his head, his gaze met Anna Mary's across the table. Gratitude and admiration shone in her eyes. His pulse quickened. He couldn't help imagining what it would be like to sit at the supper table with her every night. Her soft brown eyes mesmerized him so much he barely tasted the tangy chicken, crisp fries, or crunchy carrots and lettuce.

If only he lived near enough to spend time with her every day. He'd be willing to move here to be with her, but Daed depended on him to handle the dairy farm. Even getting away for two weeks like this meant a lot of scrambling to find replacements, and it put a huge burden on his brothers and friends. Only the urgency of Myron's request had brought Abe to Lancaster.

Unfortunately, Esther had been adamant about not traveling. Anna Mary couldn't leave her *mamm* and the younger children. Maybe when Sarah turned seventeen or so—five long years from now—she could take over. By that time, Anna Mary would be married to someone else. For her sake, Abe prayed it wouldn't be Josh.

Saddened by his conclusion, Abe attempted to lift his mood by teasing Sarah and the little ones, asking Esther questions to keep her engaged, and smiling at Anna Mary. He hoped nobody noticed him staring longingly at her while everyone else was busy eating or talking.

After the meal, he offered to help Emmie with the dishes while Sarah readied Hannah for bed and Anna Mary assisted her *mamm*. Abe normally did the dishes alone at home, so Emmie's lively antics kept him entertained. What fun it would be to have children! But he only wanted his children to have one mother—Anna Mary.

Lord, why did You bring her into my life only to make it impossible for us to get together? I've always trusted You for my future, but I can't see myself ever falling for anyone else but her.

"Abe?" Her voice behind him startled him so much he almost dropped the glass he'd been washing. "Are you all right?"

How did he answer that?

Emmie giggled. "He keeps washing that glass over and over."

Heat spread through Abe's chest and up his neck. He'd been daydreaming. And— "I—I was praying."

Anna Mary's quizzical look made it clear she could

tell it had been more than that. Did she realize he'd been thinking about her?

He broke their gaze to hand Emmie the glass to dry. "I'm almost done here. Then I should go."

"Oh."

Her soft sound of disappointment wrapped him in warmth and hope. Was it possible she felt the same way? He mentally shook himself. She'd committed to Josh, even if he wasn't much of a boyfriend. Unless and until she decided to end that relationship, Abe had no right to fall for her.

"Do you have to leave?" Anna Mary sounded as if she'd love to have him say *neh*.

Exactly what he'd love to do. "I wish I could stay, but I need to pick Tim up from work." He didn't mention what time because she might convince him to stay longer, and he really shouldn't.

Emmie made a face. "I want you to play Uno with me and read me a story."

"Maybe some other time." Abe would have enjoyed spending more time with this small spitfire. He didn't want to think about leaving Lancaster later that week.

"I'll walk you out to your buggy," Anna Mary said as Abe drained the sink.

I'd like that. Abe kept his joyful response to himself. "*Danke.* And *danke* for including me in your family meal."

"It's the least we could do after all you've done for us." Anna Mary led the way to the back door. When it swung shut behind them, she turned to him. "*Danke* for listening. You helped me so much."

"Do you know what you're going to do?"

Anna Mary sighed. "I need to give Josh a chance to explain, but—" She nibbled her lower lip. "I can't help wondering if he's still at Rachel's. If he is . . ." She looked ready to cry.

"I hope he's not, for your sake."

"That's kind of you."

Actually, it wasn't. It was a half-truth. He wanted her to be happy, and if Josh made her happy, then he'd pray the two of them would get back together. More than anything, though, he wished they wouldn't.

Anna Mary helped him hitch up his buggy. "I wish we could have talked longer." She sounded wistful. "I told you all about my problems, but I didn't have time to hear more about you."

That might be for the best. The more he got to know her, the more he shared about himself, the harder it would be to drive back to New York this weekend.

"I hope I'll get to see you before you leave town," she said shyly.

He longed for that too. But common sense told him it would be better to cut things off now. "Guess it depends on Tim's schedule." He slid the buggy door open.

Her *I see* sounded sad.

Abe wanted to turn around, to tell her he'd stay here with her, to promise he'd be back soon. He did none of those things. Instead, he climbed into the buggy and turned the horse around. Then he flicked the reins and took off down the driveway.

He couldn't resist one last peek at Anna Mary. His final glimpse showed a forlorn figure standing in the driveway. Was she upset about him leaving? Or was she pining for her missing boyfriend?

Abe had no idea, but he knew one thing for sure and certain. He'd fallen hard for a woman he might never see again. A woman who'd made a commitment to someone else. A woman he'd never forget.

Not until Abe started down the driveway did it dawn on Anna Mary that Josh had never come after her. He'd begged her to let him explain, but he hadn't bothered to follow her or set things right. He'd chosen to stay with Rachel.

Had he been there all this time? Or had he gone home, completely forgetting about his rift with his girlfriend? Or not even caring that he'd hurt her? If so, that alone told her all she needed to know about Josh's feelings for her.

He'd had hours to apologize. Instead, he'd never showed up at all.

Anna Mary's conscience twinged. What about her? Had she even thought about Josh while she sat laughing and talking with Abe? She'd thoroughly enjoyed her evening without one thought about her boyfriend. Knowing Abe, he'd probably steered the conversation to fun memories on purpose to distract her from her sorrow. He'd been so good for Mamm too. She hadn't been this engaged in weeks.

When Anna Mary entered the house, Sarah took one look and teased, "You look like you're moping for your boyfriend."

"Abe's not my boyfriend." Anna Mary regretted her sharp tone. She had no right to take out her sadness on her sister. "I'm sorry for snapping at you. Will you forgive me?"

"Of course," Sarah answered in her usual sweet way. "But when I said *boyfriend* I meant Josh. Maybe I was mistaken, though. You like Abe? I didn't know. I mean, I could tell you two—"

Anna Mary held up a hand to stop her sister. "Please don't."

"Don't what? Call Abe your boyfriend?" Sarah studied Anna Mary's downcast expression. "You want him to be, don't you?"

At her sister's question, Anna Mary's eyes burned. Although she wasn't being completely honest, she shrugged. She whirled around and headed out of the kitchen before any teardrops fell.

If she had to answer truthfully, she'd probably say *jah* to the question. She'd been attracted to Abe from the first time she met him. And the times she'd seen him since had only reinforced those feelings. His kindness when she'd been left behind, his sense of humor, his caring for her family . . . The list could go on and on.

Anna Mary shook her head to clear her wayward thoughts. She was so mixed-up right now. She'd been more drawn to Abe than she'd ever been to Josh. Still, she'd made a promise to Josh, and she intended to keep it. Unless Josh no longer wanted to date her.

Sinking onto the couch, she tried to make sense of her desires. She'd been grateful the first time Josh asked her to ride home after a singing. Deep down, she'd always feared being an *alt maedel*. She'd jumped at the chance to be part of a couple like her friends. And she and Josh got along well enough. But she'd never experienced the sparks with him that tingled through her when she spent time with Abe.

Buggy wheels crunched in the gravel driveway. Had Abe returned for something he'd forgotten? A tool maybe?

He'd fixed several things around the house when he'd been here the other day.

When he knocked at the back door, Anna Mary stayed where she was. Sarah could handle it. No sense in confusing her heart even more.

CHAPTER 9

Her sister peeked her head in the living room. "Your boyfriend's here, Anna Mary," she whispered. "Do you want to see him?"

"I told you he's not—" Anna Mary stopped abruptly when she caught sight of Josh. Her eyes widened. "I didn't think you were coming."

Instead of Josh apologizing and explaining, the way she'd expected, a question—more like an accusation—rushed from his mouth. "Is that why Abe came over? You didn't expect me? I saw Tim's buggy turning out of your driveway, but Abe was alone."

Josh's comments jabbed at Anna Mary's conscience. Although Abe's visit had been accidental, because he'd come to help her family rather than to see her, all the feelings Abe had stirred up roiled her nerves.

Perhaps Josh could read her guilt in the heat seeping into her face, but Anna Mary crossed her arms. He was one to talk. She'd caught him at Rachel's house. Not doing roof work as he'd claimed, but putting a casserole in the oven and carrying around a child.

She dug at him to cover up her own conflicted feelings. "When you didn't come right away, I figured you'd rather be with Rachel." Her attempt at indifference wobbled when she said Rachel's name.

"I'm sorry for being at Rachel's."

"You promised me you'd stay outside." Although now that she said it, she remembered she'd basically commanded him not to go inside as she'd hopped out of the buggy. Josh hadn't responded when she said it.

Now he shifted back and forth as if nervous—or maybe guilty. "I told you I didn't need to go inside for anything."

"Looked like you found plenty of reasons." *A casserole, helping Rachel with dinner, caring for a little boy.*

"I was inside for one reason, and only one." Josh emphasized the last word.

"*Jah*, to spend time with Rachel, eat with her, and—"

He held up a hand. "I went inside because of the little boy I had in my arms."

"She asked you to help her babysit? I could use your help here if you want to care for children."

"I know." Josh sounded genuinely sorry.

Anna Mary regretted making that sarcastic remark. Josh often lent a hand with her younger sisters, especially during the winter when construction work slowed down. And several times, he'd come over here to watch them when Anna Mary worked late. He'd also stepped in several times when her *mamm*—

Josh interrupted her thoughts. "You have to understand." His face grew somber. "The little boy, Zak, is Rachel's cousin's son. His *mamm* died today, and his *daed* passed a few months ago. He must miss his *daed*, because he latched onto me and wouldn't let go. I had to bring him into the house."

Although Anna Mary's heart went out to the poor boy, that didn't explain the other things she'd seen and heard.

She tried to keep the bitterness from her words, but they spewed out along with her hurt and anger. "And then you just happened to help her fix dinner too? I assume you also stayed to eat it, instead of coming here to spend time with me."

"I didn't plan to."

"Seems like you don't plan to do lots of things, but end up doing them anyway." Anna Mary cringed. Didn't she do the same thing? When Abe had asked her what was wrong, she could have kept everything to herself. Then, despite knowing she was playing with fire, she had invited Abe to dinner.

"Look, Anna Mary, I know it looked bad, but if you'd been there the whole time, you'd have seen nothing to upset you."

Could she say the same thing? She pictured her conversation with Abe. If Josh confided details about their relationship to Rachel, she'd be upset and hurt.

Too busy mentally reviewing all her interactions with Abe through Josh's eyes, Anna Mary could barely concentrate on his hurried explanation. She forced herself to listen.

"Zak stayed outside with me while I worked, and I played with him in Betty's room."

"And you didn't spend any time with Rachel?" Anna Mary most wanted to know this, even though her own conscience wasn't clear.

Josh studied the embroidered throw pillow on the sofa and didn't meet her eyes. "When Rachel and I were in the same room together, I was holding Zak, and she had the baby."

That hadn't answered her question. Just because their hands were occupied didn't mean they couldn't be exchanging secretive glances or talking about private things. She should know.

"There was nothing to it, like you seeing Abe, right?" Josh's glance flicked to her.

Now it was her turn to evade his gaze. After hesitating a few moments, she tried to adopt a matter-of-fact tone, but her words came out defensive. "He only came to say goodbye. He's headed back to New York State soon."

Josh's eyebrows rose. "And he thought you'd want to know?"

She nibbled at her lip. "*Jah*, I did want to know." *More than Josh or Abe would ever know.*

His eyes narrowed in suspicion. "You did?"

"He was very nice to me. After the volleyball game when you drove off without me, Abe understood how upset I was and comforted me. It was his idea to drive me home. I thought that was nice of him."

Josh seemed to process that. Then he narrowed in on the one thing she'd hoped he wouldn't. "Have you seen him other times?"

Anna Mary wished she didn't have to answer. She ducked her head, and when she spoke, it was barely above a whisper. "Maybe three times. Four, if you count tonight."

Looking taken aback, Josh stared at her. "How long was he here tonight?"

"About as long as you stayed with Rachel. He was here helping Sarah when I got home."

Since she was confessing, she might as well be honest about the other times. "And he came twice to fix things for Mamm and my sisters."

"I'm sorry I wasn't around to do it."

Anna Mary didn't want to think about who might have been taking up his time. To be fair, though, even if he

hadn't been at Rachel's, Josh's *daed* wouldn't let him off
work during the day. Plus, she had no right to complain
about him not being here for her when she'd been visiting
with Abe.

But Abe was leaving, and she and Josh were dating.
They needed to mend their relationship. Still, she had to
admit her worries about Josh's work at Rachel's house.

"I know you have to work long hours, Josh. I've tried
to be understanding about not having a lot of time with
you. But to find out you were spending your free time
with Rachel . . ."

"I didn't go to Rachel's to visit. I went to work. Taking
care of the little boy kept me there longer than I intended,
but I couldn't leave him. Not when he'd just lost his
mamm."

"I know." Anna Mary didn't begrudge an orphaned
boy some comfort. She had to get her jealousy of Rachel
under control. And she owed Josh an apology.

"I'm sorry for being so grumpy. It's just that I miss
you. And it's hard to give up time with you. It's so sad
the little boy lost his parents, and I know you're only
trying to help."

"*Danke* for being so understanding. I'm sorry for
causing you worry."

Anna Mary nodded, but unease lingered. "How long
do you plan to work on Rachel's house and spend time
with Zak?"

"I'm not sure. A week or two at most."

Two weeks of being sick with jealousy imagining Josh
and Rachel laughing and talking together? Remembering
the flirt's hand on Josh's arm while they were concealed
in the woods? Wondering if Josh was being faithful?
Could she deal with it?

During *Rumspringa,* the church gave the *youngie*

freedom to decide whether they wanted to join the church. That time allowed them to be sure their commitment to God and the church was strong and true. Maybe letting Josh go would give them both time to consider their connection. If they were meant to be together, it would deepen their bond.

"Maybe we should spend the next few weeks apart, praying about our relationship. Not spending time with each other might help us decide if God means for us to be together."

Josh looked surprised, but after a moment, he nodded.

Deep down, Anna Mary hoped he might protest and say they belonged together. Did it mean Rachel would win Josh in the end?

Anna Mary had some wrestling of her own to do, such as why she'd been so attracted to Abe and why she'd spilled her secrets to him. If she couldn't be that honest with Josh about her deepest feelings, should she be dating him?

Tim had two days off and insisted on taking Abe to Hersheypark one day and sightseeing the next. Although Abe would have liked to see Anna Mary one more time, he couldn't ask Tim to visit her. Besides, she'd probably worked things out with her boyfriend. Abe had prayed every night since he left her that she would have a happy relationship with the man God planned for her. He didn't include his own desires in his petitions, even though he wished he could be that man.

On Thursday night, he made a special supper to thank Myron and Tim for having him. As he pulled the pot roast from the oven and peeked under the foil, the tang of onion filled the air. He poked at the carrots and potatoes around it with a fork. They were almost done.

He loved this simple recipe of Mamm's. It only took a packet of onion soup mix, a can of mushroom soup, and a cup of beef broth. He just dumped the mixture over the meat and vegetables, wrapped everything in foil, popped it in a pan, and baked it all at low heat for three hours.

Tim strolled into the kitchen. "Smells good."

"It'll be ready in about ten minutes or so." Abe pressed the foil back into place and returned the pan to Myron's propane oven.

"My stomach's growling already." Tim's phone dinged in his pocket. He frowned at the number on the screen. "Don't recognize it." He answered with a wary *hello*.

After listening a few seconds, he held out the phone. "Some lady's asking for you."

Abe sucked in a breath. Anna Mary? Had she called to say goodbye? To talk for a while more? He grabbed for the phone.

Tim laughed at Abe's eager expression and held the phone out of reach. "It's not who you think it is. She's old."

The breath Abe had been holding whooshed out. He struggled not to let his disappointment show. Then he frowned at Tim and mouthed, *She can hear you.*

His cousin shrugged. "So what? I'm not trying to impress some old biddy."

Shaking his head, Abe took the phone, hoping Tim had been teasing about it being someone other than Anna Mary. A woman with a shaky voice, definitely elderly, introduced herself as Mrs. Vandenberg. Abe had no idea who she was. Maybe she'd mixed him up with his cousin.

"I have a favor to ask," she said. "I'd like to rent the van your driver intended to use tomorrow. I need to take several people to an out-of-town funeral. I'd return it on Monday."

"Well . . ." What could he say? "Of course you can use it. I'm sure I can find another way home."

"That's the problem. Every driver in the county is booked this whole weekend. There's a huge horse auction and several mud sales. That's why I need this van."

"I see." What was he going to do now? He'd have to figure something out as soon as he got off the phone. "I'm sorry for your loss."

"Thank you. It's always sad when the Lord takes a young mother, but to be honest, I didn't know her. I'm just transporting her relatives."

How odd. Why is this lady arranging a ride for some-one she doesn't know?

"As for you," she said, "God can turn what appears to be a setback to your gain. Trust Him."

Abe had experienced that many times. "I've found that to be true." But why in the world had she told him that? Maybe she was a bit *ferhoodled*.

"Use your time wisely," she said and hung up.

What in the world?

Tim stared at Abe's puzzled frown as he handed the phone back. "Who was that?" his cousin demanded.

"I don't know. She said her name was Mrs. Van— something."

"Vandenberg?" Tim stared at Abe in shock. "Why'd she call you?"

"That name sounds right, and I have no idea why she called." He amended his statement. "Except she wants to hire the van I had scheduled to go home in tomorrow because all the other drivers in the area are busy."

"That means you're staying longer?"

"I guess so. If Myron's all right with it. And if Daed

can get my brothers to cover a few more days. The van'll be back on Monday."

"Good. That means you'll be here for Saturday's volleyball game." Tim eyed Abe. "She say anything else?"

"To use my time wisely." Depending on what had happened between Anna Mary and Josh, maybe Abe could squeeze in one more visit before he went home. Would that be a wise use of his time?

CHAPTER 10

Anna Mary dragged into work on Saturday morning. The argument with Josh depressed her. She regretted the way she'd treated him. The tone of her voice, her cutting comments, her accusations. All of it had been because of her guilty conscience over Abe. To cover her shame, she'd lashed out at Josh. She owed him an apology, but first, she needed to spend time in prayer about their relationship.

She'd been reluctant to do that because, truth be told, she didn't want to face doing God's will if it meant making up with Josh. For the past few days, she'd been hoping Abe would stop by, but he hadn't. He must have already left for New York. She wished he'd come over to say goodbye. Though maybe it was for the best, if God's plan included dating and marrying Josh.

"What's wrong, Anna Mary?" Caroline studied her sympathetically as she entered the stand. "Your *mamm* not doing well?"

"Actually, she's a bit better."

Following Abe's visits, Mamm had improved steadily. Usually, she stayed in a low mood for several weeks this time of year, but she'd actually gotten up and dressed every day since then. She'd been asking when that nice boy would be back. Anna Mary only said she didn't know, which was true. She hated to dampen Mamm's spirits—the way her own dipped every time she realized she'd never see Abe again.

"Anna Mary?" Caroline waved a hand in front of her face. "I asked you twice already. Are you all right?"

"Sorry," Anna Mary mumbled. She didn't want to confess the real reason she felt down today. Every time her mind strayed to Abe, she estimated how far away his home was from Lancaster. If only he lived around here or she lived in New York State. She wished Mamm would take a trip to see Delores. But Mamm refused to travel outside of Lancaster. As she always said, *We have everything we could want here—food, shops, neighbors, church, community. What more do we need?*

Until this week, Anna Mary had agreed with her. Now, she longed to expand her horizons. To see other states. Or at least go as far as Stone Arabia and Fort Plain. But that would never happen.

Caroline repeated Anna Mary's name in a sharp tone. Anna Mary's head jerked up. She had to get to work.

"I'm sorry. I'll get the salads for the case."

Before she could hurry to the refrigerator, Caroline grabbed her arm. "Not until you tell me what's bothering you."

The last thing Anna Mary wanted to admit was how much she missed Abe. Caroline might not even know or remember who Abe was. Anna Mary could share one worry weighing on her, though.

"Josh and I had an argument on Tuesday night. We sort of broke up, but not exactly."

Caroline's face registered her shock. "What happened?"

Gideon glanced in their direction. "Are you planning to get the cases set up before the market opens?"

Relieved, Anna Mary scurried off. She didn't really want to repeat the nasty things she'd said to Josh or to think about him spending time with Rachel. She hadn't told anyone but Abe about finding Josh at Rachel's house.

Anna Mary slid a large metal salad container from the refrigerator. She'd volunteered to stay late last night to prep salads because she'd wanted to keep her mind off Josh and off Abe's departure.

"Don't think you're going to get away with ignoring me," Caroline warned as she lifted the broccoli-bacon salad from the lowest shelf. "Come on. Tell me," she whispered so Gideon couldn't hear.

Anna Mary shrugged. "Not much to tell. We argued about him spending time with Rachel."

"Rachel?" Caroline's squeal caught her brother's attention. She lowered her voice. "He saw her again?"

Turning her back, Anna Mary returned to the refrigerator with Caroline dogging her heels. She didn't want to share her confusion over her feelings for Abe. So she concentrated on Caroline's question. "*Jah*, he's working on her roof."

Caroline brushed that off with a quick hand movement. "That's not the same as seeing her."

Anna Mary gritted her teeth. "He was inside her house. I think he had supper there."

"*Ach*, that's not *gut*."

Heat crept up Anna Mary's neck. Would Caroline consider it bad if she knew Abe had been at Anna Mary's for supper that same night?

To escape more questions, Anna Mary rushed around filling the cases, preparing trays with silverware packets, and avoiding being near Caroline. If her friend noticed, she didn't say anything.

As Gideon left to open the market doors, Cathy Zehr scuttled up to the stand. "*Psst.* Anna Mary."

"Just ignore her," Caroline whispered, and they both kept their heads down and stayed focused on their jobs.

Cathy waved and yelled, "Anna Mary, I have to tell you something important. Something about Josh."

Anna Mary didn't want to listen to the notorious gossip, but she also didn't want news about Josh broadcast around the market. With a heavy sigh, Anna Mary set down one more packet and walked over to the counter.

Cathy bounced on her toes with eagerness. "You'll never guess who I saw when I drove in to make donuts at five yesterday morning. A van sat in Rachel's driveway and"—she smiled slyly—"who do you think had loaded a toolbox into the back?"

A sick feeling sloshed in Anna Mary's stomach. That time of morning it would still be dark, so Josh couldn't have been working on the roof. And most likely, Cathy was mistaken. He must have been taking his tools out of the van. But why before dawn? And whose van was it? Why hadn't he driven his buggy?

"I couldn't believe it!" Cathy prattled on. "Next thing I knew, he was helping Rachel carry two children to the van."

"I see." Still, Anna Mary couldn't figure out why Josh had gone to Rachel's that early.

"That wasn't all I saw." Now, Cathy bubbled with excitement. "Josh loaded their suitcases, and they all got in the van and drove off. Even Josh." She waited for Anna Mary's reaction.

How long had Cathy been sitting there? Had she pulled her buggy over to stare at them? A swift flash of anger shot through Anna Mary. Josh's behavior upset her, but she directed her irritation toward Cathy. She had one purpose for her malicious tattling—to hurt people.

Anna Mary tilted her chin. "Josh likes to help people." She hoped that would defuse this rumor spreader.

Cathy's sneer showed she saw through Anna Mary's attempt at bravado. "There's more. Rachel's *Englisch* neighbor stopped by for a dozen donuts this morning, so I asked her where Rachel was heading so early in the morning."

Of course you did. Despite her annoyance, Anna Mary had to admit she longed to know too.

"Rachel had someone come to stay at the house with her bedridden *mamm* because Rachel's headed to a funeral in Ohio."

"I know about that. Josh told me. He's been helping with the children because they just lost their mother." Anna Mary didn't really know all this for sure. She only guessed it from what Josh had said about the two children. "Their *mamm* was Rachel's cousin."

Cathy's smarmy grin deflated. Then a wicked gleam sparked in her eyes. "I can't believe you're all right with Josh going along to the funeral. Especially with a girl as pretty as Rachel."

Josh is going all the way to Ohio? And accompanying Rachel to a funeral? The churning in her stomach increased. *Is that why he didn't protest when I suggested taking two weeks apart?*

"You don't look too happy about it," Cathy gloated.

I'm not. I'm sick and upset and hurt and—

Anna Mary couldn't let Cathy get the upper hand, or she'd spread tales around the market about Josh's poor heartbroken girlfriend.

"Thanks for letting me know. But Josh and I already

talked, and we came to an agreement." She didn't have to tell Cathy what that agreement was.

"As long as you're all right with it, I guess it's all okay." Cathy couldn't mask her disappointment. "All I know is I'd never let my boyfriend go off for a weekend with a pretty flirt like Rachel. I hope, for your sake, you'll still be together after he returns."

If she wanted to, Anna Mary could make a jab about Cathy being in her thirties and still not having a boyfriend. But Anna Mary focused more on the part about Josh not staying in the relationship if he spent time with Rachel. As much as Anna Mary had doubts about things between her and Josh, she didn't want everything to end because of Rachel. They needed to make their decision because of God's leading.

People rushed into the market as Gideon opened the doors closest to them. Anna Mary had to get back to work, and she wanted to get away from Cathy with her dignity intact.

"The *gut* thing is both Josh and I plan to follow God's will for our lives, so whatever happens in the future, we'll trust the Lord." Anna Mary whirled around. "I'd better get back to work. Customers are coming in. Have a good day, Cathy."

Anna Mary hoped she'd deflected Cathy's pity, but then she almost ran into Caroline, who gazed at her with sympathy.

"I'm so sorry. I overheard what Cathy said. Is that what you and Josh argued about?"

Her throat tight with unshed tears, Anna Mary shook her head. "Not exactly."

Between customers, she told Caroline some of what had happened, but she kept the part about Abe to herself.

The less she talked about him, maybe the faster she'd forget him. At least she hoped that would happen.

"So what are you going to do about Josh?" Caroline asked.

"I don't know. We agreed to take two weeks and pray about it."

"Great idea."

Jah, it was. And Anna Mary would start now. After hearing this morning's gossip, Anna Mary definitely needed to trust God for her future.

Abe couldn't help grinning as he and Tim drove to the volleyball field. He couldn't wait to see Anna Mary again.

Tim shook his head. "You look like a cat that's cornered a mouse."

No matter how Abe tried to wipe the smile off his face, the minute he relaxed his guard, his lips curved up so much his cheeks ached. He'd never felt like this before in his life. To stop Tim's teasing, Abe forced himself to think of something serious. It didn't work.

When they reached the parking lot, he scanned every buggy for her. Suppose she didn't come today? His pulse pattered when her friend Caroline pulled into the dirt lane. Abe leaned forward to see if Anna Mary sat beside her. *Jah*, she was here.

"Are you going to be able to keep your mind on the game?" Tim growled as Abe hopped out of the buggy.

Abe couldn't guarantee he would. In fact, he was pretty sure he couldn't. Unless her boyfriend was here. Then Abe would have to avoid glancing at her. It might be best to do that anyway. After all, he didn't want any of her friends gossiping about him and causing trouble in her relationship.

Thinking of Josh sobered Abe, and the excitement in his chest fizzled.

Anna Mary stepped out of the buggy, looking downcast. His heart went out to her. She didn't look like a girl who'd mended the rift with her boyfriend. Hope filled him until he remembered he had to leave on Monday. Still, he was here now and could enjoy being with her. Maybe he could even cheer her up. But not if her boyfriend came. With each thought, his emotions dipped up and down faster than a roller coaster.

She plodded forward, head bent. When someone called out, she lifted her head and caught sight of him. She blinked several times. Then her eyes widened. Her smile broke out like sunshine after a storm.

Caroline frowned as Anna Mary hurried toward him. Abe hoped Caroline's annoyance was directed toward his cousin and wasn't because Anna Mary seemed so happy to see him.

"Abe? What are you doing here?" Anna Mary stared at him, stunned.

He probably looked like a grinning fool, but he was so overjoyed to see her. "I can't get a ride home until Monday." His spirits lifted even more when her face lit with delight. "How are things?" he asked.

"Not so *gut*." Still, she beamed at him. "But I'm glad to see you."

Jah! "And I'm glad to see you."

Tim groaned. "Would you two get moving? I have to get to work tonight. And we have a game to win."

"Don't be so sure of that," Caroline snapped, her brows still furrowed, as she studied Anna Mary. "We're going to win big tonight."

"See you after the game." Abe shot Anna Mary a special smile before he jogged off after Tim.

"All right, what's going on?" Caroline demanded.

Anna Mary didn't know how to answer. *Nothing. And everything!*

How could things be so mixed-up and uncertain, but so *wunderbar* at the same time?

She'd been so miserable she almost hadn't come to the game. And now she had a bounce in her step. The minute Abe had appeared, her parched spirit had blossomed like a flower garden after a spring rain. Birds twittered. Roses scented the air. Heavenly music filled her ears. *How can one person change my world with only a smile or a glance?*

Caroline stopped in front of Anna Mary, blocking her way forward. "I want the truth. What's going on between you and that Abe?"

Anna Mary shrugged. "We're just friends."

"Sure seems like more than that."

"I've only seen him a few times, and he lives in New York."

Tim's shout interrupted them. "I don't have all day. If you two don't come now, we'll start without you."

Caroline scowled, but she and Anna Mary rushed over to join their teammates. Seeing Abe had filled Anna Mary with energy. She jumped, spiked, and saved balls like never before. With Josh missing, she had to handle a lot more of the tricky shots. She'd never realized it, but she'd often stepped back to let him shine.

As they won the first of three, Caroline stared at Anna Mary. "What's gotten into you? I've never seen you play like this before."

Anna Mary shrugged. "Someone has to take Josh's place."

"Why don't you play like this all the time? If you did this when he's here, we'd crush Tim's team."

"Hey, Anna Mary," Tim yelled. "Where's your boyfriend?"

Suddenly, all Anna Mary's joy leaked out. While she'd been playing hard to keep Abe's eyes on her, she'd forgotten about Josh and Rachel.

Trying to sound casual, she called back, "He's away."

She must not have succeeded in acting neutral, because Caroline reached over and squeezed her hand.

"Enough lazing around," Tim declared. "Let's get the next set started. I intend to win this match."

Caroline grinned when Abe elbowed Tim. "You're not the only player on the team."

"And there's no way you'll win any of these games." She jumped to her feet. "I'm ready."

Tim glared at her. "So am I." He shot a disgusted glance at Abe. "If you'd keep your eyes on the ball instead of a certain girl, we'd win."

Abe's face flamed, and Anna Mary's heart went out to him. Tim loved to embarrass people.

On the second serve, Anna Mary jumped to make a return and twisted her ankle slightly when she landed. Abe's eyes filled with concern as she winced. He muffed an easy shot.

"Keep your eyes on the ball," Tim screamed. "She did that on purpose to distract you."

Anna Mary pinched her lips together to keep from retorting. If she did, she'd only make things worse for Abe.

He looked miserable. After flashing her an apologetic glance, he didn't look in her direction for the rest of the set until Tim's team was fighting for their final point.

Tim made the perfect setup for Abe to smash the ball over the net right at her feet. Instead, he sent it sailing softly to her. With a smile and a fluttering heart, she tapped it back to him.

For a moment, they were the only two players in the game, with the ball suspended between them and their eyes locked on each other. Anna Mary had never felt so connected to anyone in her life.

Abe couldn't take his eyes off Anna Mary. Her face glowed as she returned the ball. He wanted to forget everyone else and keep volleying the ball back and forth between them.

"What are you doing?" Tim shouted. "You could have spiked that for the point. Instead, you hit a puffball to your crush."

Abe's face burned, and he dragged his attention away from Anna Mary. *Jah*, he could have crushed that spike, but he might have hurt Anna Mary with its force, so he'd gone easy on her. He'd never put winning a match over someone else's safety, and definitely not someone he cared about.

Tim fumed as they lost the serve. "If we lose this game, it'll all be your fault."

Unfortunately, Caroline's team picked up the two points they needed to break the tie. Tim stomped around, furious.

"There's no point in even playing the next game. They've already won the match." Tim glowered at Abe. "Their second-best player is missing today, but my second-best player doesn't even bother to watch the ball."

Although Abe regretted causing the team to lose, he'd

thoroughly enjoyed every second of the game. Anna Mary's joy-filled face had enthralled him.

"She's not even pretty," Tim grumbled. "And anyway, you can't date a Lancaster girl."

Abe resented his cousin's comments. "I think she's beautiful." *Inside and out.* Strong and sturdy and not afraid of hard work, she'd be a perfect helpmeet in the dairy business. Abe loved her dark hair, and he could get lost in those brown eyes.

Tim was right about one thing, though. Abe had no chance for a relationship with Anna Mary, even if she broke up with her boyfriend. He pushed the depressing thought away. No sense in wasting time thinking about that now when he could be spending time with her.

His gaze strayed to where Caroline and Anna Mary stood by the water jug.

Dear Lord, why have You brought my attention to the perfect woman when a future with her seems impossible? Please turn my thoughts and dreams to the right partner for me.

After a disastrous third loss, Tim stormed off the court. Abe knew he should go after him, but he couldn't miss one last chance to speak to Anna Mary. She flitted toward him before he could search for her.

"Mamm has been asking about you. She really misses seeing you."

Do you miss me too? he longed to ask. Instead, he focused on her *mamm*. "How's she doing?"

"Much better ever since your visits. She's gotten up and dressed every day. That's a good start."

"I'm so glad. And how are things with you and—" He couldn't bring himself to say the name.

"Not *gut*." She bit her lip and looked about to cry. "We—we decided to not see each other for two weeks. But

I heard he went out of town with"—her voice trembled—"Rachel."

"*Ach*, Anna Mary, I'm so sorry."

"Maybe it's for the best. We decided to pray about our relationship."

"I'll be praying too." As much as he wanted to pray they'd stay broken up, he'd ask God for whatever was best for Anna Mary.

"*Danke*." She hesitated. "I know Mamm would like to see you before you leave."

She didn't say she wanted to see him too, but the invitation shone in her eyes. Abe's heart thudded in his chest. "I'd like to see all of you too."

Tim shouted, "Stop flirting and get a move on. I have to get to work."

"Maybe you could come for supper after you drop Tim off?"

"I'd like that." With a quick wave and buoyant spirits, Abe dashed off to Tim's buggy. His cousin's grousing and taunts rolled off Abe, because he looked forward to spending time with Anna Mary.

CHAPTER 11

Anna Mary couldn't wait for Caroline to drop her off at home. The minute Caroline stopped, Anna Mary hurried out of the buggy. She and Sarah prepared meatloaf, baked potatoes, and a salad. Emmie went out to pick the first peas from their garden. Anna Mary also whipped up cracker pudding for dessert and slid it into the oven to brown for fifteen minutes.

Mamm had fallen asleep on the couch, but she roused at the news Abe would be visiting. Beth bounced around setting the table, singing, "J-O-Y, J-O-Y."

"Abe will play UNO with us tonight, won't he?" Emmie asked. "He promised to do it next time."

With everyone in her family vying for Abe's attention, Anna Mary despaired of having any time to talk to him. She focused on the fact that he'd be here. That was the important part. She'd just have to share him with Mamm and her sisters.

By the time Abe arrived, the meatloaf and potatoes were ready, the peas were bubbling in the pot, and the cracker pudding was cooling on the counter.

"Perfect timing." Anna Mary smiled as she opened the

back door to let him in. Although any time Abe was around seemed to be perfect.

The appreciation gleaming in his eyes warmed her soul. She'd never felt this strong connection with Josh. Had God brought Abe into her life to show her how wrong Josh was for her? Maybe Abe would only serve as a brief example of the possibilities a true relationship could hold.

Her sisters clamored around him, sweeping him over to the table, and before he could protest, they laid out their plans for how he'd spend the rest of the evening.

"I hope this isn't too overwhelming," she whispered to him as he took his place and she leaned past him to set the meatloaf platter in front of him and Mamm.

Farther down the table, Sarah placed the peas and potatoes while Emmie set a basket of dinner rolls nearby.

"I picked the peas." Emmie slid in next to him.

Beth wasn't about to be outdone. "And I set the table."

"I'm sure you're a big help to your *mamm* and Sarah and Anna Mary." He accompanied his words with a smile at each one, but his eyes lingered longest on her.

Anna Mary's inner voice echoed the "J-O-Y" song her sister had been belting out earlier. If only Abe lived nearby. Why did she have to find someone who seemed so right who'd be leaving in two days?

After the meal and several rounds of UNO, Anna Mary and Sarah readied the little ones for bed, while Abe conversed with Mamm. Then he read bedtime stories to Beth and Emmie. Finally, Sarah and Mamm left the living room so Anna Mary could have a little time alone with Abe.

"I'm so glad you have some extra days here." Maybe she was being too forward, but Anna Mary was too happy to care.

"Me too." Abe beamed at her. "An elderly woman called and asked to use the van I'd hired to drive me home. She said all the other drivers were booked."

"All of them?" Anna Mary found that hard to believe. Not that she minded.

"*Jah.* I couldn't refuse, because she was taking people to a funeral."

Anna Mary sucked in a breath. "A funeral?"

"*Jah*, but she didn't even know the person who died. I thought that was odd."

An elderly lady wanted a van to take people to a funeral? And Josh went with Rachel in a van to a funeral yesterday?

"Do you know the lady's name?"

Abe tapped a finger to his lip. "Um, *neh.* It started with *Van*, I think."

"Vandenberg?" Anna Mary's spirits sank when Abe brightened.

"*Jah*, that was it. Vandenberg."

Anna Mary covered her face and groaned. If Mrs. Vandenberg . . .

Little details flooded back. Josh carrying Rachel's quilting at Mrs. Vandenberg's request. The letter she'd asked Anna Mary to deliver. Had Mrs. Vandenberg known Josh would be inside Rachel's house then? Most likely. She'd been the one to pay for Rachel's repairs.

"Anna Mary, what's wrong?" Abe sounded anxious.

Lifting her head, Anna Mary tried to explain about Mrs. Vandenberg's matchmaking. She listed the coincidences.

"And now, the van."

Abe's brow wrinkled in confusion. "The van?"

"A gossip told me Josh and Rachel took off in a van yesterday morning to attend a funeral together."

"Your boyfriend's going to a funeral with another girl."

Anna Mary nodded. "And the funeral's in Ohio."

"What?" The indignation in Abe's voice warmed Anna Mary. "He's going out of state with someone else? If I'd known giving up the van would hurt you, I'd never have agreed. I'm so sorry I did."

"It's not your fault. But now I don't know what to think. If Mrs. Vandenberg's trying to match Josh and Rachel . . ."

"She shouldn't be interfering in people's relationships. That's not fair. Maybe you need to talk to her. Tell her to stop meddling."

"*Neh*, Mrs. Vandenberg gets her nudges from God." Maybe this was His answer to prayer. "I prayed about my future last night, and—" Anna Mary hesitated. She didn't want to mention she'd asked God about her feelings for Abe.

"And—?" Abe prompted.

"This morning, Cathy told me about Josh and Rachel going away together. And just now, you let me know Mrs. Vandenberg set it up. So . . ."

Abe leaned forward eagerly. "So?"

"I'm wondering if God's trying to show me Josh isn't the one for me."

As soon as she said it, Anna Mary's gloom lightened. Coming to that conclusion cleared away a lot of her whirling thoughts, her questions, her doubts. Once she told Josh her decision, she could be at peace with her feelings for Abe. Except they had one major obstacle. An insurmountable obstacle.

* * *

"I'm sorry things don't seem to be working out for you and your boyfriend." Abe stopped. That felt like a lie.

Although he did feel sorry for her enduring the pain of discovering Josh had gone away with someone else, Abe rejoiced that she might be free to consider a new relationship. If Anna Mary broke up with Josh, would she be willing to consider him?

What had that elderly lady said? *God can turn what appears to be a setback to your gain. Trust Him.* Abe had thought her *ferhoodled*, but what if she'd meant exactly what she'd said? She'd given him extra time with Anna Mary. That definitely counted as a gain.

"This lady, um, Mrs. Vandenberg? You say she's a matchmaker?"

"*Jah*, she's matched almost one hundred couples."

"Wow! You think God really does give her nudges?"

"It sure seems like it. I've never heard of her making a mistake in all the years I've known her to bring couples together. Why?"

Should he tell Anna Mary what Mrs. Vandenberg had said? Or would it be better to keep it to himself? Anna Mary hadn't actually broken up with her boyfriend yet, so he had no right to interfere. Until she was free, he should keep his interest to himself.

Still, he had to say what was on his mind. "I wish I didn't have to go home on Monday."

"Me too."

Anna Mary's wistful look made him want to call Daed and schedule more time off. If only he could.

Mrs. Vandenberg had said one more thing. *Use your time wisely.* He had one more day.

"Do you have church tomorrow?"

"*Neh*, it's an off-Sunday."

"Tim's work schedule changes tomorrow. He goes in at ten in the morning."

Before Abe could ask to see her, Anna Mary jumped in. "You're welcome to come here for Sunday dinner and to spend the afternoon. I'm sure Mamm and my sisters would be happy to have you."

Her mamm *and sisters?* Abe tried not to let his disappointment show.

Anna Mary ducked her head. "I would be too," she said shyly.

Her words lit sparklers inside him. She wanted him to visit. "*Danke.* I'd like that. I enjoy spending time with all of you." *Especially you.* He kept that to himself. Unless he got confirmation she had broken up with her boyfriend, he needed to keep everything on a friendship basis.

They talked until Abe had to pick up Tim. He got up to leave reluctantly. "I didn't mean to keep you up so late."

"It's all right. I liked talking to you."

Abe had enjoyed their conversation too and couldn't wait until tomorrow. "I'll see you around eleven tomorrow."

Her bright smile in response filled him with happiness, and he whistled the whole way to the factory to get Tim. Never in his life had he experienced so much joy from being around a *maedel*.

Anna Mary could barely sleep from excitement. Tonight had been so special. And tomorrow she'd get to spend another day with Abe.

Despite her lack of sleep, she bounced out of bed the next morning filled with energy and cheerfulness. She couldn't wait until he arrived. Everyone in the family seemed more upbeat when they heard he'd be visiting.

Sarah had chopped up the leftover chicken from earlier in the week and made chicken corn soup and a chicken-and-rice casserole to stretch the meat for several meals. As the time drew closer to Abe's arrival, she put the casserole into the oven. They'd serve it with leftover salad and cracker pudding.

The clock seemed to inch forward one tiny tick at a time. When buggy wheels finally crunched in the drive-way, she flew to the door.

"Let me help you unhitch the horse," she called as she rushed to him. At the sight of him getting out of the buggy, her heart pitter-pattered. And when he turned to smile at her, her breath caught in her throat.

"*Gude mariye.*" His deep voice strummed chords in her, and the happiness on his face matched the joy in her heart.

Anna Mary spent so much time sneaking peeks at him, she fumbled with the fastenings. Once they'd freed the horse, Abe watered her and turned her out in the pasture. Anna Mary waited by the gate and walked beside him into the house, where he was quickly claimed by Beth and Emmie.

With a helpless shrug, Abe sat down on the floor to play a board game. His eyes met Anna Mary's so frequently he sometimes missed his turn. But Abe didn't seem to care. Neither did Anna Mary. And Beth and Emmie crowed about winning.

Anna Mary enjoyed the noon meal, where she could sit across from Abe and stare at him to her heart's content. His face seemed to be a natural place to rest her eyes.

Emmie and Beth kept the conversation lively, and

Mamm asked questions about the weather and Abe's traveling arrangements, while Sarah kept Hannah from smearing the casserole in her hair.

He detailed his plans and described his town and the dairy farm.

Emmie cupped her chin in her hand. "I wish we had cows."

Abe smiled at her. "They're a lot of work, and you have to get up very early to milk them."

Emmie sighed. "I don't like that. But Anna Mary's good at it."

Mamm looked thoughtful. "*Jah*, she is."

Startled, Anna Mary turned toward her mother. Mamm rarely ever gave compliments. Would Abe think she'd put her family up to this? She lowered her eyes, and her cheeks colored. When she finally glanced up, a hint of a smile lifted Abe's lips. Was that admiration shining in his eyes?

Tentatively, she returned his smile. At the joy brimming on his face, though, she broke into a full-fledged grin. Their gazes caught and held so long her food went cold.

"Aren't you going to eat?" Sarah asked.

Anna Mary forced herself to concentrate on her meal. Everyone else in the family had finished theirs. They sat waiting patiently for Anna Mary and Abe to clean their plates.

Abe set down his fork. "That was delicious. It's so nice to eat someone else's cooking other than my own."

"Then you should stay for supper tonight," Mamm said.

Anna Mary couldn't believe her mother. First, a compliment. Now, a meal invitation. Both were so unlike Mamm.

She added her own plea. "*Jah*, you're welcome to eat supper with us."

Beth clapped. "More games."

Abe's smile dipped. "I'd love to stay, but I need to pick up Tim by six."

Mamm leaned toward him. "We'll eat early enough that you can stay."

"*Danke*, but you don't have to do that."

"We want to." Sarah stood and started clearing plates.

Anna Mary caught Abe's eye and nodded to show she agreed with her sister. Then she stood to help. "Let's have dessert."

After they finished the meal, Abe offered to help with the dishes, but Sarah shooed him and Anna Mary from the kitchen. "Beth and Emmie can help me."

Mamm picked Hannah up from her chair. "I'll put her down for a nap."

Abe turned to Anna Mary. "Would you like to take a walk?"

Trying not to appear too eager, Anna Mary only nodded. A short distance from her house, a creek meandered through a lovely stretch of woods. It would be beautiful to amble along the water today with the sun shining and wildflowers in bloom.

Only one problem. Part of the treed area ran behind Josh's house and connected with Rachel's yard. If Cathy Zehr had her facts right, neither Josh nor Rachel would be home. Still, Anna Mary hesitated. Rachel's *mamm* probably couldn't see across her long stretch of lawn and into the trees from her bedroom. But Josh's brothers and their families might be visiting for Sunday dinner, and their children might be outside or even wandering in the woods.

"Is everything all right?" Abe studied Anna Mary with concern. "We don't have to walk if you're uncomfortable."

"It's not that. I'm trying to decide where to go." A rebellious streak overtook Anna Mary. *If Josh can travel out of town with Rachel, why should I worry about being seen with another man?*

She strode down the driveway toward the woods. "I want to show you the prettiest place around here."

Abe's long-legged gait easily kept up with her rapid pace. Once they entered the trees, Anna Mary slowed. Although she didn't want to admit it to herself, she'd been hoping to get here unobserved. Even though she'd made this decision, part of her worried about gossip getting back to Josh. On the other hand, they'd agreed to spend two weeks apart, so maybe she shouldn't let this worry her.

"Are you sure everything's okay?"

Abe must have sensed her uncertainty. He seemed so attuned to her moods and emotions. Anna Mary checked, and seeing nobody around, she relaxed. Her bare feet sank into the cool, lush grass, adding to her sense of calm.

She led Abe to her favorite spot. "I often used to come here when we first moved to this house after Mamm married my stepfather. Many times, when I had to make decisions, I'd sit on this rock in the creek and pray."

Since Anna Mary had started dating Josh, she hadn't spent time in the woods. Josh had negative feelings about this area and didn't even like to take a shortcut through the trees, though she had no idea why. To be respectful, she'd avoided it, but now she regretted not spending time here. Perhaps if she'd come here to pray, she'd be more certain of the right choices for her future.

"It's so peaceful here." Abe glanced around appreciatively. "Did you want to sit on the rock?"

"I'd like that."

He slipped off his shoes, rolled up his pant legs, and waded toward the rock. Then he turned around and offered her a hand. Sparks shot through him when she placed her small, soft hand in his. Though he longed to keep holding it, he released it as soon as she sat beside him on the large, flat boulder.

For a while, they sat silently beside each other. Abe bowed his head and asked God for His leading. He also prayed for Anna Mary's future. Abe wanted the best for her, even though it probably wouldn't include him.

When he lifted his head, Anna Mary had her eyes closed and her face tilted up to the sun. Her beauty and godliness pierced his soul.

As if she felt his gaze on her, she turned to look at him, her face glowing. "Whenever I come here, I turn all my problems and cares over to God. Afterward, I feel so much lighter."

"I just did that too." His heart full, Abe sent up another plea.

Lord, if she isn't the woman for me, please send me someone like her. A woman who cares about her family, works hard, and most of all, longs to do Your will.

They sat there for hours, chatting about their pasts and getting to know each other better. Abe would have liked to stay there long into the night, but they needed to get back. Reluctantly, he stood and waded partway across the creek before extending an arm to assist Anna Mary.

When they reached the shore, she squeezed his hand before letting go. He stood there, stunned. Had he imagined her sweet touch?

Neh, not from the blush blooming across her cheeks. That small reaction gave him hope. He had no idea how to make this relationship work, but if Anna Mary ended up free to date, he'd trust the Lord for direction.

CHAPTER 12

On Monday, Abe paced back and forth, waiting for the van to return. The driver texted Tim every hour with updates. The woman who'd rented his van still hadn't returned from the trip to Ohio. If Abe had known he'd be here all day, he could have made plans to see Anna Mary.

Not until almost dinnertime did the van return. Abe gritted his teeth. He couldn't ask the driver to travel through the night. They'd have to wait until tomorrow and leave before dawn.

When the driver arrived the next morning, Abe hopped in, eager to get back home. Yet, part of his heart would always stay in Lancaster. Before he'd left Anna Mary's house on Sunday, they'd exchanged addresses and promised to write to each other.

The driver handed Abe a small package. "The lady who rented this van said to give that to you."

Abe opened it to find a box of blue stationery and envelopes, several packets of stamps, and a note.

Blue is for loyalty and faithfulness. I'm sure it will come in handy. I hope you used your time wisely. Leave everything in God's hands. Remember Matthew 19:26.

How did this Mrs. Vandenberg know one of his favorite

verses? Resting his head back on the seat, Abe closed his eyes and let the words scroll through his mind: *With men this is impossible; but with God all things are possible.*

He didn't see how his longing for a future with Anna Mary could come true, but he surrendered his will to God's.

Dear Lord, only You could make this happen. If it's Your will, I'll trust You to work it all out. And if not, I'll do whatever You want me to do.

Even if God led him in a different direction, Abe wasn't sure he could ever forget Anna Mary.

The soft shushing of the car tires on the highway soon put him to sleep, and pleasant dreams of Anna Mary warmed him for most of the trip. He woke with a start when they crossed the border into New York, putting many miles and hours between him and the woman he loved.

Startled, he sat up straight. Where had that word come from? *Loved?* He'd only met Anna Mary two weeks ago. Falling in love in such a short time seemed impossible.

The word *impossible* curved his lips into a smile. Had God made it possible?

On Monday, Anna Mary rushed around the house, doing every chore she could think of to keep herself occupied. Yet nothing distracted her from missing Abe.

Being around him had soothed her. He'd listened to her recount her problems and peered deep into her soul to identify her worries and pain. Then he poured a healing balm over her frazzled nerves. She also enjoyed learning more about his life and concerns, and she'd even offered him advice too. They brought out the best in each other.

She wished she could experience that togetherness every day. If only he didn't live so far away . . .

After dinner, she sat down to write a letter. Pouring out her thoughts and feelings made her feel a little closer to him. She tucked the letter into her drawer before she went to help Sarah get the little ones ready for bed.

Mamm had gone to bed earlier, exhausted from doing too much the day before. She also seemed to miss Abe's cheerful presence. They all did, although none as much as Anna Mary.

A knock at the door startled Anna Mary, and she hurried to answer it. Maybe Abe hadn't left yet. After all, he'd surprised her by staying several extra days. She opened the door, her pulse dancing with anticipation.

"Josh?" All the eagerness and excitement leaked out of her. "What are you doing here?" She couldn't believe how rude that sounded.

"There's something we need to talk about." He shifted from foot to foot as if nervous. "May I come in?"

She opened the door reluctantly. "I thought we agreed to spend two weeks apart." She led him into the living room, but she stayed standing, praying this wouldn't take long. After her emotional day of hard work and trying to adjust to Abe's absence, she felt drained.

At first, Josh didn't say anything. He just stood there uncertainly. When he finally opened his mouth to speak, Anna Mary held up a hand.

"Please keep your voice down," she warned. "Mamm's finally fallen asleep. She had a rough day."

"I'm sorry." Guilt washed over his face. He looked sorry for more than her *mamm*. As well he should, after what he'd done.

Anger flickered in Anna Mary's chest. What right did

he have coming over here after he'd gone out of state with Rachel?

Rather than waiting for him to stop dithering, Anna Mary dove right in. "I didn't expect you to show up here again." Her words held a tinge of bitterness. "Not after Cathy Zehr saw you and Rachel driving out of town together at five in the morning. She had to go in to bake early that morning. Did you just get back?"

Josh stared down at his shoes. "*Jah.*"

Was that all he had to say? No excuses? No explanation? Did he just expect her to accept the fact that he and another *maedel*—Rachel, no less—had gone away together?

Though she should hold her tongue, Anna Mary's irritation burst from her. "So right after I say we should spend a few weeks apart to think about our relationship, you take off with Rachel for a long weekend?"

"Mrs. Vandenberg wanted me to do a job. I didn't know Rachel was going until that morning. I was supposed to do construction work. She was attending a funeral." Josh didn't meet her gaze.

He made it sound as if the whole trip had been a surprise. And as if he and Rachel had come together by accident. He just happened to have work in Ohio at the same time Rachel had to go to a funeral? So of course, they had to ride in the same van? A van hired by Mrs. Vandenberg.

"It seems odd that you'd be going out of town when you have plenty of jobs around here." Josh and his family worked long hours and often had to hire extra help, so he obviously didn't need the work.

"And you didn't protest when I suggested taking time apart." Anna Mary's voice quivered a little. "Now it all makes sense."

"It wasn't like that," he protested. Then he hesitated.

Even though she'd discovered she had more in common with Abe, it still hurt that Josh preferred Rachel to her. She'd rather not hear him admit it.

She held up a hand to stop his explanation. "Maybe it's for the best. I asked for time because I wasn't sure about my feelings for you. I don't think we're well suited."

When he didn't respond right away, Anna Mary regretted being so blunt. "I didn't mean to hurt you."

Rather than appearing wounded or disappointed, Josh looked relieved. "It's all right. I came to the same conclusion while I was gone."

Anna Mary quickly brought the conversation to a close and led Josh to the door. As he was leaving, she said, "For your sake, I hope she gives up her flirting and settles down."

As the door closed behind him, Anna Mary regretted letting jealousy rule her final words.

Lord, please forgive me.

She'd sniped at Josh not only because of jealousy but also because of her own guilt.

The next morning at work, Caroline groaned and ducked behind the refrigerator. Anna Mary turned to see what had bothered her friend, and she swallowed back a sigh of her own as Tim strutted to the counter.

Spending time with him and Abe, Anna Mary had come to like Tim a little better, and she felt sorry for his family situation. But he did like attention. He often did things to hurt people's feelings, and he prevented customers from ordering.

Rather than asking for Caroline the way he usually did, Tim homed in on Anna Mary. In his usual loud voice, he announced, "Hey, Anna Mary. Did you know your boyfriend isn't faithful?"

Customers lined up at the counter swiveled their heads to gaze at her, many with pity. Anna Mary squirmed.

"Don't believe all the rumors you hear, Tim." She kept her tone casual and indifferent.

"This isn't gossip. I saw him heading into Rachel's house early this morning."

That didn't make sense. Tim lived far from Rachel's house. She doubted he'd seen it with his own eyes. Someone else had told him. Maybe someone like Cathy Zehr.

Anna Mary didn't want Tim to know she'd broken up with Josh. He'd spread it all around, and she wasn't ready to face all the whispering behind her back and the sympathy when people found out.

"That's not surprising. He's working on her roof." Anna Mary turned to a customer.

Tim interrupted, "But he doesn't need to go inside to do that."

"Maybe he enjoys her company," she said airily and faced the customer. "What can I get you, ma'am?"

Tim stuck around as Anna Mary took the order. When she moved to the far end of the counter to dip out potato salad, he followed.

Keeping his voice low, Tim said, "Abe will be happy to hear the news."

She hoped he would, but she wasn't about to let Tim know. "What makes you think that?"

He laughed. "The poor guy fell hard for you."

"I see." Keeping her tone neutral was challenging when her heart was ping-ponging around with joy. She scurried back to her customer, wishing Tim would go.

She didn't need this distraction right now. She'd been hoping work might keep her mind off Abe. But hearing he'd fallen for her put her focus squarely back on the big empty space in her life and the one person she desperately missed.

Anna Mary had fallen for Abe too, but what kind of a relationship could they have long-distance? She was thrilled to know Abe cared, but they couldn't be more than pen pals. He had to oversee the family farm, and he couldn't leave his *daed* to do all the work alone. Besides, she'd never ask him to give up his inheritance to move down here, where she carried a heavy responsibility for the care of her mother and four younger sisters.

When Anna Mary continued to ignore him, Tim drifted toward the exit, looking lost and lonely. That made her feel sorry for him. With no other family, he must miss Abe like she did.

After Josh had left last night, she'd gone straight to bed, leaving her letter to Abe unfinished. When she got home today, she'd confide all about their breakup. Although she could never admit it to anyone else, she'd tell Abe her true feelings and confess that deep inside she'd suspected all along that Josh was interested in Rachel.

Just before closing, Mrs. Vandenberg stopped by. Anna Mary couldn't decide if she was irritated with the *Englischer* for pairing Josh and Rachel or if the matchmaker deserved a huge *danke*.

When Mrs. Vandenberg signaled she wanted to speak with Anna Mary, Gideon gave his permission for her to leave the counter.

"This won't take long," the elderly lady promised after Anna Mary joined her. "I hope you had a good weekend."

All the time she'd spent with Abe flooded back. Anna Mary's lips lifted into a smile. The best weekend ever. That last day sitting by the creek had forged an unbreakable bond.

Mrs. Vandenberg studied Anna Mary's face. "I can see you had a wonderful time. I'm so glad." She pulled a book-sized paper bag from her purse. "You might need this."

Anna Mary peeked inside. A box of pink stationery and multiple booklets of stamps.

"Pink is the color of love." Mrs. Vandenberg beamed.

"I can't accept this." As much as Anna Mary longed for it, no way could she pay for that many stamps. They'd cost a fortune.

The sweet older lady laid a hand over Anna Mary's as she tried to return them. "It's an *I'm-sorry* present for making your life miserable."

"You didn't do that." If anything, Anna Mary had caused her own rift with Josh before Rachel came into the picture.

A cheeky smile brightened Mrs. Vandenberg's face. "Like I told Abe, *God can turn what appears to be a setback to your gain. Trust Him.*"

Anna Mary's heart warmed to know she and Abe shared this message. One more thing she'd add to her letter tonight. All day long, she made mental notes of things to tell him.

Still, she couldn't accept such an expensive gift. She tried pushing the bag back across the table.

Again, Mrs. Vandenberg stopped Anna Mary's hand. For a little old lady with a wrinkled hand, she had a great deal of strength. Anna Mary didn't want to get into a package-shoving match, so she set her hands in her lap.

"I know you don't like taking gifts, but sometimes you need to be the receiver rather than always the giver. Because I'm too old for romance myself"—her wistful, regret-filled eyes rested on Anna Mary's face—"it gives me great pleasure to help along young love."

Love? Is that what she felt for Abe?

Anna Mary rolled the word over in her mind. It seemed to fit. Could you jump from an unsatisfactory relationship to falling in love in such a short time? She and Josh hadn't actually broken up until last night.

"Time doesn't count in matters of the heart." Mrs. Vandenberg laughed at Anna Mary's shock. "Some people fall in love at first sight. Others take a long time."

Somehow it seemed impossible.

"When you meet the right person, you just know." Mrs. Vandenberg's eyes twinkled. "And as for the word *impossible*—"

Anna Mary jerked back in her chair. Had this woman read her mind?

Mrs. Vandenberg laughed at Anna Mary's shocked expression. "God prods me from time to time."

Jah, Anna Mary had heard that before. She just hadn't realized what people meant. Was this even possible?

"Possible? Yes, it definitely is." Mrs. Vandenberg leaned forward. "Do you realize the word *possible* is inside the word *impossible*?"

"I never thought about it." But it was true. Was Mrs. Vandenberg saying—?

She interrupted Anna Mary's question. "I'm going to give you the same tip I gave Abe. Read Matthew 19:26 every day." The elderly lady pinned Anna Mary with a penetrating glance. "Do you believe God can do anything?"

"Of course." Anna Mary had no doubt of that.

"Good." Mrs. Vandenberg nodded in satisfaction. "Then you'll trust Him in this." Leaning heavily on her cane, she wobbled to her feet. "You need to keep reminding yourself of that verse: *With men this is impossible; but with God all things are possible.*"

Before she teetered from the table, she patted the bag filled with stationery and stamps. "You'll need this for a while, but don't give up hope. Everything will work out in God's perfect timing."

Anna Mary sat at the table for a minute, stunned. What had just happened?

She'd heard people call the elderly woman a dynamo. A hurricane or whirlwind was more like it. She blew into your life and rearranged everything you thought was settled. And after she passed through, she left your world upended. Anna Mary wasn't sure if that was a good thing.

She definitely had more sympathy for Josh now. No wonder he'd looked so confused and uncertain. Maybe he'd been blindsided the same way she had.

One thing she knew for certain. She had to share all this with Abe in tonight's letter.

CHAPTER 13

Letters flew back and forth between the two of them, sharing every detail of their days and each passing thought. At the tops of their letters, they printed: *With God all things are possible*.

Anna Mary's daily letters lifted Abe's mood at the end of his busy days. He enjoyed reading about her family, the funny and irritating market customers, and her everyday activities. Her chatty messages made him feel like he was a big part of her life.

Most of all, he loved reading her deep inner thoughts and her insights into the Scripture passages she read. He could see the growth of her faith.

Longing to be there in person, Abe penned his own thoughts, the messages he gleaned from Sunday sermons, and his prayer requests. He also tried his best to support Anna Mary emotionally and lift her heavy burdens. He clipped articles about foods, herbs, and techniques to help with her *mamm*'s depression. Nothing made him happier than when Anna Mary tried them and they helped.

In the back of his mind, the niggling thought Josh might change his mind about Anna Mary and want to get back together bothered Abe. After all, it seemed impossible anyone would fall for a girl other than Anna Mary.

Abe chuckled. Did the Scripture verse apply here? Every time he said the word *impossible*, he thought of Mrs. Vandenberg and Matthew 19:26. And Anna Mary, of course. He substituted the word *possible* and prayed it was possible Josh had fallen for someone other than Anna Mary. If he hadn't . . .

Abe didn't even want to think of what that might mean for him. For now, he thanked the Lord he had this precious connection with Anna Mary. A connection he'd have missed if she and Josh hadn't been struggling with their relationship while he was in Lancaster. Each day when he woke, he thanked God for the opportunity he'd had to meet Anna Mary, and he prayed for a way to bring them together.

Often, Abe stared off into the distance, lost in thoughts of Anna Mary or composing a letter to her in his head.

That night as they sat down for supper, Daed waved a hand in front of Abe's face. "Sohn, ever since you returned from Lancaster, you spend more time daydreaming than you do focusing on the world right in front of you."

Abe struggled to pull his attention to the canned soup and to his *daed*. "Sorry."

Daed studied him. "Are you going to tell me what's more interesting than the meal and me?"

How could Abe explain? He found it difficult to describe Anna Mary. He could list her hair and eye colors, tell about her job, explain how she cared for her family. All of those traits defined her, yet none of them caught the essence of her personality, her kindness and generosity, or the depths of her faith.

"You're doing it again." Daed laughed. "You drifted off without even answering my question."

"I had a hard time leaving Lancaster this time, and I keep remembering things that happened."

"I'm guessing this has nothing to do with your cousin. Unless you're worried about him?"

"*Neh*, Myron seems to be worried about normal *youngie* behavior." Tim was over-the-top and stretched the rules. But to be fair to his cousin, Tim hadn't gotten into any real trouble the whole time Abe had visited.

"Tim hasn't told Myron yet, but before I left, he said he's considering taking baptismal classes. He also helped me with a charity project of assisting this family of five girls whose father died."

"That's sad. I know how lonely I am since your *mamm* died. It must be hard for the mother to care for her family without a *mann* around."

"*Jah*, we tried to do what we could for her young children." *And Anna Mary.* "But Esther is lonely. And it gets her down."

"I can imagine. It was good of you to help, and I'm glad Tim participated."

"I am too. It did him good. And I think Sarah brings out Tim's softer side."

Alarm crossed Daed's face. "He hasn't joined the church. I hope you discouraged him from starting a relationship."

Abe laughed. "Sarah's a little young for him. She's only twelve. I think she reminds him of his sister."

"*Ach*, she would be about that age now." Daed shook his head, and his eyes filled with sorrow. "Not a day goes by that I don't think of her and pray she's safe and well."

"I do too." Abe pushed that worry and sadness to the

back of his mind most of the time, but it weighed on all of them.

They'd done what they could to trace her, but they'd never found her. Myron kept checking with the police so the case wouldn't go cold, but after more than a decade, it didn't seem likely she'd turn up now.

For Tim, that loss had left an aching gap that he filled with wildness, misbehavior, and sarcastic comments. Abe prayed his cousin would allow God to fill that inner hollowness. After he'd spent time with Sarah, Tim had mentioned joining the church for the first time. Maybe caring for her and the other girls would keep him on the right path.

Abe lifted his spoon to his lips while he mulled over his concerns about Anna Mary's family. "I hope Tim will continue to help the family now that I'm back here. They didn't have much food but seemed reluctant to let the church know."

Daed stroked his beard. "Hmm . . . *Hochmut* can stop people from letting others assist them."

"*Jah*, it can. And with Esther suffering from depression, she won't reach out. Her children have to handle things."

"The poor mother and children. So, tell me about this family."

Abe described the four younger girls and glossed over Anna Mary. He wasn't ready to share his deeper feelings. He didn't want to make a big deal of his budding relationship. Daed would tell his brothers, and soon all the relatives would know. They'd tease him about falling for a girl who lived so far away. One who couldn't even come for a visit.

"Abe?" Daed startled him from his thoughts. "Why don't we send Myron money and ask Tim to deliver

groceries every week? I'd rather not send money directly
to Tim."

"That might be best." Who knew what his cousin
would use the money for? Abe had one more concern. "I
don't want Myron or Tim to tell the family the food is
coming from us." The last thing Abe needed was for
Anna Mary or her *mamm* to learn he'd been providing
charity.

"Any special reason why not?" Daed eyed Abe
closely. "I've always believed in keeping giving private,
like the Scripture says, but seems you have another
reason. One connected with your daydreaming. Am I
right?"

With Daed asking a direct question, Abe had to
answer. "*Jah*. Sarah has an older sister, one about my
age. I, um . . . well, we spent some time together and—"
He certainly couldn't tell his *daed* about possibly falling
in love. "Well, we enjoyed each other's company," he
finished lamely. That didn't encompass all the feelings
Anna Mary stirred in him. It didn't even come close.

"I suspected as much." Daed sighed. "I can't afford to
lose you. The two weeks you were gone made it clear I
can't run this place without you. Your brothers are a big
help, but they don't have time to do all the cleanup after
the milking, and with my arthritis, I have trouble handling
all of it alone."

"I know." Abe tried not to show his glumness.

Daed brightened. "Why not invite her here? She could
stay with your *aenti*. Rose always enjoys company."

Abe had already considered the many places Anna
Mary could stay. "She can't leave her family. Her *mamm*
struggles with depression, so Anna Mary takes care of
her four younger sisters."

"Maybe they could all come. Rose wouldn't have

enough room, but we could work that out. A change of
scenery might do the mother good."

As much as Abe loved Daed's plan, he shook his head.
"Her *mamm* will never travel outside of Lancaster."

"That does present problems." Daed set his spoon in
his empty bowl and pushed back from the table. "Best I
can say is to pray about it. If it's in God's plan, everything will work out."

Abe had been doing that for weeks now, but nothing
had changed. He wasn't ready to give up yet, but he
sometimes wondered if this was God's way of saying *neh*
to a relationship with Anna Mary.

Several weeks had passed, and Anna Mary fought
against her discouragement. That morning, she'd received a nice long letter from Abe. While she wrote every
day, he added snippets to his letters over several days,
and then sent a thick envelope. She loved finding those in
the mailbox. They brightened her day and kept her going
until the next one arrived. But each time she slid those
blue envelopes from the box, it also reminded her of how
far apart they were.

In this letter, Abe had mentioned his *daed*'s suggestion
of having her family visit, and a twinge of sadness shot
through Anna Mary. According to Abe, they had two
people her family could stay with in addition to Mamm's
cousin Delores. But hiring a van for an out-of-state trip
was expensive, and it might take a year to save up enough
to pay for it.

Even if she had the money, Anna Mary had one other
major obstacle. She couldn't go alone and leave her
family. Not while Mamm wasn't well enough to care
for the younger girls. And Anna Mary didn't bother

asking Mamm about taking the whole family for a visit. She already knew the answer.

After Anna Mary finished all her chores, she poured all those feelings onto the page, along with her longing to see Abe again. Then she moved on to describe a peculiar happening:

Every week or so, someone has been leaving groceries on our porch in the middle of the night. I can't figure out who it is, but we're grateful for the food. Mostly, it's staples like flour and pasta and other dry goods.

The other day, I went to the bulk meat sale, planning to get some ground beef, and they said someone had put money in an account for our family. I bought beef and chicken, and Sarah and I spent all day yesterday canning and freezing the meat. That'll last for months.

As much as it bothers me to accept these gifts, I have to admit it's made life much easier. I wonder if the g'may has been doing it.

Anna Mary didn't add she'd been saving a bit from her paycheck each week because the grocery bills had gone down. After she had enough money, she'd love to surprise Abe someday . . . if Mamm ever got well enough to be left alone. She had been getting a little better, thanks to Abe's suggestions.

Picking up her pen again, Anna Mary started to tell Abe about Mamm's improvement, but then someone knocked.

"I'll get it," Sarah called as she hurried toward the door. Anna Mary's heart sank when her sister said, "Josh, come on in. Anna Mary's in the dining room."

Josh? What was he doing here?

Sarah might have thought she was whispering, but Anna Mary could hear her clearly as she told Josh, "She's writing letters like she does every night before bed."

Anna Mary wanted to get everything on paper before she forgot, so she kept writing as Sarah led Josh down the hall. She kept scribbling even after he entered the room.

"Josh is here, Anna Mary," Sarah announced.

Anna Mary had been so deep in thought, she jumped, sending pink papers fluttering to the floor. Josh bent to pick them up.

"*Neh, neh.* Leave them." Flustered, she bent and retrieved all the pages, gathering them gently and pressing them against her heart.

She hated being interrupted during the special time she set aside for Abe. She slid the papers under the stationery box to hide the words from Josh's view. When she turned to face him, she tried to tamp down her annoyance, but her words came out tart and unwelcoming. "What are you doing here?" She wished she had kept better control of her tongue.

Sarah's eyebrows rose in alarm. She disliked it when people got upset. Josh only stared at the floor and shifted uncomfortably.

A horrible fear flitted through Anna Mary's mind. What if Rachel had left Josh, and he wanted—*Ach, neh!*

The old guilt over falling for Abe before she and Josh ended their relationship flooded back in full force, and rather than Anna Mary admitting it, it sharpened her tone. "Don't tell me the flirt moved on to someone else already, and now you want to get back together." Once again, words flew out of her mouth that she should have held back. Instead, she'd gone into attack mode.

Josh only lifted sad eyes to hers and ignored her sarcasm. "*Neh,* I came to ask your forgiveness."

Forgiveness? She should be the one apologizing.

Josh's bowed head and twisting hands appeared to signal true repentance. For what? Whatever he'd come to ask, she should forgive him. She'd been taught to do that from the time she was small, but worry wiggled through her mind. Suppose he'd come here to tell her he'd made a mistake by dating Rachel?

Anna Mary had to cut that off before he asked. "If you're trying for a second chance with me, it won't work."

"I'm not here to get back together. I'm still with Rachel."

"She doesn't mind you calling on your old girlfriend?" Or maybe Rachel didn't know he'd come. If so, Anna Mary felt sorry for her.

"I'm only here to apologize." Josh looked genuinely regretful. "I wasn't the boyfriend I should have been to you, and I'm sorry for all the ways I hurt you. Will you forgive me?"

Anna Mary studied his face to be sure he meant his request. Josh's earnest expression proved he did. His heart-felt admission broke something open in Anna Mary. All her bravado and defiance crumbled. She humbled herself before God.

Dear Lord, please forgive me for the way I've treated Josh, not only tonight, but the other times I've covered up my shame by mistreating him.

Josh wasn't the only one who needed to apologize. A mountain of guilt weighed her down. Tears stung her eyes. She'd pointed a finger at him, accusing him of cheating. She hadn't used that word, but she'd meant it.

He that is without sin among you, let him first cast a stone flashed through her mind. That Scripture verse condemned her. She'd been casting a lot of stones. But she wasn't sinless.

She hadn't wanted to let Josh see those pages that had floated to the floor. *Jah*, they were private, but that wasn't the only reason. Tears trickled down her cheeks.

Anna Mary swallowed hard and struggled to get out the words. "I forgive . . . you," she gulped. "Will you . . . forgive me?"

"For what?" Josh stared at her, puzzled.

"For . . . for being . . . so grouchy . . . and mean . . . and for starting fights . . ." She hung her head. "I . . . wasn't upset . . . with you. I was . . . upset with . . . me."

"I forgive you, Anna Mary."

She lifted her head, her eyes blurry with tears. She pressed her lips together to hold back sobs. When she spoke again, her words were choked and thick. "That's not all."

"Whatever it is, I forgive you."

"You haven't heard it yet."

"It doesn't matter."

"*Jah*, it does. I said unkind things about you to others. And you didn't deserve it." Anna Mary held up a hand to stop him from responding. "There's more. I did it because I felt guilty, so I took it out on you." She lowered her eyes. "I, um, fell for Abe."

Josh's gaze fell to the pink stationery and the edges of the pages she'd been writing.

Her cheeks reddened. "*Jah*, it's a letter to Abe. I write one every night."

"That's good," he assured her.

"The thing is," she continued, "I was attracted to him the first day I met him. The day you and I had the fight at the volleyball field. I didn't want to do anything about it because we were dating."

"I'm sorry."

"*Neh*, I'm the one who should say that. Fighting those feelings made me argue and snap at you because I felt ashamed about wanting to be with someone else."

"I know how you feel. I felt guilty too."

"Will you forgive me?"

"*Jah*, and I wish you well with Abe."

Anna Mary's face crinkled, and her eyes filled with fresh tears. "He's so far away and . . ."

"Pray about it," Josh advised. "God can work things out even when we think it's impossible."

That word again. "We've both been praying. Mrs. Vandenberg keeps saying to wait for God's perfect timing."

"She thinks you and Abe will get together?"

"*Jah*, she's so encouraging."

"If it helps, Mrs. Vandenberg is an excellent matchmaker, and she comes up with some amazing ideas to match couples. If she's on your side, it's because God gave her a nudge."

"I hope you're right," Anna Mary said as she walked Josh to the door. People kept saying that, but what was taking so long? Most of the matches Anna Mary knew about had happened quickly.

After she closed the door behind him, she couldn't wait to return to her letter. She described the scene with Josh, her heart light. Confessing and asking for his forgiveness had erased a large blot from her conscience, leaving her free to pursue her relationship with Abe without guilt dragging her down.

CHAPTER 14

Before she'd left for work, Anna Mary had tucked Abe's latest letter in her pocket. She'd already read and reread it multiple times, but hearing it crackle as she worked made Abe feel closer. He'd been thrilled she and Josh had formally ended their relationship and that they'd done it on a good note.

Forgiving each other untangles all the old knots and lets you both start anew. I hope that means you're open to move forward with someone else who cares about you.

I've hesitated to express my deeper feelings for you because I didn't know for sure if you and Josh would get back together. But if you're free to date, I hope you'll consider me.

Every time she read those words, they overjoyed her. She couldn't wait to get finished with work and hurry home to write her answer. *Jah, Abe, I wouldn't consider anyone but you. You have my whole heart.*

Then she slid from delight to despair. How could they

date when they lived three hundred miles apart? She'd be faithful no matter how far the distance or how long the separation. But what if they could never be together in this life?

She reminded herself of the last few words printed at the top of the page: *With God all things are possible*.

Forgive me for doubting, Lord. Even if we never get together, I want to do Your will. I'll accept whatever future You have planned for me. And for Abe.

Even if it isn't together? a still, small voice asked.

It would rip her apart, but she had only one answer to give: *Even then, Lord. Even then.*

A weight lifted from her soul. As long as she followed God's path for her life, she'd be on the right track. But she desperately hoped Abe would be part of that plan.

She lifted her head, stepped to the counter, and met the next customer's eyes. Mrs. Vandenberg.

"I didn't want to disturb you, dear. Not when you were praying and wrestling with something that important."

The tenderness and understanding in Mrs. Vandenberg's gaze made Anna Mary ache inside. It had been so long since Mamm had been well enough to look at Anna Mary like that. If Mammi had lived, perhaps she'd have been like Mrs. Vandenberg.

"Now that you've settled your priorities," Mrs. Vandenberg continued, "I have a question for you. I need to go to Fort Plain next weekend and wondered if you'd like to accompany me."

"*Jah!*" Anna Mary squealed before thinking it over. Then her excitement dipped. "I'm not sure I can leave Mamm."

Caroline sidled up to her and leaned over the counter

to ask Mrs. Vandenberg, "Are you going to see Noah's brother, Benji?"

When Mrs. Vandenberg nodded, Caroline put a hand on Anna Mary's shoulder. "I'm sure Sarah can handle things, but if you're worried, I could stay at your house while you're gone."

"Really?" Sunshine blossomed in Anna Mary's heart. "I'll have to check with Mamm."

"Would you like me to talk to her?" Mrs. Vandenberg asked. "I can go over there now and ask her about it."

"That might help." Anna Mary hoped that if Mamm knew how responsible Mrs. Vandenberg was, she'd be allowed to go.

"What do you say about making this a surprise for Abe?" Mrs. Vandenberg asked.

How could Anna Mary possibly keep this news secret? She told Abe everything. But it would be fun to see his reaction when she showed up unexpectedly.

"All right," she agreed. "But what if he's not there?"

"Don't worry," Mrs. Vandenberg assured her. "Dairy farmers don't travel much. To be sure, I can contact one of my sources in Fort Plain and make sure he'll be home when we arrive."

After Mrs. Vandenberg left, Caroline's eyes crinkled. "You look all starry-eyed."

Jah, Anna Mary's whole body sparkled with joy. "I hope Mamm says *jah*." She drew in a quick breath. "But I can't leave you with all the work."

"We'll be fine. You won't be away for long."

By the time Anna Mary went home, Mrs. Vandenberg had come and gone.

Anna Mary couldn't believe it. Mrs. Vandenberg had convinced Mamm to agree to the New York trip.

"The poor old lady needs a traveling companion," Mamm said when Anna Mary arrived home after work. "She needs your help. A woman in her nineties shouldn't be going all that way alone."

Poor? According to market gossip, Mrs. Vandenberg owned the market and was the richest woman in Lancaster County. And from what Anna Mary had seen, Mrs. Vandenberg managed just fine on her own. Yet she'd made Mamm feel sorry for her.

Mamm leaned back on the couch and squeezed her eyes shut for a moment. When she opened them, her eyes glimmered with tears. "You know, your *daed* and I talked about moving to Stone Arabia with Delores and her husband before you were born."

"You did?" Anna Mary had never heard that before. "Why didn't you?"

Her mother's voice grew low and shaky. "I didn't want to leave here. I always wonder whether, if I'd gone, he'd still be alive."

"*Ach*, Mamm. You can't blame yourself for that. What happened was God's timing."

"It doesn't stop the guilt. Land up there was cheap. We could have bought quite a few acres if we'd sold this house. Your *daed* wanted to farm, but he stayed here to make me happy."

Suppose they'd moved to New York. *Would I have met Abe?* Anna Mary sighed to herself. If she had, they wouldn't have this huge distance between them.

Mamm swiped at her eyes. "Your *daed* took that factory job to support us—you and me and later, Sarah. I keep thinking if I'd agreed to move, he never would have been hurt on the job. He'd still be here."

Had Mamm been carrying all this guilt since Daed

died? No wonder she got so depressed whenever the anniversary of his death arrived.

Anna Mary wanted to lift her mother's burden. "You wouldn't have married Martin and had Emmie, Beth, and Hannah."

"You're right. I should count my blessings. But it's hard to feel responsible for someone's death."

"Mamm, it isn't your fault. It's the machinery's fault, the poor maintenance at the factory, the demanding boss." Anna Mary had read the newspaper clippings around the time of the accident.

"I don't know," Mamm choked out. "I just don't know."

"We can't question God's will." As soon as Anna Mary said the words, they convicted her. Hadn't she railed against the many miles between her and Abe?

Mamm's fingers pleated the fabric of her apron. "I longed to say *neh* to this trip. I don't know what I'll do without you."

Anna Mary's gut twisted into knots like the cords that bound her to Lancaster. Mamm needed her. New York was out of the question.

Staring down at her nervous hands, Mamm said so quietly Anna Mary almost didn't hear her, "I can't stand in your way. At least not for this brief visit."

"Mamm, you won't ever lose me, I promise. I'll always live where you do." Anna Mary didn't regret comforting her mother with those words, but they ended any possibility of a relationship with Abe—unless the two of them agreed to seeing each other once or twice a year for a few days.

"*Ach*, I didn't mean I'd never want you to marry." Mamm hung her head and mumbled almost under her breath, "But I'd still want you to stay nearby."

Anna Mary's insides clenched. She only wanted to marry one man. And he didn't live nearby.

Tears spilled onto Mamm's cheeks as she looked up. "I always felt like God was punishing me for insisting on not going to New York the way your *daed* wanted. I refused to pray about whether or not it was God's will."

Speechless, Anna Mary stared at her mother. She believed Daed's death was punishment for disobeying God? And she blamed herself for Daed's accident? *How can I help Mamm see the truth?*

Mamm went on. "I was afraid if I said *neh* to this trip of yours, I might lose you like I did your *daed*."

Anna Mary couldn't believe it. "Mamm, I don't have to go."

Her mother shook her head. "I prayed about it this time. I feel like God wants me to let go of my fears, stop clinging to what I want, and trust Him. I've been trying to cope with everything on my own. It's time to turn it all over to the Lord."

"I'm glad, Mamm." Anna Mary prayed Mamm's letting go of her burdens and relying on God would help with her depression. One of the articles Abe had sent explained how guilt could lead to depression. This might be an answer to Anna Mary's prayers for her mother's healing. Abe had been praying too. He'd be thrilled to know about this step forward. Anna Mary couldn't wait to tell him in person.

Anna Mary had never known about her mother's guilt. Maybe she should reread that article and share it with Mamm. Anna Mary also planned to talk to Abe about it. Together, they might be able to do more to help her mother.

"*Danke*, Lord," Anna Mary whispered as she headed to the kitchen to help Sarah with the dinner dishes.

Sarah turned and smiled. "Mamm seems better, doesn't she?"

"*Jah*. I still can't believe she's letting me go to New York." Anna Mary twirled in an excited circle. How would she control her excitement until she arrived in Fort Plain?

She hugged herself in delight and practically danced to the table where she wrote her nightly letters. She poured her heart out onto the page and told Abe how excited she was to see him in person. Because it was a surprise, she couldn't send the letter. She regretted not sharing her day right away, but she'd be able to hand-deliver it. Now her envelope would be as thick as Abe's usually were.

After she finished, she unfolded his most recent message to reread. Her eyes skimmed down the page to the place where he'd written about how much he missed her.

"I miss you too," she told him and pressed her lips to his words. "But I'll be seeing you in person next weekend. I can't wait."

On Saturday morning, Abe dragged out of the milking barn and headed for the house. No letter had come from Anna Mary for the past few days. He hoped she was all right. Suppose she'd gotten sick? How would he know? Or what if she'd changed her mind? Maybe his letter confessing his true feelings and asking about dating her had scared her off.

Or, worse, what if she'd met someone else?

A stinging pain sliced through him at that thought. She was so lovely and kind and—

He could go on about her *wunderbar* qualities all day long. Other men could be lined up at her door, begging her to go out.

He kicked off his boots in the mudroom and scrubbed his hands to rid them of barn smells before he cooked breakfast. By the time Daed stomped in and washed up, Abe had bacon and eggs ready to go.

Daed scrutinized Abe's lackluster expression. "Seems like you've lost some of your usual happiness."

Abe only grunted as he scooped breakfast onto their plates. He hadn't slept well last night. He'd been woken by nightmares. Anna Mary running away from him. No matter how much he sped up, he could never catch her. Anna Mary sitting on her couch with an assortment of different men all vying for her attention. Anna Mary smiling through the volleyball net—not at him, but at some random *youngie* who'd swept her off her feet.

"What's wrong, Sohn?" Daed asked as Abe plopped into his chair. "You look like you're carrying the weight of the world on your shoulders."

That's exactly how Abe felt. Burdened, weighed down with cares.

"This have anything to do with no pink envelopes showing up?"

"It's only been a few days," Abe said defensively. *Miserable, long, lonely days.* He tried to tell himself mail had been slow. Or the post office had delivered the mail to the wrong house and a neighbor hadn't dropped it off yet. Or—

Abe didn't want to replay those nightmares.

"Listen, Sohn, God has a plan for your life. Instead of running ahead of Him, why not surrender to His will, whatever that may be? If Anna Mary is part of God's design for your life, it'll all work out. If not, He has something better in mind."

Abe's heart clenched. He didn't want anyone or anything else but Anna Mary.

Daed finished his meal, rose from the table, and set a hand on Abe's shoulders. "I'll start mucking out the stalls. You think about what I said." He headed for the door, then turned with a sympathetic glance. "Things'll work out for the best."

Abe busied himself with clearing the table so he wouldn't have to meet Daed's searching gaze. Though Abe knew his father was right, he couldn't bear to think of living life without Anna Mary.

He wrestled with those feelings as he scrubbed the dishes. How could he accept God's will if it meant giving up Anna Mary? Abe's heart ached at the thought.

Doing what the Lord wanted wasn't always easy. Jesus had to submit to going to the cross. He'd asked for that to be taken from Him, but in the end, He did what He needed to do. The Father had a much greater plan.

And He also has the best plan for my life. Losing the woman I love in no way compares to Jesus's sacrifice. What if rebelling against God's will led to him missing out on a larger plan that would help others?

Please, Lord, make me willing to do whatever you want me to do. Even if it means a life without Anna Mary.

His heart railed against that idea, but Abe persisted, begging God to take away his resistance and give him a humble and obedient spirit.

Abe scrubbed and prayed. Scrubbed and prayed. Scrubbed until he'd almost worn through the pan's finish. Prayed until he reached the point of acceptance.

Not my will, but Yours, he said finally.

Saying those words was one of the toughest moments of his life, but he meant every one of them. And with submission came peace.

Filled with excitement, Anna Mary had risen two hours before Mrs. Vandenberg arrived at dawn. An old duffel bag holding her clothes sat by the front door, and on the table beside it, three large containers filled with an assortment of cookies waited. One each for Mrs. Vandenberg, her driver, and Abe. Anna Mary had tied them with pretty ribbons.

The containers brought back the shaft of jealousy that had shot through her when Josh mentioned Rachel baking sugar cookies for him. Now, Anna Mary smiled at the memory. Rachel could bake all of Josh's favorite cookies from now on. Anna Mary had someone she'd much rather share her cookies with. Someone who filled her heart with joy.

She did all the chores she could before Mrs. Vandenberg's Bentley was scheduled to pull into the driveway. To Anna Mary's surprise, Mamm came out of her room fully dressed.

"Have a *wunderbar* time, Dochder." Mamm infused cheer into her normal monotone. "I'll miss you, but I feel God has a reason for this trip." She paused, and sorrow filled her eyes. "Maybe this happened to make me face past pain. And to trust Him for the future."

Then she pulled Anna Mary close in a fierce hug. "I love you, Dochder."

Anna Mary blinked to clear the dampness from her eyes. Mamm had never been a hugger. Nor did she express her deeper feelings. Anna Mary felt as if she'd been given a precious gift. A gift she needed to treat with care.

Mamm didn't want to lose her. And Anna Mary had vowed to stay near her *mamm* for her lifetime. Where did that leave the relationship with Abe?

Before Anna Mary could untangle those conflicting desires, the Bentley arrived, and her sisters tumbled from their rooms to give her goodbye hugs.

"Tell Abe we miss him," Sarah said wistfully. "I wish we could all go."

"That could be arranged." Mrs. Vandenberg's crisp voice cut through the chilly morning air.

How had she heard Sarah's longing from that far away? She must have exceedingly keen hearing.

Mrs. Vandenberg's laser-like gaze landed on Mamm, who shook her head slightly. *Neh*, Mamm did not agree with that plan. She may have wrestled with old pain enough to allow Anna Mary to go this one time, but she left no doubt a family trip was out of the question.

"God has His reasons."

At Mrs. Vandenberg's ringing statement, Mamm deflated and shrank back into herself. Sarah hurried over and put an arm around Mamm's shoulders. Quiet, peaceful Sarah then did something Anna Mary had never seen her sister do.

Sarah faced Mrs. Vandenberg with steely eyes. "This is hard enough on Mamm."

First giving Sarah a caring smile, Mrs. Vandenberg faced Mamm. "Sometimes we need less coddling and more backbone, don't we, Esther?"

Mamm flinched at the steely tone of Mrs. Vandenberg's words. Then she bowed her head. After a moment, she admitted, "You're absolutely right, Liesl."

Liesl? Mamm knew Mrs. Vandenberg's first name? That shocked Anna Mary. Had they become so close during their one conversation, or had Mamm known Mrs. Vandenberg before?

Anna Mary had no time to ponder the question because Mrs. Vandenberg beckoned her to the car. Her sisters helped put the cookies and luggage in the trunk, and in a matter of minutes, Anna Mary was snuggled into the most luxurious seat ever. She smoothed her hands over the buttery leather. The driver handed her a soft cashmere blanket.

Mrs. Vandenberg turned around. "I like to nap on my trips. That makes them go faster, and when I arrive, I'm full of energy. Maybe you'd like to do the same."

It sounded like a wonderful idea, except for one minor problem. Anna Mary was much too keyed up to relax. She'd never been outside of the Lancaster area before, so she planned to drink in every bit of scenery. She'd tuck it all away to describe to her family later.

Teary-eyed, Anna Mary waved to her sisters and Mamm as the car glided down the driveway and turned onto the country lane. They were off. How was it possible to be so sad and so thrilled at the same time?

If Mamm ever agreed, could I drive away from home permanently to live so far away? Anna Mary shook her head. *Neh*, leaving this morning was hard enough, and they'd only be gone for a few days. Besides, she'd promised Mamm they'd stay together. Yet Anna Mary's heart ached to be with Abe. If only they didn't live so far apart. Or if only Abe could move to Lancaster. Sadly, that was impossible.

In what had become a daily habit whenever she said the

word *impossible*, Anna Mary repeated her favorite verse to herself. *But, Lord, what if I can't see any solution?*

That's where faith came in. She had to trust that God had a plan for her future. Her heart kept calling her to be with Abe. But what if that wasn't the Lord's will for her? She'd committed to doing whatever He wanted in her life, no matter the cost. And she intended to do just that.

CHAPTER 15

Abe walked out to the barn to join his *daed* with an uplifted spirit, but a heavy heart. Deep down, he was certain he'd done the right thing. His soul felt washed clean, filled with clarity and purpose. Even if he had to walk this earth alone without a helpmeet, he'd already set his feet on the correct path. Now he only had to go where God led him.

"You get things settled between you and the Lord?" Daed asked when Abe entered the barn.

His throat tight, Abe could barely get out an answer. "*Jah*."

"I can tell. You have a light in your eyes that shows you've spent time with God." As Abe headed for a pitchfork, Daed clapped him on the back. "Sometimes the direction God asks us to walk isn't easy, but it's always worthwhile."

Abe nodded. His *daed* had walked a lonely path ever since Mamm died. He understood about losing someone you loved. And Abe hadn't been married to Anna Mary, so he didn't have all the years of history and loving Daed had had to give up when Mamm passed. Until now, Abe had no idea of his father's suffering. Now he had a tiny inkling. And Anna Mary's *mamm* had been through it twice. No wonder she struggled to cope with life. Abe's pain paled compared to theirs.

He threw his weight behind the pitchfork, then shook the bedding through the tines. Doing familiar, mindless tasks helped to distract him from his sadness.

But he couldn't help wondering if he should have done things differently. Perhaps he'd moved too quickly from friendship to asking her to date. After all, they'd only spent two weeks together.

Jah, they'd been exchanging letters—deep, meaningful letters—for a while now, but Anna Mary had just formally ended her relationship with Josh. She might not be ready to jump into another one so soon. Or . . . A lump rose in his throat. He tried not to think about it, but the idea kept returning unbidden. A *maedel* as lovely and *wunderbar* as Anna Mary may have found someone else.

When they stopped for brunch, Anna Mary stared at the luxurious restaurant in dismay. Mrs. Vandenberg had insisted she'd be paying all the bills for the hotel and meals because Anna Mary was doing her a favor. Anna Mary refused to accept that, so she'd brought the money she'd saved. It wasn't much, but she intended to pay for herself.

When the waiter brought the menu to the linen-covered table, she gulped at the costs. Buying any meal on here would deplete almost half the money she had.

Mrs. Vandenberg leaned over. "Get whatever you want, but I'd recommend the buffet. They have so many delicious choices."

Anna Mary's gaze flew to the featured special. The buffet was the priciest item on the menu. A small box

near the bottom of the opposite page caught Anna Mary's
eye. She breathed easier. Under *Side Dishes*, she could
choose a hard-boiled egg, which she could hardly believe
cost as much as buying two whole cartons.

"I'll have a hard-boiled egg," she whispered when the
waiter returned for their orders.

"Nonsense." Mrs. Vandenberg took the menu from
Anna Mary's hands. "We'll all have the buffet. Put it on
my bill." She turned to Anna Mary. "If you only want
one egg, they have them at the buffet. It seems a shame
to ignore all the other choices, though." She rose and tottered toward the silver chafing dishes.

Anna Mary rushed after her. "Why don't I help you
with your plate?"

"That would be perfect, dear." Mrs. Vandenberg
beamed at her. "It's not easy juggling plates with one
hand while balancing on shaky legs." She tapped her cane
on the floor for emphasis.

After carrying Mrs. Vandenberg's plates and cups to
the table, Anna Mary stood transfixed beside the array of
gorgeously arranged pastries and various dishes. Once or
twice when her stepfather had been alive, he'd taken
them to Yoder's restaurant for the buffet. She'd been as
overwhelmed then as she was now.

She took small samples of everything that looked interesting. Mrs. Vandenberg encouraged her to have more
of her favorites. Anna Mary did because they'd paid so
much for it and so she wouldn't need another meal later.
She returned to the car with a full stomach and a grateful
heart.

She enjoyed riding in the comfortable car and watching the towns they passed, but after almost seven hours on
the road, Anna Mary *rutsched* around, eager for the trip to
end. She hadn't minded the riding itself or the lengthy

stops for food or for Mrs. Vandenberg to stretch her legs, except for the fact that she wanted to get to their destination as quickly as possible.

"It won't be long now," Mrs. Vandenberg assured her. "We should get there around one or so. I understand they don't start milking until four, which will give you some time with Abe."

Just hearing his name filled Anna Mary with excitement. She fingered the thick envelope she'd tucked into her purse. She'd written so much over the past few days, but now she'd actually get to hand this to him.

And she had one more thing to share with him. Her response to what he'd said in his letter: *I hope you'll consider me.*

How could he have any doubts after their correspondence? Hadn't she made herself perfectly clear?

Well, now she could dispel all his doubts in person. She hoped he'd be as thrilled with her answer as she'd been by his offer to be her boyfriend.

Now that they were so close to his farm, she had a few worries of her own. Would he be happy to see her? Or did he have so much work to do, he wouldn't have time to spend with her?

And most of all, did he like surprises?

After Abe and his *daed* had mucked out the stalls, they left the cows in the pasture, nibbling grass. The summer sunshine made a beautiful picture as it streamed through some distant trees and lit the meadow. More than anything, Abe wished he could share this peaceful scene with Anna Mary. Would she like it here? Could she ever consider it her home?

He imagined the two of them doing the milking together,

coming into the kitchen to enjoy meals, sitting together on the back porch watching the sunset. As he headed into the house to shower, he imagined all the things he and Anna Mary would do together if she came to visit. Or better yet, if she came to live here as his wife.

In that dreamlike state, he drifted downstairs to prepare a chicken-and-rice casserole for that night's supper. A meal that always reminded him of his trip to Lancaster and sitting across from Anna Mary at their table. Twice a week, he made an extra-large casserole so they'd have leftovers for the next few days. That way, they just had to heat up a portion when they came in exhausted after milking.

While waiting for it to cook, Abe wandered back into the yard, picturing how he'd take his wife's hand in his as they strolled out to check on the cows in the meadow. He leaned on the split-rail fence and tried not to lose that special feeling, but deep inside, a great gulf of loneliness opened up. What if he never had another chance to see Anna Mary again? Suppose she never answered his last letter? Abe wasn't sure how he'd go on.

Behind him, a car purred up the driveway. Probably a lost tourist stopping to ask directions. Or trying to get a closer peek at an Amish farm. He kept his back turned in case they planned to snap pictures.

The car rolled to a stop, and a door opened. Tourists usually weren't that bold. He'd started to pivot when a familiar voice called out his name. He stumbled and almost tripped over his feet. He'd spent so much time pretending she'd been with him today, his mind must be playing tricks on him.

"Abe," she called again. Pattering footsteps raced in his direction.

When he turned, Anna Mary ran to him and almost flung herself into his arms. He reached out to grasp her forearms so she didn't fall against his chest. Not that he would have minded, but they shouldn't. And if Daed were watching, Abe didn't want his father's first sight of Abe's girlfriend to be of them breaking the rules of the *Ordnung*.

He shouldn't even be touching her arms. He dropped his hands to his sides, his heart crashing into his ribs at the sight of her and the softness of her skin.

"How? What are you doing here?" He could have bitten his tongue. He hadn't meant to come across as unwelcoming. Quickly, he added, "I'm so glad to see you."

"Mrs. Vandenberg had to come to Fort Plain on business, so she asked me to come with her." Anna Mary rushed the words out, sounding as breathless and excited as he felt. "We're going to stay a few days."

"Really?" Joy flooded through him at the sight of her flushed face and the happiness in her eyes. All worries about her having fallen for someone else flew away.

"I want to learn all about milking cows and—"

Behind her, Daed belly laughed. "It's nice to see such enthusiasm for doing chores, but you might not be so eager to do it once you've actually tried it."

Anna Mary's cheeks grew fiery, and Abe longed to defend her. "Anna Mary's used to doing chores. She takes care of her four younger sisters and works at the market and—"

Daed smiled. "So I've heard. According to my *sohn*, you're quite an amazing *maedel*."

Confusion registered in Anna Mary's eyes, and it was Abe's turn for heated cheeks. "I talk about you a lot, I guess." Once he'd finally confessed to his *daed* about falling for Anna Mary, Abe couldn't stop talking about her.

"So, are you going to introduce us?" Daed demanded with a chuckle.

"Daed, this is Anna Mary. Anna Mary, my *daed*, Hank King."

"Pleased to meet you." Daed held out his hand and shook Anna Mary's.

A car door creaked open, and the driver circled the car to let out the passenger in the front seat. *Mrs. Vandenberg.*

Abe thanked God for the day he met her. And now, thanks to her, Anna Mary was standing in his driveway.

She hobbled over, leaning heavily on her cane. "Takes a while for the old legs to catch up after traveling."

After Abe introduced them, he invited them inside for lemonade. "I'm sorry I don't have time for baking, or I'd offer you cookies." He gave Anna Mary a tender gaze at the memory of the way she'd shared her last cookies with him and his cousin.

"You're in luck," Mrs. Vandenberg crowed as the driver carried two of the containers up the driveway. "Anna Mary baked enough to feed an army."

Could Abe's heart be any fuller? The answer to that turned out to be *jah*.

Before they entered the kitchen, Anna Mary reached into her purse and handed him the thickest envelope he'd ever seen. She often sent four or five pages, but this held much more than that.

"I didn't send you letters the past week because I didn't want to spoil the surprise. Plus, I wanted to hand this to you in person."

The screen door banged behind Daed, Mrs. Vandenberg, and the driver, but Abe and Anna Mary didn't follow.

He released a long sigh as he took the envelope. "I worried I'd upset you by what I said in my last letter."

"Upset me?" Anna Mary turned shining eyes up to his. "*Neh*, definitely not."

She shot him a teasing smile. "My response is in there." She pointed to the thick pink envelope.

"I have to read all this to find out?" he couldn't resist asking.

"Unless you want to ask me something in person and get an answer right away."

Her grin stole his heart, but did he have the courage to ask the question that had been burning inside him from the day he'd met her?

Anna Mary held her breath and waited. What if he'd changed his mind? At first, he'd seemed delighted to see her, but now he was hesitating.

Abe gulped in some air. "Anna Mary, I fell for you the first day I saw you. And that feeling hasn't changed. It's only grown stronger the more I get to know you. I'd like to court you, if you're willing."

Tapping one finger against her chin, Anna Mary pretended to consider, but she couldn't keep up the act. A loud *JAH!* burst from her lips. She covered her mouth. After all the times she'd scolded her friend Caroline for being too exuberant, here she was acting ten times worse. But Abe didn't seem to mind.

A wide grin spread across his face. "This has to be the happiest day of my life so far. From now on, though, I expect they'll get even better."

"They will for me." Anna Mary didn't know how she could be more joyful than she was at this moment, but agreeing to be Abe's girlfriend meant walking beside him in life. Suddenly, her spirits plunged. Dating was intended to lead to marriage, but how could they possibly be together?

"What's the matter?" Abe sounded panicked. "You haven't changed your mind already, have you?"

"*Neh*, I'd never do that. But, Abe, how can we be together when you can't move to Lancaster and my family needs me there?"

Anna Mary wished she hadn't brought up their problems so soon after they'd settled one of the most important questions of their lives. They did need to think this through, though. As much as they loved each other and wanted to be together, there was no way to do it.

He reached out with a gentle finger and lifted her chin so she looked into his eyes. "Remember what the Bible says about all things being possible."

"I know." She was just finding it hard to believe right now. Then she brightened. No point in acting gloomy when they were together for a few days. "Let's make the most of our time together."

"I intend to do that."

The smile he gave her melted Anna Mary's heart. Somehow, they had to find a way to be together.

After everyone finished their cookies, Mrs. Vandenberg and the driver stood up and prepared to take off for the hotel.

"The driver will be back to pick you up later tonight, Anna Mary," she said before leaving. "You should probably make an early night of it since you'll be back here by four tomorrow morning. If that's all right with everyone?" She glanced around, and when they all nodded, she headed for the door.

Abe couldn't believe his daydreams earlier today of having Anna Mary by his side while he worked were actually coming true. He almost wanted to pinch himself to be sure it was real. But he didn't need to do that. Anna Mary's shining face across the table proved it wasn't a fantasy.

As much as he longed to read the letter she'd given him, he'd save it for after she returned to the hotel. He wanted to focus on her every minute she was with him.

"You sure you want to come so early tomorrow?" Abe asked softly. He'd love to have her there, but he'd have little time to spend with her. She'd mostly watch, but getting up that early could be hard.

Anna Mary's head bobbed up and down with enthusiasm.

Daed gave her an approving look, but warned, "Why don't you wait and see how you feel once we've done the afternoon milking?" Then he added, "Just remember, you'll have to get up well before four to get over here on time."

"I got up at three this morning, and I'm still wide awake."

Abe could see her disarming smile charmed his *daed*. That made Abe happy. He wanted the two of them to get along well. Daed appreciated hard workers. But Abe didn't want Anna Mary to be too exhausted to spend time together later in the day. He had several places he wanted to take her tomorrow.

"If you decide to sleep in," he suggested, "you can come for part of the milking or for breakfast."

"*Danke.*" Her confident expression indicated she intended to follow through.

He sniffed the air. "The casserole's almost done. We

usually eat before milking on the nights I make the meal, then we eat leftovers after milking for a few nights."

Daed's eyes grew distant. "We always ate hot meals after milking when your *mamm* was alive. But with no woman in the house, you have to do what you can." He put on a watery smile. "I'm grateful Abe learned to cook."

Anna Mary's eyes reflected sympathy, which made Abe love her even more. If that was possible.

"I'd be happy to cook while I'm here," she offered.

Daed looked embarrassed. "I wasn't fishing for that. I just meant—" He cleared his throat. "Well, it gets lonely without a wife around."

"I understand. My *mamm* misses being married too."

"So Abe says. I'm sorry it's been hard for her."

Abe hoped Anna Mary wasn't upset about him talking to Daed about her *mamm*'s depression.

"*Jah*, it's not easy," she agreed.

Would thinking about missing people make Anna Mary reevaluate their decision to date? What if she decided she didn't want a lonely, long-distance relationship?

He stood abruptly to change the subject. "I'm going to check on the casserole. Did you want to eat supper with us, Anna Mary?"

She stared at him startled. "We just had cookies." Then she nibbled her lower lip as if reconsidering her answer. "Since I only had brunch today, I'd be happy to join you. Unless you'd rather save the leftovers for another meal."

Was she teasing him? A hint of a smile gave him the answer.

"I can always make more," he assured her. "And you can tell me if this turned out as *gut* as the casserole you served me. I used your recipe."

She burst into a smile that set his whole world on fire.

Daed rose from his chair. "I'll go herd the cows into the milking barn."

Abe shot an apologetic glance to Anna Mary. "I have to help."

"No need," Daed said. "You stay here and talk."

Abe appreciated this time alone with Anna Mary. Every minute was precious.

CHAPTER 16

Anna Mary couldn't believe she was sitting in Abe's kitchen in New York, with him across from her. His words still rang in her ear. He wanted to date her. She could hardly believe it. It seemed like a miracle.

"*Danke,* God," she whispered under her breath. She could hardly wait to milk the cows. She wanted to learn everything about it so she could picture Abe at work when she returned home.

"I'm so glad you're here." Abe's words expressed the same wonder she could hardly contain.

"Me too," she said softly. God had given her a precious gift.

Their eyes, filled with joy and caring, met and held until a burning smell came from the oven.

"*Ach!* I forgot to turn the oven to warm." Abe jumped up to pull out the smoking casserole and stared at it in dismay. "I wanted this to be a special dinner."

"It will be. Because I'm spending it with you."

"I'm so glad you feel that way." Abe shot her a grateful look before staring at the pan with a rueful look.

Anna Mary hopped up from her chair and joined him.

"It's not bad. Just a little charred around the edges. If you dip from the middle, it'll taste fine."

"If you say so." Abe looked doubtful.

"Believe me. I've had plenty of experience burning food. And I'm happy to eat the edges. I like my casseroles crunchy."

That got a loud laugh from Abe. "You're the greatest."

Anna Mary usually ate the burned parts of a meal to let Mamm and her sisters have better portions, so she was used to it. And she'd rather eat burned food across the table from Abe than eat in that gourmet restaurant where she'd had brunch.

Abe couldn't believe he'd ruined supper. He'd wanted to give Anna Mary his very best. He also couldn't believe how sweet she was being about it. Her volunteering to eat the burned parts and pretending she liked them made him smile. He'd chosen a very special woman to date. The kind of woman who'd take problems in stride and look for solutions. Who'd make a wonderful, giving wife and mother. Who'd be the perfect helpmeet by his side as they went through life. Who—

He stopped abruptly. *Who doesn't live here and never can.*

Lord, please show us a way to be together.

After Daed joined them, they prayed and ate the meal rapidly. To Abe, even the center of the casserole had a singed taste, but Daed didn't say a word, and Anna Mary claimed it tasted as delicious as hers. Abe didn't believe her, but he appreciated her kindness. Tomorrow he'd make his *mamm*'s favorite meal and hope it turned out well. He wanted to make Anna Mary's stay so pleasant she'd want to come back often.

* * *

Anna Mary could barely eat her meal, not because it tasted burned—she barely noticed that—but because her stomach flipped into cartwheels each time she glanced at Abe. She couldn't believe she was here at his table, sharing supper with him.

Hank finished his meal and stood. "I'll go out and sanitize the barn while you two wash the dishes."

He seemed to be giving them time together, which Anna Mary appreciated. Drying dishes beside Abe brought back memories of him helping in her kitchen. She pictured them in their own kitchen with children gathered around them, all occupied with their chores. But where? Lancaster or Fort Plain?

As she finished the last plate, Abe turned to her. "Ready to try milking?"

"I can't wait."

Excited, she accompanied him across the yard. She wanted to prove to Abe and his *daed* that she could be helpful.

As they reached the side-by-side milking barn, the sharp scent of bleach wafted out. Anna Mary peeked in to see rows of cows lined up on each side of the long room with low wooden beams overhead. She stepped inside eagerly. Her foot slid on wet, slippery cement.

Abe grasped her arm to keep her from falling. "Careful. Daed just disinfected and hosed down the floor." He kept a hand under her elbow, sending shivers through her, as she stepped forward.

She worried more about swooning than slipping. So much for impressing Abe's *daed*. Anna Mary regretted wearing old sneakers with so little tread. The soles were almost smooth. Whenever she had extra money, she spent

it on her sisters, so it had been years since she'd had a
new pair. If she'd known the floor would be wet, she'd
have come into the barn barefoot the way she did at home.

"I'll take off my shoes." She bent and unlaced her
sneakers, enjoying Abe's support as she stood on one foot
and then the other to remove them.

As much as she enjoyed his touch, Anna Mary fretted
about keeping him from work. Why hadn't she come in
here barefoot in the first place, the way most women and
girls did? She hoped she hadn't upset his *daed*.

Once she'd set her shoes by the door, Abe released his
hold, but the warm imprint of his fingers remained.

Trying not to let her reaction show, she pattered
toward Hank. "What can I do to help?"

With an approving smile, he glanced up from hooking
up black rubber hoses. "*Sohn*, why don't you show Anna
Mary how to clean the cows' teats? That would be a big
help."

When Abe went to fetch the solution, Hank sighed. "I
miss having young'uns running through the barn. My
little ones used to do these jobs." He looked up as Abe
approached. "I'm waiting for my *sohn* here to have
kinner. I'd love to have *kinskinder* underfoot."

At his *daed*'s words, Abe's face turned bright red. A
strange feeling fluttered through Anna Mary's chest at the
thought of being the mother of Abe's children. She stared
at the floor and couldn't meet his eyes. Her cheeks must
match his.

Abe couldn't believe Daed had said that in front of
Anna Mary. Only a few short hours ago, Abe had gotten
the courage to ask her to court. Not that he hadn't ever
had the same thoughts his *daed* had expressed, but he'd

never say them to Anna Mary. Not yet. And certainly not before they'd figured out how to be together and go on actual dates.

"Sohn, you gonna daydream about this *schee maedel* or show her what she needs to do?"

Abe's head jerked up. Was Daed deliberately trying to embarrass him in front of Anna Mary?

He frowned at his father, who only chuckled and moved on to attaching the hoses to the machinery. After taking a few seconds to compose himself, Abe gestured to the end of the row. "We'll start there and work our way up. Then we do the other side."

Anna Mary walked beside him, and he couldn't help thinking how wonderful it would be if they did this together every day.

She sniffed. "Do I smell lavender?" She sounded surprised.

"*Jah*. Our milk's organic, so we make this wash from lavender and tea tree oil mixed with castile soap."

"That's nice. It must be pleasant to make it."

The happiness in her voice made him wish he'd waited to make a batch so he could teach her. He loved the smell too, and it was much nicer to work with than the harsh ones that stunk of bleach or chemicals. He often wondered if that taste ever got into the milk in other dairies.

After they reached the first cow, he squatted down and demonstrated cleaning and drying. "We do this before milking, so the milk is clean, and again afterward, so the cows don't get infections. It's very important to be thorough."

She took the wash from him. "I can do that."

Abe steered her away from the cow's back hooves. He tried to tell himself he was only concerned with her safety, but he also couldn't resist touching her again. "Do it from here. Most of our cows are used to this, but with you being new, some might kick out." He grinned. "Never a good idea to stand behind any animal with powerful hooves, even if it seems docile."

"That's true."

Obviously, she already knew that because she took care of buggy horses. Instead of pointing it out, though, she gazed up at him with such adoration in her eyes that his heart swelled to fill his chest.

He still couldn't believe it. Anna Mary had agreed to date him. This beautiful *maedel* had said *jah* to being his *girlfriend*.

Daed cleared his throat. "You gonna help me today or not, *Sohn*?"

Reluctantly, Abe let go of Anna Mary's arm. "Coming," he called, then turned back to her. "Will you be all right?"

"I'll be fine." With a sweet smile, she turned and got to work.

He stayed for a short while to be sure she was doing it correctly and because he couldn't resist watching her dainty hands moving confidently through the task.

"We don't have all night," Daed grumbled.

Abe scurried down the aisle to pull the milking machine to the cows Anna Mary had wiped down. He attached the suction cups of the milking machine to one cow while Daed hooked up the one beside it.

Anna Mary turned at the sound of milk splashing into the metal container. Delight lit her face. "It all looks so easy."

Daed groaned. "Say that again after you've done all seventy cows. Or when it's ten degrees out, and your breath fogs the air, and you have to break off icicles to get in the barn door."

"Or after you muck out the stalls." Abe wrinkled his nose, then grinned.

"I get it." Anna Mary giggled. "I didn't mean all the work is easy, just that the machine makes the milking look easy."

"*Jah*, it's a lot better than doing it by hand."

They soon got into a rhythm of cleaning, hooking up cows, milk pinging against metal, the cart rolling down the aisle to be emptied, milk being sent through overhead hoses to the cooler. After Anna Mary finished cleaning all the cows, she went back and recleaned the ones that had been milked, but she also kept her eyes on Abe.

"You skipped that cow." Anna Mary pointed to the cow beside him.

"We can't use her milk." Abe smiled to reassure her. "See the red band around her leg? That means she's taking antibiotics for an infection."

Hank chimed in. "We're an organic farm, so we can't have anything unnatural in the milk. And we can't put infected milk into our supply."

Anna Mary studied the poor cow with concern. What would happen if she didn't get milked? The poor thing looked so uncomfortable.

Abe must have sensed her worry. "We'll milk her separately after all the good milk is collected."

Hank hooked up the next cow. "You'll also see green bands on a few cows. Those are brand-new *mamms*. They're still producing colostrum. We won't be taking their milk."

"I see." Anna Mary had a lot to learn, but she welcomed the opportunity. She wanted to understand everything about Abe's business so maybe someday she could be a part of it.

* * *

After they finished, Abe took Anna Mary for a ride in the buggy. She wanted to see where he'd grown up, so they traveled the back roads to his favorite spots. He pointed out where they went sledding in winter, where the *youngie* played volleyball and baseball, his schoolhouse, a few small local businesses.

Abe sounded almost apologetic. "It's much smaller than Lancaster."

"I like it. It's more like Gordonville or Bird-in-Hand."

"It is."

They passed a busy hardware store and a supermarket. To Anna Mary's surprise, many of the women wore heart-shaped *kapps*. It made her feel more at home to see familiar clothing.

"I see plenty of *kapps* like mine," she said in delight as she touched her own gauze prayer covering.

"*Jah*, many of the people around here came from Lancaster for cheaper farmland."

Anna Mary inclined her chin toward a woman in a long brown dress with a black bonnet. "Even her baby has a black bonnet."

"Those are the Swartzentrubers. We have quite a few around here, along with Byler and Andy Weaver Amish."

Anna Mary had sometimes seen buggies other than her own style in Lancaster, but here they passed many different kinds. Many were open with no windshield. One with a tan top and brown bottom drove by going the other way.

When they reached the outskirts of town, they passed families working in the fields and gardens, just like in Lancaster, although sometimes their clothing was different.

Many farms had homemade signs advertising honey, baked goods, lumber, eggs, and quilts. The more they drove, the more Anna Mary felt at home. Living here would be an easy adjustment. A pang shot through her. Would she ever get that chance?

Abe followed the road into a park and pulled the buggy over. "Are you up for a short hike?"

"Of course."

As Abe tied his horse to a hitching post, Anna Mary hopped out and inhaled pine-scented air. Huge birch, maple, and oak trees shaded them from the early evening sunshine. Then he led her along a trail through the woods. Fallen leaves from past autumns crunched underfoot as the sound of rushing water grew louder. At last, they reached a viewing platform.

Abe smiled. "Welcome to Canajoharie Falls."

Awestruck, Anna Mary stared at the thundering cascade of water splashing down the cliff face. "*Ach*, Abe, it's so beautiful."

As beautiful as you, he longed to say. While she stayed enthralled by the magnificent waterfall, he drank in the gorgeous picture of her enraptured face framed by towering trees and tumbling, splashing water. His heart expanded until it ached. He bowed his head and closed his eyes.

Lord, thank you for the beauty of Your creation—the loveliness of the trees, the waterfall, and, most of all, my precious Anna Mary. Danke for bringing her into my life. I'm trusting You to work out the distance between us.

"Abe?"

His eyes popped open to see Anna Mary staring at him questioningly. "I was just praying, thanking God for all this beauty."

A huge smile spread across her face, and she gazed at him with adoring eyes. "What a wonderful thing to do. I'll do that too."

Her dark lashes fanned across her cheeks as she closed her eyes, and her rapturous expression gave her a heavenly glow. Abe wanted to reach out and enfold her in his arms, to hold her close and never let her go.

When she lifted her head, her eyes glimmering with tears, Abe gripped the railing to keep his hands to himself. How he wished they could stay here for hours, but they needed to get home before Mrs. Vandenberg's driver arrived. And Anna Mary needed some rest. She'd been up early this morning, and tomorrow she'd need to rise at three if she planned to help with the milking. As much as he longed to spend more time with her, he needed to take care of her and see that she got enough rest.

"We'd better go. You need to get back to the hotel."

Disappointment flashed in her eyes. "It's so peaceful. I wish we could stay here forever."

After a brief look at all three waterfalls, from largest to smallest, he turned reluctantly to lead the way to the parking lot, the word *forever* echoing in his head. *Forever*. That's how long he intended to love Anna Mary, this special gift God had brought into his life.

CHAPTER 17

The next morning, Anna Mary rose at three and dressed in an older dress and her full apron. It seemed odd to be putting on work clothes on Sunday, but cows needed to be milked twice every day. At home, she usually had some minor chores like fixing a light meal or washing dishes on Sundays, but no intensive labor. Abe never had a day off from barn chores.

The driver tapped on her door twenty minutes later. Anna Mary slipped out of her hotel room, tucking the key card in her pocket. She'd been fascinated to discover how sliding this little plastic card over the black bump lit a green light and unlocked the door. She'd played with it for several minutes last night.

This trip had been full of firsts. Her first visit out of state, her first elegant restaurant, her first milking, her first key card, her first hotel room. This huge space with two beds for only one person seemed much too extravagant, especially after sharing a small room with Sarah. Her three younger sisters all had to crowd into the other bedroom. They'd never believe she'd slept in a bedroom this big with a couch and a small kitchen.

She'd had other firsts too. Her first waterfall . . . her

first time touching a man's hand . . . and one more first that thrilled her heart . . . her first time falling in love.

Anna Mary scurried after the driver. "I'm sorry you had to get up so early."

He grinned. "I'd do anything for Mrs. V. She set me up with my wife, so I owe her my deepest gratitude for my happiness. Plus, she makes it worth my time by paying so generously, which gives me plenty of time off to spend with my family. Not only that, I get to travel to interesting places."

He sounded so happy with his job, Anna Mary felt a little less guilty about getting him out of bed in the middle of the night.

When they arrived at the King farm, a soft light glowed from the kitchen window. Abe stood silhouetted near the stove. With a hearty thanks to the driver, Anna Mary hurried to the door Abe flung open.

"You're here. I wondered if you'd sleep in after your busy day yesterday."

Anna Mary ducked her head so Abe wouldn't see the longing in her eyes. "I want to spend every minute I can with you."

Abe reached out with a gentle finger to lift her chin. Their gazes met and held. He dropped his hand to his side, then clutched his suspenders. She needn't have been afraid to expose her true feelings. His yearning mirrored her own.

A cough in the doorway made them jump and step apart.

A hint of a chuckle in his voice, Hank asked, "Breakfast ready yet?"

The flush rising up Abe's neck and splashing onto his high cheekbones kept Anna Mary staring at him for longer than she should. Then her own face heated. What must Hank think of her?

Quickly, she bustled over to the stove. "What can I do to help?"

In a thick voice, Abe asked, "Could you set the table?"

"*Jah.*" Except she didn't know where they kept the dishes.

Hank came to her rescue. He opened a cupboard to reveal plates and glassware. "Forks and knives are in that drawer over there." He waved toward a nearby counter.

As Anna Mary prepared the table and poured orange juice into glasses, Abe took a breakfast casserole out of the oven.

"It's not burned this time," he said with a wry smile.

"Looks delicious," she assured him.

Soon they were all seated around the table for silent prayer and a rapid breakfast. Hank asked what they'd done yesterday, and Anna Mary happily recounted the fun they'd had.

"Things always seem brighter with the right person."

Hank's wistful expression tore at Anna Mary's heart. Her mother often had that same look when she recalled times with her husband.

Abe's *daed* pushed back from the table. "Lots of work to be done. I'll start rounding up the cows."

Abe stood and started to clear the table. "I'll be out shortly."

As much as Anna Mary wanted to spend this time with Abe, she couldn't interfere with his duties. "Why don't you help your *daed*? I can clean up the kitchen and do the dishes."

"Are you sure? I can help you first."

"Go on," she said, her voice gentle. "He needs company even more than he needs help."

"You noticed that too? You're a very perceptive *maedel*, my love."

Anna Mary's pulse thrummed at his endearment. For a moment, she couldn't speak. Should she confess her feelings too? Or would that start a fire neither of them could put out?

She settled for a more neutral comment. "So are you. Perceptive, I mean. Not a *maedel*." *Definitely not a* maedel. She lowered her lashes.

His voice husky, Abe said, "I'd, um, better get out there to help Daed. *Danke* for cleaning up."

"It's the least I could do after that delicious breakfast."

"You really liked it?"

"It was the best breakfast I've ever eaten." When he quirked an eyebrow, she added, "Maybe it was the company."

The grin that stretched across his face warmed Anna Mary from head to toe. She'd never known she could bring such joy to another person. Her own happiness bubbled over.

"You'd better get moving," she suggested when he stood there staring at her with an adoring expression.

As much as she wished she could stay here and bask in his loving looks, he needed to get outside to help his *daed*.

"See you in the barn," he said as he opened the back door. Then he turned and jogged toward the split-rail fence.

Through the window, Anna Mary watched the men herd the cows from the pasture to the milking barn while she washed and put away the dishes. She felt so comfortable and relaxed here in this home, in this city, in this state. And most of all, with Abe.

The rest of Anna Mary's visit moved too quickly for Abe. She assisted with the milking that morning, looking as if she'd been doing it all her life. She even mixed the ingredients for the tea tree oil wash after he gave her the measurements, and she helped feed the cows and turn them out in the pasture.

After they finished mucking out stalls, which Anna Mary insisted on doing too, he drove her to Stone Arabia, where she admired the rolling hills and beautiful vistas. They walked the Revolutionary War battlefield to see the stone church built in the 1700s. He'd been here before, but visiting this historical site with her electrified him. Everything seemed brighter, rosier, and more interesting.

What would life be like if she lived here and they could enjoy each other's company every day?

Anna Mary seemed to reflect his joy. She beamed at him and had a bounce to her step as she kept pace with him. And she eagerly pointed out details he might have missed. Butterflies flitting around a bush filled with pink flowers. Roses and ivy climbing the old stone walls.

The delight on her face as she discovered each new thing did strange things to his insides. And it made him love her even more than he already did. If that was even possible.

As they drove back from Stone Arabia, Anna Mary sighed. "I should have asked Mamm for Cousin Delores's address. Coming all this way without visiting Mamm's favorite relative doesn't seem right."

"I should have thought of that." Abe regretted not

considering Anna Mary's mother. "If we had more time, we could look for her."

"But we need to get back. It's almost milking time."

Abe appreciated that she seemed so attuned to his schedule, but he should have done more for her. "Bring Delores's address along next time you come. I'll make that visit our first stop. I'd like to meet her too." He prayed Anna Mary could make another visit, since he wasn't able to get away.

After they returned home, Anna Mary prepared supper while Abe and Daed moved the cows into the milking barn. She put the meal in the oven to bake before she joined them in the barn.

As Anna Mary pitched in to help with the evening milking, Abe couldn't help thinking how wonderful it would be if they did this together every day, but he warned himself to guard against getting used to her help. She'd have to leave before long. When would she be able to return? He hoped it would be soon.

Her spirits heavy, Anna Mary went to the Monday morning milking, knowing this was her last day here with Abe. Mrs. Vandenberg would pick her up soon for the trip home.

They'd just finished letting the cows back into the pasture when car tires crunched up the gravel drive. Hank hurried out to greet Mrs. Vandenberg and the driver, but Anna Mary and Abe lingered behind the barn.

"I wish you didn't have to go," he said, echoing her thoughts.

"I'd love to stay here." If only it could be forever. "I don't know when I'll be able to get back." Anna Mary would have to save for years to afford to pay for a trip herself.

"I wish I could come to Lancaster, but now that it's June, none of my brothers can get away from their farms until after the fall harvest."

Both of them stared at each other despondently.

"I'll miss you, Anna Mary." His words rang with heartfelt sadness.

She choked back the lump in her throat and blinked to clear her stinging eyes. "I'll miss you too, Abe."

Hank strode around the barn. "You two ready? Mrs. Vandenberg is eager to get on the road. She has things to take care of in Lancaster."

Reluctantly, Anna Mary rounded the barn, got into the car, and waved until Abe was out of sight.

The ride to New York had been so thrilling, filling her with anticipation. Now, although she was happy to be heading back to see her family, the trip overwhelmed her with gloom. When would she ever get to see Abe again?

As Mrs. Vandenberg dropped Anna Mary off, three of her sisters raced from the house and threw their arms around her.

"You're back," they chorused.

Emmie danced around Anna Mary, and Beth soon copied her, making Anna Mary smile, though her heart was heavy.

"Hannah's napping," Sarah explained, "or she'd be out here too. She kept looking around and calling your name. She'll be glad to see you."

Her sisters' warm welcome cheered Anna Mary, but nothing could touch the ache deep inside at missing Abe.

As soon as she went inside, Mamm wanted to hear all about the trip. Anna Mary described the farm, the milking, and the scenery in such vivid detail that Mamm and her sisters hung on every word.

"I wish we could see it," Sarah said after Anna Mary had finished.

"You didn't visit Delores?" Mamm frowned a little.

"I didn't have her address, but Abe wants to stop there next time."

The creases in Mamm's brow deepened.

Ach. Anna Mary had let wishful thinking get the better of her. Mamm had agreed to one trip. Still, Anna Mary couldn't help recalling Abe's comment about stopping at Delores's next time.

When he'd said that, her pulse had stutter-stopped. She'd been thrilled Abe was already anticipating another visit, but how likely was that? Judging from Mamm's expression, probably never.

Anna Mary's spirits plummeted.

"We missed you when you were gone," Emmie said plaintively.

"I missed you too." Anna Mary had, but she'd been so busy having fun with Abe during the day and evening, she hadn't missed her family until she was alone in the big hotel room at night.

"When I was in the hotel, I wished you all could be there with me." She described the room with its two double beds, little kitchen, desk, couch and chairs. But she left out the huge TV across from the bed. Better not upset Mamm more than she already had. Anna Mary had never touched it and had no desire to, but that might not be enough for her mother.

Beth's eyes sparkled with wonder. "Two of Mamm's beds in one room?"

Emmie shook her head. "No room's that big."

"I could hardly believe it myself. And guess how I got into the locked room?" Anna Mary held up her fingers to demonstrate. "I swiped a card a little smaller than an UNO card over this bump on the door. When the green light flashed, I could open the door."

Emmie crossed her arms. "I don't believe you."

"You'd have to see it for yourself."

"No child of mine will be going to any hotel room. Never again. And definitely not one in another state." Mamm's sharp comment sliced through the conversation, cutting off all possibility of a return trip.

The finality in her voice chilled Anna Mary to the bone.

"Furthermore, I don't like the idea that you used electricity."

"Electricity?"

"How do you think that door lock worked?"

Anna Mary hadn't thought about it, but was that fair? The electricity hadn't been installed in her own home. She swallowed back the protests rising to her lips. She didn't want to spoil her special trip with an ugly argument.

Inside, though, her thoughts churned. Mamm had used electricity anytime she went in an *Englisch* supermarket or visited an *Englisch* neighbor or used their phone. To be fair, Mamm hadn't done any of those things since their stepdad had died, but still . . .

And she didn't have a problem with people riding in a car when they had packages or large grocery orders to bring home, even though the *Ordnung* forbade cars.

"Tell us more," Beth begged.

Mamm pulled herself shakily to her feet. "I think you've all heard enough. I don't want Anna Mary filling your head with this nonsense." She herded Beth and Emmie from the room.

Sarah sent Anna Mary a sympathetic glance before balancing Hannah on her hip and following Mamm.

Anna Mary slumped into the chair like a balloon with all the air let out of it, her happiness and excitement draining away. *Mamm will never let me go to New York ever again.*

CHAPTER 18

Anna Mary pined for Abe. She threw herself into the chores at home, hoping to ease some of her loneliness and longing. Missing Abe like this helped her understand her mother's grief. At least Abe was alive and well, even if they were far apart. But after what Mamm had said, they might remain separated forever.

Now that Anna Mary had seen what Abe's life was like, she could understand why he wasn't able to visit. She poured her heart out on paper for hours Monday night and told him everything she'd thought and felt while she visited, everything she missed about being with him, and everything that had happened since she'd ridden away from his house. Everything, that is, except what Mamm had said about no more New York trips.

On Tuesday morning, she left for work early to make up for some of the time she'd been gone. Caroline took one look at Anna Mary and rushed over to put an arm around her shoulders.

"*Ach*, I'm so sorry the visit didn't go well." Caroline gave Anna Mary a quick side hug. "Want to talk about it?"

Anna Mary wished she could shake her head, but Caroline would only persist until she got the full story.

"The trip was wonderful. Abe and I had the best time. I helped with the milking. We went sightseeing and had great conversations." She paused and closed her eyes to relive the magical moment. "And he asked to court me."

"He did?" Caroline's squeal carried around the market.

At least Gideon hadn't opened the doors for customers yet, but many of the other stall owners and staff stared in their direction.

"Can you keep your voice down?" Anna Mary whispered. "I don't want everyone in the market knowing my business."

"Oops, sorry." Caroline clapped a hand over her mouth. She lowered her volume a few decibels, but her words were still louder than Anna Mary preferred. "Well, what went wrong, then?"

"Nothing. Everything was perfect. Up until it was time to leave. I miss him so much."

"I can imagine."

"But when I got home, Mamm said none of us can ever go out of state again."

"*Ach, neh*, she can't mean that."

"She did. She was very upset about my hotel stay, and I think she missed me." Anna Mary's eyes stung. "Abe can't get away to come here, so . . ."

She whirled around before Caroline spotted the tears. Hurrying to the refrigerator, she bent to take out salad ingredients. Thank heavens they had to make all fresh salads on Tuesdays because the market had been closed since Saturday afternoon.

"I'll start on the broccoli salad," she said in a choked voice as she searched for raisins and bacon to put in it.

"I brought boiled potatoes and macaroni from home, and I fried and crumbled bacon yesterday to make our prep easier. The bacon's on the top shelf of the refrigerator."

As if sensing Anna Mary didn't want to talk, Caroline stayed silent for a while as she prepped potato salad, then macaroni salad. Anna Mary moved on to the garden salad. Slicing ingredients with a sharp chop of her wrist helped release a little of the ache around her heart.

"Maybe your *mamm* will change her mind," Caroline said softly.

"You know my *mamm*." Anna Mary tried not to snap at her friend, who was only trying to be comforting. "Do you think that's likely?"

"*Neh.*" Caroline's face sank into glum lines that matched Anna Mary's mood.

That reminded Anna Mary she'd forgotten to thank Caroline. "I should have said this when I first came in. *Danke* for spending time with Mamm and the girls this weekend."

"I'm happy to do it anytime you need a break."

The only time Anna Mary wanted a break might be to spend time with Abe, but that was out of the question. She wouldn't be taking Caroline up on her offer.

Farther down the aisle, the employee door burst open, and a large group of chattering *Englischers* entered the market.

Caroline glanced around. "Gideon must be upstairs in his office. I guess I'd better go head off those people to let them know the market doesn't open for forty-five minutes."

The group looked pretty unruly and rather tough. Many of them sported multiple tattoos and nose, eyebrow, and lip rings. Maybe Caroline would need some backup.

"Want me to go with you?" Anna Mary offered.

"Sure." Caroline threw Anna Mary a grateful glance. Together, they headed up the aisle but stopped when

Mrs. Vandenberg tottered out from behind the crowd. "All right, listen up, everyone." She pulled a clipboard from her purse.

"Caroline," she called, "where's Gideon?"

"Upstairs, I guess."

"Well, you and Anna Mary will do." She turned slightly. "Aisha and Danika, you'll be working at Hartzler's Chicken Barbecue." She waved toward Caroline. "These are your coworkers, Caroline and Anna Mary."

"Huh?" Caroline stared at Mrs. Vandenberg.

"You and your brother agreed to take two workers from the STAR center, remember?"

Caroline blinked. "Oh, right. You twisted Gideon's arm—" She yelped when Anna Mary poked her in the ribs.

Anna Mary stepped forward. "Welcome. I'm Anna Mary." She held out her hand.

At first the girls didn't respond. Then one of them broke into an uneasy smile.

"Hi, I'm Danika. This is Aisha." She shook Anna Mary's hand firmly.

Caroline had recovered her manners and introduced herself. "So you're from the STAR center?"

Both girls nodded.

"Come on, I'll show you around." Caroline led the way to the booth.

Anna Mary had heard a lot about the STAR center, which Caroline's sister-in-law Nettie and her new husband, Stephen, ran. Mrs. Vandenberg started it to keep young children off the streets and out of gangs. Then she expanded it to getting young adults out of gangs. These girls must be from that program.

By the time Gideon arrived, Caroline had shown the girls around and explained the various jobs they did before the market opened. Aisha, who'd worked in a restaurant kitchen for a year, chopped vegetables for the garden salad like a pro. Anna Mary was demonstrating how to prep trays with silverware packets. Then she and Danika made fast work of that job.

Gideon stepped back, startled, when he saw the girls. Caroline mouthed, *STAR*, and he nodded. She performed the introductions. Then they worked out what jobs the girls would do.

Gideon asked Danika to help unload baked goods and fill the cases. Both girls did their jobs but seemed nervous and uncomfortable, and they said little.

But when Nick, who ran the candy counter at the end of their stand, arrived with his son Aidan, the girls perked up.

"Hey, Aidan," Aisha said.

He stopped in his tracks, blinked, and then came rushing toward them. "What are you two doing?"

"Working here."

That was the most Anna Mary had heard Aisha say at one time. She beamed at Aidan as if he'd rescued her from danger.

"Want me to teach you to do the fries?" he asked, and they both nodded vigorously. "I have to help my dad set up the candy counter, but I'll be back once the market opens to show you."

Both girls seemed eager to work and did whatever they were asked to do. Caroline explained how to fill pint and quart salad containers for customers, then the girls both prepped small salad containers to put on lunch trays.

"We store them in the refrigerator so we don't have to dip them out," Anna Mary explained. "It saves a lot of time."

"Plus, it keeps the sliding doors in the cases out front free for the person who's dipping out large salad containers. Anna Mary came up with the idea. It's been brilliant." Caroline smiled at her.

Before the market opened, Mrs. Vandenberg wobbled to the counter, said hello to the STAR girls, and told them she'd be praying for them. Then she beckoned to Anna Mary. After studying her face for a moment, Mrs. Vandenberg mused, "I thought you'd be glowing after your weekend trip."

"I am, but—" Anna Mary bit her lip. She didn't want Mrs. Vandenberg to think she wasn't grateful. "I had a wonderful time. *Danke* for all you did for me and for Abe."

"I understand your sorrow over parting and over being so far apart, but it's something more than that."

How does Mrs. Vandenberg always seem to know my secrets?

After taking a deep breath, Anna Mary spilled out the truth. "Mamm says I can't ever go out of state again." The last words almost became a wail. She steadied herself. "I don't know what to do. That means I can never spend time with Abe again. And he can't get away from the farm to come here."

"My, my, that does sound like a crisis. I can tell you haven't prayed about it yet, have you?"

Anna Mary hung her head. "*Neh.*"

"I'd suggest doing that before you panic. And trust Abe with the truth. If you start hiding things from each other, you'll never make a lasting marriage."

How did she guess that?

She was right. She and Josh had hidden things from each other, and that ended up driving a wedge between them. She couldn't take the chance of that happening with Abe. She loved him too much.

"Other people may be stronger than you think." Mrs.

Vandenberg waggled her fingers in a goodbye wave, then called over her shoulder, "Keep the faith. And remember what God says about *impossible*."

Anna Mary did remember, but she didn't see how being with Abe could ever be possible.

"You don't have to see it," Mrs. Vandenberg's voice carried from across the room. "All you have to do is believe it."

How did you believe something you couldn't see? Something that seemed impossible?

Anna Mary turned to find Danika studying her curiously. "How old are you?"

"Twenty-one."

"And ya still let yer ma tell you what to do?"

Anna Mary's brows drew together. "Of course." Didn't everyone? If you lived at home, you obeyed your parents. Even if you left home, you still honored them.

Danika stared at Anna Mary as if she'd dropped from another planet. "I ain't listened to my old lady since I was nine."

"Nine?" Anna Mary wasn't sure she'd heard right.

"Maybe eight. I jest do my own thing. Seems to me yer old enough to decide when to see yer boyfriend. I assume he's yer boyfriend."

"He is, but I can't disobey my mother."

Danika shook her head. "Yer a grown woman. Make up yer own mind."

Mamm had been upset about the hotel key card. What would she think about Anna Mary taking advice from an ex–gang member with three tattoos and a nose ring?

Right after Anna Mary left, Abe opened the letter he'd been saving all weekend. The words on the page sounded so much like Anna Mary did in person that he could hear her tone and inflection. After each paragraph, he closed his eyes and pictured the words coming from her mouth. It made him feel as if she were still here with him.

He hoped she'd be able to visit often. Did Mrs. Vandenberg plan to bring Anna Mary for more visits? That thought filled Abe with longing.

Reaching into his desk drawer, he pulled out the blue stationery Mrs. Vandenberg had given him. He was running low. Maybe he'd better buy more the next time he went to town. He smoothed a sheet onto the desktop and began to write:

Dearest Anna Mary,

Abe couldn't believe he could write those words now. She'd given him a special gift this weekend when she answered *jah*. Now he could let the love in his heart flow onto the page.

He jotted down all his thoughts and feelings about the weekend and wrote that he looked forward to reading hers. He told her how much he loved her and how happy it made him to know she was his girlfriend. Then he closed with his plans for her next visit to Fort Plain and listed all the sites he wanted to show her.

Daed called Abe's name.

"Coming." Abe folded the letter, slid it into an envelope, addressed it, and put a stamp on it. He'd get it in the mail now so it would go out first thing tomorrow morning. That way she wouldn't have to wait for his week's worth of news.

"Abe?" Impatience laced Daed's tone. "I've called you four times now. The cows can't wait."

Clutching the letter, Abe jumped up and headed down

the hall. "Coming. I just need to put something in our mailbox."

He jogged down the driveway to the mailbox at the end of the lane. With great care, he propped the envelope inside and lifted the red metal flag to alert the letter carrier. Then he went to help Daed, but the only thing on his mind was figuring out a way to get Anna Mary to Fort Plain permanently.

Weeks flew by and letters zinged back and forth, but Abe came no closer to finding a solution. And Anna Mary's *mamm*'s reaction to the trip had made it less likely Anna Mary would be allowed to come to New York.

Then during Daed's monthly call with his brother, Myron mentioned an electrical fire had destroyed equipment in Tim's section of the factory, so he was out of work and seemed to be running wild again. Myron begged for Abe to come, but Daed had a better idea. Why not send Tim to New York? They'd put him to work milking cows and keep him out of trouble.

Abe groaned when he heard the plans. Why couldn't Daed have sent him to Lancaster?

"Sohn, I know you would have preferred for this to be different, but we can't ask your brothers to do the milking when they're so busy on their own farms."

"*Jah*." Abe understood Daed's reasoning. But silently, he mumbled, *Why, Lord? Why are You keeping us apart?*

"You know, Sohn, in the Bible it says Jacob worked seven years for Rachel, and that time seemed to him like a few days, because of his love for her."

Suppressing another groan, Abe asked, "So I'll need to wait seven years to be with Anna Mary?"

Daed tried to hide a smile, but he wasn't successful. "I mean you need to put this in perspective. It's only been a few weeks."

"It already feels like it's been seven years." Abe sighed. "And look what happened to Jacob after all that time. He ended up getting the wrong woman and had to work seven more years to marry his true love."

Abe stood and headed for the door. He'd taken to pacing outside the pasture as he prayed. He needed more time with the Lord after this disappointment.

The cows lowing in the field, the warm sunshine, and the scent of sweet meadow grass soothed Abe. He loved his home and his work, but he'd give it all up for Anna Mary. Like Jacob, if someone asked him to work seven years to marry her, he'd do it. He'd even work fourteen years for a guarantee they'd be together.

But his situation was so open-ended, he had no idea how long or even if they could ever be together. What he wanted was certainty. But it seemed God wanted to teach him patience—and faith.

CHAPTER 19

Anna Mary read Abe's letter about his *daed*'s Biblical example and Abe's declaration that he'd be willing to work for her for fourteen years. He loved her that much? That made her heart sing. But the song hit discordant notes for her as well as Abe over the indefinite future. She didn't want to wait forever.

Would God expect them to take some action?

Danika's question kept playing in Anna Mary's mind. Most *Englischers* didn't seem to worry about obeying their parents after a certain age. But Anna Mary's conscience wouldn't let her defy Mamm. Besides, Sarah couldn't take over the household or make enough money to pay bills, so Anna Mary wasn't free to leave. Maybe in two years, after Sarah graduated from eighth grade, they might consider it.

Pen scratching across the paper, Anna Mary revealed all these thoughts to Abe. She found that discussing her internal questions and conflicting ideas helped her sort things out. One advantage of being so far away was that they delved into things they might not have talked about in person. When they were together, the pleasure of being in each other's company overtook this deeper musing. Maybe that's what God wanted them to discover.

After jotting all that down, Anna Mary went back to Abe's letter. Tim would be heading to New York. She checked the date of the letter. Tomorrow.

> *Myron arranged for a car to bring Tim up here, but you know my cousin. He's furious that Myron told the driver to pick him up at six. Tim doesn't want to get out of bed that early. Since he hasn't been going into work, he's taken to staying out late and sleeping in. I worry he's going to be even angrier when he learns Daed expects him to help with milking.*

Anna Mary chuckled. She could just imagine Tim's face when she found that out. She probably shouldn't be laughing, but Tim had made plenty of mocking comments about her best friend, Caroline. A few weeks of milking cows might lessen some of his swagger.

> *If only I could take Tim's place. I'd love to be up there doing that.*

Abe had told her his *daed* missed her help. She couldn't go, but—

She jumped up and rushed to the kitchen and plunged into a baking and cooking frenzy. Sarah asked what she was doing, then pitched in to help. Thanks to the generosity of the donor who left groceries, they had plenty of ingredients. Yesterday, someone had left three times the usual amount of dry goods, along with a big cooler filled with meats.

Hours later, the counter held cookies, coffee cakes,

loaves of homemade bread, cinnamon rolls, and several casseroles. Anna Mary froze the meals along with some homemade ice packs. Then they packed a box with baked goods. She and Sarah had done some canning from their garden, so they prepared another large box with an assortment of canned vegetables, homemade soups, and strawberry jam.

Anna Mary surveyed their handiwork with satisfaction. "Tomorrow morning, we can put the casseroles and ice packs in the cooler. I'll drop it off in the morning before six."

She hurried back upstairs to add more to her letter to Abe. Then she tucked it into the box under a jar of soup and went to bed early.

When Anna Mary woke, she dressed hurriedly. The aroma of baked goods still perfumed the air, and when she reached the kitchen, she discovered Sarah removing a pan of cinnamon rolls from the oven. The counter was dotted with treat-filled plastic bags.

"What's this?" she asked.

Sarah's face held a sweet smile. "We made so many things for Abe, but what about Tim? He has a long trip."

"That was thoughtful."

Her sister's cheeks pinkened. "He's so nice. He deserves to have some treats too."

Tim? So nice? Anna Mary choked back her laughter. Sarah was probably the only person in the world who'd call Tim nice.

While Anna Mary packed the casseroles, took the boxes out to the buggy, and hitched up the horse, Sarah wrapped the cinnamon rolls in foil to keep them warm and gathered cookies, homemade granola bars, and fruit rolls in a brown paper grocery bag. She even penned a note on it: *Have a nice trip!*

Anna Mary took off for Tim's house and arrived a little after five thirty. A light glowed in the kitchen, illuminating a sulky Tim, shoveling boxed cereal into his mouth. His uncle stood nearby, hands on hips, appearing to scold him.

They both looked up when Anna Mary tapped at the door.

Myron threw open the door, saying, "See, I told you the driver might get here early. I was right." He stepped back, mouth open, when he caught sight of Anna Mary. "You're the driver?"

"*Neh*, I came to see Tim."

That didn't soften Myron's expression. And Tim's face hardened.

"What do you want?" he demanded. "To tag along on my trip to New York?" He flashed her a sardonic smile.

Myron gasped. "You will not be taking your girlfriend with you on this trip."

"She ain't my girlfriend. She's Abe's."

"Even so, you may not ride all that way alone with a girl."

"We won't be alone. We'll have a driver," Tim taunted his *onkel*.

Anna Mary cut through the tension. "I'm not going to New York. I just came to ask Tim if he'd deliver some things to Abe and Hank."

Tim smirked. "I won't deliver any kisses, if that's what you have in mind."

"Tim!" Myron thundered. "That is enough. I won't have that kind of talk in my house."

"You already did," Tim pointed out. He hopped up from the table. "I'm not sure I want to take your *gifts* to Abe."

"Sarah sent some treats for your trip too."

Tim visibly melted at Anna Mary's words. "She did?"

"*Jah*, she got up hours ago to make you cinnamon rolls so they'd still be warm."

"Where are they?" Tim headed eagerly for the door. "It'd be better than this slop I have to eat for breakfast."

Myron snapped back, "You could learn to cook your—"

The back door slammed shut behind Tim, cutting off the rest of Myron's sentence.

A car purred into the driveway as Tim and Anna Mary reached her buggy. She pulled out the brown bag and handed it to him. Tim read the note, peeked into the bag, and blinked.

"She made this for me?" He sounded close to tears.

Suddenly, Anna Mary felt sorry for him. Maybe nobody had ever done nice things for him.

The driver approached them. "Any bags to load?"

Tim cradled the bag close. "*Jah*, this."

Myron stepped out onto the porch, carrying a duffel bag. "You forgot your clothes."

Tim's mouth tightened. Then he glanced down at the bag in his arms, and his face softened a little. "Thanks, Myron."

His *onkel* appeared shocked. He put the bag in the open car trunk while Tim set the paper bag on the front seat. The driver helped Anna Mary transfer the boxes and cooler.

Myron shuffled near the car as the driver got in. "Have a safe trip," he said gruffly, then spun on his heel and strode inside.

Anna Mary waited until the car took off before turning her buggy in the driveway and heading home. She still had an hour until she had to leave for work. She'd throw in a load of wash, help Sarah get the younger girls ready, see if Mamm needed anything, and have a bite to eat before driving to the market.

She was still a bit tired from the marathon bout of baking last night and the extra early rising this morning, but it cheered her to imagine Abe's face when he received the boxes. She hoped he could feel the love she'd poured into everything she'd sent.

"I hope Tim's not going to be a problem," Daed said as they milked that morning. "Myron says Tim avoids work and is insolent."

Abe wasn't sure what to say. His cousin could be a handful, but Tim had a reason. And Myron could be abrasive. Abe couldn't say that to Daed, who didn't like Abe to criticize his elders.

"He works hard at the factory. They promoted him right before the fire."

"*Gut.*" Daed nodded his approval. "I hope he'll have the same work ethic here."

Abe wasn't so sure. He suspected Tim might not enjoy being around cows, but better not to worry Daed.

When Tim did arrive, he pulled out his duffel bag and waved nonchalantly to the trunk. "Someone sent you those boxes." At Abe's puzzled look, Tim laughed. "Check inside. You'll figure it out."

Abe only knew one person in Lancaster well besides Abe and Myron, but she couldn't afford to send him this many cartons. He lifted the flap of one box and spied cookies. The cookies Anna Mary knew were his favorites.

"Wait." He grabbed his cousin's arm. "Anna Mary sent all this? How?"

Tim shrugged. "I dropped off three weeks of groceries

in case I'm here that long. I didn't expect her to waste them all on you." He reached into the front seat of the car and eased out a grocery sack.

Before he flipped it around to face his chest, Abe glimpsed the words, *Have a nice trip!* "That from Anna Mary too?"

"Nope," Tim said airily. "All these presents ain't enough for you? You gotta try to take mine?"

A frisson of relief slid through Abe. Not that he should be jealous if Anna Mary had packed Tim some snacks—at least that's what Abe guessed was in the bag—and wished him a good trip. Anna Mary would be thoughtful like that.

But the tender way Tim held the bag piqued Abe's curiosity. "So . . . who's that from, then?"

"None of your business."

Hmm. Did his cousin have a girlfriend? Abe didn't have time to find out. He had to unload the things Anna Mary had sent and get the cows into the milking barn.

Daed's eyes widened as Abe carried everything into the kitchen and transferred the casseroles to the freezer, the canned goods to the pantry, and the baked goods to the counter. Abe couldn't believe it either. He and Daed hadn't had home-canned vegetables and soup since Mamm passed. And Abe never had the time or energy to attempt more than basic meals.

"That girl's a keeper," Daed exclaimed as he set jars of homemade soup and tomato sauce on shelves next to store-bought cookies and tins of soup and vegetables. "You've got to find a way to keep her in New York."

Daed's words pierced Abe. He spent every waking hour trying to come up with a solution. "Her *mamm* needs her. And she won't let Anna Mary come to New York again."

Abe hadn't shared that information from Anna Mary's first letter after she'd returned home.

"I wish I could talk to her *mamm*. I understand her loneliness and her need to cling to her daughter, but is she thinking about what's best for everyone?"

"You mean us?" Abe had to grin.

"I meant her daughter, but, *jah*, it would benefit us too." Daed chuckled.

"If we're counting who benefits, Anna Mary's *mamm* has more people on her side. She has four younger daughters."

Daed pulled a face. "I guess that makes us the losers."

"Sure does." Abe sobered. "Plus Sarah's only twelve, so she isn't ready to take Anna Mary's place yet."

Tim pounded down the last three steps of the stairway and burst into the kitchen. "Sarah's very competent. She does a lot of the work and takes care of the little ones."

Abe held up a hand to show he hadn't been criticizing Sarah. "I know she does. I didn't mean she wasn't helping. It's just that she can't get a job to pay bills."

His cousin huffed out a breath. "But she does everything she can. And she's good and kind and—"

"She certainly is." Abe didn't want to argue with Tim. And his cousin spoke the truth. Sarah was a sweet, remarkable twelve-year-old. A younger model of the wonderful, special Anna Mary.

Apparently satisfied that everyone appreciated Sarah's virtues, Tim slouched against the doorjamb. "I went upstairs and picked a room. Hope that was okay. You both seemed too busy talking. I didn't want to interrupt." Jealousy flashed across his face, then wistfulness.

Abe hadn't meant to make his cousin feel left out. Poor Tim hadn't had a father figure since he was small. Myron did his duty, but he was prickly. A crusty old bachelor set in his ways, unused to children. Tim never had proper guidance, only lectures and criticism.

Daed went over and slung an arm around Tim's shoulders. "You haven't been here since you were seven, but you're still part of this family."

Tim *rutsched* uncomfortably. "*Jah*, guess you're stuck with me."

"We're *blessed* with you." Daed's firm words emphasized the family love.

Sensing Tim's discomfort with sentiment, Abe tried to lighten the mood. "We're also glad you're here so we can stick you with the worst milking chores."

Tim made a face, but relief at being rescued flickered in his eyes.

Daed patted him on the back. "Abe's just trying to scare you. Anna Mary loved those jobs when she was here."

"If Anna Mary loved them," Tim warbled in a mocking, falsetto tone, "then I'm sure I'll dislike them."

Abe rubbed his hands together as if he couldn't wait to make Tim's life miserable. "Well, guess what? You arrived in perfect time to try."

Daed glanced at the clock. "Time to round up the cows for milking. No time for an early supper."

For once Abe didn't regret not having a leftover casserole to reheat. "We can warm up Anna Mary's spaghetti soup afterward."

To Abe's surprise, Tim took to the milking right away. He did a thorough job of cleaning the cows and begged to learn how to hook up the milking machine. Afterward, he even volunteered to assist with cleanup, and he scrubbed and disinfected the hoses and metal containers carefully.

Daed glanced at Abe over Tim's bent head and raised his eyebrows in approval. Like Abe, Daed had sensed praise made Tim uncomfortable, so he settled for a low-key *nice job*.

A flush of pride colored Tim's face before he settled on a scowl. But Abe and Daed had both seen Tim's pleasure.

"Why don't you go inside and start dinner, Abe? Tim and I can see the cows get back into the pasture."

Abe noticed Daed had avoided the usual *sohn*. He too must have sensed Tim's envy of their relationship. Maybe spending time alone with Daed would give Tim some of the fatherly advice and care he needed.

As Abe made his way to the kitchen, he whistled. He might not have Anna Mary here yet, but eating things she'd made brought her a little closer and gave him hope for the future.

CHAPTER 20

Abe's first letter after Tim arrived gushed with thanks for the gifts Anna Mary had sent him. She hugged the pages to her chest as if she could sense Abe's presence. Then she eagerly devoured the rest of the message.

Tim seemed to have bonded with Abe's *daed*, and the two of them spent time alone together, talking and doing jobs around the property. Abe used his spare time to write longer letters, which thrilled Anna Mary.

Tears sprang to her eyes when Abe recounted his father's comments about her. Hank really liked her and wanted her in New York. That made Anna Mary even more determined than ever to find a way.

Abe closed with a scrawled PS from Tim:

*Please tell Sarah thank you for the snacks.
They were delicious!*

After that, Abe had added:

*Sarah has a big fan. Tim still keeps the empty
bag with her message on his dresser. Having a
sweet little sister has softened Tim's heart.*

When Anna Mary relayed Tim's message to Sarah, she ducked her head to hide her smile.

After she heard Tim still had the bag, she grinned. "I'm so glad he liked it. He's so nice. And he needs somebody to take care of him."

"That's what Abe says too," Anna Mary agreed. "I think Abe's *daed* is trying to be a father to him. It's too bad they didn't take Tim in when he was little."

"They wanted him, but Tim stayed here in case his sister came back."

Anna Mary stared at her sister in surprise. "How do you know that?"

"Tim told me. He really wanted to go to New York, but he couldn't. Not without his sister."

So Tim had sacrificed his happiness for his sister. A sister who'd never returned.

How sad! Anna Mary prayed staying with Abe and his *daed* would give Tim some of the family life he'd missed. Being on their farm would benefit Tim in so many ways. What Anna Mary didn't realize was how much it would benefit her too.

Abe spent extra time cooking and doing dishes to allow Tim to be alone with Daed. The two got on so well, and Tim remembered being here as a youngster, so the milking jobs came easily to him. And Daed, instead of napping in the afternoons as he usually did, took Tim with him to do chores around the farm or sat in the living room discussing life and spiritual things with Tim.

Following one of those discussions, Tim came into the kitchen with damp eyes. "Hank wants some milk and cookies."

Abe studied him with concern. "Is something wrong?"

"*Neh*, I'm better than I've ever been." At Abe's questioning glance, he explained, "I got right with God. It feels good to confess all my sins and let go of controlling my life. I was messing everything up anyway."

After Tim left with two cups of milk and an assortment of snacks, Abe smiled to himself. His cousin was probably the one who wanted the treats. Leave it to Daed to notice and ask for them for himself.

That was one of the many things Abe loved about his father—his sensitivity and his wisdom. Make that two things. Abe could list many, many more. And he was glad Tim was finally getting good, supportive parenting. Already it had set his cousin on the right path.

Tim entered the barn willingly, did all the chores eagerly, and, for the first time ever, made no complaints, criticisms, or sarcastic comments.

Abe pulled Daed aside to ask about it.

"Surrendering to God made a huge difference. I've also offered to pay a detective to search for his sister. He wanted to pay something toward it, but I told him he could pay me back by doing his best here at the farm."

"He's sure done that," Abe said admiringly.

"Very much so," Daed agreed. "In fact, I was thinking Tim and I could handle the work together without you for the next two weeks or so."

Abe stepped back, his feelings hurt. He'd encouraged all Tim's special time alone with Daed, but he hadn't expected to get cut out of the loop. "You don't need me?" Abe said around the lump in his throat.

Daed shook his head. "For goodness' sake, Sohn, I thought you'd be overjoyed."

"Huh?" How would Daed's not wanting him . . . ?

Suddenly, light dawned. "You really can do without me?"

"Only for two weeks. Don't get carried away." Daed grinned. "But I could scrape by until Tim has to return."

Abe wanted to leap in the air and shout *hallelujah!*

He managed to rein in the impulse. He needed to prove he could make rational, well-thought-out decisions. His enthusiasm drooped. A driver would be too expensive.

Please, Lord, You've given me an opportunity I never thought I'd have. I'll trust You for the cost.

Tim entered and interrupted them. "Isn't it about time to get the cows in the barn?"

"Could you start on that, Tim? Abe and I will be out shortly."

"You want me to do it by myself?" Tim stood there, stunned. Hesitant.

Abe stared at him in shock. He'd expected his cousin's usual show of bravado. Instead, he sounded humble. Unsure of himself.

"I trust you can do it."

Tim straightened his shoulders and strode out the door. Not his usual swagger, but firm, confident steps.

By the time Abe turned back to Daed's amused smile, he had the solution. "A train or bus might be less expensive."

"Sounds *gut*. Edna will take you to the station in Amsterdam as soon as you've packed."

"You already called her?"

"What do you think?"

Abe couldn't believe it. "*Danke, danke, danke,*" he called over his shoulder as he raced up the stairs to throw his clothes in a bag and stuff his savings into his wallet. He'd just finished filling a thermos and a plastic bag of cookies when the driver pulled in.

"You're off to Pennsylvania, huh?" Edna asked as he tossed his bag in the back seat and slid in next to her.

Too excited to answer, Abe nodded. If he didn't have to wear a seat belt, he'd have been on the edge of the seat the whole way.

"Have a safe trip, Sohn. Myron's expecting you tomorrow morning."

Had Daed set everything up there too? If Abe had ever wondered whether Daed would accept Anna Mary as his future *dochder*-in-law, this trip proved he was one hundred percent behind their match.

Daed slipped Edna some money. "I added extra for the short notice and your help."

"I can pay," Abe protested.

"Save your money for your dates with Anna Mary."

Edna opened her purse, put the bills inside, pulled out some folded papers, and handed them to Abe. "Here are your tickets. I printed them out."

She continued to chatter as she turned the car around and headed for the station. Abe barely heard her.

"The Amsterdam station's small and unstaffed, so you need to have your ticket ahead of time." She gestured to the papers he clutched. "You'll see you have to switch trains twice. Once in New York City. The other in Philadelphia. You'll have a few hours' layover there, but you should get to Lancaster by six thirty tomorrow morning."

If he could get a ride to the market from Myron's, maybe he could surprise Anna Mary before work the way she'd surprised him.

Edna rambled on about times and switching trains, but Abe had drifted off into daydreams of all the things he and Anna Mary would do together. While she worked, he could do things to help her family. And Abe intended to convince Esther to let Anna Mary visit New York again. Not just once, but many times.

The ride to the station seemed to take hours. Abe was impatient to be on his way. But when Edna pulled up to the station, Abe stared at the tiny brick building near the train track. He'd always pictured stations as bustling places filled with trains whooshing by every few minutes. This was about the size of their toolshed with Daed's small office attached. Inside, it held a row of chairs.

Abe took a seat two seats away from the lone occupant. He flopped his bag on the empty place next to him and closed his eyes to wait. If Jacob's seven-year wait seemed like a few days, Abe's eleven-hour trip to reach Lancaster should seem like seconds. Somehow, it didn't. Each minute ticked by with the hand on the clock inching in tiny increments around the clockface.

Finally, a loud whistle blasted, the windows rattled, and, with an earsplitting squeal of brakes, the train arrived. Abe boarded, and they sped through the early evening until nightfall. The train rocked, and scenery whizzed by, making Abe's eyes ache. From time to time, they stopped to pick up other passengers. He drew in a relieved breath when they pulled into the New York station.

He followed the crowd into a cavernous building with elevators and numbers and arrows. Bewildered, he threaded his way through the crowds, trying to figure out where to go. The noise was overwhelming. People rushed in every direction, brushing past him, bumping into him, elbowing him out of the way as he gawked.

Finally, he approached a friendly-looking man to ask where to go.

After a quick glance through Abe's paperwork, he said, "You're in Penn Station. Moynihan Hall is across

Eighth Avenue. You'll go there to wait for your next train. It'll arrive in about two hours." He beckoned to Abe. "Come on. I'll show you."

They glided down escalators, passed stores and restaurants, and stepped outside into a cacophony of pounding music, honking horns, and hustling crowds. Behind them the glass walls glowed. Farther down the street, neon signs in garish colors pulsed on and off. Abe's eyes ached from so much light.

The man smiled at Abe. "I could have taken you through the concourse, but I thought you might like to see New York City at night."

"Thank you," Abe managed to say, too disoriented to do more than swivel his head from side to side, taking in the chaos. A few trees grew on the sidewalk, but everything else around him seemed to be glass, steel, or concrete. How did people live here? Where did they rest their eyes? Or their ears?

He thanked the man again after he pointed out where to catch the next train. Two hours later, Abe boarded the train for Philadelphia. Because the trip only lasted a little over an hour, he worried about closing his eyes and missing his stop. When the train pulled into the station, he stumbled toward the hard wooden benches for his three-hour layover and fell asleep.

Bleary-eyed, Abe woke with a jerk to hear them calling for Lancaster. He stumbled toward the final train of his trip. Actually, if he'd been at home, he'd have been up more than an hour ago for milking. That and knowing only an hour's ride separated him and his beloved Anna Mary kept him awake during the last leg of the journey. He overflowed with joy as the sun painted the horizon in vibrant pinks and oranges before they screeched into the final station.

He exited the train and headed into the Lancaster station. A woman waved to him and held up a sign: *Abe King*. She was here for him.

With a toothy grin, she approached him. "Abe?" When he nodded, she thrust out her hand. "I'm Marilyn. Your uncle sent me. He figured you'd be exhausted after your trip."

"I am," Abe admitted, grateful for Myron's thoughtfulness. Abe's body begged for rest, but he wanted to see Anna Mary. He didn't want to waste a single minute of his time in Pennsylvania.

Anna Mary enjoyed training Danika and Aisha. Unlike Caroline, who was the baby of her family, Anna Mary had taught her younger sisters most of their household skills. Gideon noticed her teaching talent, so he asked her to take over that job. He even increased her pay.

Aidan had taught them to make fries, and Fern had showed them how to make boxes and package bakery orders. Today, under Anna Mary's watchful eyes, they'd filled all the display cases, prepped lunch trays, and loaded the refrigerator with salad cups for the trays. She moved on to teaching them to make the various salads whenever they had a lull in customers.

Before the market opened, she had them mix up the oil-and-vinegar dressing they used for several salads and made sure they added a bit of sugar. "We'll use it for three-bean salad and sauerkraut salad."

"Eww." Danika wrinkled her nose. "Sauerkraut is stinky. I don't want to make that."

"I'll do it," Aisha volunteered. "What ingredients do I need?"

"Diced celery, green pepper, and onion."

Gideon went to unlock the market doors, and people poured into the market. Caroline had stationed herself at the counter, so Anna Mary scrutinized the workers. As usual, Aisha chopped the vegetables with skill, but Danika was much clumsier.

"Why don't you rinse the beans and put together the salad ingredients? Aisha can chop extra green pepper and onion."

Behind them, Caroline sucked in a breath. Anna Mary whirled around.

"What's wrong?" She searched for what had upset her friend and saw a familiar form striding toward her. It couldn't be.

She blinked, sure her eyes were playing tricks on her. She'd been missing Abe so badly she must have mistaken a stranger for him. He couldn't possibly be here in Lancaster.

But when she lifted her lashes, he'd reached the counter. It truly was Abe. Here. In person.

"But—but how?" she stammered.

"How did I get here?"

His tender smile started a slow burn inside.

"By train."

She shook her head. "*Neh*, how could you take time off? How can your *daed* do the milking without you? How did—?" Her questions tumbled out one after another.

Abe held up a hand. "I'll tell you all about it when you have a break."

Caroline nudged Anna Mary's shoulder. "Go on and sit at the café tables. We don't get really busy for an hour or so. Aisha and Danika can help until then. You can come over if we get swamped."

Anna Mary hesitated, but Caroline insisted, so with a

wide smile, Anna Mary joined Abe at a table, where he caught her up on Tim's visit, his train trip, and his plans. Joy gushed into her words as they discussed what they'd do together for the next two weeks. Two whole weeks together.

Mrs. Vandenberg strolled by, her cane tapping a jaunty rhythm. "Didn't I tell you to trust God?"

Abe stared at Anna Mary. "She didn't cause the fire at Tim's factory, did she?"

Anna Mary dissolved into peals of laughter. "I'm sure she didn't. But maybe she knew it would happen."

The elderly lady gave them a knowing smile. "I expect Tim is settling in well."

Abe stared at her. "How did you know that?"

"I have my ways."

"Tim seems to like doing the milking. And Daed is giving my cousin some much-needed attention."

"Ahh, that's exactly what I prayed would happen." She looked like a cat who'd tipped over a milk pail to lap up cream. "God has a special future planned for that young man."

"Tim?" Anna Mary and Abe chorused in unison, both of them incredulous.

"You don't believe God can work miracles?"

"Of course He can," Anna Mary said automatically. She pinched her lips shut to stop the words itching to be spoken. *But with Tim?*

"Don't look so surprised," Mrs. Vandenberg chided them. "It may take a few years, but God has two wonderful young ladies who'll influence Tim in the right direction."

Anna Mary couldn't help wondering if one of them was her sister.

Abe must have had the same thought, because he mouthed, *Sarah?*

Mrs. Vandenberg leaned toward Abe. "Your father has offered to help Tim find his sister, right?"

"*Jah.* How did you know?"

Mrs. Vandenberg's angelic smile held a touch of mystery. "Here." She reached into her huge purse, dug around, and pulled out a business card. "Have him contact my detective. He's already begun looking into the case."

Abe took the card, still looking stunned. "*Danke.* I'm sure Tim will appreciate it."

"It might take a while, but we'll find her." With that confident remark, she waved a hand and headed off. "I don't want to waste any of your precious time together, so we can talk later."

Before she reached the door, she stopped and teetered on her cane. "I'm sure you'll be persuasive, Abe."

His head jerked back, and Anna Mary studied him. "Are you hoping to persuade *me* of something? If so," she said teasingly, "it won't be hard." She'd be happy to do whatever he wanted.

Abe couldn't believe he was here with Anna Mary, and the trusting, loving glance she gave him made him feel like the luckiest man in the world. If anything, the power to persuade rested in her hands. He'd do anything to ensure her happiness.

But he had come to Pennsylvania with one major goal in mind, besides spending as much time as he could with Anna Mary. "Actually"—Abe *rutsched* in his chair—"I hope to convince your *mamm* to visit her cousin and bring all of you along. Do you think Mrs. Vandenberg approves of my plan?"

"Sounds like it." Anna Mary's face grew enraptured.

"If anyone can do it, you can. Mamm thinks so highly of you. She's always asking when you'll be back for a visit."

"I'm glad." Perhaps that might make his job easier.

"You encouraged her to get out of bed when none of us could. Though she still takes an afternoon nap, she gets up every day and has started helping with housework and caring for the little ones."

Abe couldn't wait to see the improvements. Anna Mary had mentioned many of them in her letters.

People milled around the café tables. Lines formed at the counter. Anna Mary jumped to her feet, a reluctant look on her face.

"I need to get back to work."

"I understand. I'll be here when you get a lunch break."

CHAPTER 21

For the next few hours, Abe leaned back in his chair, which he'd angled to face the counter of Hartzler's. The sizzle of fries and crisp, crackling aroma of barbecued chicken drifted over to Abe, making his stomach rumble. He hadn't eaten anything since he finished the last of Anna Mary's cookies in the New York train station.

He could order something, but he wanted to have lunch with Anna Mary, so he waited. Meanwhile, he enjoyed the carefully choreographed dance of Gideon, Caroline, Anna Mary, and two new girls Abe hadn't seen before. They dodged and ducked and sidled past each other and around the teenage boy tending the fries. Gideon basted and bagged chickens. Caroline took the money while Anna Mary filled the trays with the two girls' assistance.

I'm sorry I can't spend much time with you, Anna Mary mouthed.

That's all right. I'm fine.

Of course, he'd love to talk to her, spend time with her, but he was content to sit here and watch her flit from job to job, flashing her gorgeous smile at each customer. She saved a special smile for him each time their eyes met.

The closer the clock moved to noon, the busier the stand grew. Abe began to wonder if she'd ever get a meal break. Not until two o'clock did the crowds thin. Caroline sent the two new girls out for lunch first. Abe sighed. He should have grabbed something to eat.

When the girls returned, Gideon and Anna Mary took a break.

She made a beeline for Abe. "I have to be back by three so Caroline can eat and attend the auction—or, more likely," she said with a grin, "watch the auctioneer."

"Is that Noah who was watching the game—the one where Tim splashed mud all over Caroline?"

Anna Mary grimaced. "*Jah*. Poor Caroline." She sighed. That had been so humiliating for her friend. "Anyway, the stand always gets busy a little after three, once school lets out. Parents and teachers stop in. Later, workers come by on their way home, so I won't be able to spend time with you again until after work."

She looked so disappointed, Abe wanted to raise her spirits. "What do you want to eat?" he asked.

Anna Mary laughed. "Anything but chicken."

"Lead the way." He waved in front of him.

"Let's get pizza." She motioned to the left, and they walked beside each other past the stairway and down the aisle.

Abe loved pizza. Had she chosen it because he'd told her it was one of his favorite foods? He appreciated her thoughtfulness, but he wanted to get something she preferred. She always spent time thinking of others, caring for others, working for others. He longed to lift some of those burdens and spoil her with some special treatment.

* * *

Abe had just started to ask Anna Mary something when Cathy Zehr popped out from behind the quilting booth.

"Ooo . . . who's this, Anna Mary?" Had Cathy been waiting there to waylay them?

Anna Mary longed to say, *None of your business*. But she couldn't be rude. Besides, she had nothing to hide. Still, she didn't relish being the topic of gossip. Whatever she said would be whispered about all over the market and the town.

"A friend." She bit back her exasperation. "Abe King. Abe, this is Cathy Zehr."

"Nice to meet you," Abe said, his tone polite, but he'd stiffened beside Anna Mary, evidently sensing her discomfort.

"A friend, eh?" Cathy's eyes gleamed. "You mean *boyfriend*?"

Abe shot Anna Mary a questioning glance before answering. When she nodded, he said, "*Jah*, I'm Anna Mary's boyfriend."

"I thought so." Cathy's triumphant look grated on Anna Mary.

"Well, we'd better hurry," Abe said. "I'm glad to meet one of Anna Mary's friends, but she has a short lunch break. I want to be sure she gets something to eat." He steered Anna Mary past Cathy's avid gaze.

She scurried to keep up with them. "Where are you from?"

"New York." His crisp answer cut off further inquiries. "Are you sure you want pizza, Anna Mary? It's your lunch break."

"New York?" Cathy sounded breathless from trying to keep up with their hurried pace. "The city or the state?"

"State." Abe stared down at Anna Mary inquiringly, waiting for an answer to his question.

"I love pizza," she assured him. She appreciated him wanting to please her.

"You don't know she likes pizza?" Cathy acted shocked. "You must not have dated for long. Anna Mary often comes down here for lunch. When she doesn't bring one from home, that is."

"Good to know." Abe gave Cathy a brief smile and got in line. "What kind do you want?"

"Pepperoni."

That elicited a huge grin. "My favorite."

The two of them stared into each other's eyes until the *Englischer* behind them cleared his throat. The line had moved up, but they hadn't. They scooted forward.

"So what town do you live in, Abe?" Cathy moved into place beside him.

"Fort Plain."

"Hey, lady," the *Englischer* groused. "You can't cut in line like that."

"I'm not. I'm just talking to my friend here." She waved at Abe. "I'm not buying pizza."

"You'd better not." The man crossed his arms.

When they ordered, Abe turned to Cathy. "Can I get you something?"

Anna Mary's jaw tightened. Abe had made a fatal mistake. Now Cathy would assume she'd been invited to eat with them. She didn't blame Abe. He was just being polite. But Cathy knew exactly what she was doing.

"I'll take a slice of cheese." Cathy simpered up at Abe.

What was she doing? She was in her late thirties. Surely

she wasn't trying to cause trouble in their relationship. But she had broken up other couples with her rumors.

The *Englischer* elbowed his way between Cathy and Abe. "Oh, no, you don't. Cancel that pizza," he ordered. "She needs to go to the end of the line. I'm next."

A woman behind him agreed. "He's right. She cut in front of us."

Flustered, the poor counter girl looked from one to the other.

Anna Mary's heart swelled when Abe took charge. "I'll pay for her cheese pizza, but to be fair to the others, I'm sure she plans to wait her turn." At Abe's convincing smile and soft *sorry*, along with the other customers' glares, Cathy slunk to the end of the line.

When Abe and Anna Mary started off without her, Cathy yelled, "Hey, wait for me."

"I'm sorry," Abe said firmly, "but Anna Mary has to get back to work on time."

"Oh, Abe." Anna Mary sighed in relief. "*Danke*. She's such a gossip, and it's so hard to get rid of her." Anna Mary couldn't believe how politely he'd managed it.

Cathy couldn't fault Abe for excluding her. He'd been kind and paid for her pizza. Then he'd put her on the spot. If she'd refused to go to the end of the line, she'd have appeared rude. And that *Englischer* might have even dragged her there.

"I could tell," Abe said. "From the way you bristled when she first came toward us, I sensed she might be trouble."

"I bristled?" Anna Mary couldn't believe he'd noticed her slight stiffening.

"Don't worry. Nobody else would ever notice, but I

noticed the small changes in how you stood. It seemed like you wanted to run away."

"I did." If Abe could read her that well, what else was he picking up on? "You're starting to remind me of Mrs. Vandenberg."

Abe had a hearty laugh at that. "I can't read minds like she does. But when I really care about someone, I can pick up what they're feeling."

"That's a gift." A gift he'd used the day he first met her. He'd sensed her distress, known when to tell Tim to stop mocking her, soothed her hurt feelings over Josh.

They sat at a table near Hartzler's and shared their pizza.

Anna Mary wondered about his comment. "You said you pick up those things when you care about someone, but you did it after that first volleyball game."

"I tuned into you from the moment I met you. At first, it wasn't hard because all your feelings showed on your face, but . . ." Abe bit into a slice of pizza and chewed thoughtfully. He didn't meet her eyes. "To be honest, I fell for you right away. I tried not to because you had a boyfriend, but I wanted to go after him and demand he treat you right."

"You did?" Anna Mary had been overwhelmed by an instant attraction that she had fought too. "I felt so guilty because I'd rather be with you than with Josh."

"I'm so glad things worked out the way they did."

"So am I. Josh is happier with Rachel, and being with you has been . . ."

Caroline signaled for Anna Mary. She shot out of her seat.

"It's been the most wonderful experience of my life," she said quickly before she hurried to relieve Caroline.

* * *

Anna Mary rushed off before Abe could respond, but he'd have echoed what she'd said. He couldn't believe she was his girlfriend or that he'd be spending the next two weeks with her.

He settled back in his seat to enjoy watching his beloved. They spent so much time making eye contact, Caroline had to nudge Anna Mary out of the way or point to jobs she should be doing.

Their eyes locked again, and Anna Mary walked into the teen, who was turning with an order of fries. They showered down. He and Anna Mary both leapt back to avoid being burned, and she collided with one of the girls carrying a salad container. At least it was empty.

But her boss's lips thinned.

Anna Mary apologized and rushed for a broom while the teen filled another bag with fries.

Abe got up from his chair and strolled off to the right. He didn't want to run into Cathy Zehr. By sitting here, though, he'd become a distraction. Tomorrow he wouldn't come into the market. The last thing he wanted was for Anna Mary to lose her job because of him.

He'd been in the market a few times with Tim, so he remembered some of the stands. He'd like a soft pretzel, but that was at the other end of the market. It was two aisles over from Cathy. Should he chance it?

Anna Mary liked raisin pretzels. She'd mentioned that in a letter. He kept a wary eye out as he passed the staircase, but he didn't see Cathy. He ordered seven pretzels, in case Anna Mary invited him back to her house after work. Then he wandered down to the other end of the market and loitered there until closing time.

* * *

Anna Mary missed Abe when he walked away, but now she could concentrate on her job. She hoped he hadn't gone home. She'd planned to invite him to have supper with them.

He strolled into view as Gideon went to lock the doors for the day, and her heart picked up the same joyous pace as it had earlier when he'd entered the market. Two whole weeks! If only she didn't have to work.

Gideon stopped by the table and said something to Abe. Would he shoo Abe outside? No customers were allowed in the building after hours.

To her relief, Gideon shook Abe's hand and headed for the other end of the market to lock up.

"Why don't you go home?" Caroline suggested. "I doubt you'll be any help here when you can't take your eyes off the café tables," she teased. When Anna Mary didn't move, Caroline pushed her gently to the booth exit.

"Are you sure?"

"I'm positive. Go on. Abe's waiting. And if those are pretzels, they're getting cold."

Elated, Anna Mary rushed over to Abe. "They're letting me go home early." She'd make up the time by coming in early tomorrow. "Do you want to come to our house for supper?"

"I was hoping you'd ask." He held up the bag. "I got pretzels for your *mamm* and sisters too." A sheepish look crossed his face. "Myron dropped me off on his way to work, so I don't have a way home."

"You have a way home," she said firmly. "To a home where everyone will be happy to see you."

"I hope so." He shook the bag. "That's why I bought a bribe."

"They'd be thrilled to see you even without the pretzels." Anna Mary's mood soared higher at the joy in Abe's eyes.

The two of them chattered during the whole trip, and when they got to the house, he helped Anna Mary take care of her horse.

"Don't let them see you," she said as they approached the door. She opened it a crack and called out, "Who'd like a surprise?"

Emmie and Hannah both yelled, "Me," and raced toward her.

Staying out of sight, Abe thrust the bag of pretzels through the gap.

"Pretzels, pretzels, pretzels." Emmie twirled in delight.

"What about another surprise?" Anna Mary asked and pushed the door open to reveal Abe.

Emmie and Beth tackled his legs. Sarah clapped a hand over her mouth to hold back a squeal.

"Abe?" Mamm's eyes glowed. "*Kumme* in, *kumme* in."

"He's here for a two-week visit." Anna Mary led him to the kitchen, where he placed the bag in the center of the table.

Mamm trailed after them. "No pretzels until after supper, girls."

Anna Mary caught Abe's eye, and they both smiled. Her *mamm* sounded like a real mother. It had been a long time since Mamm had issued any orders or taken charge. Was she doing it for Abe's benefit? Anna Mary didn't care why. She was just glad to see Mamm take over some mothering duties.

The dinner followed the pattern of those they'd had during Abe's previous visits. After the meal, Sarah insisted on doing the dishes so Abe and Anna Mary could go for a walk. When they returned, Abe played a few card games, then read bedtime stories to Emmie and Beth while Sarah got Hannah ready for bed. Mamm insisted she needed no help and headed off for an early bedtime.

Sarah hovered in the background, bringing out snacks and coffee or sometimes joining the conversation. Anna Mary was so wrapped up in talking to Abe, she barely noticed, but Abe thanked her and tried to include her.

After Sarah yawned several times, Abe stood. "I should let you get some sleep."

Anna Mary jumped up. "I'll drive you back." She didn't want to miss one precious second of his company.

"I'd like that." He hesitated. "I think it'd be better if I don't bother you at work tomorrow."

As much as she disliked admitting it, Abe was right. And she needed to make up all the time she'd taken yesterday. "But I'll see you tomorrow after work?"

"If it's all right with your family, I'll be here when you get home."

Sarah answered shyly from the doorway. "We'd all like that. Why don't you come for breakfast so you can see Anna Mary before work?"

"*Danke.* I can use Tim's buggy, so nobody'll need to pick me up in the morning."

That would be more practical, but Anna Mary would miss the chance to ride over here with him, so she made the most of their ride home.

CHAPTER 22

Abe woke early the next morning with one main goal in mind—besides spending time with Anna Mary, of course. He wanted to convince Esther to take a trip to Stone Arabia. Mrs. Vandenberg seemed to endorse his idea yesterday, but Abe realized he hadn't asked for heavenly guidance.

Lord, if this idea is from You, please give me a chance to talk to Esther and direct my words.

Before he left for Anna Mary's, he fixed a hearty breakfast for Myron, which his *onkel* appreciated.

"No offense to Tim, but is there any chance your *daed* would consider switching *sohns* permanently?"

For a moment, Abe's heart leapt. Maybe this was God's solution to being with Anna Mary. Daed would never go for it, though. And Tim would never agree to stay in Fort Plain. His cousin wanted to remain in Lancaster, where he'd last seen his sister. Still, God could make anything possible.

With a light heart, Abe set off for Anna Mary's. He enjoyed breakfast with her, but it ended too soon. He walked her out to the barn and helped her hitch up the horse.

"The market closes at four on Saturdays, so I should

be back by five thirty. I'm so glad I have off Sunday and Monday so we can spend all day together."

"I am too." He'd miss her while she was gone, but maybe he could make some headway with his plan.

Once she set off, Abe helped Sarah and Emmie with the dishes. Then he went into the living room to talk to Esther, but the little girls begged him to play games.

He sat on the floor with them, but when Esther asked about his trip, they stopped setting up the board and listened, enraptured, to tales of the train and the cities where he'd stopped.

Esther's face wrinkled in distress. "*Ach*, what a long, hard trip. And so many hours on the road."

Abe regretted mentioning the length of the trip and all the hustle, bustle, and noise he'd encountered. And instead of stressing the fun of the new adventure, he'd made the cities and layovers sound overwhelming.

He tried to backtrack. "It wasn't a bad trip. And you can take faster trains with fewer stops." He rushed on, hoping to correct his mistake. "I took that one because it was the only train out of Fort Plain that night."

"I want to ride on a train," Emmie declared. "And I want to see your cows."

"You can see cows all around here, Emmie." Esther's sharp tone didn't deflate her daughter.

"But they're not Abe's cows," Emmie insisted stubbornly.

Sarah, ever the peacemaker, smiled at Abe. "Anna Mary told us all about milking your cows. She really seemed to like it."

Emmie thrust out her lower lip. "I'd like it too."

"I'm sure you would, Emmie." Sarah tousled her younger sister's hair.

"Can I milk your cows, Abe?" Emmie asked.

"Of course." Was this the opening he'd been waiting for? "All of you are welcome to visit and help out at the farm." He turned to Esther. "If your *mamm* will let you."

Grabbing Beth's hands, Emmie pulled her to her feet. The two of them danced around their mother. "Can we, Mamm? Can we?"

Esther's lips tightened. "If you girls are that excited about milking, I'm sure we can ask the Fishers down the road to let you help."

Emmie's face fell. So did Abe's spirits. Had he doomed his chances with today's conversation?

Gideon came over to Anna Mary on their break. "I met your young man yesterday. He seems nice." He hesitated, and worry lines grooved the skin around his mouth and eyes. "Wasn't he one of that group hassling Caroline?"

"That was his cousin Tim. Abe isn't like Tim at all."

"You can tell people's characters from the company they keep."

Mrs. Vandenberg came up behind Gideon and patted his shoulder. "Not always."

He turned toward her.

She flicked her eyes toward the two girls helping Caroline. "I'm sure people don't judge your sister-in-law Nettie when she spends time around gang members. Am I right?"

Embarrassment flashed across his face. "*Jah*, you are."

"Sometimes people may be helping others turn their lives around," Mrs. Vandenberg continued.

"Exactly." Anna Mary jumped in to defend her boyfriend. "Abe's *onkel* asks him to come to Lancaster when Tim's in trouble. Abe's a good influence on him."

Gideon inclined his head. "I apologize. I only wanted to make sure you're safe, Anna Mary."

That was sweet of Caroline's brother to look out for her. "*Danke.*" But she didn't need to be protected from Abe. He was her protector. A smile blossomed inside. And he'd come to be with her for two weeks.

"Also," Gideon said, drawing Anna Mary's attention back to the conversation, "I wanted to let you know you don't have to do any cleanup after work while your boyfriend's here. He said he has to head back to New York in two weeks."

"That's thoughtful of you, Gideon." Mrs. Vandenberg beamed at him. "But I wouldn't have expected any less from the manager I put in charge of my market. I hope having two new workers will also allow Anna Mary to take time off for visiting Fort Plain."

"I'm sure that can be worked out." Gideon nodded to her and excused himself.

"I can't—" Anna Mary started to explain that Mamm wouldn't let her go, but Mrs. Vandenberg waved aside the protest.

"You know, dear, you only need faith the size of a mustard seed."

That took Anna Mary aback. Was Mrs. Vandenberg implying that Anna Mary wasn't trusting God? To her chagrin, she realized Mrs. Vandenberg was right.

Jah, she prayed many times a day, but deep down inside, did she really believe it would happen?

Dear Lord, I'm sorry for not believing You can do anything. Please help my unbelief.

Mrs. Vandenberg's face smoothed into satisfaction as she studied Anna Mary.

"Maybe now you're ready for what I brought." Mrs.

Vandenberg reached into her purse and removed an envelope addressed to Abe. "He might need this." She snapped her purse shut. "Keep the faith," she reminded Anna Mary before heading off.

Those words echoed through Anna Mary's mind as she headed home. *Keep the faith. Keep the faith.*

Abe rushed out of the house as soon as buggy wheels clattered up the driveway. He'd helped the girls with their chores, done a few household repairs, and driven to Myron's an hour ago to put a casserole in the oven for his dinner. He'd apologized to his *onkel* for hurrying off, but Myron only laughed and said he remembered courting Sadie years ago.

"You never know how much time you'll have with each other. Make the most of it." His eyes held a wistful look. His fiancée had died a few weeks before their wedding, and in the twenty-five years since, he'd never courted anyone else.

Abe intended to make the most of it and to find a way to bring their two families together. Right now, though, he wanted to spend as much time as possible with his sweet girlfriend.

She stepped out of the buggy, bringing her sunshiny smile with her. Abe longed to wrap his arms around her and cradle her close. Instead, he concentrated on helping her unhitch the horse.

When they finished, they started for the house, but Anna Mary stopped. "Wait. I have something for you." She handed him a letter.

"You're writing me letters when I'm right here?"

She laughed. "I wouldn't have time at work, but I thought about you all the time. This is from Mrs. Vandenberg."

Curious, Abe tore open the envelope. He read the message once, then reread it. "I can't believe it."

He scanned it a third time:

You prepare the soil and plant the seed. I'll do my part to water it. Trust God for the growth.
  I have business in Fort Plain and have reserved a van for the day you head home. There'll be plenty of room for you and all those you invite to accompany you. No charge to anyone.

Abe sat dumbfounded. He wouldn't have to take the train. Thank the Lord. And there'd be room for Anna Mary's family, but—

"What's the matter?" Anna Mary's brow furrowed in concern. "You looked so happy. Now you're frowning."

He passed her the note. Her quick indrawn breath told him she'd read about the van.

"Oh, Abe," she said breathlessly. "It would be a dream come true if only Mamm . . ." Her voice trailed off the way his own excitement had.

"It'd be perfect. But how do we convince your *mamm*?"

Mamm had to say *jah*. She just had to. But like Abe, Anna Mary stared at the note, uncertainty and disappointment swirling through her. They had less than two weeks to convince Mamm to take the whole family to New York.

"I tried earlier today," Abe confided, "but giving the details of my train trip didn't help. And when Emmie said she wanted to milk my cows, your *mamm* said she could do that at your neighbor's farm."

"*Ach*, Abe, she's so set against it. I don't see how we can ever change her mind."

He removed the letter from her hand and read the first paragraph again. Then he repeated the last line, "*Trust God for the growth.*"

That gave Anna Mary's spirits a big bump. Mrs. Vandenberg's last words to her had been *keep the faith.* "She reminded me today that we only need faith the size of a mustard seed."

"So . . ." Abe grinned. "The seed we need to plant only has to be mustard-seed size."

"They're so tiny. We can do that." Anna Mary didn't know how, but she'd follow Mrs. Vandenberg's advice and trust the Lord.

Abe glanced at the note again. "I wonder what she means about doing the watering. Unless she means supplying the van."

"For now, we just need to figure out our part." Mustard seed? What seed could they plant? What would make Mamm want to go to New York?

Anna Mary was still pondering that when they reached the kitchen. Immediately, she was swept into the meal preparations. Abe offered to help, but Sarah shooed him into the living room.

"Mamm's alone out there," Sarah said. "Why don't you keep her company? And could you take Hannah with you?" She peeled the little girl's hands off her leg. "Thing's will get done faster."

"I'd be happy to."

Anna Mary stopped to watch as Abe bent down and

lifted Hannah into his arms. She snuggled her face against his shoulder. Daydreams of Abe holding their future children filled Anna Mary with love and anticipation. He'd be a *wunderbar daed*.

He smiled at her over Hannah's tousled curls, and the love-light shining in his eyes told her he'd had similar thoughts. With a quick thumbs-up, he headed into the living room.

Later, as they sat around the table, Abe smiled at Emmie. "You know what Anna Mary's favorite thing was in New York?"

You, she mouthed and bit back a grin when she flustered him.

He shot her a *you're-supposed-to-be-helping-me* plea with his eyes.

She sobered. He was trying to plant a seed, and she was distracting him.

Abe turned his full attention back to Emmie, who was trying to guess.

"The waterfalls," he said finally. "Do you know what they are?"

Emmie shook her head.

Anna Mary hurried to explain. Her little sister's mouth opened at the description of water cascading over a mountain. Then Emmie peppered them with questions. Sarah and Beth joined in.

"Have you ever seen a waterfall?" Abe asked Sarah.

She shook her head. "*Neh*, but I'd like to see one."

Mamm's sharp tone sliced through the excited chatter. "If you want to see a waterfall, there's one in the Lancaster County Central Park."

Emmie bounced up and down in her seat. "Can we go there, Mamm? I want to see a fallwater."

"Waterfall," Mamm corrected. "There are plenty around here."

"I don't think any of the ones around here are sixty feet high." Maybe Anna Mary shouldn't have risked irritating Mamm by pointing that out. "Canajoharie Falls has three waterfalls. The other two are thirty and ten feet high, but they're all beautiful."

Emmie giggled. "That's a funny name."

Abe chuckled. "It is. Try saying it three times fast. Canajoharie. Canajoharie. Canajoharie."

Beth and Emmie turned it into a tongue-twister amid peals of laughter.

"Tell us more about Fort Plain," Sarah begged.

Was God giving them an opening to convince Mamm? It sure seemed that way. Anna Mary and Abe took turns describing the beautiful scenery, the old church in Stone Arabia, the rolling countryside, and the small towns.

"It's a lot like here," Anna Mary said. "A lot of women have *kapps* like Mamm and me. It made me feel right at home."

"I wish we'd had more time to see more things while Anna Mary visited." Abe described several other tourist attractions.

"I wish I'd seen those," Anna Mary said wistfully after he finished.

"Me too," Emmie said.

Sarah nodded. "I wish we could all go to New York." She stood and began clearing plates.

As Anna Mary rose to join Sarah, her heart echoed her sisters' wishes.

"I wish I could show you around my area," Abe said, "and it would be fun to have Emmie's help with our cows. Anna Mary did such a good job. She could show you how to do it."

The deep creases in Mamm's forehead didn't bode well for a future trip. Anna Mary sent up a quick prayer. *Please, Lord, if this is Your will, soften Mamm's heart.*

To her relief, Abe, with his keen understanding of people's feelings, sensed they were upsetting Mamm. When he changed the subject, Anna Mary sent him a silent *danke.*

As they'd talked about New York attractions, Esther grew more and more tense. And when her daughters started clamoring about visiting, a thundercloud descended over her features. Abe needed to turn this discussion in a different direction.

Keeping his voice light, he addressed Emmie. "The fun thing about traveling is seeing new places. That's why I like coming to Lancaster." He added a teasing tone to his voice. "Besides seeing all of you and my family."

Emmie's face folded into a pout.

Abe needed to do a balancing act here—keep Emmie interested while reassuring Esther he didn't want to steal her girls away. Well, only one of them. He scrambled to think of things Emmie might think of as fun.

"What about Lapp Valley Farms? They let you watch the milking." He and Tim had gone there, and Abe had talked to the men milking the cows. "But the best part was the ice cream."

Now he had Emmie's attention. She licked her lips. "Can we get ice cream, Mamm?"

Anna Mary set servings of apple crisp in front of him and her *mamm*. But Abe's words had arrested Sarah's attention. She stood, unmoving, two plates extended.

"We used to go there a lot when Emmie was little. We haven't been there since . . ." Her chin wavered.

Ach, Abe hadn't meant to cause distress. They probably hadn't had enough money to go after their *daed* died.

He hurried to make amends. "Why don't we take the little ones there on Monday when Anna Mary has off?" When Esther moved as if to forestall the plan, Abe added, "It'll be my treat since you've fed me at every meal."

"Can we? Can we?" Beth and Emmie pleaded.

"We'll see." Esther didn't sound enthusiastic.

"It would be fun, Mamm. And the little ones can play on the playground and see the animals."

"I said we'll see." Esther's firm tone ended the requests.

Abe picked up a different thread, describing some places they might be familiar with, like the bulk goods store and the farmer's market. But an idea had taken shape in Abe's mind.

While Anna Mary worked, he could take the girls on small local trips. Maybe they'd be able to convince Esther to accompany them. She probably hadn't been out much except for church since her second husband's death. It might get her over her fears about going new places. At least he could try. And trust the Lord for the rest.

CHAPTER 23

Two *wunderbar* things happened on Monday. Anna Mary could hardly believe it. Abe took the whole family for ice cream at Lapp's, and he convinced Mamm to come along. She seemed to enjoy herself as much as the little ones, although several times, she stared off into the distance, her eyes sad, as the girls played on the playground.

Then, when they pulled into the driveway, Abe stopped by the mailbox so Anna Mary could get the mail. Ordinarily, she did it first thing in the morning, eager to see if Abe had sent a letter. Now while he was here, she hadn't been checking as regularly. Today, though, she was glad she had. One envelope came from Delores.

Mamm opened it and read as they headed for the barn. While Anna Mary and Abe took care of the horse and put away the buggy, Mamm meandered down the walk, engrossed in the letter. Two tiny lines deepened between her eyes.

"Is something wrong?" Anna Mary asked when she returned to the house to find Mamm rereading the letter.

"Delores's daughter and son-in-law and their children are moving to Indiana this week. They want her to go with them, but she doesn't want to leave her home. It has too many memories of her husband. If she stays, she'll be all alone in that big house."

"That's a hard decision."

Mamm nodded. "When her daughter first talked about it, I suggested she move back here. She says Lancaster is too crowded and touristy now. She likes the quieter country living. I don't know what she's talking about. Our area is quiet."

"We do have a lot of tourists," Anna Mary pointed out. "Maybe not back here on the country roads, but even in the small towns like Gordonville, people often lean out of car windows to snap pictures." Until today, Mamm hadn't been outside much for years.

"Poor Delores. I can't imagine being all alone in that big house."

"I bet she'd welcome some company." Anna Mary tossed out the idea casually. When Mamm narrowed her eyes with suspicion, Anna Mary hastened to smooth things over. "I'm just thinking of what I'd want if I were alone after having a big family around me."

"I guess." Mamm's words had a sour edge.

Anna Mary changed the subject. "Would you like lasagna or hamburgers tonight?" She'd planned special meals for every night while Abe was here. Usually, they had soup and salad for supper. Lately, with all the groceries arriving, they'd added grilled cheese or a bit of meat. But with the huge amount of food they'd gotten last week, they had so many options.

"Why don't you ask Abe? After all, he treated us today." Mamm's face softened as she smiled at him.

Mamm really seemed to like Abe a lot, which made Anna Mary happy. If only she could convince her *mamm* to visit New York.

"I'm glad you enjoyed it, Esther. I hope while I'm here, you'll let me take the girls on more trips. It's lonely without family around, and Myron isn't one for visiting the attractions."

"I'm sure the girls would like that." But worry lines marred her agreement.

"And you could come with them."

Anna Mary loved the gentle way Abe coaxed her *mamm* to try new things.

With a heavy sigh, Mamm said, "I don't want the girls to get too used to exploring new places or having daily treats. They'll miss those things when you're gone. I don't like stirring up a desire for things they can't have."

Abe looked thoughtful. "I've often found after I take trips, I appreciate being home much more."

"Really?" Mamm didn't sound convinced.

Anna Mary chimed in. "That's true." She'd loved being with Abe, but her own bedroom had seemed more welcoming when she got back. "There's something about returning to a familiar place that's comforting. It's how I felt after coming back from New York."

Abe smiled at her. "And as much as I enjoy being in Lancaster with all of you, going home is like being wrapped in a warm blanket." He laughed. "Even if it's twenty degrees out. Like it was during last winter's trip after I stayed with Tim."

Even Mamm laughed at that.

"As for the meal, lasagna sounds delicious." Abe's eyes met hers and held, and Anna Mary drowned in the depths of love they revealed. She had trouble breaking away. Then she floated into the kitchen as if on air. God had given her a special gift when Abe arrived in her life.

* * *

The rest of the week, Abe alternated between helping with household chores and organizing outings. He spent the rest of his time gazing into Anna Mary's eyes, taking private walks with her, and fixing meals for his *onkel*. The days flew by, and they'd made little headway with Esther. She seemed to enjoy the trips, but her disapproval of a New York trip remained high.

Mrs. Vandenberg arrived on Friday after Anna Mary had headed for work. Abe was helping the younger girls get ready for a train ride on the Strasburg Railroad. The forty-five-minute trip from Ronks made a circle through Amish farm country. The old-fashioned steam engine didn't zip along like the trains Abe had ridden to Lancaster, but he thought it might calm Esther's fears about being on a train. Not that they'd need to travel by one if they took Mrs. Vandenberg up on her offer of a van ride.

"Do you have a minute?" she asked Esther, then settled into a chair without waiting for an answer.

Abe hovered outside the living room as he and Sarah packed sandwiches and snacks to take along with them. He wanted to learn how Mrs. Vandenberg would persuade Esther to go to Fort Plain.

To Abe's surprise, Mrs. Vandenberg brought up Delores right away.

"Esther, I'm concerned about your cousin. She'll be all alone by the end of next week."

"You know about that?"

"I keep up with all the couples I match."

So Mrs. Vandenberg had matched Delores and her husband? How long had she been doing this?

Esther's voice shook. "Can you get her to move back here?"

"It would be best for you to go there. God has another

man in mind for Delores, so she needs to stay where she is."

"I can't go to New York."

"Even if that's where the Lord wants you?"

Esther sobbed softly. "Why would God want me to leave my home?"

"Perhaps there's something He needs to show you in New York. I suggest you pray about it."

"I want to do God's will, but—"

Mrs. Vandenberg pushed herself shakily to her feet. "You know what I've always said about *but*. Whenever you follow something with a *but*, you don't mean what you said before that. I hope you don't mean you won't do God's will."

Esther sucked in a breath. "I can't do this. How can I leave my home and travel to a strange place?"

"Read Philippians 4:13. *I can do all things through Christ which strengtheneth me.*" With those words, Mrs. Vandenberg hobbled toward the door.

Esther was still shaking her head when Sarah and Abe entered the room with the cooler and a thermos of water. Emmie followed with a sippy cup for Hannah. Beth dragged the diaper bag behind her.

"Mamm?" Sarah asked in alarm. "Are you all right?"

"I'm not sure."

To give her some time to recover, Abe volunteered to hitch up the horse.

"I don't think I'm going." Esther's voice wavered. "I need to go back to bed."

"*Neh*, Mamm." Sarah was practically in tears. "You've been doing so well. And Abe's only here for a few days."

Esther waved her hand. "You girls go. I'm not needed. You and Abe can handle everything without me."

"We don't want to." Abe kept his tone gentle, but forceful. "Your daughters want you to come, and so do I." He needed her to see that train rides weren't scary in case Anna Mary had to ride in one to visit him sometime. "We could wait until tomorrow if you'd rather."

A flurry of *nehs* came from the girls.

Emmie grabbed her *mamm*'s hand and tried to pull her to her feet.

"Not now, Emmie. I have a lot to think about."

Sarah's eyes brimmed with tears. "Please come, Mamm. We don't want to ride the train without you. Can you think in the buggy and on the train?"

Esther looked at the pleading faces circled around her and blew out an exhausted sigh. "I doubt I'll be able to do much thinking."

"We'll be real quiet," Sarah promised. "Won't we, Emmie?"

Although Emmie appeared as doubtful as her mother, she nodded.

Abe stepped closer. "Do you need a hand?"

A wan smile crossed Esther's face. "I always seem to need a hand. Maybe it's time I did something on my own. Or, as Mrs. V reminded me, with God's help."

All four girls clapped and cheered, including Hannah, who, although she didn't seem to know why, patted her chubby little hands and babbled happily.

Sarah shushed her sisters and picked up Hannah. "We need to let Mamm think."

An hour later they boarded the train. The girls had *oohed* and *aahed* in the gift shop and stared at the loco-motive with awe. Myron had told Abe to request a stop at Groff's Grove for the picnic area and playground.

Esther paled and drew in a breath when they boarded

and when the train jerked to a start. The girls stared out the windows, breathless with excitement and a bit fearful as the train swayed.

Sarah, her face tight, put an arm around Beth, and Esther held Hannah. Abe sat across the aisle, letting Emmie have the window seat. She had none of her family's worries as she bounced up and down. The chugging engine and loud whistle and plumes of steam all fascinated her.

By the time they reached the picnic grove, all of them had become seasoned travelers. During their hour layover, the girls played on the wooden replica train and ate their lunch. Even Esther had a slight smile when the train clacked into sight to take them back.

That evening, when Anna Mary arrived home, Emmie and Beth tumbled out the door in the race to be first to tell her about their adventures.

"You went on a train?" Anna Mary turned incredulous eyes to Abe.

"Just a short ride."

"But you didn't tell me."

Abe headed to the barn with her. "I wasn't sure your *mamm* would agree to go."

Anna Mary screeched to a halt and stared up at him. "Mamm went too?"

"After Mrs. Vandenberg talked to her."

"Mrs. Vandenberg came here?"

"I have a lot to tell you." Abe smiled down at her sisters. "Emmie, why don't you and Beth help Sarah with dinner while Anna Mary and I take care of the horse?" Once the two little ones had trotted off to the house, Abe relayed the whole story.

"*Ach*, Abe." Her eyes brimmed with tears. "Even if we don't get Mamm to New York, this is a miracle."

Abe didn't intend to stop here. He wanted to get Anna Mary's family to his farm, and today's train trip was the first step toward the final destination.

CHAPTER 24

The rest of Abe's visit, the girls and Mamm went on short outings with Abe. Anna Mary accompanied them on her days off. She and Abe also played volleyball against each other. Without Tim, though, Caroline's team crushed the opposition. The two of them also played baseball with her youth group and attended singings together.

Josh, chatting with Rachel, beamed at Anna Mary when she entered with Abe. He appeared genuinely happy for her. And though a little twinge of jealousy shot through her at Rachel's beauty, after Abe nodded at the couple, friendly but disinterested, he made it clear he had eyes only for Anna Mary. Her happiness brimmed over.

The past two weeks had been a dream, but the next morning Abe would head home. That night, they all went to bed early.

Anna Mary couldn't sleep. She sat up in bed and hugged herself. Tomorrow, when Abe took off in Mrs. Vandenberg's van, Anna Mary and her whole family would go with him for a three-week stay with Aunt Delores. Anna Mary still couldn't believe Mamm had agreed.

Between Abe, Mrs. Vandenberg, and many, many prayers, Mamm had changed her mind. Now Anna Mary begged God that Mamm would enjoy her visit so much, she might want to go again. Even if she didn't, Anna Mary hoped she'd be allowed to make the trip from time to time. For now, she'd enjoy her next three weeks as much as she had Abe's time in Lancaster.

Mrs. Vandenberg arrived at dawn the next morning, and Abe hopped from the van to help load suitcases and the many treats the girls had baked and canned. Abe had helped pick vegetables and fruit in the garden and even assisted with the canning. He'd explained to Sarah he wouldn't have time to do that very often once he got back home, but he appreciated learning many of the tasks Anna Mary did every day. And she loved doing them with him.

The only thing Anna Mary wasn't really looking forward to was seeing Tim. He always rubbed her the wrong way. But she had to be nice to him because he was Abe's cousin. She prayed for patience with his teasing and critical comments.

To her surprise, after an uneventful trip with many stops for the little ones to stretch and plenty of time for Anna Mary and Abe to talk in the back seat, she came face-to-face with a smiling Tim. He looked delighted to see them all, especially Sarah.

Abe introduced him to her *mamm* and made introductions a second time after his *daed* emerged from the barn.

Hank greeted everyone, then headed over to Mamm. "Esther, I just want to thank you for the lovely young lady you raised. My Abe couldn't have picked a better girlfriend."

Mamm blushed prettily. "I didn't have that much to do

with it. Anna Mary's done most of it herself since my—my husband passed." Her eyes sparkled with tears.

"Abe mentioned that. I'm sure it wasn't easy losing two husbands and having five girls to raise. I know how lonely it can be. I lost my wife two years ago."

"I'm so sorry." Mamm gave him a sympathetic glance.

"I didn't have it as hard as you. My children, all except Abe, were already grown and married. You had little ones." His eyes ranged over Hannah, sleeping in Mamm's arms, to Beth and Emmie.

"It's been a challenge," Mamm admitted. "I couldn't have done it without Anna Mary and Sarah." She stared down at the ground, a shamed expression on her face. "I wish I'd been stronger for them." She nibbled at her lower lip. "I struggle with depression."

Anna Mary couldn't believe Mamm was confessing this to a stranger. She must have sensed Hank was as perceptive and understanding as his son. Anna Mary had done the same with Abe the first day she met him—spilled out her heartache, her argument with Josh. Abe had even seen her tears.

Now Mamm was doing the same thing. Nobody else had noticed. Abe had taken Emmie and Beth to the pasture fence to see the cows. Tim was talking to Sarah, and Mrs. Vandenberg stood by the van with a serene smile as if she had orchestrated the whole wonderful picture. With God's help, of course. Which she had indeed.

Abe boosted Emmie and Beth up on the split-rail fence so they could watch the cows nibbling in the meadow. A sense of contentment flowed over him. He had four little sisters he loved already, and he was head over heels for their older sister. Daed and Esther were getting along well, and Tim had lost some of his hard, cruel edges. Abe wasn't sure how much came from Daed's influence and how much was due to Sarah's sweet sisterly care, but either way, it was a pleasant change.

Anna Mary seemed to be listening to her *mamm*'s conversation as well as Mrs. Vandenberg's talk with Tim while the driver unloaded bags and boxes.

"Sorry, girls." He lifted them to the ground. "Stay right here. I have to help with the boxes." He hurried over, hefted several boxes, and carried them into the house. He returned for the cooler. All the food he put in the pantry and freezer.

Mrs. Vandenberg insisted she'd be treating everyone to pizza for supper. She planned to eat with them, then drive Anna Mary's family to Stone Arabia. So Abe only had to unload his duffel and a few souvenirs he'd picked up for Daed.

As he headed out the door to get those, Anna Mary shouted, "No, Emmie. Get down."

Abe pushed open the screen door. Emmie had climbed to the top rail and was trying to balance. She reached over to pet a calf and tumbled headfirst over the fence.

Emmie shrieked. Daed reached her in a few strides. He hopped over the fence. Abe was a few steps behind. He vaulted the top rail too. Everyone else crowded around.

Daed knelt beside Emmie. "What hurts?"

"Everything," she yowled as she tried to push herself up with one arm.

"Wait a minute." His voice gentle, Hank asked her to stay still until he checked her head and neck.

She shook her head so vigorously, he laughed. "I'd say those are all right. Does anything else feel sore?"

"My hand," she wailed.

"Let's roll you over and see." Daed grimaced when he

took a look. He twisted around to meet Esther's eyes. "Her wrist."

"I'm so sorry," Abe said to her and Anna Mary. "I should have been watching her."

"*Neh*, I should have," Anna Mary and Sarah said in unison.

"It's my fault." Esther's face mirrored their guilt.

"Nobody's to blame," Daed soothed.

But Abe still blamed himself, even though the others acted as if it were their fault.

Abe gently supported Emmie's hand and wrist as Daed lifted her into his arms. "Best use the gate this time."

Together, they got her through, and Esther took Abe's place.

Mrs. Vandenberg motioned them to the van. "We'll run you to the emergency room."

"Sohn, you, Tim, and Anna Mary will have to handle the milking," Daed said as he got into a bench seat with Esther.

By the time they returned several hours later, the milking had been completed, Sarah had fixed a salad and dessert while Hannah and Beth napped, and Mrs. Vandenberg had picked up pizza.

Daed came in holding Emmie, Esther hovering beside them. With a pained smile, Emmie lifted an arm encased in a blue cast.

"That's *gut*," Daed said. "Keeping it up is helpful." He turned to Abe. "Milking go all right?"

"Of course. Anna Mary did a great job, and Tim's learned a lot."

"Hey," Tim protested. "Admit it. I did a *wunderbar* job."

Abe had to agree. And between the three of them, they

finished only a little later than usual. Abe had enjoyed being in charge. Someday, he'd take over, and he'd love to have Anna Mary beside him. Maybe Tim too—as long as his cousin kept his temper and teasing in check.

Mrs. Vandenberg's face showed her exhaustion, and she and the driver left as soon as they finished eating and Abe loaded the suitcases into Daed's buggy. Daed had volunteered to drive Esther and her children to Stone Arabia.

A short while later, all of Anna Mary's family sat with his family. Abe would love to have the supper table stay like this every night.

Danke, Lord, for working out this trip. Please help our future meals to look like this, if it is Your will.

When they piled into Hank's buggy, Anna Mary and Sarah squeezed into the back with Beth and Hannah on their laps, and Mamm held Emmie. Anna Mary waved to a forlorn Abe.

I'll be back for morning milking, she mouthed, making him brighten.

"Tell you what," Hank said to Mamm as they started off, "tomorrow why don't we get my horse used to you and Anna Mary. Then you can take my buggy back and forth. Abe and I can share his while you're here."

"We couldn't do that," Mamm protested.

"Don't worry. I'm sure the horse will adjust. Checkers is docile."

"*Neh*, I meant we couldn't put you out like that."

"All right. I can get up at three to run over to pick you up if you'd rather."

Mamm's eyes widened. "I didn't mean to make you run over to Stone Arabia every day."

"You don't want me to get you?" He put on a wounded look.

Mamm hid a smile. "I'm trying not to be a burden."

"It'd never be a burden to pick up you and your lovely family. It's a pleasure."

"Even after spending hours in the emergency room?" Mamm's voice had a light and teasing note Anna Mary had never heard before.

"Even then. I told Anna Mary how much I miss having *kinner* in the milking barn. It'll be a joy to have them here for the next few weeks." Hank sounded wistful.

They traveled a bit in silence, and the three little ones drifted off to sleep.

Hank, his voice barely above a whisper, broke the quiet. "You're lucky to have young ones still at home. I miss the patter of little feet in the hallway."

"Oh, that must be hard." Mamm's words oozed sympathy.

"It is. As a parent, you raise them so they can start their own families. When they do, you've done your job well, but it doesn't mean you don't miss them."

When Mamm sat thoughtfully for a moment, Anna Mary held her breath. Was Hank trying to point out it was time to let her older daughter move on? Would her mother get his point?

Mamm hung her head. "I've not done a *gut* job of that."

"What do you mean? Anna Mary is a *wunderbar* young lady. She's mature and responsible. From what I've seen, she's a hard worker, an excellent cook, takes great care of children, knows how to clean, and, best of all, has a loving heart."

Anna Mary squirmed. She'd never heard anyone list her *gut* points before. She tried not to dwell on the compliments. It might puff her up too much. Mamm would warn her against *hochmut*.

"And Sarah," Hank went on, "she's very much like her older sister. She too has the virtues of a *gut* wife and mother."

"That's not my doing," Mamm burst out. "I haven't been the *mamm* I should be to them."

"Don't be so hard on yourself. You did what you could in a difficult situation."

"You don't understand." Mamm's anguish bled through each word. "I stayed in bed for weeks at a time, sunk in my own depression."

"That sounds like a dark time." Hank's nonjudgmental response was what Mamm needed.

Abe saw the good in everyone, the way his *daed* did. Maybe Hank's gentle acceptance could help Mamm heal her deep wounds.

Anna Mary prayed God would use their time here to bring Mamm back to herself.

She repeated his words. "A dark time? *Jah*, it was. Instead of relying on God, I wallowed in my grief."

"Most people sink into self-pity during painful losses. I had cows that needed to be milked every day. It's really the only thing that kept me going. That and prayer. And Abe, of course."

"You don't understand. My children should have kept me going, but I left them and all the household chores to Anna Mary and Sarah."

"It's *gut* you'd trained them well enough they could take over some of the work."

"Not some. All," Mamm choked out.

"Who trained your girls what to do and how to do?" Hank couched his question in gentleness.

She lifted her head and stared at him. Shock and

wonder flitted across her face. "*Ach*, Hank. You don't know what a weight you've lifted from me." A tear trickled down her cheek. "I still feel guilty for not being there for my girls, but I did do things in their earlier years to give them the skills."

"Of course you did. Your daughters prove you've been a fine mother. And you've come out of those dark times, haven't you?"

Mamm turned her head away to stare out the window. Anna Mary ached for her mother. She'd confessed to so many things. Would she be honest about this? Hank had Abe's gift of making you want to bare your soul. He seemed to be drawing out the long-held poison of self-reproach. Anna Mary whispered a prayer Mamm would tell the truth.

"Only recently," Mamm admitted. "Every year, around the times of their deaths and around our wedding anniversaries . . ."

"Those are the hardest to bear." Hank's tone made it clear he understood the depths of her grief. He'd traveled that road himself. "And you went through it twice."

"I also have to face those times knowing I killed my first husband." Her words dripped with anguish.

To Hank's credit, he didn't recoil. Anna Mary's respect for him skyrocketed.

"Want to talk about it?" Hank asked.

Abe had asked her that same question, and she'd poured out her heartbreak over Josh's betrayal. His empathetic listening had lessened her pain. Maybe Mamm would respond to Hank's question the same way and heal her own suffering.

And she did. Through tears, she recounted the story she'd told Anna Mary.

As her mother finished, Hank pulled into Delores's

driveway and stopped. He turned toward Mamm and laid a gentle hand on her arm.

"Esther, it seems like you've paid for this every year since. We don't always know why God arranges our lives the way He does. But one thing I know for sure. If God had intended for your husband to move to New York, you could never have stood in the way of the Lord's will."

Mamm hung on Hank's words. "I never thought about it like that." She laughed shakily. "It makes me sound prideful. Like I think I'm more powerful than God."

Hank gave her arm a squeeze and let go. "Maybe it's time to ask for God's forgiveness for all the guilt and blame you've been carrying." He hesitated. "And it might also be time to forgive yourself."

Eyes full of wonder, she stared up at him. "I can't tell you how much this has helped. *Danke* for everything you did tonight." She tilted her chin toward Emmie's cast.

"I'm glad I could help." He slid his door open. "Stay there, and I'll take Emmie so you can get out."

All the worry and fear for Mamm that had been weighing down Anna Mary's soul lifted and floated away like a butterfly taking flight. She was grateful to Hank for being so understanding and for raising his son to be perceptive too. The Lord had given her whole family a blessing when He brought Abe into her life.

CHAPTER 25

Delores stood on the porch of an elegant three-story mansion, holding the door wide. Light from the propane lamp spilled out from the entryway behind her, illuminating thick white columns. She stared toward the buggy with an anxious expression. When Hank lifted the sleeping Emmie with a cast on her arm, Delores dithered on the steps.

"*Ach*, what happened?" she cried.

"Emmie had a little accident." Mamm tried to soothe her cousin's anxiety. "She'll be fine." Then she mumbled in an undertone, "And so will I. Thanks to you." She smiled up into Hank's eyes. "And to God."

"I'm so glad," he whispered, before turning to carry Emmie to the house. He called over his shoulder, "If you girls wait, I can get the other two."

But Mamm pulled the front seat forward and took Hannah from Sarah. After Sarah exited, she held Beth so Anna Mary could get out, but then Mamm didn't hand Beth back. All of them hurried after Hank, who had already introduced himself to Delores.

"Where do you want her?" He gestured with his chin to Emmie.

"Right up here." Delores motioned to the sweeping central staircase of the grandest mansion Anna Mary had ever seen. The ceilings soared at least twenty feet above them to embossed decorations surrounding an unlit chandelier dripping with crystal teardrops.

All of them stood in the spacious foyer, their mouths open, staring around at the marble floor, the intricately carved mahogany newel post and spindles, the unlit gold filigree sconces on the walls. Carved rosettes curved along the top edges of two matching love seats covered in maroon velvet nestled into niches on either side of the stairs.

Delores laughed nervously. "I forgot you'd never been here. I know it's a little odd for an Amish home."

Mamm recovered first. "When you said you and Paul had bought an abandoned house, I never pictured anything like this."

"*Jah*, well, it was quite the bargain. The furniture came with the house, but we bought it because Paul wanted the farmland." Her eyes grew sad. "He farmed it until the day he died."

Anna Mary tried to imagine a farmer with muddy boots tromping into this house, and she had to hold back a giggle.

"If only we'd had sons," Delores continued. "Neither of our daughters married farmers. I've been renting the land to an Amish neighbor."

Anna Mary tried to imagine the rest of the house. The only thing that didn't fit in the cavernous room was a rolling propane light like the one they used at home.

Delores noticed Anna Mary's gaze. "We didn't pull out the electricity because this is a historic home, but we've never had it turned on while we were here."

Hank nodded. He seemed to be the only one not gawking at the grandiose house. "Must need a lot of upkeep, eh?"

"For sure and certain." Her cheeks colored. "A carpenter-handyman from our *g'may* often stops by to do repairs." She motioned them to the stairs. "Let's get the little ones to bed."

They followed her up the wide staircase that wound upward to a floral-carpeted hallway. More sconces lined the walls. A carved table with lion's feet held several battery-powered DeWalt lights.

Delores picked one up. "Anna Mary, since you aren't carrying anyone, perhaps you could take another."

They padded down the hall with fifteen-foot ceilings to a door with a gold knob engraved with flowers. Delores opened it and ushered them inside. "I put the three little ones in here together."

The room held an old-fashioned white iron crib and two double beds with matching wrought iron headboards tucked under arched windows. Two massive armoires etched with floral designs on their doors rose majestically on either side of the room.

Anna Mary turned down the covers and removed Emmie's shoes. Hank slipped her onto the bed, covered her, and propped her cast on a pillow while Sarah lowered Hannah into the crib and pulled a light blanket over her. After Anna Mary helped Mamm get Beth into bed, Hank thrust his hands in his pockets.

"I'd better go. I'll bring in your suitcases." He turned to Anna Mary. "I'll be here at three thirty if you want to help with milking." He smiled. "But Abe and I will understand if you'd rather sleep later in these comfy beds."

"*Neh*, I want to go."

"Fine. I'll be here. Anyone else who wants to join us is welcome." He sent a questioning glance Mamm's way.

"Not tomorrow." She looked regretful. "I need to unpack, get the girls settled in, and catch up with Delores." She directed a fond smile at her cousin. "Perhaps we can bring the girls over to watch the afternoon milking."

"I'll look forward to that." Hank strode from the room. "I meant what I said about enjoying having children in the barn."

Delores called after him, "Take a DeWalt if you need one." Then she showed Sarah and Anna Mary to the bedroom they'd share and gave Mamm a room across from the three little ones. Hank distributed the suitcases and bags to the correct rooms and said one more goodbye.

Sarah and Anna Mary took a quick tour of the huge room with its own attached bathroom containing a claw-foot tub.

"Whoever built this house sure liked lions," Sarah said. "And flowers."

Anna Mary laughed, a sound that echoed around the high ceilings and bounced off the intricate floral wallpaper. They could explore more over the next few weeks, but now she needed some sleep. She couldn't wait to get back into the routine of milking with Abe. Tomorrow held so much promise Anna Mary wasn't sure she could relax enough to fall asleep. But she drifted off instantly to dreams of a future with Abe.

Abe's mouth dropped open when he reached Delores's house. Had he come to the right place? Daed had told him it was huge, but he was unprepared for this massive mansion. No wonder Delores didn't want to be alone in it. Why did people need such large homes?

When Anna Mary opened the door, he was glad he'd insisted on taking Daed's place this morning. It had been well worth it to wake an hour early. He'd have time alone with her as they drove back to the house. She told him about his *daed* helping her *mamm*, and once they pulled into his driveway, they prayed for her together. It was wonderful to have a spiritual connection along with their friendship and their love.

Abe smiled at her so often during breakfast that Tim teased him unmercifully. He and Anna Mary ignored Tim until he gave up. Milking went swiftly with four of them working.

After they'd all cleaned up, Abe and Anna Mary followed Daed's buggy to Delores's, where all her sisters rushed out the front door, begging to go to the farm. Esther gave them permission to return with Abe and Anna Mary. His *daed* planned to drive Esther a little later.

That hadn't been the original plan, but Abe didn't complain. He liked having the girls for company, and he hoped Daed might have some impact on Esther's decisions about Anna Mary.

He leaned close to her to whisper, "So Daed plans to talk more to her about children growing up and going off on their own."

She shifted Emmie on her lap to tip her head closer to his. "Great! Mamm seemed to understand his earlier hints." She was holding Emmie to make more room in the back seat and to keep Emmie's cast from getting banged and bumped.

Emmie didn't seem to worry about that. She barreled out of the buggy as soon as it stopped and raced her sisters to the pasture fence.

"Don't you dare climb that fence again, Emmie." Anna Mary's words cracked out like a whip.

Emmie halted for a second, then sprinted to keep up with Sarah and Beth. One fist clenching Anna Mary's dress, Hannah toddled beside her older sister as she helped Abe unhitch the horse.

"I'll watch them," Sarah called, and Anna Mary nodded.

When they finished, Abe scooped up Hannah. "Why don't we go for a walk?"

Anna Mary glowed. "*Jah.*"

They strolled past the kitchen window. Tim's sad face stared out as they passed. He must not have heard the buggy pull in.

Abe stopped and mouthed, *Sarah*. He pointed to the backyard.

Tim raced out the back door like a shot. When he noticed them watching him, he slowed and ambled around, acting as if he hadn't noticed the three girls by the fence.

"Stop watching him," Anna Mary murmured. "He won't walk over there until he's sure we aren't spying on him."

"You're making me feel like Cathy Zehr," Abe complained.

She laughed. "You don't look anything like her."

"That's not what I meant, and you know it." He paused. "But I must admit, I'm more like Cathy than I care to admit. I'd love to know what Daed and your *mamm* are talking about."

"I hope they're talking about letting me visit more often. Or even . . ." Anna Mary hesitated, as if saying her thoughts aloud might cause something bad to happen.

When he gave her a questioning look, she clammed up. "Come on. I tell you everything."

"I woke with an idea this morning. Delores mentioned she wants to turn her house into a bed-and-breakfast."

"House? Mansion, you mean?"

"*Jah*, mansion. And she doesn't like being alone. I could offer to stay and work with her. I'd miss Mamm and my sisters if they went back. And my best friend, Caroline. But now that they have help at the stand—"

Abe didn't give her time to finish her thought. He cut in. "That's a brilliant idea. Why don't we ask your *mamm* when she gets here?"

"Maybe we should wait until I check with Delores. She does dislike being alone in that big house. All right, mansion." She corrected herself before he could. "So she might be willing to have company even before she converts it."

Abe's pulse rapped triple-time at the thought. If Anna Mary lived nearby, they could—

He didn't get to finish his future plans, because Daed and Esther turned into the driveway, chatting and beaming at each other. They seemed to be getting along really well. Maybe too well? If that was possible.

Anna Mary studied them closely. "Do you think . . .?"

"I was wondering the same thing." Maybe he was only imagining things because he was in love himself, but Daed and Esther seemed to be having more than a friendly conversation. How might that impact Abe's relationship with Anna Mary?

On the one hand, they'd probably get to spend more time together. On the other, it would be odd if Daed and Esther married. *Whoa.* Where had that thought come from? Abe pushed it from his mind.

Perhaps Daed was only charming Esther to ensure Abe could see more of Anna Mary. He relaxed. Daed would never do anything to mess up their relationship. But the bothersome thought returned when his father stayed so absorbed in his conversation he didn't get out of the buggy.

When Daed did finally step out, he and Esther unhitched the horse together, and he escorted her into the barn to get the horse accustomed to her. Should he and Anna Mary follow them?

Abe smirked.

"What's so funny?" Anna Mary demanded.

"What would Cathy Zehr do now?"

Anna Mary burst out laughing.

In the end, they didn't trail their parents, though they both wanted to. Anna Mary loved every minute of being with Abe, and hoped Delores's bed-and-breakfast might be the key to her future with Abe.

Hank grinned from ear to ear when the girls begged to accompany him to do the milking. He shot Mamm a triumphant look. "My dream come true."

Mamm looked happier and prettier than Anna Mary remembered seeing her in years. She stood in the doorway to the milking barn, cradling Hannah, as Hank and Abe taught the girls to wipe udders and squeegee the floor.

Emmie whined because she couldn't do the milking machine, but even cleaning udders proved challenging with one hand. When her arm ached, Hank improvised a sling using an old towel.

He tied it around her neck and patted her shoulder. "Maybe this'll help."

After he finished, Emmie threw her other arm around his neck and hugged him. "*Danke.*"

His eyes sparkled with moisture when he rose, and Mamm stared at him as if he were a hero.

Again, they finished in record time.

"Many hands make light work," Abe said as they turned the cows into the pasture. "If I had this many assistants every day, I could double the number of cows."

Anna Mary checked Mamm's reaction. A sad, faraway

look entered her eyes, but it disappeared when Hank swept everyone into the mudroom to clean dirty feet and boots, and she bustled into the kitchen to help Sarah with supper while the milkers went to clean up.

That night after the sun went down, Hank lit a fire in the pit in the yard, and they all sat around it toasting marshmallows and making s'mores. Anna Mary relaxed back beside Abe, mesmerized by the crackling flames, inhaling the smoky air as her sticky-faced little sisters stamped out stray sparks and giggled as they chased fire-flies.

Stars twinkled overhead. Logs snapped and popped. Crickets chirped and frogs croaked. The night sounds washed over Anna Mary, bringing a deep, abiding peace. Her soul sang along with nature's lullaby. How she wished they could do this every night.

The summer days drifted by in a haze of joyful mo-ments and companionship. Even Emmie, who usually caused disasters or got into trouble, mellowed out. Per-haps the hard work and early hours of milking drained her restless energy. She'd taken to following Hank around like a shadow, and he often stood with one hand on her shoulder. Or she tucked a hand in his as he walked the perimeter to check the fencing. She hovered beside him, handing him tools when he did repairs.

The whole family came for morning milking and stayed until nightfall. Even Delores had taken to join-ing them for the noon and evening meals. The women took turns cooking, and every meal was more delicious than the last.

"Do you miss making supper?" Anna Mary teased Abe one night.

He laughed. "What do you think? I'm eating better than I have since I started cooking, and milking's so much easier with all the extra hands. I feel lazy."

They all went to church together on Sunday, and Anna Mary accompanied Abe to singings. Even Tim joined them. It reminded Anna Mary of the first time she'd ridden with Tim and Abe, but now Abe drove and she sat up front next to him with Tim in the back.

Anna Mary still hadn't approached Delores about the bed-and-breakfast, but Abe and Anna Mary both paid close attention whenever Delores discussed her future plans. One Monday, her handyman friend scheduled a time to look over the building to take measurements and discuss renovations.

Abe offered to drive Delores home to meet with him. Anna Mary slid into the back seat to let her mother's cousin ride up front. Delores chattered to Abe about everything she wanted to do. Then she hit them with a bombshell.

"If I'm opening to *Englischers*, I wonder if it'd make sense to have electricity. The wiring's all there, although it may be too old and need to be replaced."

Anna Mary swallowed hard. "Electricity? Would your bishop agree?"

"I doubt it."

Gut. Anna Mary relaxed. Mamm had gotten upset about the hotel key card. She'd never let Anna Mary stay in a house with electricity.

Abe swallowed hard and looked reluctant to criticize. "Tourists often like to have the full Amish experience. My friends from church who rent out rooms to *Englischers* say they like to do chores."

"*Jah*, we have places like that in Lancaster." Anna Mary backed him up. "They're always booked full."

Delores laughed. "If people are looking for an authentic Amish experience, they won't book rooms in a historic mansion. They'd expect cows, horses, and chickens. I can't offer that. I only have one tired old buggy horse."

True. Thank heavens the bishop wouldn't agree.

The contractor had already arrived when they pulled in, and Delores ushered him into the formal dining room. Anna Mary and Abe joined them at the twenty-person dining table under another unlit chandelier. On this one, golden angels perched on an ornate filigree base and held tulip-shaped glass cups aloft. The heavy walnut furniture had carved leaves and flowers.

Peter, a quiet, unassuming Amish man, entered with a clipboard and pen. He jotted notes as Delores spoke. Occasionally, he'd offer an opinion.

When they reached the bathroom renovations, he suggested keeping all the original fixtures. "But I'm concerned about the hot water heater. The propane one you have handled your family and a few guests, but it's more than twenty years old. And *Englisch* guests won't be frugal with water. Not in a house that looks like this."

Together, they made lists of renovations.

"The heating system may need to be replaced as well," he said as he stood. "I'll work up the costs for that."

"One other thing." Delores didn't meet his eyes. "What would it cost to upgrade the electrical system?"

Peter's jaw dropped. "You can't be serious. Bishop Yoder would never allow it."

"I want a price," Delores insisted.

Clutching his clipboard, Peter spoke each word like a bullet. "I. Will. Not. Put. In. Electric."

"You know how to do it. You've installed it in all the homes in that new development."

"*Jah*, I know all about putting it in, but I won't do it in an Amish home. Especially not yours." His eyes held a world of hurt. "I can't believe you even asked."

She gave him a defiant look. "I'll find someone else who will."

"If you do, get them to do all these repairs. I won't touch any of them." He headed for the door. "Think long and hard about this. I don't want you to be shunned."

Would Mamm's cousin really defy the *Ordnung*? Anna Mary sat there in shock. If Delores went ahead with this, Mamm would never set foot in this house again. Nor would she let her daughters.

Anna Mary's perfect idea for staying near Abe had just gone up in smoke.

CHAPTER 26

When Abe and Anna Mary took Delores back to the farm, they both stayed silent as she reviewed the updates she hoped to make. She didn't seem to notice they weren't responding. Both of them had been excited about Anna Mary's plan to stay in New York. Now their hopes had been dashed.

They arrived back in time for afternoon milking. Afterward, they all gathered around the table. As they passed around a basket of homemade potato rolls Mamm had made, Hank smiled at her.

"These are delicious, Esther." He leaned over to help Emmie butter her roll. "That reminds me. The doctor in the emergency room said the cast should come off in about four weeks. Did you want me to make the appointment?"

Mamm's eyes expressed her gratitude for his thoughtfulness, but she shook her head. "We'll have to get it done in Lancaster. Our three weeks will be up soon."

"Couldn't you stay a little longer?" His question held a pleading note. "It would be best for the same doctor to see her."

Delores caught Mamm's eye. "You're welcome to stay as long as you want. I'm enjoying your company."

Abe eyed Anna Mary across the table. Once Mamm found out about the electricity, she might pack them up and drag them home.

The lines of disappointment on Hank's face smoothed into happiness. "You have a place to stay."

"As much as I'd love to stay"—her eyes met his—"Sarah starts school soon after we get back. And Anna Mary has already taken too much time off from her job."

"I see." Hank swallowed hard and stared down at his plate. "I'd hoped . . ."

Nobody got to hear what he'd hoped, because Beth upset her water glass. Emmie yowled when water splashed across her dinner plate.

Emmie pointed to her soggy roll. "Look what she did."

Hank placed a hand on her shoulder as Mamm and Anna Mary rushed to stop the flood. "We'll get you another one, Emmie."

Beth bawled. "My dress is all wet."

"We don't have any dry clothes here. We'll have to go back to Delores's." Flustered, Mamm dabbed at the puddle on the table with a dish towel.

Anna Mary used a cloth to dry the chair and swipe at Beth's dress. Sarah ran for the mop to clean the floor.

Over her shoulder, Mamm flashed Hank a sardonic look. "You said you missed having children around. How about now?"

With a serene smile, Hank kept a comforting arm around a sobbing Emmie as he buttered another roll. "This is what I missed most."

"Oh, you." Mamm turned back around. "We'll leave as soon as you finish your supper, Beth."

Sarah, who rarely complained, protested, "But we're having another fire tonight."

"We'll have to do it another time." For the first time in a long while, Mamm was firm and decisive. At Mamm's frown, Beth toned down her wail to sniffles and tried to eat her meal.

Anna Mary wanted to object, too, because they'd all have to go home in the buggy together. This day was turning into a nightmare.

Abe wasn't sure what he could do to help. Daed had comforted Emmie. Anna Mary and her *mamm* were cleaning and calming Beth. At the other end of the table, Hannah had fallen asleep with her head in the mashed potatoes. Abe hopped up and headed toward her before she slid off the stack of books with a pillow on top that she was seated on.

Cradling her in his arms, he carried her to the sink and sponged off her curls. When the damp cloth touched her forehead, she added her wail to those of the other two.

"Sorry," Abe said as everyone glanced in his direction. "I was trying to help."

Delores scraped her plate clean and rose. "We need to hitch up the horse. These kids are all overtired. The past few weeks of getting up early and staying up late is making them all cranky. Me too."

"Can someone hold Hannah?" Abe asked her. "I'll take care of the buggy."

To his surprise, Tim volunteered. Winning a smile from Sarah was his reward.

In a flurry of movement, the whole roomful of people scurried outside while Abe hooked up the buggy. Anna Mary jumped in to help.

Hank carried Emmie. "Delores is right. The children need more sleep. Everyone should sleep in tomorrow." He searched the crowd for Esther. "You too."

Anna Mary lifted a sad gaze to his. "I don't want to miss the milking tomorrow, but we'll all have to come together."

"*Neh*, you don't," Abe insisted. "I'll come get you. And you can stay now too. I'll run you home later."

Her joyous expression lit fireworks in his soul.

For the next few days, the little ones and Mamm slept in while Anna Mary and Sarah rose early to help with milking. Everyone else arrived mid-morning to assist with mucking out the stable while Mamm and Delores prepared the noon meal. Then they shared lunch at the picnic table in the yard, and after that, Abe took them sightseeing. They used two buggies to visit the falls, the old church, and other scenic sites. Everyone, including Mamm, enjoyed the trips.

Seated beside Hank in the buggy behind Abe's, Mamm sat straight and tall, a contented smile on her face. Whenever Anna Mary glanced back, Mamm and Hank appeared deep in conversation. Sometimes, they wandered off by themselves, just the two of them. Anna Mary and Abe did the same whenever they could.

After the outings, they all pitched in with afternoon milking while Mamm and Delores cooked supper. Mamm often made excuses to slip out to the milking barn, where she'd stand and watch everyone working together with a longing expression on her face. She especially loved watching Hank teaching Emmie and Beth.

Hank's gentleness and patience reminded Anna Mary of Abe. He, too, would make a caring father. If only they could stay this close after their three weeks ended. Everyone was obviously much happier together.

The only sad thing about each day was that it meant they were one day closer to going home. Anna Mary's heart railed against the coming departure. She didn't want to leave. Fort Plain now felt more like home than Lancaster.

The only one who seemed to want to head back was Mamm. Yet, when she spent time around Hank, she appeared delighted with his company.

So far, Delores hadn't moved forward with her renovation plans. She might be waiting until they left so the house wouldn't be under construction while they were staying here. She hadn't even mentioned the updates to Mamm. She probably realized Mamm would object. Anna Mary prayed Delores was reconsidering the electric.

Those hopes were dashed on the day before their departure.

While Abe and Hank were at Delores's that evening to put the little ones to bed, Peter arrived to drop off supplies. Anna Mary held the door, and Abe assisted him with carting in ladders, tools, and painting supplies.

"I'm glad you've given up that other fool idea," Peter said to Delores as he lugged in two ten-gallon paint containers.

Her jaw set in mutinous lines. "I'm not asking you to do it."

Peter stopped dead in his tracks, and Abe almost impaled him with a stack of two-by-fours. Abe pivoted to one side, just missing a lamp with a stained-glass shade. Anna Mary released a long breath of relief.

"Turn around and take those back to my truck," Peter commanded Abe, who stood there, confused.

"I told you I wouldn't do this job if you're installing electric."

"I'm not," Delores said. Then, after he passed, she muttered, "Not yet."

Her words shocked Anna Mary. "You lied to him?"

Delores turned prickly. "I didn't lie. Not exactly."

Under Anna Mary's searching gaze, Delores grew defensive. "I haven't made up my mind. And until I do, no electricity's being put in *yet*."

"Shouldn't Peter know that you're considering it?"

"My decisions are none of his business. Or yours."

She was wrong. It was Anna Mary's business. Until she had a commitment that Delores would never install electricity, Anna Mary couldn't offer to work here. Her future happiness depended on that promise, but more than that, she cared about Delores. "I don't want to see you do anything against the *Ordnung* or be shunned."

"That's my choice." Delores whirled around and stalked off.

Abe came upon Anna Mary standing in the hall, staring at a door that still vibrated after being slammed. "What's wrong?"

"I upset Delores. And on our last night here." Anna Mary turned toward him, her expression miserable. "I feel terrible after all she's done for us."

"I can't believe you'd do anything to hurt anybody. She probably took it wrong." He reached out to touch her arm to reassure her, but lowered his hand before he fell into that temptation. "You can always apologize."

Anna Mary nibbled her lip in that cute way she did when she was thinking. "I don't know if I can."

"Want to talk about it?" When she nodded eagerly, he motioned to the front door. "Why don't we take a walk?"

He'd been planning to ask her on a romantic, last-night-together stroll in the moonlight. He pushed aside his own desires. Right now, listening to Anna Mary's distress was more important.

His *daed* and Esther had headed into the garden earlier to talk, so to give them, as well as Anna Mary and himself, privacy, Abe escorted her outside and to a woodland path. Tall oaks and maples surrounded them, enclosing them in a quiet space.

"So what happened?" he asked once they entered the pine-scented bower.

Anna Mary repeated her conversation with Delores. "I guess she really is going through with it."

"Seems like we can't change her mind. But we can pray."

"You're right." Anna Mary glanced up at him gratefully. "I keep forgetting to turn my problems over to the Lord."

"Remember the verse Mrs. Vandenberg suggested to us. God can change an impossible situation to possible." He gave her a tender look, expressing all the love that filled him. "After all, I got a long trip to Lancaster, and you had three weeks here. Neither of us thought those visits were possible."

"That's true."

The magnetic pull of her moonlit eyes drew him toward her. He thrust his hands into his pockets to keep from reaching out and enfolding her in his arms the way he longed to do.

His voice husky, he tried to reassure her and himself. "If God made those miracles happen, He can work out other things, including more time together. And changing Delores's mind."

Anna Mary's soft sigh brought his attention to her kissable lips. If they stayed here any longer, he might forget all about the *Ordnung*'s rules.

"Maybe we should go back." *Before I give in to temptation.*

"*Jah*, Mrs. Vandenberg will be here at dawn tomorrow morning." Anna Mary's sad smile held a trace of humor. "I guess that means I'll get to sleep in."

Her words cut deep. It also meant that tonight was goodbye. He'd be milking when she drove away in the morning. "I'm going to miss you."

"I'll miss you too." Anna Mary's plaintive voice wrenched his insides.

Dear Lord, please help us find a way to stay together permanently.

CHAPTER 27

After Abe walked her back to the house and they said their final goodbyes, Anna Mary waved until he was out of sight. Then she shut the solid oak door and leaned her forehead against it, letting sadness crash over her in waves. Loneliness and loss overshadowed all the happy memories of the past three weeks.

For a long while, she drowned in despair. When would she see Abe again? Why did so many things seem to conspire against them? She'd been so happy here. If only she could find a way to stay. Mamm didn't know about Delores's tentative plans for electricity. If Anna Mary kept them a secret, she might be able to convince Mamm to let her stay here to work with Delores.

She shook her head. *Neh*, she couldn't lie to Mamm. Besides, Mamm needed her. Mamm had gotten so much better while she was here, but what if she fell apart when she got home? Sarah couldn't cope without Anna Mary's job and help. She had to go back to Lancaster, but everything in her ached to stay here. Here where her heart had found a home. Here where she'd be with her true love.

Anna Mary wrestled with her desires, but eventually surrendered to God's will for her life.

Please direct my steps, Lord, and make me willing to do whatever You have planned for me.

Although she should go up to bed, the solidness of the wood against her forehead reminded her of the Lord's strength and security. A phrase from the book of John kept running through her head: *I am the door.* In the tumult that was her life, Anna Mary clung to that steadiness of the Savior.

Lord, I'm leaning on You to get through this. I don't know why we live so far apart and have to endure so many separations, but I'm trusting You to work things out.

A still, small voice whispered to her heart: *Say the whole verse.*

Anna Mary tried to remember the rest. When it came to her, she smiled. It was as if that verse had been written for her situation. *I am the door: by Me if any man enter in, he shall be saved, and shall go in and out, and find pasture.*

Was this God's answer to her pleading heart? *Jah,* she believed the part about entering in and being saved, but she'd never paid attention to the rest. She had been going in and out. And back and forth. She loved the ending. *Find pasture.* The one place she longed to be had a pasture. Was the Lord sending her a sign?

The doorknob jiggled, and Anna Mary leapt back. Who would be coming in at this time of night?

Shoulders slumped and eyes filled with tears, Mamm fumbled her way in the house. With her hand over her mouth, she stifled small sobs.

"Mamm?"

A strangled scream came from Mamm's throat, and she pressed her hands to her chest. "Anna Mary?" she choked out. "I thought everyone would be in bed by now."

"What's the matter?"

Her mother shook her head and didn't answer. Anna Mary went to Mamm and laid a hand on her arm. Until now, Anna Mary hadn't realized how much she towered over her fragile, petite mother, who'd hunched over and shrunken into herself, making her even tinier.

"Come," Anna Mary said gently and led her mother to one of the Victorian settees.

After assisting Mamm onto it, Anna Mary sat close to her mother and took her hand. "What is it?"

Mamm pinched her lips tight. When Anna Mary pressed her again, her mother's clipped words cut off communication. "This is not something to discuss with a child."

"I'm grown now," Anna Mary pointed out. "Did Hank do something to hurt you?"

With a constricted *jah*, Mamm covered her face with her hands and hunched over as if in pain.

"What did he do?" Anna Mary's desperate whisper carried fear. Hank seemed so gentle, so kind. What could he have done to hurt Mamm like this? "Please, Mamm, tell me."

Each word seemed to be wrenched from her. "He . . . he asked me to . . . marry him."

Anna Mary sat in stunned silence. *Marry him?*

Why had that upset her mother? *Jah*, the suddenness of the proposal might be shocking. But it wouldn't leave Mamm crying.

Between tearful gasps, she explained, "He worries about me . . . being alone . . . with young children . . . to raise. He wants . . . to take care . . . of me . . . and the girls."

"But that's *wunderbar*. You and Hank get along so well."

"*Jah*, we do. He's . . . he's everything I've ever

wanted . . . in a man. Strong, but gentle . . . caring and
kind . . . God-fearing . . . upbeat . . . funny . . ."

Anna Mary interrupted the list of Hank's stellar attrib-
utes. From the sound of it, Mamm could go on and on. "If
he has all these *gut* qualities, why are you crying?"

Through Mamm's muffled wails, Anna Mary made
out the words *marriage of convenience.*

"He . . . he . . . must not . . . *love* . . . me."

Had Mamm fallen for Hank? Was that why his proposal
made her cry?

Anna Mary patted Mamm's shoulder. "He cares enough
to ask you to marry him. I'm sure he's met other widows
with children. He didn't offer to take care of them."

"He . . . pities me."

"Hank enjoys your company. I've never seen pity in
his eyes when he's around you."

Mamm didn't seem to hear Anna Mary's comment. "I
can't bear . . . another marriage . . . of convenience."

Another? Anna Mary stared at her weeping mother.
"Daed?" she asked hesitantly.

"*Neh.* Martin."

Martin? Anna Mary's stepfather?

"I thought . . . we'd get closer . . . after we married.
We . . . never did."

Looking back, Anna Mary recalled the coldness between them. Mamm had started her downward spiral into
depression soon after Emmie was born.

"I tried . . . so hard. But he never . . . responded."

Anna Mary squeezed her eyes shut to stop her own
tears. She'd buried those memories deep down after his
funeral, but now her stepfather's discontented, irritated
face swam before her.

Mamm swiped at her eyes. "People say love . . . can
grow . . . from friendship. But so can . . . resentment."

"It doesn't have to be that way."

"I couldn't stand it . . . if Hank glared at me. If he picked at . . . every little thing I did wrong. If he . . ."

"I don't think Hank is like that."

"Not now. But what if . . .?"

Anna Mary cut her off. "There's no way to know the future. Maybe you should pray about it."

"You're right." Mamm pushed herself to her feet on shaky legs, but her words were brisk. "We need to get to bed."

"Mamm?" Anna Mary hesitated, then spoke her mind. "Don't let the past interfere with your future."

"Easy for you to say. You didn't have to live through it."

"I just meant . . ."

"Leave it alone, Anna Mary." Mamm headed for the stairs. "Forget I said this. I never should have told you anything. Less said, sooner forgotten."

Anna Mary trailed her mother up the stairs, her mind whirling. Did Mamm mean she intended to forget Hank's proposal? It certainly sounded that way.

Abe and Daed did the morning milking in silence. Only the splash of milk against steel, the glug of the milker, and restless cows stomping or lowing made noise in the barn's stillness. Tim tried a few joking remarks, but he fell quiet when nobody responded.

Daed cleared his throat. "It's too quiet in here. I miss the girls' lively chatter."

So did Abe. And even more, he missed the lovely smiles he exchanged with Anna Mary as they worked.

After they turned the cows out into the pasture and mucked the barn, Abe went in to clean up and start the meal. Everywhere he went brought reminders of Anna

Mary. The canning jars lining the shelf. Her place at the table. The way she stood at the stove to cook. The loaf of bread on the counter she'd baked.

Daed came into the kitchen before Tim and sank into his chair. "I loved having everyone at the table. Even with the spills and messes and noise." He sighed heavily. "Guess we'll never have that again."

Abe turned from the grilled cheese sandwiches he was frying. He missed having Esther and Delores in the kitchen for every meal.

"I'm sure they'll be back. They seemed to enjoy themselves." Even Esther, who'd been so reluctant to travel, had blossomed into a relaxed, smiling woman.

Daed groaned and put his head in his hands. "I muddled that all up. I'm sorry, Sohn."

"What do you mean?"

"I misread things and made a terrible mistake."

Abe didn't understand his father. "Everything went well while they were here." Unless . . . Daed had offended Esther when the two of them were alone.

"I hope this doesn't mess things up between you and Anna Mary."

What could Daed have possibly done to hurt the relationship? "Even if you and Esther had a tiff, it won't come between Anna Mary and me, don't worry."

"It will if Esther won't let Anna Mary visit or be with you ever again."

"What did you argue about?" Nothing Daed did could break him and Anna Mary up permanently.

"We didn't fight about anything." Daed's voice dipped so low Abe could barely hear him. "I asked her to marry me."

"You what?" Unsure what else to say, Abe stared at

his *daed*. After only being with Esther for three weeks, Daed had proposed to her?

"I knew it was too soon. And sure enough, she turned me down."

For goodness' sake, what had his father expected?

"It was a peaceful God-given night strolling through the garden, and we were enjoying each other's company so much, I got ahead of myself. *Neh*, I got ahead of God. She was so upset she left me standing in the garden and rushed into the house without saying goodbye or even turning around."

"I'm sorry." Abe could sense Daed's deep hurt. Now wasn't the time to point out how inappropriate his actions had been or how startled Esther might have been when she'd only known him a short time. Later, after Daed could think more rationally, they could talk about it.

Until then, Abe had to clear up one thing. "Why would this affect my relationship with Anna Mary?"

Daed rubbed his forehead. "Before she ran inside, I asked if we could still stay friends, maybe write to each other or visit from time to time. She said she didn't want to hear from any of us again. Ever. It sure sounded like she was including you."

Esther might have spoken out of shock or disgust, but surely she didn't mean to include Abe in her angry statement. He refused to believe she'd forbid Anna Mary to see him again.

CHAPTER 28

The ride home from Fort Plain was somber. Not even Mrs. Vandenberg's jokes or Emmie's excited chatter about all their fun at the farm, punctuated by Beth's happy exclamations, lifted Mamm's or Anna Mary's moods.

After they sat at the restaurant table for lunch, Mrs. Vandenberg faced them both with a stern expression. "You two are acting as if God can't work miracles."

Anna Mary wanted to respond, *You don't know what we're dealing with.*

"I know perfectly well." Mrs. Vandenberg pinned Anna Mary with a searing gaze. "Until you have faith and trust God, how do you expect this to work out?"

She turned her attention to Mamm. "It's time you stopped feeling sorry for yourself and started paying more attention to others' needs. You might find your own get met too. But if you continue hiding in your shell to avoid getting hurt, you're going to end up a lonely, shriveled old lady."

Mamm's head snapped up. "What?"

"You know very well what I mean. All your thoughts are about protecting yourself. Think about what's best for everyone else involved."

A wounded look crossed Mamm's face. Then she ducked her head to study the menu. "I'll pay for my family's meal."

"It's already been paid for. If you want to pay me back, spend some time asking yourself what each person in the situation needs and wants. Consider what you can do to care for them, even if it frightens you."

"I don't know what you mean."

"Yes, you do. Stop hiding from the truth." Mrs. Vandenberg turned to Emmie and Beth. "What would you two like to eat?"

It seemed the discussion was over. Mrs. Vandenberg kept the conversation light and fun while they ate, and when they returned to the van, she said gently, "You two should do some soul-searching and spend time in prayer. I won't bring this up again, but I will be interceding for both of you. God will show you the next steps to take if you open your hearts and minds to all He has in store for you."

Anna Mary squirmed uncomfortably each time she remembered Mrs. Vandenberg studying her. As much as Anna Mary longed to have even mustard-seed-sized faith, each time she thought about Delores's electric and Mamm's refusal of Hank's offer, worry and doubt seeped in.

She needed to counterbalance that. For the last hour of the trip, she listed all the miracles in her life, all the good things that had happened, everything that brought her joy. As she expressed gratitude for each blessing, her happiness grew. So did her surety that whatever God brought into her life would work out for good, even if she couldn't see it right away.

* * *

The next day, Abe and his *daed* sat across from each other at the kitchen table, both writing letters. While Abe scribbled down all the thoughts in his head—all his happy memories of his time with Anna Mary, his longing to be with her, everything he missed about being together, his sorrow over being separated, and his daily activities since she'd left—Daed's stationery remained blank. Brow furrowed, he stared off into space.

He let out a long breath. "This is so hard."

"Write what's on your heart," Abe advised.

"That's what caused the trouble in the first place. I'm trying to figure out what went wrong. And how I can fix it."

"Why not just apologize?"

Daed brightened. "That would be a good start." He bent his head and scribbled quickly. After he stopped to reread it, he scribbled out places and squeezed in different wording.

Abe prayed Daed would get the right message across. It would be awkward if his father and Anna Mary's mother couldn't be around each other. At least they didn't live close to each other, where they'd run into each other every day. For the first time, Abe thanked the Lord for the one thing he'd railed against the most—the distance between himself and Anna Mary.

He jotted that thought in his letter to her and described his father's agony over the message he planned to send to her *mamm*.

> I hope your mamm *will find it in her heart to forgive him. He's really broken up about this. I've never seen him this distressed since Mamm died. He hasn't said so, but I think he fell hard for your* mamm. *He also really misses your sisters. The barn is so quiet. Much too quiet without them. And it's a lonely place for me without you here.*

On the other side of the table, Daed crumpled a page into a ball and tossed it toward the trash can. It bounced off the rim and landed on the floor. "Figures," he muttered as he went to retrieve it.

Abe had never seen his *daed* so upset with himself. After dropping the paper in the garbage, Daed sat, eyes closed and head bowed, for a long time. Abe joined him in prayer.

When Daed lifted his head, his eyes shone. "All I can do is confess the truth and ask forgiveness."

This time when he picked up his pen, it flew across the page. He even smiled when he finished. "I don't know how she'll take this, but being honest clears my conscience." He folded his paper and slid it into an envelope.

Abe did the same with his. After he addressed it, he slid it across the table so Daed could copy the information. Then Abe picked up both envelopes, added stamps from his supply from Mrs. Vandenberg, and whistled as he took the letters out to the mailbox. As he lifted the red flag, he hoped Anna Mary would be pleasantly surprised to receive a letter so soon after she went home. Abe didn't want to hold on to the news about his *daed* asking her *mamm* to marry him. And he couldn't wait to find out if Esther had told Anna Mary about it or had kept it a secret. He only hoped their parents' actions wouldn't drive a wedge between them.

Abe's letter arrived along with one addressed to Mamm from Hank. Nervousness gnawed at Anna Mary's stomach as she carried both envelopes into the house. She half expected Mamm to throw hers away unread, but her mother uttered a small cry and turned it over and over in her hands as if afraid of what it might contain.

Anna Mary took hers to her room to savor it in privacy.

She'd settled into the rocker and opened the flap when Mamm uttered a heartrending cry. Anna Mary tossed her letter on the bed and raced out to the living room, where Mamm sat, her hands covering her face. Her shoulders shook, and tears dripped out from between her fingers.

"Mamm?" Anna Mary sat beside her mother and slipped an arm around her shoulders, reminding her of their last night in Stone Arabia.

All her sisters raced into the living room and stood in a circle a short distance from Mamm, distress written on every face.

"I've been a fool," Mamm blubbered.

The letter had floated to the floor, and Anna Mary stared at the heartfelt words in disbelief.

Dear Esther,

I'm so sorry for springing my proposal on you. I acted impulsively because I'd fallen in love with you and didn't want to lose you. I never considered what an impossible situation I'd put you in. I thought by offering marriage it might give you time to come to love me in return. But I should have realized your feelings may never match mine. Can you ever forgive me?

I understand if you never want to speak with me again. But I hope we can put this behind us and go back to being friends. I really enjoyed my time with you, and you seemed to have fun too. If nothing else, can we at least be cordial acquaintances for the sake of our children?

Very truly yours,
Hank

Anna Mary squirmed with guilt for reading Mamm's private letter. But now that she had, she might be able to help her mother better. Mamm had not wanted a marriage of convenience. Hank had dispelled that fear. Her mother should be overjoyed.

"Mamm, I'm sorry. I shouldn't have done it, but I just read the letter. Hank says he loves you."

"That makes it even worse."

Worse? How could finding out someone loved you make anything worse? Unless Anna Mary had misunderstood Mamm's feelings for Hank.

"You don't love him?" Anna Mary asked as gently as she could.

Mamm ignored her question. "Maybe it's for the best. If I'd known he loved me, I'd have accepted his proposal right then. Thinking he was asking for a marriage of convenience stopped me. I didn't want to go into another marriage with a man who pitied me."

"So now that you know the truth, you'll—"

"That kept me from making a huge mistake."

"Mistake?" Anna Mary was confused. If they both loved each other . . .

"I don't want to live in New York." Mamm emphasized each word.

Emmie pouted. "We do. We all like it there."

"And I don't want ever to marry." A shrill note crept into Mamm's tone. "I can't go through that again."

Anna Mary wanted to be understanding, but she couldn't follow Mamm's reasoning.

"Besides . . ." Mamm sniffled. "He took back his marriage proposal. He wants to be acquaintances. I can't do that."

So many *I can't*s. Anna Mary shook her head. Mrs.

Vandenberg had once scolded Caroline for saying *I can't*.
Anna Mary repeated Mrs. Vandenberg's wise words,
"You can do anything with God's help."

"Maybe I should have said I don't want to." With a
whimper, Mamm snatched up the letter and retreated to
her room.

Anna Mary stood there uncertainly. Should she go
after Mamm? Or leave her alone for a while? Maybe
giving her some time to sort out her feelings would be
best.

She hurried to her room and read Abe's letter. He reinforced his *daed's* feelings for Mamm. Anna Mary's heart
ached for Hank. And for Mamm. They both cared for
each other, but seemed to be working at cross-purposes.

Anna Mary poured her confusion at Mamm's reaction
onto the page. *I'll talk to her later to find out why she's
so set against marrying your* daed *when she seems to
care for him.* Anna Mary avoided the word *love* despite
being pretty sure that most closely represented Mamm's
true feelings.

But later, after Mamm had calmed down, Anna Mary
confronted her mother. "You love Hank, don't you?"

Mamm set her lips and refused to answer, but Anna
Mary persisted until Mamm finally said, "That's what
makes this so hard." She refused to meet Anna Mary's
eyes.

Anna Mary followed her into the kitchen. "What's hard
about it? You didn't want a marriage of convenience.
Abe's saying it's not."

"I don't want to get married again. And I certainly
can't be friends with Hank."

"Why not?"

Mamm stared up at Anna Mary as if she wasn't one
hundred percent. "I can't be around him without letting

my real feelings show. If he finds out I lo—care for him, he'll persist. One thing I know for sure and certain: Hank King won't let the matter drop if he finds out the truth."

Anna Mary couldn't believe Mamm was denying herself happiness. It made no sense.

Her face set in tortured lines, Mamm said, "I think it's best if we cut off contact completely with the whole King family, including Abe."

"You can't forbid me from seeing my boyfriend because you're afraid of your feelings for his *daed*. That's unfair."

"I don't want you going to New York again. I can't afford to lose you."

No way would Anna Mary accept that ultimatum. She had to honor her mother, but did that commandment count if your parent made an unjust decision?

When Anna Mary's letter describing her *mamm*'s decision arrived, Abe read through it several times. None of it made sense to him. He waited until after morning milking to approach his father.

"Daed, I have to go and see Anna Mary. Straighten things out. Even if it's just for a few days."

"What's the problem?"

Many emotions chased across Daed's face as Abe explained what Anna Mary had written. "Sounds like I need to go too." Sad lines deepened the crevices in Daed's weather-beaten face. "But you should be first. As long as Tim's here, we can handle the milking. It'll go a lot slower, but this is important. I'll call Myron tonight."

And that night, Abe once again found himself on a train to Lancaster. Only this time, he didn't stand in the stations bewildered. He strode to where he needed to go with purpose and determination.

Last time, he'd been determined to persuade Esther to let Anna Mary come to New York, and with Mrs. Vandenberg's and God's help, Esther had brought the whole family to Fort Plain for three weeks. His goal for this visit was to convince Esther to lift her ban on spending time with his family, and deep down, he also hoped to plead his father's case. If Anna Mary was right and Esther did love Daed, Abe and Anna Mary needed to find out what was holding her back. Only God could change Esther's heart and mind, but Abe planned to do whatever he could to assist. Perhaps he could also enlist Mrs. Vandenberg. With divine intervention and earthly helpers, Abe hoped they could resolve this misunderstanding and bring happiness to both families.

CHAPTER 29

When he walked into the Lancaster station, expecting his *onkel*'s driver to pick him up again, Abe came face-to-face with Mrs. Vandenberg.

"Don't tell me," Abe said, "God warned you that I'd be arriving here this morning."

Mrs. Vandenberg's chirpy laugh attracted several glances. "This time, God sent me a phone call from a human. Your father suggested you might want some backup."

"Daed?" Abe couldn't believe it.

"He and I had some conversations about my match-making. But if he hadn't contacted me, I'm sure God would have given me a nudge. You're the key to several romances I'm assisting Him on."

Abe blinked at her. What on earth—?

"Don't look so shocked. In God's timing, you'll see."

At the moment, Abe only had one romance on his mind. Well, maybe two.

"Two to start," she assured him. "But I know of four you'll play a hand in. Maybe five."

Huh? Abe didn't even know three couples he could match besides Daed and him.

"Sometimes you might just be the messenger. Other times you'll play a bigger role." She motioned for him to follow her out of the station. "No time for lollygagging. We have work to do. I imagine you'd like to see Anna Mary."

That quickened Abe's steps. He took Mrs. Vandenberg's arm to help her over the uneven ground outside, and the driver assisted her into the Bentley. When they pulled up outside the market, she turned to him.

"We'll wait, but don't take too long. Saturdays are extremely busy. We'll drop you at Myron's and then bring you back to the market at closing time."

Abe had been hoping to stay longer at the market, but it was packed. He couldn't even get near Hartzler's chicken stand. As he stood there trying to figure out how to attract Anna Mary's attention without distracting her from all the customers, a hand clamped on his arm.

Abe jerked away, but the hand gripped like a vise. He turned to see the gossip, Cathy Zehr.

"Come with me," she commanded. "I have something for you."

He wasn't sure he wanted anything she had to offer, but if he jerked away, he'd knock into someone in this crowd. Cathy dragged him past the quilt stand and into a small niche beyond it. A wooden sign decorated with musical notes and reading *Dough-Re-Mi* was displayed above a small glass case filled with donuts.

When she saw him staring at her sign, she explained, "I love to sing, so . . ."

Abe had to admit it was clever, but he needed to get away.

Cathy must have sensed he wanted to escape, because she looked at him with pleading eyes. "Could you take something to your *onkel* for me?"

"Myron?" What in the world?

"Do you have any others?" she asked tartly.

Actually, Abe had plenty, but only one in the area. He waited while she filled a box with a dozen donuts. Then she placed an envelope on top.

"I need him to do something for me. I hoped this might sweeten him up."

Abe gulped. He hoped she wasn't trying to attract his *onkel*'s attention. The last thing Myron needed in his life was a gossip like Cathy. Not that he'd take notice of any woman, but if he did, Abe guessed she'd be at the bottom of the list.

"*Danke*," she called after Abe as he wove his way back to Hartzler's.

Anna Mary's mouth flew open when she caught sight of him. He couldn't get close enough to talk to her, so he mouthed that he'd see her at closing. She nodded, her eyes dancing and her face alight. He stood near the exit doors gazing at her beauty as people pushed past him. Not until he'd been elbowed by six or eight people did he wave goodbye and head out to the Bentley.

Mrs. Vandenberg smiled at the bakery box in Abe's hands. "I see Cathy found you." She nodded in satisfaction. "I told her I'd be bringing you by this morning."

Had she set up this meeting? Abe hoped not. Otherwise, it didn't bode well for his *onkel*.

"Cathy has an ingenious idea. She always did have an unusual way of looking at the world. It might actually work well if you can convince Myron to agree."

Abe preferred to suggest his *onkel* run the other way, but if Mrs. Vandenberg wanted him to help, he'd at least try.

When they arrived at Myron's house, he wasn't home. He'd left a note saying he had a meeting, but he'd be back by noon. Abe set the bakery box on the kitchen counter, dropped his duffel bag in the bedroom where he usually stayed, and fixed several sandwiches. He also warmed up some chicken corn soup for his *onkel*.

Myron did a double take when he walked in and spotted two bowls on the table. "You're eating here?"

His *onkel*'s obvious pleasure bothered Abe's conscience. "I'm sorry I wasn't around much last time I was here."

"Didn't expect you to be. You're here for a reason, and that reason's over there." Myron waved a hand in the direction of Anna Mary's house.

"I shouldn't have ignored you. I'm sorry."

"Nothing to be sorry about. That *maedel* should have all your attention. It's only right and fair."

Neh, it wasn't. Although Abe wanted to be with Anna Mary every second of the day, he shouldn't have neglected his *onkel*. He stirred the noodles. Bits of celery and carrot floated to the surface of the broth, scenting the air with chicken.

"I want to be with you too," Abe said as his *onkel* pulled out a chair. He should make time for Myron as well as Anna Mary and her family.

"I'm honored." His *onkel*'s voice grew husky.

Abe ladled the soup into the bowls and set sandwiches on their plates. Then he sank into his usual chair.

When they lifted their heads following the prayer, Myron studied Abe's face. "What's the matter? You look so glum."

Abe spilled all the details about his *daed* and Esther. How they'd fallen for each other and how Daed had asked her to marry him.

Myron nodded. "Your *daed* told me he planned to do

that. He didn't mention a word about it afterward, so I figured it must not have gone well."

"You were right. While Esther visited, Daed was happier than I've ever seen him since Mamm passed. But Esther has cold feet. She's lost two husbands. Anna Mary says her mother fears marrying again and losing a third."

Rubbing his chin, Myron stared at the table. "I understand how she feels." He cleared his throat. "Guess I'm not the best person to give advice on this because I've done the same. Shut myself off from pain. When you do that, you wall yourself off from all love."

If anyone should know about that, it'd be Myron. After his fiancée had died, he never dated anyone. But he also might have some thoughts on how to break through that fear. It couldn't hurt to ask. "Do you have any idea how to help her?"

Myron gazed off into the distance. "Only thing I can suggest is give her time."

How much time? Myron had shut down for twenty-five years after his loss. Daed couldn't wait that long. Neither could Abe and Anna Mary.

"You know," Myron said, his voice rusty, "I've been thinking I made a mistake. God didn't mean for a man to be alone. If I had a wife, maybe Tim would of turned out better."

Abe started to protest, but Myron held up a hand. "If I'd married, Tim woulda had regular meals, someone to read him bedtime stories, someone to tuck him in bed at night, someone to—" Myron's voice broke.

Abe's heart went out to his *onkel*. "You did what you could."

Myron shook his head. "*Neh*, I failed him in so many ways. I was too wrapped up in my sorrow to help him deal

with his. I hope Esther doesn't make the same mistake."
He fell silent, lost in thought.

Abe didn't want to interrupt Myron's contemplation,
so he sat quietly, even though he was itching to get up
and return to Anna Mary.

After a while, Myron came out of his reverie. "Regretting the past won't change the future. Only doing things
differently in the present can do that." He finished the last
of his chicken corn soup and stood.

That wisdom made sense. What could Abe do differently now that might change his future?

"What's that big box on the counter? Snacks from
your trip? Anything we can have for dessert?"

Abe started. "*Ach*, I was supposed to give you that."
He hopped up and brought the box to the table. "Cathy
Zehr from the farmer's market asked me to give this to
you."

At her name, Myron's lip curled slightly. He straightened it out, obviously regretting he'd made his distaste
obvious.

His *onkel*'s reaction surprised Abe. Cathy wasn't in
their *g'may*. "You know her?"

"*Neh*. But I know *of* her. Tim's had some run-ins with
her. I understand she's an awful gossip." He picked up
the envelope. "A note too?"

He read it, his eyes widening. "What is this? A prank
Tim cooked up?"

"*Neh*, it's really from Cathy."

"Please don't tell Tim this because it might encourage
him to do more, but I think this is one of his cruelest
jokes." Myron looked crushed. "I can't believe you agreed
to take part after everything I just confided in you."

"Myron, I don't know anything about this. What does
the note say?"

"Read it for yourself." He tossed it toward Abe.

Abe stared in shock. The handwriting was definitely a woman's. But at her request, Abe's stomach turned. She asked if she could meet Myron tomorrow after church to ask his advice. Her nephew, a single father, needed her to watch his two unruly boys, ages seven and eight. She'd like to talk to Myron about how he parented Tim after he adopted him at age seven.

Poor Myron. How could Cathy be so cruel? Everyone in the family and the *g'may* knew Myron had struggled to raise Tim. They had such an antagonistic relationship, Tim often threatened to run away and had disappeared several times. He always came back, insisting he'd only returned because he wanted to be around here for his sister. Tim did care deeply about his sister, but Abe suspected Tim had run out of money or a warm, safe place to sleep.

"I'm sorry. I never would have brought this home from the market if I'd known." Abe crumpled the note and threw it away.

"Take the box to your girlfriend's family. I can't bear to throw away food, but I'll never touch one of those woman's donuts. The little girls don't need to know the poison that came with those sweets."

Although Abe had no idea why Cathy had done something to hurt Myron, he intended to protect his *onkel*. If Cathy showed up tomorrow, she'd face both Abe and Myron.

Myron stood. "Best get the dishes cleared away so's you can get back to your girlfriend."

Abe grabbed his plate and glass and headed for the sink, but Myron blocked his path.

"I'll take those. You go on. Spend as much time as you can with your girl."

"*Danke*." Abe intended to follow that advice. Mrs. Vandenberg had just pulled in to the driveway.

As he headed for the door, Myron said, "If you think it would help, I could talk to Esther."

It couldn't hurt, and Myron might give Esther something to think about. "That'd be great if you want to try." So far, Abe and Anna Mary hadn't been successful in convincing Esther to give up her fears.

"And don't forget to pray," Myron called before the door swung shut.

That was the best advice ever, and Abe followed it right then and there.

Anna Mary's heart skipped a beat when Abe returned just before closing. She couldn't believe he was here again. God really had made all things possible. Abe helped with the cleanup so she'd get done faster, and Gideon thanked him for scrubbing the rotisserie, which was the worst job of all.

Abe laughed. "It doesn't compare with mucking stalls." He whispered to Anna Mary as they headed for the buggy, "When you're working beside me, any job seems easier. I've missed you in the milking barn."

She swallowed the lump in her throat. "I feel the same way. I hope we can convince Mamm to let me visit New York again." She stopped to stare up at him. "That is why you're here, isn't it?"

"*Jah*, and to see if there's a way to change your *mamm*'s mind about Daed."

Anna Mary nodded. "I guess the donuts are for the girls. They'll be thrilled."

"Actually," Abe said, "they're from Myron." At her surprised frown, he explained.

She shook her head. "Cathy often hurts people's feelings with her bluntness and her rumors, but I can't believe she'd be that cruel. I guess we'll find out tomorrow afternoon."

Abe's face lit up. "You're coming?"

"I want to be there for your family the way you've been there for mine."

He looked as if he wanted to take her in his arms, and Anna Mary wished for a moment she were *Englisch* and could hug him back. How long would they have to wait until they could marry?

She drew her thoughts up short. Abe hadn't even asked her that question yet. They'd only started courting officially a short while ago, and they'd still had to find a way to make a future together with all the obstacles in their way.

When they got to her house, Anna Mary again asked him to stay out of sight when she first opened the door and held out the bakery box. The last time she'd surprised her family with Abe's visit, he'd brought soft pretzels. This time, he had a dozen donuts, courtesy of Cathy Zehr.

Her sisters squealed when they saw the donuts, but their shrieks increased when Abe appeared. Mamm rushed into the kitchen to see what was going on.

"Abe?" she faltered. "I—I thought . . ."

"You'd never see me again?" Abe finished her sentence. "Not allowing Anna Mary to come to New York ever again won't keep us apart, Esther. We'll find a way to be together because we love each other."

Mamm winced at the word *love*, but Anna Mary's spirits fizzed with gladness.

"Time for supper," Sarah announced, setting one more place at the table.

Everyone clamored to sit by Abe. Only Mamm stood apart, stoic and pale.

Conversation stayed light during the meal and dessert. Abe helped with dishes and bedtime stories, but once the little girls had gone to bed, Mamm excused herself, saying she was tired.

Abe looked disappointed. He must have hoped to talk to her tonight, but Anna Mary wanted time alone with him. They went for a walk and discussed what they'd say to Mamm.

Tomorrow would be a busy day. After church, they'd save Myron from Cathy's nastiness and then confront Mamm. Anna Mary rejoiced that there'd be one bright spot after their draining afternoon—going to the singing with Abe. She couldn't wait for that. As for the rest, they prayed about it together.

CHAPTER 30

Anna Mary loved seeing Abe sitting across from her in church. Her gaze strayed in that direction too many times, and she had to keep pulling her focus back to the minister. She longed for the day when she and Abe would be in the same church together every Sunday. With him here in Lancaster today, it suddenly seemed much more possible.

During their long separation, she'd thought being with him would be impossible, but like the Scripture promise Mrs. Vandenberg kept reminding them of, God had made it possible for them to see each other often. In fact, over the past two months, they'd spent more time together than apart. That alone was a miracle!

Now she and Abe were praying for two more miracles—changing Mamm's mind about her ban on travel to New York and about turning down Hank's proposal. Anna Mary said a quick prayer that God would work things out for the best, then turned her attention back to the next sermon.

After the church meal, Anna Mary and Abe headed to Myron's. He'd arrived home from his church before them and was pacing up and down in the living room.

He wrung his hands. "I should have told her *neh*. Why didn't I?"

Abe leaned close to Anna Mary and whispered in her ear, "He usually does his best to avoid being around women. So this, plus discussing his parenting of Tim, is doubly hard."

Anna Mary nodded. The strained lines on Myron's face made her pity him. She still couldn't believe Cathy had done something this hurtful.

At the crunch of buggy wheels outside the window, Myron winced. He managed a semblance of a smile when she strode to the front door bearing a bakery box.

She thrust it at him. "They're day-olds, of course, but I thought I should give you something for the help you'll be giving me."

Without being invited, she marched past Myron into the living room and plopped onto a chair. Her eyebrows rose a little when she noticed Anna Mary and Abe. "You two coming for some parenting advice too?"

Anna Mary gasped. Abe hurried over and took the bakery box from his *onkel*, whose nerveless fingers were about to drop it. He set it on the kitchen counter and returned to take a seat on the couch near Anna Mary, but not within touching distance. She released a silent sigh at his discretion. No need to give Cathy anything more to gossip about.

"I'm Cathy Zehr." She thrust out her hand to Myron, who looked as if someone had asked him to pet a poisonous snake.

"I know." He gave her a limp handshake, rushed to the farthest spot across the room, and dropped into a rocker.

Cathy cleared her throat. "I wasn't sure you knew me. You've never stopped at my market stand." She almost seemed hurt. "I guess you got my message?" Without waiting for a response, she plowed on. "As I said in my note, my nephew needs me to watch his boys." She swallowed hard, and her eyes misted.

Anna Mary felt a stab of pity for the lonely gossip. She truly cared about her nephew.

"He—he . . ." Cathy took a breath that did little to calm the underlying trembling in her voice. "He'll be going to Mexico for several months for a cancer treatment. I've never spent much time around children, so I need some advice."

Take-charge, bossy Cathy asking for advice seemed so out of character. Anna Mary tried not to gape.

Myron shook his head. "I'm the last person who can help. I knew nothing about parenting when Tim and his sister came to live with me, and I still don't."

"That's exactly why I chose you."

All three of them stared at her.

"Tim was unruly just like my two nephews. And he was around seven, right? My nephew's two boys are seven and eight. Almost the same situation."

"*Jah*, he was seven and quite a handful. But I already told you, I didn't know what to do, how to handle him. And—"

Cathy cut him off. "Perfect. So we're in the same situation. I don't have any idea how to handle them either."

"I don't see how I can help you." Myron hung his head. "I failed with Tim. He rebelled and ran wild. I—"

"Perfect. You're exactly what I need."

Myron's eyes bugged out. "That doesn't make sense. I'm the last—"

Again, she cut him off. "You made mistakes. Bad mistakes raising Tim. I want you to tell me everything you did. Then I won't make the same mistakes."

The other three sat in stunned silence. Had she just said that?

Myron's low groan ended on a snicker. Then a rusty chuckle came from deep within his chest and grew to a full-blown belly laugh. Finally, he wiped his eyes and spoke. "First time I was ever asked that. Might be the smartest way to go about it. If that's the kind of advice you're after, I have plenty of it."

"*Gut.*" Cathy stood. "When do you want to meet for our first lesson?"

He gulped and looked trapped. "Um . . ."

Anna Mary thought he might say *never*.

As usual, Cathy took charge. "Tomorrow after we both get off work?" She glanced at Abe and Anna Mary. "I'm guessing you'll be spending the whole day together since the market's closed."

Abe and Anna Mary's eyes met, and they both hesitated. Neither of them wanted to share their plans with a gossip.

Without waiting for a response, Cathy galloped on. "I'll bring supper since I assume they"—she waved toward Anna Mary and Abe—"will be too busy. I hope you like spaghetti and meatballs and garlic bread."

Myron gurgled something that might have been a *jah*, or possibly a hairball stuck in his throat.

Cathy sailed to the door. "See you at six." A few seconds later, the door slammed behind her.

The chair rocked back, and Myron groaned. "She sure don't give you time to answer her questions."

Abe studied his *onkel*. "You're really going to do this?"

"Seems like I don't have much choice."

"You could tell her *neh*," Anna Mary suggested.

Myron chortled. "She don't seem like a woman to take

neh for an answer." Then he sobered. "Might make up for the many errors I made with Tim. Perhaps God's giving me a second chance to get things right."

"Second chances can be a good thing," Abe said.

"Definitely," Anna Mary agreed. Abe had been her second chance at love, and what a *wunderbar* experience that had been. "Sometimes it takes a mistake to make things much better the next time."

Abe beamed at her. Was she thinking what he was thinking? He'd been her second chance. It delighted him that she'd had a much better experience this time around.

"Speaking of second chances," Myron said, "don't we have someone else who needs one?"

They sure did. Now that Myron had gotten his, it was time to concentrate on Daed's. Abe bowed his head.

Lord, if it's Your will for Daed and Esther to get together, please give us the right words to say to help Esther see the truth.

When he looked up, Myron was smiling at him. "*Gut* idea. We can use all the heavenly help we can get." He picked up the box of donuts and handed them to Anna Mary. "If your sisters won't mind day-old donuts?"

"They'll love them. *Danke.*"

"Don't thank me. Thank Cathy Zehr."

As they exited the house, Anna Mary whispered to Abe, "I wonder what Cathy would think if she knew my sisters were eating all her donuts."

He laughed. "We won't tell her."

On that light note, they got into her buggy, and she passed him the bakery box. Myron followed behind so they wouldn't have to drive him home before the singing. Abe still couldn't believe he'd be going to another singing with Anna Mary. This time in Lancaster. Last time, they'd been in Fort Plain. He thanked the Lord for all the chances they'd had to be together and prayed for many more.

When they arrived at Anna Mary's house, the little girls swarmed the bakery box he held. Abe was happy to see Esther hadn't retreated to her bedroom for a nap. He introduced his *onkel*.

Then he added, "He's my *daed*'s brother."

"I could tell." Tiny creases formed between her eyes. After a quick handshake and hello, she looked away.

Maybe Myron's resemblance to Daed bothered her. Myron was a rougher cut version of his father, but they had many of the same mannerisms.

"I can see why my *bruder* fell in love with you."

Myron's boldness shocked Abe. His *onkel* had always been awkward around women, but that comment had been tactless and inappropriate. He hoped Cathy's visit hadn't scraped away the few manners his *onkel* had.

To Abe's surprise, Esther colored and seemed pleased by the compliment. "He's a *wunderbar* man."

"Why don't we go into the living room?" Anna Mary suggested. She put a few donuts on a plate for their company and whispered to Sarah to keep the girls in the kitchen with the rest of the box. Her sister nodded, and the adults filed out of the kitchen.

Once they'd settled into their seats, Myron opened the conversation. "It's been painful hearing my *bruder*'s heartache over losing you."

Esther drew in a sharp breath, and her face contorted. "I can't . . ."

"Do you love him?"

At Myron's probing question, Esther hunched into herself. "I don't think that's your business."

"It is if my *bruder*'s suffering."

She flinched, but didn't respond.

Myron plunged on. "If the answer's *neh*, I'll tell him to stop torturing himself and move on."

Esther paled and twisted her hands in her lap. That comment seemed to have hit her like a blow.

But his *onkel* didn't let up. "So what's the answer? *Jah* or *neh*?"

Head down, words barely audible, Esther admitted, "*Jah*." Then she murmured, low enough that only Abe, who was sitting closest to her, heard, "With all my heart."

Abe's heart ached. Had she ever told his father that? Most likely not, or Daed would have been on her doorstep instead of Abe. And Daed would never stop until he'd persuaded her to marry him.

Anna Mary had written to Abe, saying she believed her *mamm* was in love, but Daed had dismissed that as an attempt to comfort him. If only he'd heard it from Esther's lips. Abe wished Daed could be here with them now.

Myron asked the question Abe had been wondering about. "Have you ever told Hank?"

Esther's fingers pinched ridges in her apron. "*Neh*," she mumbled.

"Don't you think he deserves to know? He's broken-hearted over you rejecting him, convinced he'll never be *gut* enough for you."

She gasped. "That's not true. I'm the one who's not *gut* enough for him. I—"

He waved a hand to cut her off. "If you've never told him that or that you love him, what else would he think?"

"I never wanted him to think this is his fault," Esther cried. Distress carved lines in her face. She held out an imploring hand.

Abe wanted to comfort her, but his *onkel* pressed on before Abe could stop him.

"What else is he supposed to think?"

"I—I don't know."

At her plaintive voice, Anna Mary leaned over to take her *mamm*'s hands in hers.

"Don't coddle her," Myron commanded.

Abe frowned at his *onkel*. If this was an example of Myron's parenting techniques, no wonder Tim had turned out rebellious.

Anna Mary ignored Myron's barked order, and Abe smiled at her to offer his support.

He turned to his *onkel*. "A little love and caring can sometimes encourage people to change."

"Cathy Zehr taught me a lesson today about confronting people."

Esther's head jerked up and she mouthed, *Cathy Zehr?*

At her puzzled look, Abe smiled and nodded.

Myron grinned. "*Jah*. She showed me pointing out the error of people's ways can be freeing."

"Not always," Abe said dryly.

"Well, if somebody had forced me to face up to things years ago, my life might have been different. And I'm not going to stand by and let this couple ruin their lives."

Before Abe could get a word in edgewise, Myron pinned Esther with a question. "So you love him and he loves you. What's holding you back?"

Esther went mute. Once again, she bowed her head and twisted her fingers together.

"Fear can cause you to make foolish mistakes. It can make you deny yourself new opportunities and happiness."

Anna Mary bit her lip and examined Esther anxiously. Abe longed to be seated next to Anna Mary, to curl his arm around her shoulders, to protect her. She'd always coddled her mother. It must be hard for Anna Mary to hear Myron challenge her *mamm*.

Myron waited for a response, but when none came, he confessed, "I should know. I've spent twenty-five years walling myself off from hurt. It doesn't protect you. In the end, it only leaves you lonely."

A tear trickled down Esther's cheek. "I know."

"Hank feels that loneliness now. Maybe he always will. Does it make sense for two people to hurt each other like this when they could be spending their days loving and supporting each other?"

"I didn't mean"—Esther gulped—"to hurt him."

"But you did. And you're hurting yourself too. And your children. Wouldn't they be better off with a loving, caring father?"

Esther covered her face with her hands, and her shoulders shook with sobs. "But . . ."

When she stopped, Abe wondered if she'd remembered Mrs. Vandenberg's warning about the word *but*.

Her words came out in a wail. "I've lost two husbands. I can't bear to lose another."

"I understand that pain." Myron gentled his voice. He sounded close to tears. "I lost my fiancée."

"I'm sorry," Esther said. "The hurting never stops."

"What's worse is when you let it keep you from experiencing life, from trying again with someone new. Instead, you hide it inside and let it shrivel you and dry you up until you're nothing more than an empty shell."

Esther cried harder. "I'm sorry." She stood and stumbled toward her bedroom.

"Don't run away from it, Esther. You can never run far enough to escape."

Anna Mary jumped up and put an arm around her *mamm*.

Myron shook his head. "Anna Mary, I think you've overprotected her too much. She needs to face up to things."

"I'm just going to walk her to her bedroom." In the doorway, Anna Mary hugged her mother. "I love you, Mamm."

Anna Mary's tenderness choked Abe up. He'd found the most wonderful, loving woman in the world. He could hardly believe she'd agreed to date him.

"Esther," Myron called, "God gives second chances."

"What about third chances?" Esther's snappy reply boded well for her bouncing back. She shut the door behind her with a loud click.

"I think she took it to heart," Myron said.

Abe wouldn't have pushed Esther this way, but his *onkel*'s bluntness seemed to have made an impact.

Myron stood. "Now I need to go home and do what Esther's doing. Wrestle with God." He muttered as he walked to the door. "This old fool"—he bounced a finger off his chest—"was lecturing himself more than speaking to Esther."

Abe shot Anna Mary a sympathetic glance after his *onkel* walked out the door. "I hope he didn't upset your *mamm* too much. If I'd known he'd go after her like that, I never would have suggested he come."

"Maybe he's right. I do coddle Mamm. Makes me wonder if she'd have been stronger if someone had confronted her like your *onkel* did. I don't think I ever could have done it, but it might have made a difference."

"I can't see you lecturing anyone the way Myron did. You're too sweet and gentle."

* * *

Oh, Abe, if only you knew.

As much as she appreciated Abe's loving words, Anna Mary's conscience prickled. She hung her head. "Not really. You bring out the best in me. At the singing tonight, ask Josh if I'm sweet and gentle. I'm sure you'll hear an earful."

Abe gritted his teeth. "After the way he treated you . . ." He growled deep in his throat. "He deserved anything you flung at him."

"I'm not so sure." Mrs. Vandenberg's reminder to always be honest flashed through Anna Mary's mind. She hoped she'd never treat Abe the way she treated Josh, but Abe deserved to know all of her. "I'm not proud of it, but I treated him worse than Myron treated Mamm. Much, much worse."

"I find that hard to believe."

"It's true. I'm just warning you I can be a pain."

"If you're trying to change my mind about loving you, nothing you tell me will do that. I love all of you—good, bad, and in-between."

"*Ach*, Abe, I haven't done anything to deserve that."

"You don't have to do anything to *deserve* love. After all, God loved us while we were still sinners."

Anna Mary had thought nothing could make her love Abe more than she already did. She'd been wrong. Her heart expanded with so much love for him and for God that her chest ached. She whispered words of thanksgiving to the Lord who had brought them together.

CHAPTER 31

Mamm didn't come out of her room for supper, and she hadn't emerged by the time Anna Mary and Abe returned after the singing. A tiny sliver of light shone under her door. She must have her DeWalt turned on.

"Do you think I should go in and check on her?" Anna Mary asked him. "It looks like she's awake."

"If she's doing what Myron suggested and talking to the Lord, it might be best to leave her alone until she's ready to come out."

Instead of bothering Mamm, Anna Mary prayed, but when her mother didn't come out for breakfast the next morning, Anna Mary worried. She went to the bedroom door and knocked softly.

No answer.

Anna Mary turned the knob. Locked. Was that Mamm's signal she didn't want to be disturbed? Inside, she panicked. Should she try to get the door open?

Myron dropped Abe off as she debated. Anna Mary rushed outside and explained her dilemma.

"I'm tall enough to see in the window. Want me to check if she's all right?"

Relief flooded through her at his suggestion. "*Jah*." She followed him around the house.

He stayed a few feet from the window and stood on his toes. A smile spread across his face as he stepped back. "She's fine. The Bible's open on her lap, and she's reading."

"Thank the good Lord." Anna Mary hurried into the kitchen to inform Sarah, whose tense face relaxed.

"That's *gut*. I'll take care of the little ones while you and Abe go out. Perhaps Mamm will leave her room soon."

Anna Mary and Abe had planned a full day together and were eager to be on their way. She'd prepared a picnic basket and taken an old quilt. They set off after breakfast to their first destination—the Lancaster park with a waterfall.

"This won't compare to Canajoharie Falls, but I love the sound of rushing water while picnicking. Let's start with the Garden of Five Senses."

She led the way to a lovely area of flowering plants, trees, and a water fountain, where birds sang and rippling water flowed from the fountain, a waterfall, and a stream. They sniffed the flowers and the mystery scents along the path. They ate at a picnic table and then talked while hiking trails through the woods and along creeks.

Anna Mary sighed in contentment. This time together gave her a perfect rest. And she couldn't think of anyone she'd rather share it with than Abe. "I rarely have a chance to relax like this."

He agreed. "I don't get full days off either, so we should make the most of it."

Anna Mary spread the quilt on a grassy spot under the trees. They sat together listening to the water splashing and birds trilling.

"Once we're in charge of the milking business, we'll need to hire enough help to let us take days off just to be together to appreciate nature." He sent her a loving smile. "And to appreciate each other."

"When do you have to go back?" She wished his answer could be *never*. Or, better yet, that Mamm would let her go to New York.

"Daed didn't say. I can't leave him for long. Tim does fine, but Daed has to take on most of the work to get everything done on time. If they don't, they could miss the milk truck."

"I hope I'm not the cause of that."

Abe gazed at her as if she were a beautiful painting. "It would be worth it."

For Anna Mary, life couldn't possibly be sweeter. Abe was everything she ever wanted and dreamed of in a man, and he returned her love. All they needed was to be together every day.

When they returned, Sarah reported Mamm hadn't come out of her room all day. Abe accompanied Anna Mary to her *mamm*'s bedroom door. Her knocks remained unanswered.

Abe tried knocking. "Esther?"

Rustling came from inside, and the door flew open. Esther glanced around. Seeing only them, her radiant face slid into disappointment.

"Esther?" Abe said again.

Her voice dull and flat, she said, "You sound so much like your *daed*."

"You thought I was Daed?"

She nodded, then said shakily, "That was foolish, wasn't it?"

"*Neh*," Abe assured her. "Sometimes I want to have Anna Mary with me in New York so much, I imagine I hear her voice. Or I see a flash of a Lancaster dress and *kapp* turning the corner in the market, and I rush after the woman, only to find it's a stranger."

Mamm turned assessing eyes on Abe. "You understand, don't you?"

"*Jah*, I do. That's why I traveled all this way just to spend a few days with your *dochder*."

"I see." And the way she met his eyes, it seemed as if she really did.

Sarah came rushing from the kitchen. "Mamm, I thought I heard your voice. Supper's ready."

"I guess I'd better eat."

"You haven't had anything since the church meal." Sarah led the way to the table.

Emmie and Beth raced to hug their mother around the knees. A wan smile crossed Esther's face. She sank into her chair, but she didn't speak during the meal.

When Anna Mary and Abe rose to assist Sarah with the dishes, Esther motioned for Anna Mary to stay seated.

"Do you usually see Mrs. Vandenberg at the market?" Esther asked.

Abe bent to take the plate Emmie had carried to the sink. "*Danke*." He strained to hear the conversation.

"If she's there tomorrow, ask her to come to see me. I have a question to ask her. She always has wise advice."

That was for sure. Mrs. Vandenberg had arranged Anna Mary's visit to New York. Abe hoped she'd do that again.

But when Mrs. Vandenberg showed up the next day, she had a suggestion Abe didn't want to hear. He'd stopped by to visit Esther and the girls, hoping to coax them all out on another sightseeing trip.

But Esther asked him to take the girls somewhere while she spoke with Mrs. Vandenberg. When they returned, the elderly lady was saying her goodbyes.

"Abe, time for you to pack up and head home tomorrow. Your *daed* needs you."

"But I—" Abe couldn't express his deepest desire of staying here with Anna Mary as long as possible. The words stuck behind a lump in his throat. A lump so large he thought he might never be able to swallow it down.

"Be ready by five thirty. My driver will be here to pick you up. I can't go. I have business here tomorrow."

"Can Anna Mary go along?"

"Not this time."

Her answer dashed his dreams. Yet, it gave him a little hope for the future.

The rest of the day he spent with Anna Mary proved bittersweet. He loved every minute, but as each second ticked down, the end of their time together drew nearer. When she drove him back to Myron's and he said goodbye, they had no idea when they'd see each other again.

"She did say *not this time*?" Anna Mary asked for the fifth time that night.

Abe assured her those were Mrs. Vandenberg's exact words. "I wish she'd said how soon next time would be."

"Me too."

He replayed Anna Mary's response and Mrs. Vandenberg's promise as he waved and watched her buggy disappear. He'd cling to even the smallest shred of possibility.

After tossing and turning all night, Abe stumbled out to the Bentley before dawn. He greeted the driver, tossed his duffel onto the back seat, climbed in after it, and sank back into the comfy seat, intending to sleep.

At movement in the passenger seat, his eyes snapped open. Mrs. Vandenberg had said she wouldn't be coming. Had she changed her mind?

Abe shoved his duffel aside and scooted over to check. A woman sat, rigid and upright, staring straight ahead. Abe would recognize that profile anywhere.

Esther.

A sense of doom washed over Anna Mary when she woke on Wednesday morning. Last night came flooding back. She'd said goodbye to Abe. By now, he was almost an hour away.

She dragged down to the kitchen and started breakfast. After she and Sarah finished the girls' bobs and dressing, Anna Mary tapped at Mamm's door. It squeaked open. Mamm must not have latched it.

"Mamm?" Anna Mary peeked into the room. Her mother's bed had been made. Everything was in its proper place. Everything except the envelope propped on the dresser. An envelope with Anna Mary's name.

She approached it with dread. The short note inside began:

Myron was right. I have a few things I need to make clear to Hank. It's better to do this in person rather than in a letter.

Anna Mary's pulse sped up. Had Mamm gone to tell Hank her true feelings?

The next sentence dashed her hopes:

I won't be gone long.

If Mamm had gone to let Hank know she loved him, she'd want to spend time with him, not return quickly. Despondent, Anna Mary skimmed the rest of the message:

Please take care of the girls. Sarah's old enough to watch them while you're at work, but Barbara Reich has invited them to spend the day with her children on Thursday. I hope to be back late that night, depending on the driver's schedule.

Mamm would arrive in Fort Plain today and be back tomorrow. That barely gave her two half days to talk to Hank. Not the actions of a woman in love.

Wait. If Mamm went today, she must have gone with Abe. Why hadn't Mrs. Vandenberg told them?

Anna Mary simmered with resentment. If Mamm hadn't decided to go today, Abe could have stayed longer. Not only did her mother plan to cut off ties with Hank, she'd also shortened Anna Mary's time with Abe. The two of them had planned another trip for her day off today.

Throughout the day, while she and Sarah did chores, Anna Mary prayed. First, that God would give her grace to forgive her mother. As her heart softened toward Mamm, Anna Mary prayed for her mother's and Hank's well-being. Then she lifted her relationship with Abe up to the Lord. And finally, at day's end, she found peace.

Tension filled the ride to Fort Plain. Abe tried to make conversation with Esther, but she sat rigid, hands twisting in her lap, and gave one-word answers. It was obvious she didn't want to be disturbed, so he lapsed into silence.

When they pulled into the driveway, Daed hurried out to greet Abe but stopped, his face a mask of agony, when he spied Esther. Rather than turning toward him, she stared straight through the windshield, her jaw set.

The driver got out and came around to open the door. "Do you want me to take your bag to Delores's?"

Her neck stiff, Esther bobbed her head up and down. To Abe, it looked as if her heart had turned to stone and so had her body. Or maybe a pillar of salt, like Lot's wife. She kept her gaze on the past, rather than the future.

Oh, Lord, please heal her heart. And Daed's.

Abe wasn't sure if Daed could take another blow. She'd already rejected him once. Now it seemed as if she'd come to do it again in person.

Although Abe pitied Esther for all the tragedy she'd been through, he wished she hadn't come to inflict more on Daed.

The driver stood waiting by Esther's car door. When she didn't move, he shifted uncomfortably. "Do you want me to take you to Delores's too?"

A barely noticeable shake of her head was Esther's only response. She fumbled with her seat belt and stepped out of the car, her whole body rigid.

"What time do you want me to return?" the driver asked.

Daed cleared his throat. "Either Abe or I can take her to Delores's."

Esther didn't acknowledge that, and only said through tight lips, "Tomorrow afternoon."

After the car backed out, she turned in Daed's direction but kept her eyes lowered, focused on his work boots.

"Can we talk?" Each word dropped out like a stone, controlled and emotionless.

"Of course." Longing and caring infused Daed's answer.

Abe feared his father would get his heart broken all over again. *Lord, please protect him.*

At first, Abe didn't want to pray for the woman who'd come to hurt his father, but she was Anna Mary's *mamm*, and he'd come to care for Esther during the time he'd spent with her, so he added, *And please heal Esther's pain from the past.*

"Do you want to come in?" Daed asked, every word dripping with love and hope.

She shook her head. "Could we walk?" She pointed to the worn path along the pasture fence.

"*Jah.*" Daed moved to her side, but she inched away, putting a greater distance between them.

Abe's heart sank. This didn't bode well. He wanted to hover nearby, ready to protect his father from the blows Esther was about to inflict.

Daed must have sensed Abe's plan, because he turned and, with a quick flick of his head, indicated Abe should go into the barn.

From time to time, snatches of conversation drifted in when Daed and Esther walked past the barn. She did all the talking, her words rapid and tense.

The first time, she was describing her marriage of convenience and the pain it had caused her. Anna Mary had written about it, but Esther went into depth, making Abe ache with sympathy. Daed must be doing the same.

On their second pass, Daed's voice rose. "So you plan to punish me and yourself because of your guilt?"

Esther pleaded, "Please understand."

"I do understand, Esther, maybe better than you know."

By the third pass, she'd moved on to describing her fears of losing someone she loved and how that kept her from loving again.

Abe strained to hear Daed's response, but they'd moved too far away. That brought Abe's attention back to the barn.

Tim acted as if he were mucking stalls, but he hadn't made much progress. In fact, he was still in the same stall where he'd started. Over the past few weeks, Abe had noticed his cousin did one stall in the time it took Daed to do four. Abe, being younger than Daed, moved even faster and could do five or six.

"You planning to clean that stall, or are you just pretending to?" Abe took on Myron's tone.

Tim jumped and turned around, a startled expression on his face. "You sounded just like *Onkel*."

"Don't change the subject. You dawdle instead of mucking your stall so Daed and I get stuck with most of the work."

His cousin had the grace to look ashamed. "*Jah*, I hate doing it."

"So do we."

"Wow." Tim stared at Abe. "Your weekend in Lancaster sure changed you."

His cousin must mean the assertive behavior. "I spent some time with Myron."

Tim shook his head. "Never a good thing." But he did pick up his pace.

Abe struggled with guilt because he slowed his own work down to hear the conversation outside when Daed and Esther passed by. They paced the length of the fence and then returned.

This time, Esther was recounting Myron's visit.

Daed's laughter rumbled from deep in his chest. "My brother gave you relationship advice?"

"*Jah*, and it turned out to be some of the best advice I've ever gotten."

"Well, I'll be." Daed sounded bemused.

Esther's answer trailed off as they moved past the barn. The only words Abe caught were *fear* and *foolish mistakes*. As they turned, another phrase floated in: *shrivel and dry up until you're nothing more than an empty shell.* Almost an exact quote of what Myron had said.

Tim poked his head over the stall wall. "You eavesdropping?"

Abe went back to work with a mumbled *jah.*

"Thought so." Tim sounded triumphant. Then his face fell. "You think they'll get together?"

"Not unless God works a miracle," Abe muttered.

"Too bad. Hank's been miserable since she left. While she was here, they seemed like they'd make the perfect couple."

"*Jah*, they did. Sometimes fear causes people to put up barriers to love."

Tim's face crumpled, and he turned away. When he spoke, his words were muffled. "Yeah, it can do that."

Abe hadn't meant that as a dig at his cousin, but Tim must have taken it that way. Tim and Myron had both erected huge walls against love. So had Esther. Often, nobody could scale those barriers to reach someone's heart. Only God could remove those blocks. Abe prayed that would be the case for Esther and Daed.

* * *

Later that night, Abe sat at the table, jotting down all his thoughts and the scraps of conversation he'd overheard. Daed had done the afternoon milking while Esther sat on a rocker on the porch, staring despondently at the empty meadow. Neither of them ate supper. Instead, they resumed walking. This time, Abe had no excuse to stay in the barn to listen.

They still hadn't come in when Abe and Tim went to bed. In the wee hours of the morning, buggy wheels crunched down the driveway. Daed wouldn't get much sleep before the morning milking.

Daed sleepwalked through his chores and left to pick up Esther. They didn't come back to the house, so Abe had no chance to assess the relationship's status.

His father returned for the afternoon milking without Esther.

When Abe inquired about her, Daed's answer was clipped. "She's gone."

Gone back to Lancaster forever?

But his *daed* seemed to be carrying a heavy burden, so Abe didn't ask. Daed skipped supper again and took off in the buggy for an errand. After he returned, he sat at the table for a long time struggling to write a letter. Though he placed his hand over the envelope to conceal the address from Abe, enough peeked through to reveal it was to Esther.

A goodbye? A plea to reconsider?

Maybe Anna Mary's next letters would offer an explanation.

Meanwhile, his father walked around in a daze, wearing a strange expression. Abe couldn't put a finger on it. Confusion. Bewilderment. Uncertainty. Worry.

Esther must have ended the relationship, and it seemed

Daed couldn't figure out why. He misplaced things, did the same jobs over again, stared into space instead of working.

Abe's hope for the future sank as Daed's absent-mindedness increased.

32

CHAPTER 32

When Mamm returned from Fort Plain, she refused to talk about her trip. Instead, she flew into a flurry of housecleaning—weeding out closets, scrubbing the insides of cupboards and drawers. She moved through the house like a whirlwind, as if trying to erase any traces of thoughts or feelings.

At Abe's letter describing his *daed*'s behavior, Anna Mary's spirits plummeted. They obviously hadn't fixed the rift in their relationship. Where did that leave her and Abe?

Anna Mary returned home from work one day to find Mrs. Vandenberg and her mother having a serious discussion on the porch. The two of them sat on the rockers, both with frown lines on their faces.

That night at supper, Mamm signaled for all of them to stay at the table after they finished eating. "It's time I told you what happened in New York. Hank asked me to marry him, and I promised to let him know in one week. The week will be up tomorrow, and I plan to tell him in person."

Tell him what?

Mamm refused to say. "Aunt Delores begged to have

you all come to stay again. I don't think it's wise, but Mrs. Vandenberg insisted all of you should go. Except you have to stay and work, Anna Mary."

They'd all go to Fort Plain without her?

Anna Mary swallowed back tears. "If you're all going, I want to go too." She wouldn't miss this chance to spend time with Abe, even if it meant losing her job.

Despite Mamm's protests, Anna Mary marched out to the phone shanty and left a message on Gideon's answering machine. The market was closed tomorrow, so he'd have a day's notice to get someone. Even without a replacement, the two new girls should be able to handle things.

When they arrived at Delores's the next day, Mrs. Vandenberg's driver dropped the girls and their luggage off, then drove Mamm to Hank's farm.

Anna Mary and Sarah chattered together. What answer would Mamm give Hank?

Their mother's stern, forbidding face didn't seem like that of a woman about to say *jah* to the man she loved.

A Bentley pulled into the driveway after they'd finished the afternoon milking, and Esther emerged. What was she doing here? Had she come back to torture Daed? Abe wanted to stop her from inflicting further heartbreak.

"Esther?" Daed stared at her with longing eyes. "You've come to give me your answer?"

She nodded, and Abe could tell it wasn't good news. So could Daed. His face fell.

"Let me get cleaned up, and then we'll talk." He pivoted and, shoulders slumped, headed into the house.

After Daed returned, the two of them again paced back

and forth on the path, their heads together, arguing. Abe wished he could hear the conversation.

At dusk, Abe went out for a walk of his own, praying for his father and Esther as well as for himself and Anna Mary. He was coming back up the driveway when Daed escorted Esther to the buggy. He must be taking her to Delores's. Neither of them appeared happy.

Abe used the phone in Daed's office to place a call to Delores's house. She'd installed a phone for her business. He wasn't sure she'd answer or if she used an answering machine, the way Daed did.

To his surprise, she picked up on the first ring. "Oh," she said, disappointed when she heard his voice. "I was expecting— Never mind. I'll go get Anna Mary."

Anna Mary's lilt when she answered lifted Abe's sadness over their parents.

"Want me to pick you and your sisters up in the morning for milking?"

"I'd love that. How did things go?"

"Not well." He sighed heavily. "I hope this won't interfere with us."

"It'll never change our feelings for each other."

"Of course not. I just meant whether or not we'll get to spend time together."

"I hope not." Her voice quavered. "I need to hang up. Delores is waiting for a call. I'll see you in the morning."

Abe couldn't wait to see her again. He'd spend whatever time he could with her.

Mamm's lips thinned when she heard about their plans for the next day. "I don't want the girls getting used to going to the Kings' house."

Anna Mary noted she hadn't said *Hank's* house.

"As long as we're here," Mamm insisted, "we should spend our time helping Delores. She wants to open her bed-and-breakfast next month. There's a lot of work to do."

If she had to stay here, Anna Mary wouldn't get to spend much time with Abe.

When she told him that the next morning, he offered to join her and Sarah in fixing up Delores's mansion. That perked Anna Mary up. Even Tim offered to assist when he found out the plan.

Delores was delighted to have two strong young men to move furniture. It didn't give Anna Mary much time with Abe, but as she washed all the dishes in the floor-to-ceiling cupboard and polished the furniture, she could at least watch him muscling dressers up the stairs or carting old furniture to the basement. His smiles when he passed her made it all worthwhile.

They all did the afternoon milking and returned to Delores's for dinner and to work. When the younger children went to bed, Abe and Anna Mary sat together in one of the parlors to talk, and before he left, they planned the same schedule for tomorrow.

Abe took care of the horse and headed out of the barn. Daed's voice carried on the clear night air. Abe didn't want to interrupt him and Esther, so he melted into the shadows to wait until they passed.

"So this is goodbye?" Daed's words ached with sorrow. "You came all this way to tell me I'm the most *wunderbar* man you've ever met, and you don't want me to blame myself for what went wrong between us?"

"I—I couldn't let you think this was your fault."

"And you don't want to marry again because you can't face losing another husband?"

A barely audible *jah* reached Abe's ears. He shouldn't be listening to their private conversation, but if he moved now, he might interrupt something important.

"I lost my wife and never want to go through that agony again either. But is it really better to hide from pain and stay lonely the rest of your life? Or is it better to take a risk and be happy even for a short time?"

"You're braver than I am."

"It takes more than courage to make a commitment like this. It takes faith to follow God's leading."

"I—I haven't prayed about it because I'm afraid. What if God says *jah*? I can't bear to lose someone I love."

"You love me?" Daed sounded stunned.

Esther's *jah* came out small and ashamed. "I fell hard the first day I met you."

"And you ran from me so you wouldn't get hurt? *Ach*, Esther. Suppose we both live into our eighties or even nineties? You want to be alone all those years?"

Her only answer was a sob.

Daed put a finger under her chin and lifted it so he could gaze into her eyes. "Will you do me one favor? Pray about it. If the Lord tells you *neh*, I'll accept that it's over."

At her nod, he said in a choked voice, "Why don't I drive you home now? You can give me your answer to-morrow."

Abe slipped into the darkness beside the barn and flattened himself against the wooden boards as they entered the barn for the buggy. Once they were inside, he high-tailed it for the house and spent his night in prayer.

Evidently, Daed did too, because he emerged for morning milking looking haggard, but peaceful. Determination pinched his lips together, and he seemed ready for a blow.

A blow that never came.

When Esther drove up the driveway as they emerged from the barn, her face radiant, they had their answer.

A tornado had blown through Anna Mary's life, uprooting her and everything around her. In the space of a few months, she and Abe had gone from believing they'd be separated forever to living a short distance apart. Mamm had gone from a depressed single mother to a blushing bride. And Anna Mary had gone from being part of a busy family to living alone with Aunt Delores in a huge mansion.

Mamm and Hank had decided it would be inappropriate for Anna Mary and Abe to live under the same roof, so after a painting frenzy, all four of her sisters had moved into rooms in Hank's large house. And they all helped in the barn.

The only time Anna Mary saw them and Abe was at milkings. Otherwise, she stayed busy at the B and B, working long hours with little time off. Peter had convinced Delores not to install electricity, at least while Esther's daughter was staying there, so Anna Mary didn't have to worry about having that confrontation with Mamm.

But now that Abe lived only a few miles away, they were seeing less of each other. Or at least it seemed that way. Sometimes Abe would stop by the B and B to help out or trail Anna Mary around as she did her chores, but she was always in too much of a rush to spend much time with him.

One morning after milking, Anna Mary waved a quick goodbye to Abe, but he stopped her.

"I don't have much time," she said regretfully. "We have a party of ten arriving after breakfast and six check-outs. All the rooms need to be ready before lunchtime. They paid extra to get in early."

"Slow down," Abe said. "Take a breath. I've arranged for Sarah to take your place today."

"You what?"

"Anna Mary, you deserve a break. Take Sarah with you back to the B and B. After we both clean up, we're going for a picnic and to have a relaxing day together."

"*Ach*, Abe." Anna Mary couldn't believe it. A whole day off. Other than church Sundays, she hadn't had time off in months.

She hurried back to Delores's and got ready. Then she and Sarah cleaned up after breakfast and did a few rooms together so Sarah could learn the routine. By that time, Abe had arrived to pick up Anna Mary.

"*Danke* you for doing this," she said to Sarah, then beamed at Abe. "And *danke* you for arranging it."

He surprised her by driving to Canajoharie Falls, where they enjoyed a picnic and hiked the trails. They had a lovely day together. Before they needed to get back for the afternoon milking, they took a short walk to admire the falls.

"Anna Mary." Abe turned and gazed at her with admiration. "You look so beautiful standing there with the spray behind you."

At the desire in his eyes, Anna Mary's pulse matched the rapidly pounding water. She'd always compared her beauty to that of other girls and found herself lacking. But Abe saw both her inner and outer beauty, and had eyes only for her.

"I love you so much and want to spend the rest of my life with you. Will you marry me?"

"*Ach*, Abe, I love you too." Then, her soul overflowing like the waterfall behind her, she answered his question with a heartfelt *jah* that barely expressed all the joy and love bubbling up inside.

The two of them had been on a long journey of separations and reunitings, but now they would be together forever. And they would enjoy every minute spent in each other's company for as many years as God gave them.

EPILOGUE

Anna Mary, her infant son strapped in a baby carrier in front of her and three-year-old Leah clinging to her apron, stepped inside the new, larger milking barn to be greeted by the sharp smell of bleach and wet floors. Her husband and father-in-law had all the cows lined up in the barn.

Abe looked up from assembling the hoses. The smile that lit his face thrilled her. Even after five years of marriage and two children, the look in his eyes set her heart afire. He looked tenderly at his daughter as she padded toward him.

Taking her hands in his, Abe showed her how to hook up the hoses.

After they finished, Leah beamed. "I helped, Mamm."

"And now you can help me. We need to mix up more wash to clean the cows."

Hank stared down at his sweet granddaughter, joy on his face. "Just what I always dreamed of." His gaze moved to the baby carrier. "Soon he'll be toddling around here ready to help. I told you several years ago I wanted *kinskinder* in the barn, and now . . ." His eyes filled with moisture.

Then he gazed around at Sarah, Emmie, Beth, and Hannah, all working diligently. "And I said"—he swallowed hard—"I missed having *kinner* helping me. Now I have five *wunderbar* daughters. God is so good."

"And God brought you into our lives." Anna Mary's eyes misted. "You've made Mamm and my sisters so happy."

Anna Mary couldn't get over the changes in her mother. Mamm went through her days humming and singing. And nobody could miss the love shining in their eyes when she and Hank gazed at each other.

Abe and Hank had expanded the barn to one hundred cows, and she and Abe had built a house on the land next door to his *daed*'s property so they could be close to the barn and the rest of the family. They usually all ate their meals together.

Although Sarah worked full-time at the B and B, she also spent time at the milking barn on her days off. At seventeen, she had joined the church and caught the eye of many admirers in her youth group, but an older *mann* had his eye on her. A *mann* she'd long admired, but who, until now, had always considered her like a younger sister.

As they emerged from the barn, a Bentley pulled into the driveway. Everyone crowded around Mrs. Vandenberg as she stepped out. Even little Leah toddled toward the old lady she called *Miz Vee*. Mrs. V held a special place in everyone's heart. She'd united two couples here and made everyone happier by her presence.

She greeted each one in turn, then turned her attention to Tim, who hung back behind the chattering girls. She beckoned him forward. "I have some information for you." In her hand, she held a manila envelope.

At the dumbfounded expression on his face, Sarah sucked in a breath.

"It's taken a long while, and your uncles, Myron and Hank, both helped."

"Myron?" Tim's eyebrows shot up.

"Yes, Myron's been looking for your sister ever since she disappeared. He turned over all the facts he'd gathered, which gave us a good start."

Tim stared at her. "Myron was looking for"—Tim swallowed hard—"Ivy all that time? He never told me. I thought he didn't care."

"He didn't want to disappoint you if all his searches led nowhere. Many of them did. But that helped us avoid those pitfalls."

His lips pressed into a tight line, Tim kept shaking his head. "I don't believe it. All this time I resented Myron for not caring about my missing sister. I thought . . ." He choked back a sob. "I owe him an apology."

"I'm sure he'd appreciate that. He regrets his harshness and the way he raised you."

"*Jah.*" Tim focused on his barn boots. "He apologized for it when he came for my baptism, but I didn't quite believe him."

"I'm sure you two will work things out. Meanwhile, we need to figure out what to do about that packet." Mrs. Vandenberg waved toward the envelope.

"Where is she?" He tore into the envelope.

"Before you get too excited, this isn't a sure thing. But it's the most reliable information we've found so far."

Tim devoured the pages. When he reached the last one, he glanced up at her, disappointment brimming in his eyes. "Mexico?"

"I know you don't fly, but if you'd like to go, we can figure out a way."

Tim clamped his teeth down hard on his lower lip and met Sarah's eyes. When she nodded, he said, "Let's try a letter first. If it seems like it's really her, we can decide from there."

Abe moved close to Anna Mary and reached for her hand. Hidden behind her full skirt, their fingers intertwined, giving her comfort and strength. She prayed this would be a genuine source. Mrs. Vandenberg's researcher had hit so many dead ends over the past few years, but maybe this finding held promise.

"I hope Tim finds out the truth." Abe leaned close to whisper in Anna Mary's ear. "Maybe then he can finally settle down and let go of all the hurt from his childhood."

"The way your *daed* helped my *mamm* let go of her past pain."

Abe squeezed her hand. "I'm so glad she and Daed found true love. And I found mine." He set a gentle hand on his sleeping son's head, then met Anna Mary's gaze, his eyes overflowing with tenderness. "Love heals so many wounds."

"So does God's grace. And we can trust Him to lead us to our perfect love."

"He led me to mine, and I thank Him every day that she said *jah*."

"And she's thrilled she did. And she's ever so grateful you asked."

Abe drew her back into the shadows, away from prying eyes, enfolded her in his arms, and kissed her thoroughly. "Do you think the children's *mammi* would be willing to put the little ones to bed this evening? I'd like to take my wife to a special place tonight."

"My *mamm* would be delighted, and we have plenty of other babysitters who'd beg for a chance to watch our children. And there's nowhere I'd rather be than spending time alone with you."

A few hours later, the two of them walked hand in hand to the spot where Abe had asked her to marry him. As the sun slipped behind the trees, bathing the landscape in pastel hues of lavender, apricot, and rose, Abe drew Anna Mary close and in a low, throaty voice whispered, "You'll never know how much I wanted to hold you that night. Now I can."

Abe drew Anna Mary close, one hand gently cradling the back of her head as he brought his lips to hers in a tender kiss. She melted into his embrace, her arms encircling his broad shoulders, thrilled at the familiar sensation of his beard brushing against her skin.

They held the kiss for a long moment, the rest of the world fading away until it was just the two of them alone amidst the tranquil beauty of God's creation and the comforting lull of the cascading waterfall in the background. When their lips finally parted, Abe rested his forehead against Anna Mary's, the contented smile on his face matching hers.

"I love you," he murmured in a husky whisper. Anna Mary rejoiced at the words, as wondrous to her now as the first time he had uttered them.

"And I love you," she whispered back as she snuggled into her husband's embrace, perfectly at peace. This was exactly where she belonged.

The last rays of the sun glinted on the falling water, creating tiny rainbows in the mist. Rainbows of promise. God's promise. And the promise they'd made to each other on their wedding day. Vows they would renew every day for the rest of their lives.

Visit our website at
KensingtonBooks.com
to sign up for our newsletters, read
more from your favorite authors, see
books by series, view reading group
guides, and more!

Become a Part of Our
Between the Chapters Book Club
Community and Join the Conversation